About the Authors

USA Today bestselling, RITA-nominated, and critically acclaimed author **Caitlin Crews** has written more than 150 books and counting. She has a master's and a PhD in English Literature, thinks everyone should read more category romance, and is always available to discuss her beloved alpha heroes. Just ask. She lives in the Pacific Northwest with her comic book artist husband, is always planning her next trip, and will never, ever, read all the books in her to-be-read pile. Thank goodness.

Pippa Roscoe lives in Norfolk near her family and makes daily promises that *this* is the day she will leave the computer and take a long walk in the countryside. She can't remember a time when she wasn't dreaming of gorgeous alpha males and misunderstood heroines. Totally her mother's fault of course – she gave Pippa her first romance at the age of seven! She is inconceivably happy that she gets to share those daydreams with you! Find out more at: @PippaRoscoe and pipparoscoe.com

Carole Mortimer was born in England, the youngest of three children. She began writing in 1978 and has written over 170 books for Mills & Boon. Carole has six sons, Matthew, Joshua, Timothy, Michael, David and Peter. She says, 'I'm happily married to Peter senior; we're best friends as well as lovers, which is probably the best recipe for a successful relationship. We live in a lovely part of England.'

Ruthless Rivals

April 2026
Tempted by the Boss

July 2026
Consequences of Desire

May 2026
Bound by Vows

August 2026
Taming the Cowboy

June 2026
Back for Revenge

September 2026
Deal with the Enemy

Ruthless Rivals: Tempted by the Boss

CAITLIN CREWS

PIPPA ROSCOE

CAROLE MORTIMER

MILLS & BOON

All rights reserved including the right of reproduction in whole or in part in any form. This edition is published by arrangement with Harlequin Enterprises ULC.

This is a work of fiction. Names, characters, places, locations and incidents are purely fictional and bear no relationship to any real life individuals, living or dead, or to any actual places, business establishments, locations, events or incidents. Any resemblance is entirely coincidental.

Without limiting the exclusive rights of any author, contributor or the publisher of this publication, any unauthorised use of this publication to train generative artificial intelligence (AI) technologies is expressly prohibited. HarperCollins also exercise their rights under Article 4(3) of the Digital Single Market Directive 2019/790 and expressly reserve this publication from the text and data mining exception.

® and ™ are trademarks owned and used by the trademark owner and/or its licensee. Trademarks marked with ® are registered with the United Kingdom Patent Office and/or the Office for Harmonisation in the Internal Market and in other countries.

First Published in Great Britain 2026
by Mills & Boon, an imprint of HarperCollins*Publishers* Ltd
1 London Bridge Street, London, SE1 9GF

www.harpercollins.co.uk

HarperCollins*Publishers*
Macken House, 39/40 Mayor Street Upper,
Dublin 1, D01 C9W8, Ireland

Ruthless Rivals: Tempted by the Boss © 2026 Harlequin Enterprises ULC.

Castelli's Virgin Widow © 2016 Caitlin Crews
Expecting Her Enemy's Heir © 2023 Pippa Roscoe
At the Ruthless Billionaire's Command © 2017 Carole Mortimer

ISBN: 978-0-263-42160-6

Printed and Bound in the UK using 100% Renewable Electricity
at CPI Group (UK) Ltd, Croydon, CR0 4YY

CASTELLI'S VIRGIN WIDOW

CAITLIN CREWS

To my wonderful editor, Flo Nicoll,
for our fantastic year together!

Thank you so much for taking such
great care of me – and my books!

CHAPTER ONE

"Please tell me this is a bad attempt at levity, Rafael. A practical joke from the least likely clown in Italy."

Luca Castelli made no attempt to temper his harsh tone or the scowl he could feel on his face as he glared across the private library at his older brother. Rafael was also his boss and the head of the family company, a state of affairs that usually did not trouble Luca at all.

But there was nothing *usual* about today.

"I wish that it was," Rafael said from where he sat in an armchair in front of a bright and cheerful fire that did nothing at all to dispel Luca's sense of gloom and fury. "Alas. When it comes to Kathryn, we have no choice."

His brother looked like a monk carved from stone today, his features hewn from granite, which only added to Luca's sense of betrayal and sheer *wrongness*. That was the old Rafael, that heavy, joyless creature made entirely of bitterness and regret. Not the Rafael of the past few years, the one Luca greatly preferred, who had married the love of his life he'd once thought dead and was even now expecting his third child with her.

Luca hated that grief had thrown them all so far back into unpleasant history. Luca hated grief, come to that. No matter its form.

Their father, the infamous Gianni Castelli, who had built an empire of wine and wealth and brusque personality that spanned at least two continents, but was better known around the world for his colorful marital life, was dead.

Outside, January rain lashed the windows of the old Castelli manor house that sprawled with such insouciance at the top of an alpine lake in Northern Italy's Dolomite Mountains, as it had done for generations. The heavy clouds were low over the water, concealing the rest of the world from view, as if to pay tribute to the old man as he'd been interred in the Castelli mausoleum earlier this morning.

Ashes rendered ashes and dust forever dust.

Nothing would ever be the same again.

Rafael, who had been acting CEO of the family business for years now despite Gianni's blustery refusal to formally step aside, was now indisputably in charge. That meant Luca was the newly minted chief operating officer, a title that did not come close to describing his pantheon of responsibilities as co-owner but was useful all the same. Luca had initially thought these finicky bits of official business were a good thing for the Castelli brothers as well as the company, not to mention long overdue, given they'd both been acting in those roles ever since the start of their father's decline in health some years back.

Until now.

"I fail to understand why we cannot simply pay the damned woman off like all the rest of the horde of ex-wives," Luca said, aware that his tone was clipped and bordering on unduly aggressive. He felt restless and edgy in his position on the low couch opposite Rafael, but he knew if he moved, it would end badly. A fist through a wall. An upended bookshelf. A broken pane of glass. All highly charged reactions he did not care to explore, much less explain to his brother—given they smacked of a loss of control, which Luca did not allow. Ever. "Settle some of Father's fortune on her, send her on her way and be done with it."

"Father's will is very clear in regard to Kathryn," Rafael replied, and he sounded no happier about it than Luca felt. Luca told himself that was something anyway. "And she is his widow, Luca. Not his ex-wife. A crucial distinction."

Luca nearly growled but checked it at the last moment. "That's nothing but semantics."

"Sadly not." Rafael shook his head, but his gaze never left Luca's. "The choice is hers. She can either accept a lump settlement now, or a position in the company. She chose the latter."

"This is ridiculous."

It was something far worse than merely ridiculous, but Luca didn't have a word to describe that gnawing, hollow thing inside him that always yawned open at any mention of his father's sixth and final wife. *Kathryn.*

The one who was even now in the larger, more formal library downstairs, crying what appeared to be real tears over the death of a husband three times her age she could only have married for the most cynical of reasons. Luca had seen them trickle silently down her cheeks, one after the next, as they'd all stood about in the frigid air earlier, giving the impression she could not manage to contain her grief.

He didn't believe it. Not for a second.

If Luca knew anything, it was this: the kind of love

that might lead to such grieving was rare, exceedingly unlikely and had never made a great many appearances in the Castelli family. He thought Rafael's current happiness was perhaps the only evidence of it in generations.

"For all we know, Father found her hawking her wares on the streets of London," he muttered now. Then glared at his brother. "What the hell will I do with her in the office? Do we even know if she can read?"

Rafael shifted, the dark eyes that were so much like Luca's own narrow and shrewd. "You will find something to keep her busy, because the will assures her three years of employment. Ample time to introduce her to the joys of the written word, I'd think. And whether you like her or not is irrelevant."

Like was not at all the word Luca would have used to describe what happened inside him at the mention of that woman. It wasn't even close.

"I have no feelings about her whatsoever." Luca let out a laugh that sounded hollow to his own ears. "What is one more child bride—acquired solely to cater to the old man's ego—to me?"

His brother only gazed at him for a moment that seemed to stretch on for far too long. The old windows rattled. The fire crackled and spat. And Luca found he had no desire whatsoever to hear whatever his older brother might say next. He'd preferred Rafael when he'd been lost in a prison of fury and regret, he told himself, and unable to concentrate on anything outside his own pain. At least then he'd been a known quantity. This new Rafael was entirely too insightful.

"If you are determined to do this," he said before Rafael could open his mouth and say things Luca would have to fend off, "why not set her up with something in Sonoma? She can get a hands-on experience at the vineyards in California, just as we did when we were boys. It can be a delightful holiday for her, far, far away."

From me, he did not say. *Far, far away from me.*

Rafael shrugged. "She chose Rome."

Rome. Luca's city. Luca's side of their highly competitive wine business. The marketing power and global reach of the Castelli Wine brand were, he flattered himself, all his doing—and possible in large part because he'd been left to his own devices for years. He had certainly not been required to play babysitter for one of his father's legion of mistakes.

His father's very worst mistake, to his way of thinking. In a lifetime of so very many—including Luca himself, he'd long thought. He knew his father would have agreed.

"There's no room," he said now. "The team is lean, focused and entirely handpicked. There's no place for a bit of fluff on sabbatical from her true vocation as an old man's trophy."

Rafael was his boss then, he could see. Not his brother.

And entirely pitiless. "You'll have to make room."

Luca shook his head. "It may set us back months, if not years, and cause incalculable damage in the process as we try to arrange the team around such a creature and what are sure to be her many, many mistakes."

"I trust you'll ensure that none of that happens," Rafael said drily. "Or do you doubt your own abilities?"

"This sort of vulgar nepotism will likely cause a riot—"

"Luca." Rafael's voice was not loud, but it silenced

Luca all the same. "Your objections are noted. But you are not seeing the big picture."

Luca tried to contain the seething thing within that pushed out from the darkest part of him and threatened to take him over. He thrust his legs out in front of him and raked a hand through his hair as if he was languid. Indolent. Unbothered by all of this, despite his arguments.

The role he'd been playing all his life. He had no idea why it had become so difficult these past couple of years to maintain his profoundly unconcerned facade. Why it had started to feel as if it was more of a cage than a retreat.

"Enlighten me," he said, mildly enough, when he was certain he could manage to speak in his usual half bored, half amused tone.

Rafael did not look fooled. But he only picked up his glass from the antique side table and swirled the amber liquid within.

"Kathryn has captured the public's interest," he said after a moment. "I shouldn't have to remind you of that. *Saint Kate* has been on every cover of every tabloid since the news of Father's death broke. Her grief. Her selflessness. Her true love for the old man against all odds. Et cetera."

"You will excuse me if I am skeptical about the truth of her devotion." At least he sounded far more amused than he felt. "To put it mildly. The truth of her interest in his bank account I find a far more convincing tale, if less entertaining."

"The truth is malleable and has little to do with the story that ends up splashed across every gossip site and magazine in existence," Rafael said, and there was the hint of a rueful smile on his face when he looked at Luca again. "No one knows this better than me. Can we really complain if this time the coverage is not exactly in our favor?"

Luca wasn't sure he found his latest stepmother's obvious manipulation of the press to be in the same realm as the stories Rafael and his wife, Lily—who also happened to be their former stepsister, because the Castelli family tree was nothing if not tangled and bent back on itself—had told to explain the fact she'd been thought dead for five years.

But he thought better of saying anything.

After a moment, Rafael continued, "The reality is this. Even though you and I have been running things for years now, the perception from the outside is very different. Father's death gives anyone and everyone the opportunity to make grand claims about how his upstart, ungrateful sons will ruin what he built. If we are seen to shun Kathryn, to treat her badly, that can only reflect negatively on us and add fuel to that fire." He set his glass down without drinking from it. "I want no fuel, no fire. Nothing the tabloids can sink their dirty little claws into. You understand. This is necessary."

What Luca understood was that this was a directive. From the chief executive officer of Castelli Wine and the new official head of his family to one among his many underlings. The fact that Luca owned half of the company did not change the fact he answered to Rafael. And that none of this sat well with him didn't alter the fact that Rafael wasn't asking his opinion on the matter.

He was delivering an order.

Luca stood abruptly, before he said things he wasn't

sure he meant in an effort to sway his brother's opinion. Rafael stayed where he was.

"I don't like this," Luca said quietly. "It can't end well."

"It must end well," Rafael countered. "That's the whole point."

"I'll remind you that this was entirely your idea when it becomes a vast and unconquerable disaster, sinking the whole of Castelli Wine in the wake of this woman's incompetence," Luca said, and started for the door. He needed to *do* something. Run for miles and miles. Swim even farther. Lift very heavy weights or find a willing and eager woman. Anything but stay here and brood about this terrible new reality. "We can discuss it as we plummet to the bottom of the sea. In pieces."

Rafael laughed.

"Kathryn is not our Titanic, Luca," he said, and there was a note Luca did not like at all in his voice. Rafael tilted his head slightly to one side. "But perhaps you think she's yours?"

What Luca thought was that he could do without his brother's observations today—and on any day, should those observations involve Kathryn, who was without doubt the bane of his existence.

Damn that woman. And damn his father for foisting her upon his sons in the first place.

He left Rafael behind in the private library with a rude hand gesture that made his brother laugh, and headed downstairs through the grand old hallways of the ancient house that he hardly noticed the details of anymore. The portraits cluttering the walls. The statuary by this or that notable Italian artist flung about on every flat surface. It was all the same as it had been before Luca had been born, and the same as it would be when Rafael's eldest son, Arlo, was a grandfather. Castellis endured, no matter the messes they made.

He imagined that meant he would, too, despite this situation.

Somehow.

He heard Lily's voice as he passed one of the reception rooms and glanced in, seeing his pregnant sister-in-law, some six months along, having one of her "discussions" with eight-year-old Arlo and two-year-old Renzo about appropriate behavior. Luca hid a grin as he passed, thinking the lecture sounded very similar to ones he'd received in the very same place when he'd been a child. Not from his mother, who had abdicated that position as quickly as possible following Luca's birth, or from his father, who had been far too important to trouble himself with domestic arrangements or child rearing. He'd been raised by a parade of well-meaning staff and a series of stepmothers with infinitely more complicated motives.

Perhaps that was where he'd learned his lifelong aversion to complications.

And to stepmothers, for that matter.

Luca had grown up in the midst of a very messy family who'd broadcasted their assorted private dramas for all the world to see, no matter if the relentless publicity had made it all that much worse. He'd hated it. He preferred things clean and easy. Orderly. No fusses. No melodrama. No theatrics that ended up splashed across the papers, the way everything always did in the Castelli family, and were then presented in the most hideous light imaginable. He didn't mind that he was seen as one of the world's foremost playboys—hell, he'd cultivated that role so no one would ever take him seriously, an asset in business as well as in his personal life. He didn't break hearts—he simply didn't traffic in the kind of emotional upheavals that had marked every other member of his family, again and again and again. *No, thank you.*

But Kathryn was a different story, he thought as he made his way to the grand library on the ground floor and saw the slight figure standing all alone in the farthest corner, staring out at the rain and the fog as if she was competing with it for the title of Most Desolate. Kathryn was more than a mess.

Kathryn was a disaster.

He wasn't the least bit surprised that *Saint Kate,* as she'd been dubbed around the world for her supposed martyrdom to the cause that was old Gianni Castelli and his considerable fortune, was all over the papers this week. Kathryn did *convincingly innocent* and *easily wounded* so well that Luca had always thought she'd have been much better off dedicating her life to the stage.

Though he supposed she had, really. Playing the understanding mistress and undemanding trophy wife to a man so much older than her twenty-five years was a performance all its own. What Luca couldn't understand was why an obvious trollop like Kathryn made his skin feel too tight against his frame and his hands itch to test the smoothness of hers, even now. It didn't make any sense, this stretched-taut, heavy *thing* in him that nothing—not time, not space, not the odious fact of her marriage to his own father, not even the prospect of her polluting the refuge of his office in Rome—ever eased or altered in any way.

He glared at her from the doorway, down the length of the great room with so many books lining the floor-to-ceiling shelves, as if he could make it disappear. Or barring that, make *her* disappear.

But he knew better.

It had always been like this.

Luca's father had made a second career out of marrying a succession of unsuitable younger women who'd let him act the savior. He'd thrived on it. Gianni had never had much time for his sons or the first wife he'd shunted out of sight into a mental institution and mourned very briefly after her death, if at all. But for his parade of mistresses and wives with their endless needs and worries and crises and melodramas? He had been always and ever available to play the benevolent God, solver of all calamities, able to sort out all manner of troubles with a wave of his debit card.

When Gianni had arrived back in Italy a scant month after his fifth wife had divorced him with his sixth wife in tow, Luca hadn't been particularly surprised.

"There is a new bride," Rafael had told him darkly when Luca had arrived in the Dolomites as summoned that winter morning two years ago. "Already."

Luca had rolled his eyes. What else was there to do?

"Is this one of legal age?"

Rafael had snorted. "Barely."

"She's twenty-three," the very pregnant Lily had said reprovingly, her hands on the protruding belly that would shortly become Renzo. She'd glared at both of them. "That's hardly a child. And she seems perfectly nice."

"Of course she seems nice," Rafael had retorted, and had only grinned at the look Lily had thrown at him, the connection between them as bright and shining as ever, as if Castellis could actually make something good from one of their grand messes after all. "That is her job, is it not?"

Luca had prepared himself for a stepmother much like the last occupant of the role, the sharp blonde creature whom Gianni had inexplicably adored despite the fact she'd spent more time on her mobile or propositioning his sons than she had with him. Corinna had been nineteen when she'd married Gianni and already a former swimsuit model. Luca hadn't imagined his father had chosen her for her winning personality or depth of character.

But instead of another version of fake-breasted and otherwise entirely plastic Corinna, when he'd strode into the library where his father waited with Arlo, he'd found Kathryn.

Kathryn, who should not have been there.

That had been his first thought, like a searing blaze through his mind. He'd stopped, thunderstruck, halfway across the library floor and scowled at the woman who'd stood there smiling politely at him in that reserved British way of hers. Until his inability to do anything but glower at her had made that curve of her lips falter, then straighten into a flat line.

She doesn't belong here, he'd thought again, harsher and more certain. Not standing next to his old, crotchety father tucked up in his armchair before the fire, all wrinkles and white hair and fingers made of knots, thanks to years of arthritis. Not wringing her hands together in front of her like some kind of awkward schoolgirl instead of resorting to the sultry, come-hither glances Luca's stepmothers normally threw his way.

Not his *stepmother*.
That thought had been the loudest.
Not her.
Her hair was an inky dark brown that looked nearly black, yet showed hints of gold when the firelight played over it. It poured down past her shoulders, straight and thick, and was cut into a long fringe over smoky-gray eyes that edged toward green. She wore a simple pair of black trousers and a cleanly cut caramel-colored sweater open over a soft knit top that made no attempt whatsoever to showcase her cleavage. She looked elegantly efficient, not plastic or cheap in any way. She was small and fine boned, all big gray eyes and that dark hair and then, of course, there was her mouth.

Her mouth.

It was the mouth of a sulky courtesan, full and suggestive, and for a long, shocking moment, Luca had the strangest notion that she had no idea of its carnal wallop. That she was an innocent—but that had been absurd, of course. Wishful thinking, perhaps. No *innocent* married a very rich man old enough to be her own grandfather.

"Luca," Gianni had barked, in English for his new wife's benefit. "What is the matter with you? Show some manners. Kathryn is my wife and your new stepmother."

It had filled Luca with a kind of terrible smoke. A black, choking fury he could not have named if his life had depended upon it.

He hadn't been aware that he was moving, only that he'd been across the room and then was right there in front of her, looming over her, dwarfing her with his superior height and size—

Not that she'd backed down. Not Kathryn.

He'd seen far too much in those expressive eyes of hers, wide with some kind of distress. And awareness—he'd seen the flare of it, followed almost instantly by confusion. But instead of simpering or shifting her body to better advantage or sizing him up in any way, she'd squared her slender shoulders and stuck out her hand.

"Pleased to meet you," she'd said, her English-accented voice brisk. Matter-of-fact. The sound of it had fallen through him like a hail of ice and had done nothing to soothe that fire in him at all.

Luca had taken her hand, though he'd known it was a terrible mistake.

And he'd been right. It had been.

He'd felt the drag of her skin against his, palm to palm, like a long, slow lick down the length of his sex. He should have jerked his hand away. Instead, he'd held her tighter, feeling her delicacy, her heat and, more telling, that wild tumult of her pulse in her wrist. Her lips had parted as if she'd felt it, too.

He'd had to remind himself—harshly—that they were not only not alone, she was also not free.

She was something a whole lot worse than *not free*, in fact.

"It is my pleasure, *Stepmother*," he'd said, his voice low and dark, that terrible fire in him shooting like electricity all through his limbs and then into her. He'd seen her stiffen—whether in shock at his belligerence or with that same stunned awareness that stampeded in him, he'd never know. "Welcome to the family."

And it had been downhill from there.

All leading him here. To the same library, two years later, where Kathryn stood like a lonely wraith in a simple black dress that somehow made her look fragile and too pretty at once, her dark hair clipped back and no hint of color on her face below that same inky fringe that kissed the tops of her eyelashes.

She was gazing off into the distance through the windows that opened up over the lake, and she looked genuinely sad. As if she truly mourned Gianni, the man she'd used shamelessly for her own ends—ends that, apparently, included forcing herself into Luca's office against his will.

And it enraged him.

He told himself that was the thing that washed over him then, digging in its claws. *Rage.* Not that far darker, far more dangerous thing that lurked in him, as much that terrible hunger he'd prefer to deny as it was the familiar companion of his own self-loathing.

"Come, now, Kathryn," Luca said into the heavy quiet of the book-lined room, making his voice a dark and lazy thing just this side of insulting, and taking note of how she instantly stiffened against it. Against him. "The old man is dead and the reporters have gone home. Who is this maudlin performance for?"

CHAPTER TWO

LUCA CASTELLI'S TRADEMARK GROWL, his English laced with an undercurrent of both his native Italian and that particular harsh ruthlessness that Kathryn had only ever heard directed at her, jolted through her like an electric shock.

She jerked where she stood near the library window, actually jumping in a way he'd be unlikely to miss, even from all the way on the other side of the long, luxurious, stunningly appointed room.

Well done, she thought, despairing of herself anew. *Now he knows exactly how much he gets to you.*

She didn't expect that anything she did would make this man *like* her. Luca had made it clear that could never happen. Over and over and over again, these past two years. But she wanted him—*needed* him—not to actively hate her as she started this new phase of her life.

Kathryn figured that was better than nothing. As good a start as she could hope for, really. And her mother certainly hadn't raised her to be a coward, despite how disappointing she knew she'd always been. Rose Merchant had never let hardship get between her and what needed to be done, as she'd reminded Kathryn at every opportunity. Forging ahead into the corporate world the way Rose hadn't been able to do with a child to raise all on her own was, truly, the least Kathryn could do to honor all of her sacrifices.

And to assuage the guilt she felt about her marriage to Gianni—the one time "honoring her mother's sacrifices" had allowed her to do something purely for herself, too. But she couldn't let herself think about that too closely. It made her feel much too ungrateful.

Kathryn straightened from her place at the window, aware that her movements were jerky and awkward, the way she always seemed to be around this man, who noticed every last embarrassing detail about her and never hesitated to use each and every one of them against her. She nervously smoothed down the front of her dress. Nervously and also carefully, as if the dress was a talisman.

She'd agonized over what to wear today because she'd wanted to look as unlike the gold-digging whore she knew the family—*Luca*—thought she was as possible. And still, she was terribly afraid she'd ended up looking rather more like a poor man's version of an Audrey Hepburn wannabe instead. The papers would trumpet that possibility, call it *an homage to Audrey* or something equally embarrassing, and Luca would assume it was all part of a deliberate campaign toward some grim end he believed she'd been angling toward since the start, rather than simply riding out the attention as best she could. The cycle of his bitter condemnation would continue, turning and turning without end...

But she was delaying the inevitable. She'd always wanted a chance to prove herself, to work on the creative side of a corporation and try her hand at something fun and interesting like marketing or branding instead of the deadly dull figures at which she was utterly hopeless. She'd spent her whole marriage excited at the prospect of working in the family company with Luca and his creative genius.

Even if, other than that corporate flair of his, he was pretty much just awful. She assured herself powerful men often were. That Luca was run-of-the-mill in that sense.

Kathryn took a deep breath, resolutely squared her shoulders and turned to face her own personal demon at last.

"Hello, Luca," she said across the acres of space that separated them in this vast room, and she was proud of herself. She sounded so calm, so cool, when she was anything but.

For any number of reasons, but mostly because looking at Luca Castelli was like staring directly into the sun. It had been from the start.

And as usual, she was instantly dizzy.

Luca moved like a terrible shadow across the library floor, and tragically, he was as beautiful as ever. Tall and solid and impressively athletic, his rangy form was sculpted to lean, male perfection and was routinely celebrated in slick, photo-heavy tabloid exultations across at least five continents. His thick black hair always looked messy, as if he lived such a reckless, devil-may-care life that it required he run his hands through it all the time and rake it back from his darkly handsome face as punctuation to every sentence—despite the fact he was now the chief operating officer of the family company.

Even here, on the day of his father's funeral, where he wore a dark suit that trumpeted his rampant masculinity and excellent taste in equal measure, he gave off that same indolent air. That lazy, playful, perpetually relaxed state that only a man cresting high on the wealth of generations of equally affluent and pedigreed ancestors could achieve. As if no matter what he was actually doing, some part of him was always lounging about on a yacht somewhere with a cold drink in his hand and women presenting themselves for his pleasure. He had the look of a man who lived forever on the verge of laughter, deep and whole bodied, from his gorgeous mouth to his flashing dark eyes.

Kathryn had seen a hundred pictures of him exactly like that, lighting up the whole of the Amalfi Coast and half of Europe with that irrepressible *gleam* of his—

Except, of course, when he looked at her.

The scowl he wore now did nothing to make him any less beautiful. Nothing could. But it made Kathryn shake deep, deep inside, as if she'd lost control of her own bones. She wanted to bolt. She might have, if that wouldn't have made this whole situation that much worse.

Besides, if she'd learned anything these past two years, it was that there was no outrunning Luca Castelli. There was no outmaneuvering him. There was only surviving him.

"Hello, *Stepmother*," he said, that awful dark thing in his voice wrapping around her and sinking hot and blackened tendrils of something like shame into every part of her body, so deep it hurt to breathe. He seemed unaffected as ever, sauntering toward her with his usual deceptively lazy deadliness and those dark eyes so burning hot she could feel them punching into her from afar. "Or should we concoct a different title for you? *The Widow Castelli* has a certain gothic ring to it. I think. I'll have it engraved on your business cards."

"You know," Kathryn said, because she was still entirely too light-headed and not managing her tongue the way she should, "if you decided not to be horrible to me for five minutes the world wouldn't *actually* screech to a halt. We'd all survive. I promise."

His face was like stone, his full lips thin with displeasure, and he was closing the distance between them much too fast for Kathryn's peace of mind.

"I have no idea why you feel you need to bring this particular performance of yours into an office setting," he said as he drew closer. "Much less mine. I'm certain there are any number of hotel bars across Europe that cater to your brand of desperation and craven greed. You should have no trouble finding your next mark within the week."

That he could still hate her so much should not have surprised her, Kathryn knew, because Luca had been remarkably consistent in that since the day she'd arrived in Italy with Gianni two years ago. And yet, like that cold winter morning when he'd charged at her across this very same floor, dark and furious and terrifying in a way she hadn't entirely understood, it did.

Though *surprise* wasn't really the right word to describe the thing that rolled inside her, flattening everything it touched.

"I suppose the world really would end if you accepted the possibility that I might not be who you think I am," she said now, straightening her spine against the familiar rush of pointless grief that was her absurd response to the fact this angry, hateful man had never liked her. Kathryn channeled that odd, scraped-raw feeling into temper instead. "You'd have to reexamine your prejudices, and who knows what might happen then? Of course a man like you would find that scary. You have so many of them."

The truth was that she hardly knew Luca, despite two years of having forced, unpleasant interactions with him. What she did know was that he'd taken an instant and intense and noticeable dislike to her. On sight. Why she'd subsequently spent even three seconds—much less the whole of her marriage to his father—trying to convince him that he was wrong about her was a mystery to her. It no doubt spoke to deep psychological problems on her part, but then again, what about her relationship with this family didn't?

But she did know that poking at him was unwise.

Kathryn had a moment to regret the fact she'd done it anyway as Luca bore down on her, striding across the expanse of polished old floors and priceless rugs tossed here and there below rows of first editions in more languages than she'd known existed, all as smug and wealthy and resolutely untouchable as he was.

"This is as good a time as any to discuss the expectations I have for all Castelli Wine employees who work in my office in Rome." Luca's voice was dark. Cold. And as he moved toward her he regarded her with that sharpness in his eyes that made her feel...fluttery, low in her belly. "First, obedience. I will tell you when I am interested in hearing from you. If you are in doubt, you can assume I prefer you remain silent. *You* can assume that will always be the case. Second, confidentiality. If you cannot be trusted, if you are forever running off to the tabloids to give whining interviews about the many ways you have been wronged and victimized, *Saint Kate*—"

Kathryn flinched. "Please don't call me that. You know that's something the tabloids have made up."

Her mum had sniffed at the name and the image more than once, then reminded Kathryn that *she* had given Kathryn everything and received little in return, yet had never been called a saint by anyone. She'd even suggested that perhaps it had been Kathryn who'd come up with that name and that obnoxious storyline in the first place. It hadn't been.

That wasn't to say she hadn't played to it now and again. She'd always been fascinated with a good brand and widespread global marketing.

The fact that no one believed she hadn't made it all up herself, however, she found maddening. "*Saint Kate* has nothing to do with me."

"Believe me," Luca said in that quiet, horrible way of his, "I am under no delusions about you or your purity."

An actual slap would have hurt less. Kathryn blinked, managed not to otherwise react and forced herself to stay right where she was instead of reeling at that. Because his opinion of her aside, this was her chance to do something she really, truly believed she'd be good at instead of what other people thought she *ought* to be good at. She knew he hated her. She might not know why, but it didn't matter in the end. Kathryn had never wanted status or jewels or whatever the stepmothers before her had wanted from Gianni. She'd wanted this. A chance to prove herself at a job she knew she could do, in a company that had international reach and a bold, bright future, and to finally show her mother that she, too, could succeed in business. *Her* way, not Rose's way. This was what Gianni had promised her when he'd persuaded her to leave her MBA course in

London and marry him—the opportunity to work in the family business when the marriage was over.

This was what she wanted. She knew that if she did what every last nerve in her body was shrieking at her to do and broke for the door, she'd never come back, and Luca, certainly, would never give her another chance, no matter what it said in Gianni's will.

Her mother would never, ever forgive her. And the lonely little girl inside Kathryn, who had never wanted anything but Rose's love no matter how out of reach that had always been, simply couldn't let that happen.

"Luca," she said now, "before you really warm up to your insults, which are always *so* creative and comprehensive, I want to make sure you understand that I have every intention—"

"May the angels save me from the intentions of unscrupulous women." He was almost upon her, and one of the most unfair parts of this was that she couldn't seem to keep herself from feeling something like mesmerized by the way he moved. That impossible, offhanded grace of his he didn't deserve, and she shouldn't *notice* the way she did. It made her limbs feel precarious. Uncertain. "Third, my father's will says only that I must accommodate your desire to play at an office job, not what that job entails. If you complain, about anything at all, it will get worse. Do you understand?"

She felt a dark, hard pulse inside her then. It felt like running. Like fright. It gripped her, hard. In her temples. In the hollows behind her knees. In her throat.

In her sex.

Kathryn didn't have any idea what was happening to her. She struck out at him instead.

"Oh, what fun." She stared back at him when his

scowl edged over into something purely ferocious, and she made no attempt to rein in her sarcastic tone. Gianni was dead. The gloves were off. "Are you planning to make me scrub the floors? Let me guess, on my hands and knees with a toothbrush? That will teach me… something, I'm sure."

"I doubt that very much," he gritted out. He stopped a few feet away from her. *Too close*. Luca stood there then, in all his male fury while that dark thing that had always flared between them wound tighter and tighter around them and stole all the air from the graceful room. "But if I ask you to do it, whatever it is, I expect it to be done. No excuses."

Kathryn forced herself to speak. "And what if it turns out you're wrong about me and I'm not quite as useless as you imagine? I'm guessing abject apologies aren't exactly your strong suit."

His hard mouth—that she shouldn't find so *fascinating*, because what was wrong with her? She might as well find a shark cuddly—shifted into a merciless curve that was entirely too harsh to be a smile. "Have I ever told you how much I hate women like you?"

That word. *Hate*. It was a very strong word, and Kathryn had never understood how everything between them could feel so *intense*. She wasn't any clearer about that now. Nor why it scraped at that raw place inside her, as if it mattered deeply to her. As if he did.

When of course, he couldn't. He didn't. Luca was a means to an end, nothing more.

"It was rather more implied than stated outright," she replied, fighting to keep her voice even. "Nonetheless, you can take pride in the fact you managed to make your feelings perfectly clear from the start."

"My father married ever-younger women the way some men change their shoes," Luca said darkly, as if this was news to either one of them. "You are nothing but the last in his endless, pointless game of musical beds. You are not the most beautiful. You are not even the youngest. You are merely the one who survived him. You must know you meant nothing to him."

Kathryn shook her head at him. "I know exactly what I meant to your father."

"I would not brag, were I you, about your calculating and conniving ways," he threw back at her. "Especially not in my office, where you will find that the hardworking people who are rewarded on their merits rather than their various seduction techniques are unlikely to celebrate that approach."

Luca shook his head, judgment written in every line of his body in that elegant suit that a man as horrible as he was shouldn't have been able to wear so well. *Seduction techniques*, he'd said, the way someone might say *the Ebola virus*. It offended her, Kathryn thought.

He offended her.

Maybe that was why she lost her mind a little bit. He'd finally pushed her too far.

"I spent most of my marriage trying to figure out why you hated me so much," she bit out, heedless of his overwhelming proximity. Not caring the way she should about that glittering thing in his dark eyes. "That a grown man, seemingly of sound mind and obviously capable of performing great corporate feats when it suited him, could loathe another person on sight and for no reason. This made no sense to me."

She was aware of the grand house arrayed behind him, its ancient Italian splendor pressing in on her from all sides. Of the crystal clear lake that stretched off into the mist and the mountains that rose sharp and imposing above it. Of Gianni, sweet old Gianni, who she would never make laugh again and would never call her *cara* again in his gravelly old voice. Even this rarefied, beautiful world felt diminished by the loss of him, and here Luca was, as hateful as ever.

She couldn't bear it.

"I'm a decent person. I try to do the right thing. More to the point—" Kathryn raised her voice slightly when Luca made a derisive noise "—I'm not worth all the hatred and brooding you've been directing at me for years. I married your father and took care of him, the end. Neither you nor your brother had any interest in doing that. Some men in your position might *thank* me."

It was as if Luca expanded to fill the whole of the library then, he was so big, suddenly. Even bigger than he already was. So big she couldn't breathe, and he hadn't moved a muscle. He was simply dark and terrible, and that awful light in his eyes burned when he scowled at her.

"You were one more in a long line of—"

"Yes, but that's the thing, isn't it?" He looked astonished that she'd interrupted him, but Kathryn ignored that and kept going. "If you'd seen the likes of me before, why hate me at all? I should have been run-of-the-mill."

"You were. You were sixth."

"But you didn't despise the other five," Kathryn snapped, frustrated. "Lily told me all about them. You liked *her* mother. The last one tried to crawl into bed with you more than once, and you laughed each time you dumped her out in the hall. You simply told her to stop trying because it would never happen with you—you didn't even tell your father. You didn't hate *her*, and you *knew* she was every single thing you accuse me of being."

"Are you truly claiming you are not those things? That you are, in fact, this unrecognizable paragon I've read so much about in the papers? Come now, Kathryn. You cannot imagine I am so naive."

"I never did anything to you, Luca," she hurled at him, and she couldn't control her voice then.

There were nearly two years of repressed feelings bottled up inside her. Every slight. Every snide remark. Every cutting word he'd said to her. Every vicious, unfair glare. Every time he'd walked out of a room she entered in obvious disgust. Every time she'd looked up from a conversation to find that stare of his all over her, like a touch.

It was true that on some level, it was refreshing to meet someone who was so shockingly *direct*. But that didn't make it hurt any less.

"I have no idea why you hated me the moment you saw me. I have no idea what goes on in that head of yours." She stepped forward, far too close to him and then, no longer caring what his reaction would be, she went suicidal and poked two fingers into his chest. Hard. "But after today? I no longer care. Treat me the way you treat anyone else who works for you. Stop acting as if I'm a demon sent straight from hell to torture you."

He'd gone deathly still beneath her fingers. Like marble.

"Remove your hand." His voice was frozen. Furious. "Now."

She ignored him.

"I don't have to prove that I'm a decent person to you. I don't care if the world knows your father forced you to hire me. I *know* I'll do a good job. My work will speak for itself." She poked him again, just as hard as before, and who cared if it was suicidal? There were worse things. Like suffering through another round of his character assassinations. "But I'm not going to listen to your abuse any longer."

"I told you to remove your hand."

Kathryn held his dark gaze. She saw the bright warning in it, and it should have scared her. It should have impressed her on some level, reminded her that whatever else he was, he was a very strong, very well built man who was as unpredictable as he was dangerous.

And that he hated her.

But instead, she stared right back at him.

"I don't care what you think of me," she told him, very distinctly.

And then she poked him a third time. Even harder than before, right there in that shallow between his pectoral muscles.

Luca moved so fast she had no time to process it.

She poked him, then she was sprawled across the hard wall of his chest with her offending hand twisted behind her back. It was more than dizzying. It was like toppling from the top of one of the mountains that ringed the lake, then hurtling end over end toward the earth.

Her heart careened against her ribs, and his darkly gorgeous face was far too close to hers and she was *touching* him, her dress not nearly enough of a barrier to keep her from noticing unhelpful things like his scent, a hint of citrus and spice. The heat that blazed from him, as if he was his own furnace. And that deceptively languid strength of his that made something deep inside her flip over.

Then hum.

"This, you fool," Luca bit out, his mouth so close to hers she could taste the words against her own lips. She could taste *him*, and she shuddered helplessly, completely unable to conceal her reaction. "This is what I think of you."

And then he crushed his mouth to hers.

CHAPTER THREE

HE DID NOT ASK. He did not hesitate. He simply *took*.

Luca's mouth descended on hers, and Kathryn waited for that kick of terror, of unease, of sheer panic that had always accompanied any hint of male sexual interest in her direction before—

But it never came.

He kissed her with all that lazy confidence that made him who he was. He took her mouth again and again, still holding her arm behind her back and then sliding his free hand along her jaw to guide her where he wanted her.

Slick. Hot.

Deliciously, wildly, stunningly male.

He kissed her as if they'd done this a thousand times before. As if the past two years had been leading nowhere but here. To this hot, impossible place Kathryn didn't recognize and couldn't navigate.

There was nothing to do but surrender. To the molten fire that rolled through her and pooled in all the worst places. A heaviness in her breasts, pressed hard against his chest. And that restless, edgy, weighted thing that sank low into her belly and then pulsed hot.

Needy. Insistent.

And Kathryn *forgot*.

She forgot who he was. That she had been his stepmother for two years, though he was some eight years older than she was. She forgot that in addition to being her harshest critic and her bitter enemy through no fault of her own, he was now going to be her boss.

She forgot everything but the taste of him. That harsh, sweet magic he made, the way he commanded her and compelled her, as if he knew the things her body wanted and could do when she had no idea. When she was simply lost—adrift in the fire. The greedy, consuming flames that licked all over her and through her and deep inside her and made her meet every stroke of his tongue, every glorious taste—

He set her away from him. As if it hurt.

"Damn you," he muttered. Followed by something that sounded far harsher in Italian.

But it seemed to take him a very long time to let go of her.

Kathryn couldn't speak. She didn't understand the things that were storming through her then, making her blood seem like thunder in her veins and her skin seem to stretch too tight to contain all the *feelings* she didn't know how to name.

They stared at each other in the scant bit of space between them. His face was drawn tight, stark and harsh, and it still did absolutely nothing to detract from his sheer male beauty.

"You kissed me," Kathryn said, and she could have kicked herself.

But her lips felt swollen and she had the taste of him in her mouth, and she didn't know how to process that hot and slippery feeling that charged through her and then concentrated between her legs.

If possible, that dark look on his face got blacker. As if he was a storm.

"Don't you dare try that innocent game on me," he gritted out.

"I don't know what that means."

"It means I know the difference between a virgin and a whore, Kathryn," Luca said, the fury in him like a brand that pressed into her, searing her flesh, and she didn't understand how she could feel it the same way she had that desperate kiss. "I can certainly taste it."

She realized she had absolutely no idea how to respond to that.

"Luca," she said, as carefully as she could when her entire body was lost in the tumult of that endless kiss. When she had no idea how she was even capable of speech. "I think we should chalk that up as nothing more than an emotional response to a very hard day and—"

"I will not be your next target, Kathryn," Luca told her, a frozen sort of outrage in his voice and pressed deep into the fine lines of his beautiful face. "Hear me on this. *It will not happen.*"

"I don't have targets." She blinked, the room seeming to shimmer everywhere he was not, as if he was a black hole. "I'm not a weapon. What kind of life do you lead that you think these things?"

He reached over and took her upper arm in his hand, pulling her close to him again, and that fire that hadn't really banked at all blazed. Fierce and wild. Almost knocking her from her feet.

"I don't want you in my office," he growled. "I don't want you polluting the Castelli name any more than you already have. I don't want you anywhere near the things that matter to me."

Kathryn's teeth chattered, though she wasn't cold.

"That would probably be far more terrifying a threat if you weren't touching me," she managed to point out, though her voice wasn't nearly as cool as she'd have liked. "Again."

Luca laughed, though it bore no resemblance to that carefree, golden laughter that had helped make him so beloved the world over, and released her. If she didn't know better, if he'd been some other man with the usual collection of weaknesses instead of a monolith where his heart should have been, she'd have thought he hadn't meant to grab her in the first place.

"I will never lower myself to my father's discards," he told her, horribly, his gaze hard on hers in case she was tempted to pretend she hadn't heard that. "Nor will I allow you to corrupt the good people in my office with your repulsive little schemes. Your game won't work on me."

"Right," she said, and maybe it was because this was all so out of control already. Maybe that was why she couldn't seem to keep herself in check any longer around him. What was the point? She'd tried to *rise above* him for two years, and here they were anyway. "That's why you kissed me, I imagine. To demonstrate your immunity."

Luca went very still.

So still that Kathryn stopped breathing herself, as if the slightest noise might set him off. His dark eyes were fixed on her as if she was the kind of target he'd mentioned before, and she'd never felt more like one in her life. Between them, that spinning, tightening, desperate and dangerous electric band seemed to wrap tighter, pull harder. So hard it pulsed inside her, insistent and rough. So lethal she swore she could see it stamped across every tightly held, hard-packed muscle on his sculpted form.

Rain clattered against the windows behind her, and off in some other part of this massive house, little Renzo let loose one of his ear-piercing toddler screams that could as easily be joy as peril.

Luca shook his head slightly, as if he'd been released from a spell. He stepped back, his expression shifting from whatever that harsh, hard thing was to something far closer to disgust.

"You will regret this," he promised her.

She swallowed. "You'll have to be more specific. That could cover a lot of ground."

"I will make sure of it," Luca told her, as if she hadn't spoken. "If it's the very last thing I do."

His voice had the ring of a certain finality, and it clanged inside her like a gong. She stood there, stricken, her mouth still aching from his kiss and her body lost in its own strange riot, and watched as he simply turned and began to walk away from her.

She wanted nothing more than to forget all about this. To take the lump payment Rafael had offered her and disappear with it. She could have any life she wanted now. She could be anyone she wanted, far away from the long shadow of the Castellis where she'd lived for so long.

But that would mean the past two years of her life had been for nothing. That she'd simply thrown them away for cash. It would mean she was exactly the woman Luca thought she was—and that all her mother's sacrifices would have been for nothing in the end. That there was nothing to Kathryn's own life but guilt and falling short.

And Kathryn could bear a lot of things. She'd had no choice, given what a failure she'd turned out to be in her mother's eyes. She simply didn't have it in her to make it that much worse. There was that part of her that was convinced, after all this time, that if she tried hard enough she could make her mother love her. If she could just do the right thing, for once.

"I'm so glad we had this talk," she called after him, directing her not-quite-sweet tone straight toward the center of his tall, broad back. He wanted to play target practice? She could do that. "It will make Monday so much better for everyone."

He didn't turn back to face her, though he slowed. "Monday?"

If she was the good person she'd always believed herself to be, Kathryn thought then, surely she wouldn't take *quite* so much pleasure in this tiny little moment, this almost pointless victory.

"Oh, yes," she said, with deliberate calm and that triumph right there in her voice. "That's when I start."

He should never have touched her.

He should *certainly* not have tasted her.

But he had always been a fool where that woman was concerned, and in case he'd been tempted to doubt that, she haunted him all the way back to Rome.

Luca drove himself into the city from the family's private airfield, risking death in an appropriately sleek and low-slung car that made Rome's famously chaotic traffic a game of wits and daring and delicious speed. And he regretted it when he arrived at the Renaissance-era villa that housed both his business and his home, because playing games with his life at high speeds through the streets of the ancient city he loved was far preferable—and much less dangerous—than letting himself think about Kathryn.

Though he supposed both edged into that same dark place inside him, as if he was as much of a damned mess as every other Castelli in history down deep, beneath all the controls he'd spent his life putting into place to prevent exactly that.

He tossed his keys to the waiting attendant in his garage and stalked into the building, only to find himself standing stock-still in his own empty reception area, his head filled with those damned *eyes* of hers, turned a dreamy slate green after he'd kissed her, and that sulky mouth—

Luca muttered a chain of curses. He raked both his hands through his hair as he headed into the offices that sprawled across the first two levels of this lovingly maintained building in Rome's Tridente neighborhood, a mere stone's throw from the Spanish Steps and Piazza del Popolo.

His office. His one true love. The only thing he'd ever loved, in point of fact. The only thing that had ever come close to loving him back, with one success after the next.

He lived in the penthouse that rambled over the top two levels, and that was where he headed now, taking his private lift up into the rooms he'd furnished with steel and chrome, wide-open spaces and minimalist art, the better to play off the history in every bit of stone and craftsmanship in the walls and the high, frescoed ceilings and every view of gorgeous, sleepless, frenetic Rome out of his windows. He tore off his clothes in his rooftop bedroom of glass and steel before making his way out to the pool on the wraparound terrace that surrounded the master suite and offered a three-hundred-sixty-degree perspective on the Eternal City.

If Rome could stand for more than two and a half thousand years, surely Luca could survive the onslaught of Kathryn. She had no idea what she was setting herself up for. Luca was a tough boss at the best of times, demanding and fierce, and that was what the loyal employees he'd handpicked said about him to his face. What could a former trophy wife know of the corporate world? She might have some fantasy of herself as a businesswoman, but it was unlikely she'd last the week.

Of course she won't be able to handle it, he thought with something a great deal like relief—how had he failed to realize that earlier? He was called upon to indulge her whim, not alter the whole of his carefully controlled existence. The sooner she understood how ill suited she was to a life that involved more work than play, the sooner she'd drift off to find her next conquest. The problem would take care of itself.

Luca still felt edgy and entirely too messed up, despite the chill of the winter evening and the kick of the wind. Out of control. Jittery and appalled with himself. He told himself it must be grief, though he hadn't been close with his father. He might have wished, from time to very rare and sentimental time, that he'd had a better understanding of the man whose shadow had fallen over him all these years—but he never had.

Perhaps the funeral had hit him harder than he'd realized.

Because he could not understand why he'd kissed Kathryn. What the hell was the matter with him?

How could he—a man who prided himself on always, *always* keeping his life clean and trimmed down and free from anything even resembling this kind of emotional clutter—have no idea?

He dived into the pool then, cutting into the heated water and then pulling hard as he began to swim. He lost himself in the rhythm of his strokes, the weight and rush of the water against him and the growing heat in his body as he kept going, kept pushing.

Lap after lap. Then again.

He swam and he swam, he pushed himself hard, and it was no good. She was still right there, cluttering up his head, reminding him how empty he was everywhere else.

Wide gray eyes. All that dark hair and that fringe that made her seem more mysterious somehow. All of her, wedged in him like a jagged splinter he could never remove, that he'd never managed to do anything but shove in that much farther. She worried at him and worried at him and he had no idea anymore who he was when he was near her. What he might do.

Luca stopped swimming, slamming his hands down on the lip of the pool, sending water splashing everywhere.

He did not dip his quill in his company's ink, ever. He knew better than to throw grenades like that into the middle of his life. He did not touch his employees, and he certainly did not avail himself of his father's leftovers. He had been a loud, angry child often abandoned by his single living parent for months at a time in the old manor house because of the trouble he'd caused. He'd gotten over that kind of behavior while he'd still been a child. This kind of mess was precisely what he'd spent his adult life avoiding.

This was a nonissue.

Luca climbed out of the pool and wrapped himself in one of the towels his staff kept at the ready, and then made his way back inside, hardly noticing the way the sun had turned the rambling old city orange and pink as it sank toward the horizon. Not even when he stood at one of the high windows that looked out over the winding, cobbled streets that led toward Piazza di Spagna and the famous Spanish Steps, where it seemed half of Rome congregated some evenings.

He saw nothing but Kathryn, dressed in her funeral clothes like some waifish fairy tale of a widow, and it had to stop. She'd already had two black marks against her before today. Her marriage to his father in the first place. And the unpalatable fact of her tabloid presence, the endless canonization of *Saint Kate*, nauseatingly described as the plucky English lass who'd bearded any number of dragons in his twisted old-Italian family.

It repulsed him. He told himself she did, too.

That kiss today was the third black mark. He couldn't pretend he hadn't started it, hauling her to him with the kind of heedless passion he'd been so certain he'd completely excised from his life. How many times had he seen this or that foolish longing lay his father low? How often had he rolled his eyes at his brother's enduring anguish over Lily? How many times had his own pointless emotions bit him in the ass as a child? He'd promised himself a long time ago that he would stay clear of such quagmires, and the truth was, it had never been particularly difficult.

Until Kathryn. And the truth remained: he'd been the one to kiss her. He accepted that failing, even if he couldn't quite understand it.

The problem was the way she'd kissed him back.

The way she'd melted against him. The way she'd opened her mouth and met him. The way she'd poured herself into him, against him, until he'd very nearly forgotten who and where they were. That she was his stepmother, his father's widow, and that they'd been standing much too near the family mausoleum where the old man had only just been interred.

Luca was sick, there was no doubt about that—and the fact he was hard even now, at the mere memory of her taste, proved it.

But what game had she been playing?

She was good, he could admit it. She'd tasted like innocence. He still had the flavor of her on his tongue.

That was the most infuriating thing by far.

And Luca vowed, as the last bit of winter sun fell down behind Rome's enduring skyline, that he would not only make this little corporate adventure for his father's child bride of a widow as unpleasant as possible— he would also do much worse than that.

He would take Saint Kate's halo and tarnish it. And her.

Irredeemably.

By the time Kathryn made it to the ornate Castelli Wine offices in one of the most charming neighborhoods in Rome that Monday morning at exactly nine o'clock sharp, she'd prepared herself.

This was a war. A drawn-out siege. She might have lost a battle in that library far to the north in all those forbidding, foggy mountains, but that meant nothing in the scheme of things. It was a small battle. A kiss, that was all.

The war was what mattered.

The receptionist greeted her in icy Italian and pretended not to understand Kathryn's halting attempts to speak the language—then picked up the phone and spoke in flawless English, staring at Kathryn all the while. Her expression was impassive when she ended the call, but Kathryn was certain she could see triumph lurking there in the depths of the other woman's haughty gaze.

She ordered herself not to react.

"How lovely," Kathryn said, her own tone cool. "You speak English after all. Please tell Luca I'm here."

She didn't wait for the other woman's response. She went and sat in one of the rigid antique chairs that lined the waiting area and pretended to be perfectly comfortable as she waited. And waited.

And waited.

But this was a war, she reminded herself. And it had occurred to her at some point over the weekend that for all his bluster, Luca had no idea who she was or what he was dealing with. All he saw was his image of her as the gold digger who'd snared his father. That meant, Kathryn had decided, that she had the upper hand. So if he wanted to leave her stranded in purgatory all morning, cooling her heels in his waiting room as some childish gesture of pique and temper, let him. She wouldn't give him—or his receptionist, for that matter—the satisfaction of looking even the slightest bit impatient.

She kept her attention on her mobile, keeping her expression as smooth as glass as she dutifully emailed her mother to let her know she'd started work in Castelli Wine as planned, then thumbed through the news. For an hour.

When Luca finally appeared, she sensed him before she saw him. That dark, thunderous, electric thing that made every hair on her body leap to attention, filling the whole of the great cavern of a waiting room that had until that moment been bright with the Rome morning, light pouring in from the windows to dance across the marble floor. She forced herself to take her time looking up.

And there he was.

He was even more devastatingly gorgeous today, in a more casual suit than the one he'd worn at the funeral, the open white collar of his shirt offering her a far too tempting glimpse of the expanse of his olive skin and the hint of that perfect chest she knew—from the tabloid pages dedicated to him and that one Castelli family outing to Positano that had involved a boat and Luca without his shirt, God help her—had a dusting of dark hair and all those finely carved ridges in his abdomen.

She told herself she was starting to find that scowl on his face almost charming. Like a love song from an ogre.

"You're late," he said.

That was astoundingly unfair at best, but Kathryn didn't have to look to the smug receptionist to understand that there was no point arguing. Besides, Luca had warned her not to complain. She wouldn't. Kathryn stood, smoothing out her skirt as she rose.

"I apologize. It won't happen again."

"Somehow," Luca replied, sounding very nearly merry—which was alarming, "I doubt that."

Kathryn didn't bother to reply. She walked toward him, telling herself with every click of her heels against the hard floor that she remembered nothing from last week in that old library up north. Not his taste. Not that thrilling, masterful way he'd simply *taken* her mouth with his. Not the searing, impossible heat of his hand against the side of her face and that deep stroke of his clever tongue—

She hadn't dreamed those things. They hadn't kept her wide-awake and gasping at the ceiling, not sure how to handle the riot all those searing images and memories had caused inside her. *Certainly not.*

Luca's expression was unreadable as she drew close to him, and she hated that she had no idea what was going on behind his gleaming dark eyes as he ushered her deep into the heart of the Castelli Wine offices. She thought she felt him glance over her outfit, a pencil skirt and a conservative silk blouse that could offend no one, she was sure, but when she sneaked a look at him, his attention was focused straight ahead.

He stopped at the door to a large glassed-in conference room and waved a hand at the group of people sitting around the table inside. *My coworkers*, Kathryn thought—with what she realized was an utterly naive surge of pleasure when she realized not a single one of them was looking out at her with anything approaching a smile on their faces.

She froze beside Luca, who already had his hand on the door.

"What did you tell them?" she asked.

"My people?" He sounded far too triumphant, mixed in with that usual hint of laziness that she was beginning to suspect was all for show. "The truth, of course."

"And which truth is that?"

"There is only the one," Luca said. Happily, she thought. Again. "My father's petulant trophy wife has insisted she be given a job she does not deserve. We do not have jobs hanging about without anyone to fill them, so there was some reshuffling required."

"I assumed you'd be giving me janitorial duties." She arched a brow at him. "Wasn't the idea to make sure this was as unpleasant for me as possible?"

"I made you my executive assistant," Luca replied smoothly, his dark eyes glittering. "It is the most coveted position in this branch of the company." He shifted back slightly. Relaxing, she realized. Because he was obviously enjoying himself. That sent a shiver of ice straight down her spine. So did his smile—which she was close enough to see did not reach his eyes. "It is second only to me, you see. That's quite a bit of power to wield."

She frowned at him. "Why would you do that? Why not make me file things in some basement?"

"Because, *Stepmother*," Luca said in that slow, dark way of his that should not have gotten tangled up in all her breathless memories of that kiss, not when it was clearly meant to be a blow, "that would only delay the inevitable. I am quite certain you won't make it the allocated three years. But if you leave after three days? Three weeks? All the better."

She stiffened. "I won't leave."

He nodded toward the group of people inside, all eyeing her with ill-disguised hostility.

"Each and every person in that room was handpicked by me. They earned their positions here. They function together as a tight and usually congenial team. But I have informed them that all of that is a thing of the past, as you must be shoehorned in whether we like it or not." He turned his gaze on her. "As you can see, they're thrilled."

Kathryn's stomach sank to her feet, because she understood what he'd done. Her pathetic little fantasies of distinguishing herself somehow through hard work in some forgotten corner of the office where she could quietly shine crumbled all around her.

Her mother would be furious. She'd claim that this was exactly what had happened when Kathryn tried to defy her and strike out on her own. Kathryn felt a sinking feeling in her gut, as if maybe Rose was right.

And maybe it was hideously disloyal, maybe it made her a terrible person and an ungrateful child, but Kathryn really, really didn't want that to be true.

"You painted a target on my back," she said now, her lips feeling numb. "You did it deliberately."

This time, Luca's smile reached his eyes, but that didn't make it any warmer. Or this situation any better. "I did."

Then he pushed open the conference room door and fed her straight to the wolves.

CHAPTER FOUR

THREE HARD WEEKS and two days later, Kathryn boarded the Castelli family private jet on the airfield outside Rome, this time in her capacity as the most hated employee in Luca's office. She marched up the folded-down stairs with her back straight and her head high—because that title, of course, was an upgrade compared to her previous role as the most hated stepmother in Castelli family history.

She thought she had this being-loathed thing under control.

It was all about the smile.

Kathryn smiled every time conversation halted abruptly when she entered a room. She smiled when her coworkers pretended they didn't understand her and made her repeat her question once, then twice, so she'd feel foolish as her words hung there in the air between them. She smiled when she was ignored in meetings. She smiled when she was called on to answer questions about past projects she couldn't possibly know anything about. She smiled when Luca berated her for allowing unrestricted access to him and she smiled brighter when he let his people in and out the side door of his office himself, so he could do it all over again.

She smiled and she smiled. The benefit of having been splashed across a thousand tabloids and held to be *so good* and *so self-sacrificing* was that she found she could use *Saint Kate* as a guide through each and every one of her chilly office interactions. Especially because she was well aware that the less she reacted, the more it annoyed her coworkers.

Luca, of course, was a different issue altogether.

She ducked into the plane and made her way into the upgraded living room space, smiling serenely as she took her seat on the curved leather sofa that commanded the center of the room. Luca was already sprawled out at one of the tables to the side that seated three apiece in luxurious leather armchairs, one hand in his hair as usual and the other clamping his mobile to his ear.

He eyed her as he finished his conversation in low Italian, and didn't stop when it was done.

"You're still here," he said. Eventually.

She smiled brighter. "Of course. I told you I wouldn't leave."

"You can't possibly have enjoyed these past few weeks, Kathryn."

"You certainly went out of your way to make sure of that," she agreed. She showed him her teeth. "Much appreciated."

He frowned, and she smiled, and that went on for so long, she was tempted to turn on the big-screen television and ignore him—but that was not how an employee would behave, she imagined.

"You were at the office when I arrived this morning," he said gruffly.

"Every morning."

"I beg your pardon?"

"I'm at the office when you arrive *every* morning," Kathryn said mildly. "Your assistant can't be late the way I was that first day, can she? It sends the wrong message."

She didn't expect him to admit that he'd deliberately kept her waiting that day, simply so he could chastise her for tardiness. He didn't disappoint her, though there was a gleam she didn't quite understand in his dark eyes as they remained level on hers.

"Surely you have other things to do with your time." He waved a hand at her, as if she was displaying herself in a tiny string bikini rather than wearing another perfectly unobjectionable blouse and skirt, chosen specifically to blend in with everyone else and be unworthy of comment. "Trips to the places rich men frequent, the better to identify your next target, for example."

"I had that all planned for this weekend, of course," she said in her sweetest, most professional tone, "but then you scheduled this trip to California. I guess the gold digging will have to wait."

He didn't speak to her again until the plane reached its cruising altitude and the single, deferential air steward had set out trays of food for their dinner on the dark wood coffee table that sprawled in the center of the jet's deeply comfortable and faintly decadent living room. Kathryn's stomach rumbled at her, reminding her that she'd worked through lunch. And breakfast, for that matter, not that her dedication ever seemed to make a difference in Luca's slippery slope of an office, where she literally could do no right.

You're used to that, aren't you? a voice inside her asked—but she shoved it away. Her mother's disappointment in her hurt, yes, but it wasn't invalid. Kathryn was well aware of her own deficiencies, and not only because she'd heard about them so often.

If she hadn't been so deficient, she reminded herself, she wouldn't have found marrying Gianni to be such a perfect option for her. She'd have excelled at her MBA the way she'd been supposed to do.

"Tell me the story," Luca said after they'd eaten in silence for a while, surprising her.

He had a plate on the table before him and was lounging in his leather armchair as he picked languidly at it, but his seeming nonchalance didn't make her heart beat any slower. Nor did it help matters that they were trapped in a plane together, and Kathryn couldn't seem to make herself think about anything but that. All the gilt edges and wood accents and noncommercial setup and decor in the world couldn't change the fact that she and Luca were suspended above the Atlantic Ocean in the dark, with no buffer between them.

Alone.

That hit her like a punch then slid down deep into her belly and pulsed there, as worrying as it was entirely too hot.

She had never actually been alone with Luca before.

There had always been someone else around. Always. Gianni. Some other member of the Castelli family. Staff. All the people in his office, especially because they all lived to catch her out in a misstep as she muddled her way through her first weeks on the job. Rafael and his family the week of the funeral, never more than a room or two away, liable to walk in at any moment.

This was the first time in over two years that it had ever been just the two of them.

There's a pilot, she told herself as her heart slowed, then beat too hard against her ribs. *You're not really alone.*

But she knew even as she thought it that it didn't mean anything. Neither the pilot nor the air steward would disturb Luca unless he summoned them himself. She might as well have stranded herself on a desert island with the man.

That, she reflected helplessly, her mind suddenly full of images of a half-naked Luca gleaming beneath some far-off tropical sun, *is not a helpful line of thought.*

And there was a certain hunger in that dark gaze of his that made her think he was entertaining the same rush of images that she was.

"What story?" she asked, and hated how insubstantial her voice was. And the way his dark gaze sharpened at the sound, as if he knew why.

"The lovely and touching fairy tale of how an obviously virtuous young woman like yourself fell passionately in love with a man who could easily have fathered your parents, of course. What else?"

That was meant to insult her, Kathryn knew. But he'd never asked her that before. No one had. The entire world thought they knew exactly why a younger woman had married a much older man—and that wasn't entirely untrue, of course. There were reasons, and some of those reasons were financial. But that didn't mean it had been as cold or as calculated as Luca was determined to believe.

"It wasn't a fairy tale," she told him, tucking her feet up beneath her on the butter-soft leather sofa and smoothing the edges of her skirt down farther toward her knees. She frowned at him. "It was just…nice. I met him very much by accident at a facility that caters to seniors and people with degenerative health challenges."

He didn't *quite* snort at that. "How touching."

"Surely you know that your father wasn't well, Luca." She shrugged. "He was visiting a specialist. I was in the waiting area and we got to talking."

"You were there, one assumes, to gather some extra polish for your halo and crow about it to the tabloids?"

Kathryn thought of her mother, and the way her body had betrayed her, growing so old and knotted before her time. She thought of the gnarled hands that had scrubbed floors to give Kathryn every possible chance—*I had plans for my life, Kathryn*, Rose had always said in that sharp way of hers, *but I put them aside for you.*

How could Kathryn do anything less than the same in return for her?

"Something like that," she said now, to this man who didn't deserve to know anything about her mother or her struggles, or the choices Kathryn had made to honor the sacrifices that had been made for her, no matter how badly she'd done at that sometimes. "I do so prefer it when my halo shines, you know."

Luca laughed—and it was *that* laugh. That famous spill of light and life and perfection, illuminating his face and making the air between them dance and shimmer for a long, taut moment before he stopped himself, as if he hadn't realized what was happening.

But she could hoard it anyway, Kathryn thought, feeling dazed. She could hold it close. An unexpected gift she could take out and warm herself with during her next sleepless night—and this was not the time to ask herself why she thought anything this man did was a gift. Not when she knew he'd hate her even more for thinking such a thing.

"And a driving, inescapable passion for a septuagenarian overtook you in this waiting area?" he asked, his voice darker than before, his gaze much too shrewd. "I hear that happens. Though not often to young women in their twenties, unless, of course, you were discussing his net worth."

"I liked him," Kathryn said, and that was the truth about her marriage, no matter the extenuating circumstances. She shrugged. "He made me laugh and I made him laugh, too. It wasn't seedy or mercenary, Luca, no matter how much you wish that it was. He was a good friend to me."

A better friend than most, if she was honest.

"A good friend."

"Yes."

"My father. Gianni Castelli. *A good friend.*"

Kathryn sighed, and set her plate down on the coffee table, her appetite gone. "I take it you've decided in your infinite wisdom that this, too, must be impossible."

Luca's laugh this time was no gift. Not one anyone in her right mind would want anyway.

"My father was born into wealth, and his single goal was to expand it," he told her harshly, the Italian inflection in his voice stronger than usual. "That was his art and his calling, and he dedicated himself to it with single-minded purpose from the time he could walk. His favorite hobby was marriage—the more inappropriate, the better. Do not beat yourself up. Most of his wives misunderstood the breakdown of his affections and attention."

"I don't think you knew your father very well," Kathryn suggested. She lifted up her hands when Luca's eyes blazed. "Not in the way I did. That's all I mean."

"You're speaking of the two years of your acquaintance with him, as opposed to the whole of my life?"

"A son can't possibly know the man his father was." She lifted a shoulder then dropped it. "He can only know what kind of father he was or wasn't, and piece together what clues he can about the man from that. Isn't that the history of the world? No one ever knows their parents. Not really."

She certainly didn't know hers. Her father had buggered off before she was born, and her mother had given up everything that had mattered to her so Kathryn wouldn't have to bear the weight of that. Kathryn knew the sacrifice. Her mother reminded her of what she'd left behind for Kathryn's sake at every opportunity, and fair enough. But she still couldn't say she understood the woman—much less the way she'd treated Kathryn all her life.

A muscle leaped in Luca's lean jaw.

"I knew my father a great deal longer than you did," he gritted out after a moment. "He had no friends, Kathryn. He had business associates and a collection of wives. Everyone in his life was accorded a role and expected to play it, and woe betide the fool who did not live up to his expectations."

"Is that what this has been about all this time? All the hatred and the nastiness and the threats and so on?" she asked. She tilted her head to one side and said the thing she knew she shouldn't. But she couldn't seem to stop herself. "You…have daddy issues?"

The crack of his temper was very nearly audible. If the plane itself had been thrown off course and sent into a spiraling nosedive toward the ocean, she wouldn't have been at all surprised—and it took Kathryn a long, tense, shuddering moment to understand that the jet they sat on was fine. The plane flew on, unaffected by the minor explosion that had taken over the cabin—and the aftershocks that were still rolling through her.

The only steep and terrible free fall was in her stomach as it plummeted to her feet.

Luca hadn't moved. It only felt as if he had.

She watched, as fascinated as she was alarmed, as he tamped that bright current of fury down. He still didn't move. He stared back at her as if he'd very much like to throttle her. One hand twitched as if he'd considered it. This suggested to her that she'd been more on target than she'd imagined when she'd said it.

But then he blinked and the crisis passed. There was only the usual force of his dislike staring back at her. That and the leftover adrenaline trickling through her veins, making her shift against the sofa cushions.

"Why me?" he asked, his dark voice a spiked thing as it slammed into her. "I've made no secret of my opinion of you. What sort of masochism led you to throw yourself in my path when you must know you'd have had a much better time in another branch of the company?"

"Is that a thinly veiled way of asking if I'm pursuing you for my usual gold-digging ends?" she asked, unable to tear her gaze from his and equally unsure why that was. Why did he *invade* her like this? Why did she feel as if he had more control over her than she did?

"Was it veiled, thinly or otherwise?" he asked, his voice soft. If no less harsh. "I must be doing it wrong."

Kathryn's smile felt forced, but she didn't let it fade. She had the wild notion, suddenly, that it was all she had.

"I considered working for your brother, of course," she said quietly. "I doubt he's particularly fond of me, but there's certainly none of…this." She waved her hand between them, in that too-thick air and that taut electric storm that charged it. "It would have been easier, certainly."

"Then, why?" Luca's mouth curled into something much too dark to be any kind of smile, and the echo of it pulsed inside her. "To punish us both?"

"The fact is that your brother maintains the business and he's very good at it," Kathryn said. "He will make certain the Castelli name endures, that no ground will be lost on his watch. He's a very steady hand on the wheel."

"And I am what?" Luca didn't quite laugh. "The drunken driver in this scenario? I drive too fast, Kathryn. But never drunk."

"You're the innovator," she said quietly. It felt… dangerous to praise him to his face. To do something other than suffer through his darkness. "You're the creative force in the company. Never satisfied. Always pushing a new boundary." She shrugged, more uncomfortable than she could remember ever having been around him before, and that was saying something. "My personal feelings about you aside, there's no more exciting place to work. You must know this. I assume that's why all your employees are so—" Kathryn smiled that little bit brighter, and that, too, was harder than it should have been "—fiercely protective."

Luca looked thrown, which she might have considered a victory at any other time—but there was something about the way he gazed at her then. It seemed to sneak into her, wrapping itself around her bones and drawing tight. Too tight.

"Can you do that?" he asked, his voice mild but with that *something* beneath it. "Put your personal feelings aside?"

She met his gaze. She didn't flinch.

"I have to if I want this job to mean something," Kathryn told him, aware as she spoke that this might have been the most honest she'd ever been with him. As if she had nothing to lose, when that couldn't be further from the truth. This was her only chance to prove that she could make something of herself without her mother's input or directives. This was her only chance to honor her mother's sacrifices—and also stay free. "And I do. Unlike you, I don't have a choice."

The Castelli château, the center of Castelli Wine's operations in the States, perched at the top of Northern California's fertile Sonoma Valley like a particularly self-satisfied grande dame. The vineyards stretched out much like voluminous queenly skirts, rolling out over the hills in all directions, seeming to take over this part of the valley all the way to the horizon and back. Tonight the winery gleamed prettily through the crisp winter night, bright lights in every window as a line of cars snaked down the long drive between the marching rows of cypress trees.

Luca loved the unapologetic spectacle of it—the high Italianate drama in every detail, from the epic sweep of the house itself to the grounds kept in a condition to rival the Boboli Gardens in Florence, delighting the tourists on their wine-tasting tours of Sonoma—despite himself.

Tonight was the annual Castelli Wine Winter Ball. This was the reason Luca had flown across the world, landing only a scant hour earlier, which he was sure Rafael would think was cutting it a bit close. He and Rafael needed to make it abundantly clear to all and sundry that nothing had changed since Gianni's passing. That everything was business as usual at Castelli Wine.

And as with most things in life, the more elegant and relaxed and attractive the face of a thing, the more people were likely to believe it.

Kathryn, Luca thought grimly, certainly proved that rule. And so did he. He banked on it, in fact.

He checked his watch for the fifth time in as many seconds, unreasonably irritated that she hadn't been waiting for him when he'd emerged from his bedroom suite, showered and dressed and as recovered from their flight as it was possible to be in such a short time. He could already hear the band in the great ballroom and the sound of very well-heeled enjoyment below, all clinking glasses and graceful laughter, wafting up into the far reaches of the family wing and down the long hall to this remote set of rooms set apart from the rest.

Luca glared at Kathryn's door, as if that might make her appear.

And when it did—when it started to open as if he'd commanded it with that glare—he scowled even more.

Until she stepped out into the hall, and then, he was fairly certain, all the blood in his head sank with an audible thud to his sex.

"What—" and his voice was a strangled version of

his own, even from the great distance that ringing in his ears made it sound "—*the hell* are you wearing?"

Kathryn eyed him with that cool expression of hers that he was beginning to think might be the death of him. It clawed at him. It made him want nothing more than to heat her up and see what lurked beneath it.

"I believe it's called a dress," she said crisply.

"No."

She stood there a moment. Blinked. "No? Are you sure? The last time I checked a dictionary, the word was definitely *dress*. Or perhaps *gown*? A case could be made for each, though I think—"

"Be quiet."

Her mouth snapped closed and she had no idea how lucky she was that he hadn't silenced her in the way he'd much prefer. He could already taste her again, as if he had. Luca pushed off the wall opposite her door, unable to control himself. Unable to *think*.

A red haze of sheer lust kicked through him, making everything else dim.

Yes, Kathryn was wearing a dress. Barely. It was in an off-white shade that should have made her look like a ghost, with that English complexion of hers, but instead made her seem to glow. As if she'd been lit from within by a buttery shimmer. It had a delicate, high neckline and no sleeves, and an elegant sort of wide belt that wrapped around her waist before the full skirt cascaded all the way to the floor.

None of that was the problem. *That* could have been Grace Kelly, it was all so effortlessly tasteful and stylish.

It was the damned cutouts that made his entire body feel like a single, taut ache. Two huge wedges that edged in at sharp angles from the sides, cutting into the lower bodice of the dress and showing sheer acres of her bare skin in that sweet spot below her breasts and above her navel, then flaring out over the curves of her sides.

Luca wanted to taste her everywhere he saw skin. Right here. Right now.

He didn't realize he'd said that out loud until her eyes went wide and turned that fascinating slate-green shade, and then it didn't matter anyway, because he'd lost his mind—and worse, his control. He backed her into her own closed door, bracing himself over her with a hand on either side of her head.

"You can't," Kathryn said. *Whispered*, more like, her voice a rough little scrape that he could feel in the hardest part of him. "Luca. We *can't*."

Luca didn't ask himself what he was doing. He didn't care. That dress pooled around her, seductive and impossible, and he was lost in the elegant line of her neck and the hair she'd swept back into a complicated chignon at her nape.

"Did my father give you these diamonds?" he asked, trying to force this red-hazed lust out of him by any means possible. But it didn't shift at all, not even when he lifted a finger to trace the sparkling stones she wore in both her ears. One, then the next.

All of this was wrong. That pounding ache in his sex. This impossible hunger that stormed through him, casting everything else aside—including his own good intentions. He knew it. He still couldn't seem to care about that as he should. As he knew he would eventually.

"Answer me," he urged her, his mouth much too close to the sweet temptation of that tender spot behind her ear, and he couldn't identify that dark, driving thing that had control of him then. "What did you have to do to earn them, Kathryn?"

She jerked her head to the side, away from his fingers and the way they toyed with the delicate shell of her ear, but it was too late. He could see the way she shivered. He could see the pulse that fluttered madly in her neck. He could see the goose bumps that ran down her bare arms.

There was no ordering himself to pretend he hadn't seen those things. Or that he didn't know what they meant.

"You are meant to be here as my assistant, nothing more," he reminded her, his voice a low throb in the otherwise quiet hallway. "This is not meant to be an opportunity for you to flaunt your wares and pick up new customers."

"You're disgusting."

The icy condemnation in her voice poured over him, gas to a flame.

"That is an interesting choice of words," Luca murmured, his lips the barest breath away from her warm neck, and she shuddered. "What is more disgusting, do you think—the fact that I do not want you parading around the château, contaminating my family home and my father's memory? Or the fact you have no qualms about wearing a dress that makes every man in the vicinity think of nothing but you, naked?"

She turned her head to face him then, and her hands came up, shoving futilely at his chest. Luca didn't budge, and he had the distinct pleasure—or was it pain, he couldn't tell—of watching the color rise in her exquisite cheeks.

"Only you think that," she snapped at him, mutiny

and feminine awareness and something hotter by far in her furious gaze. "Because only you live your life with your head in the gutter. Everyone else will see a lovely dress by a well-known designer and nothing more."

"They will see my father's widow in white, with her naked body on display," he corrected her. "They will see your complete disregard for propriety, to say nothing of the memory of your very dear *friend*."

She laughed. It was a high, outraged sound.

"What should I have worn instead?" she demanded. "A black shroud? What would make you happy, Luca? A tent of shame?"

His hands shook and he flattened them against the wall, because he knew. *He knew.* If he touched her again, he wouldn't stop. He didn't care how much more he'd hate himself for it.

He wasn't sure he'd even try to stop himself.

"You told me your laughable story," he reminded her. "An unlikely friendship struck by chance in a far-off waiting room, between one of the wealthiest men in the world and you, our favorite saint." He studied the way her lush mouth firmed at that, the way her eyes flashed and darkened. "I think I saw the syrupy cable-television movie you based that absurd nursery rhyme on. What is the real story, I wonder?"

"I can't help it if you're so cynical and so jaded that all you see in the world is what you put into it," she threw at him with something more than mere temper in her eyes—and it fascinated him. That was his curse. *She* fascinated him, damn her. Maybe she had from the start. Maybe that was the truth he'd been burying for two years. "Here's a news flash, Luca. If you spend your life looking for ulterior motives and cruelty, that's all you'll ever see. It's a self-fulfilling prophecy."

"Do you know why I hate you, Kathryn?" He didn't wait for her answer. "It's not that you married my father for his money. So did everyone else. It's that you dare to act offended when anyone calls that spade the spade it is. It's that you believe your own tabloid coverage. *Saint Kate* is a myth. You are nothing like a saint at all."

She made a frustrated sound and shoved at him again. "I can't control what you think of me. I certainly can't control what the tabloids say about me. And this might come as a giant shock to you, but I don't *care* if you hate me or not."

Somehow he didn't believe her, and he couldn't have said why that was.

And something inside him cracked. A chain broke, and he shifted, leaning in closer and then reaching down to trace the cutout angle of her dress that was closest to him. He sketched his way from the tender skin at the juncture of her shoulder and chest down, skating around the tempting swell of her breast, then cutting in with the line of the fabric toward her belly.

Her breath came hard. Broken.

But she didn't tell him to stop. She didn't shove at him again. Her hands curled into fists and rested there against his lapels, urging him on.

Luca concentrated on the task of this. Of his fingertip against her insane, impossible smoothness. Of the fire that danced between them, the flames stretching ever higher, until he was wrapped up in the sensation of her skin beneath his and the scent of her besides. The hint of something tropical in her hair and the subtle, powdery notes that whispered of the very expensive perfume he now associated with her so strongly that the hint of it in places she wasn't made his body clench down hard in awareness.

Once in a distant resort in the Austrian Alps. Once in a seaside hotel in the Bahamas. She hadn't been in either place, but she was here. Tonight, she was here.

And this was no different. *This is madness*, he told himself.

He didn't kiss her. He didn't dare risk the possibility that he wouldn't stop this time. But he leaned in closer anyway, until their breaths were the same breath. Until he could see every last thing she felt as it moved through her expressive eyes. Until the fact he *wasn't* taking that mouth with his, that their only point of contact was his finger as it danced along that edge where fabric met skin, became erotic.

It became everything.

And he wanted this too much. He wanted *her*. Luca wanted to lose himself inside her, to hurl them both straight into the heart of this wildfire that was eating them both alive.

"This," he said softly, "is what a whore wears when she wishes to announce she's available again. Discreetly, I grant you. But the message is the same."

He felt the way she stiffened, and then he indulged himself and wrapped the whole of his palm over the exposed indentation of her waist, and, God help him, the smooth heat of her blasted into him. It ricocheted inside him. It lit him on fire.

It made that hunger in him shift from an insistent pulse to a roar.

But even though he could feel the deep, low shudders that moved through her body, that told him she felt the same need that he did, she shoved at him again. Much harder this time, using her fists. He grunted and backed up.

He didn't remove his hand.

"What's your plan, Luca?" Her gaze was dark, and he couldn't read her. Her chin edged higher, and her voice was cool and hard. That was what penetrated the red haze, like shards of ice deep into him. "Are you going to prove I'm a whore by acting like one yourself? Do you think that's how it's done?"

Luca dropped his hand then, with far more reluctance than he cared to examine just then. He stood away from her, lust and longing and that greedy kick of need making him scowl at her. Making him wish too many things he shouldn't.

Making him wonder why she was the only thing he couldn't seem to control—or, more to the point, his reaction to her.

"I don't need to prove the truth," he gritted out. What the hell was happening to him? How had she gotten the better of his control? He tried to shake it off. "It simply is, no matter how you pad it out and pretend otherwise to make yourself look better."

She straightened, only that flush high on her cheeks and the hectic glitter in her too-dark eyes to mark what had happened here.

What had *almost* happened.

"I think you'll find that math doesn't work," Kathryn said crisply, and she might as well have shoved a knife deep into his side. He felt as if she had. "Whorish behavior always adds up to two whores, Luca. Not one dirty whore and an innocent with dirty hands by accident, almost but not quite corrupted by doing the exact same thing. No matter what lies you tell yourself."

And then she pushed past him and started down the hall, her every movement as graceful and elegant as if she was a damned queen, not the grasping little gold digger they both knew full well she was.

CHAPTER FIVE

The party was long and bright and painful.

Of course, it always had been. Kathryn told herself that, really, this was no different than the other times she'd had to parade around the Castelli château in this gorgeous little pocket of the Northern California wine country, acting as if she neither heard nor saw the whispers and the overlong, unpleasantly speculative looks.

This was merely part and parcel of being notorious, she told herself. Something every other member of the Castelli family had found a way to handle. Why couldn't she do the same?

But, of course, she knew.

It was Luca. At every other party she'd ever been to with him, he'd kept as much distance between them as possible, as if he feared too much proximity to her would contaminate him. But this time she was his assistant, no longer his stepmother. That meant her place was at his elbow, no matter what had happened between them in that hallway.

And worse, what had *almost* happened. What she told herself she absolutely would not have allowed to happen—but she could feel the hollowness of that assertion tying her stomach into knots.

He'd caught up to her on the stairs that led down toward the ballroom and had slid a dark, fulminating look her way as he'd fallen into place beside her.

"I think you should leave me alone," she'd told him. Through her teeth.

"With pleasure," he'd replied silkily. "Does this mean you quit?"

She'd glared at him, and he'd caught her by the arm when she'd very nearly missed a step, and then held her fast when she would have yanked herself away from him.

"Careful," he'd warned her. "We are no longer in private. And in public, you are my father's widow and my current assistant."

"That is, in fact, all I am anywhere." She'd shaken her head at him. "Except for the sewer inside your head, of course."

"One scandal at a time," he'd told her, sounding something very much like *grim*. He'd let her go when they'd reached the ground floor. "Tonight I think the fact the Widow Castelli has joined the workforce will have to carry the gossip news cycle, don't you? Unless you'd like to use this opportunity to update your global dating profile by announcing to the world that your hunt for a protector has begun anew."

"And by *hunt*," she'd retorted icily, "am I to understand you mean something like you manhandling me in a hallway? Was that your version of an audition?"

Luca's mouth had curved in that lethal way that was nothing so palatable as a smile.

"It's a tragedy for you that you can't manipulate me, I'm sure," he'd said, sounding anything but tragic. "Make sure you schedule time in my calendar for me to care about that. Maybe next month? In the meantime—" and he'd switched then, from the obnoxious Luca she'd come to expect into the COO version of Luca that she'd only ever seen in action over the past few weeks in his office "—you stay next to me. You do not speak unless spoken to directly. Just smile and look pretty and make sure you remember every detail of every conversation we have so we can compare notes later."

She'd blinked. "Uh, what details am I looking for?"

He'd stared down at her, and it was getting harder and harder for her to imagine how anyone saw him as a lazy, lackadaisical playboy when the truth of him was stark and obvious and stamped right there on his intensely beautiful face.

"All of them, Kathryn," he said, as if she was an idiot. She hated that he made her feel like one—and simultaneously feel as if she needed to prove him wrong. Then again, she'd had a great deal of experience with that feeling. "You never know which little detail will make all the difference."

And then he'd strode ahead of her straight into the ballroom, and the moment he'd entered it, become that other Luca. As if he'd flipped a switch.

Affable and approachable. Quick to make everyone around him laugh. He always had a drink in his hand and appeared to be ever so slightly tipsy, though this close to him, Kathryn discovered that he didn't actually drink much. He slapped backs and kissed cheeks. He flirted with everybody. He was delightful and about as unthreatening as a man who looked like him and moved like him and wore black tie as easily as he did ever could.

Kathryn didn't have to ask him why he bothered to

put on such an elaborate act. The *why* of it became clear almost instantly.

She'd spent a great deal of time smiling prettily next to Gianni, too, and no one had found him particularly delightful. They'd always been guarded. Distant and cagey. Especially if they were somehow involved in the business.

But it was as if no one could believe that *this* Luca Castelli, who commanded the attention of the whole party simply by entering it, was the same one who ran the Rome office with such a deft hand. This bright, gleaming, careless creature. Even though there was no other name on that door in Rome but his.

Kathryn had heard the rumors. That it was Gianni himself who'd propped up Luca's office—except, of course, for the small problem that an old man with dementia could not possibly have run anything. Perhaps he simply had a particularly good team to support him, the rumor mill had countered. But no matter what people speculated about in private, when they were in Luca's presence, they basked in it. In him. In that effortless sort of sunshine he spread about him so easily.

And they told him everything.

Secrets. Rumors. Things their supervisors—who were often standing across the room—would kill them for saying out loud.

Everyone succumbed to the golden myth of Luca Castelli, Kathryn saw. Everyone. Captains of industry, wine connoisseurs and college-age caterers alike lost in the perfection of his inviting smile.

Watching him in action told her a great many things, but most of all, it made her feel better about herself for falling so completely under his spell every time he got too close to her. It wasn't something fatal in her own design, as she'd imagined. It wasn't that weakness in her that her mother had always despaired of and had gone to such lengths to stamp out of her. It was *him*.

She ducked into the mostly hidden powder room off the main ballroom when Luca got into an intense discussion about a documentary Kathryn had never seen with a handful of very intellectual types who'd made it clear they both recognized her and thought her beneath them. *Far* beneath them. She was happy to let them think so.

Inside the luxurious bathroom suite, she sat down on the couch in the lounge area and took a little breather. Away from the crush of the crowd, most of whom looked at her with nothing but ugly supposition on their faces. Away from Luca, whom she really should hate.

Why didn't she hate him the way she should? The way he unapologetically hated her?

"Being fascinated with him is only making everything worse," she snapped at herself, out loud—and then jumped when the door to the lounge swung open.

"Oh," Lily said. She looked around as if she expected there to be more people in the room—or as if she'd heard Kathryn talking to herself like a crazy person. Kathryn trotted out her smile automatically. "I didn't realize anyone was in here."

"Only me," Kathryn said mildly. "Depending on your point of view, that may or may not count."

Rafael's wife laughed, then smoothed her hands over the swell of her pregnant belly, looking resplendent in a gleaming blue gown. And happy. That it took her a moment to recognize what that expression meant made something inside Kathryn catch. As if happiness was so foreign to her.

"Don't pay any attention to Luca," Lily said, her eyes meeting Kathryn's in the mirror then moving away. "The man is *such* a control freak. He can't stand surprises, that's all."

She ran the water in the sink and then smoothed her damp palms over the coils of heavy braids she wore, all collected into a fat bun at the back of her head. Kathryn had always liked Lily. She was the least judgmental member of the Castelli family. She'd been the most welcoming to Kathryn, and Kathryn had even imagined that under different circumstances they might have been friends. Perhaps that, too, was naive.

She was beginning to realize that *she* was naive, in every possible way—something she'd have thought was impossible, given how hard her mother had worked to wring that out of her. And yet.

"Am I a surprise?" she asked, when she was sure she could keep her voice light and easy. "I don't think that's the word Luca would use."

Lily slanted an amused look at her. "Everything about you is a surprise," she said. "From the day you arrived. You refuse to slot yourself into one of Luca's depressingly functional and supernaturally clean boxes. He hates that."

"He hates surprises?" Kathryn laughed lightly. Very lightly, which was at odds with how her heart punched at her, as if this information about Luca was the most important detail of all she might have collected here tonight. "Here I thought the only thing he hated was me."

It was Lily's turn to laugh, though hers seemed far less for show.

"He hates messes," she said. "He always has. If he hates you? It's because you're messing things up for him, and he doesn't know how to handle something he can't sanitize and shelve somewhere. And between you and me, that's probably a good thing."

Then she smiled her goodbyes and went back out into the crush, leaving Kathryn to mull that over.

But not for long. Her mobile buzzed in her clutch and she knew it was Luca, which got her moving out of the bathroom lounge and back into the party before she even looked at the display.

"Are you taking a holiday?" he growled into the phone when she answered, all spleen and fury. "If not, you'd better be right here when I turn around. I'm not paying you to gallivant around the château like one of the guests."

"Are you paying me at all?" she asked mildly, spotting him several groups away and moving around them as she spoke. "I thought your father set up a trust for me so you couldn't hold a paycheck over my head. Or maybe for other reasons, and that's just a happy accident?"

"I'm turning around now," he said, and she came to a stop before him as he did.

Their eyes met. Held.

It was harder than it should have been to pull herself away. To concentrate on tucking her mobile back in her clutch. To tell herself there was nothing at all in his dark eyes but what there always was: some or other form of fury, brightened up with dislike.

She didn't understand why no one could see the truth about him but her. She told herself she was making it up. That it wouldn't be there when she looked up at him again—that he'd be that half lazy, half obnoxious man he should have been and nothing more.

But it was still there. That fury, that need. That hunger that terrified her and intrigued her in equal measure. A whole world in that gaze of his, and she had no earthly idea what to do about it.

"I think you're being paged," she told him, nodding toward a bejeweled woman in a slinky dress made entirely of sequins, who was bearing down on Luca from afar. "You wouldn't want to disappoint your fans with this show of seriousness, would you?"

"It's not a show. It's business. Not a concept I expect you to comprehend."

"I'm sure that's what you tell yourself," she said unwisely. So very unwisely. "But it's interesting that you're so determined to hide part of yourself away wherever you go, don't you think?"

She had no idea why she'd said that. Luca looked frozen into place for a long, taut moment, an arrested expression on his darkly gorgeous face. Then he blinked, and there was nothing but his usual darkness again, leaving Kathryn faintly dizzy.

"Careful, Stepmother," he said softly. Lethally. "Or I might be tempted to truly give them something to talk about tonight."

She didn't believe he'd do anything of the kind—of course she didn't—but she still had to fight to restrain a shiver at the thought. And she was sure that Luca knew it, that the unholy gleam of something like gold in his dark eyes was that pure male knowledge Kathryn was very much afraid would be her undoing.

But then he turned away, his public smile at the ready, that intensity gone as if it had never been.

And Kathryn reminded herself that it didn't matter what this man's sister-in-law, who had once been his stepsister, had said in the bathroom lounge. It didn't matter what happened in remote hallways in the château. The only truth that mattered was that she was his assistant now, and if she couldn't do that job as well as she should, everything else he'd ever said about her was true. And not just him.

You've had more opportunities than I could have dreamed of having! her mother had said the last time she'd seen her, at Christmas, with that look on her face that had told Kathryn that once again she'd failed Rose terribly, as she'd always managed to do. "And look what you've done with them."

Kathryn hadn't known what to say or how to defend herself. Because Rose had been the one to encourage Kathryn into marrying Gianni in the first place.

"The world is filled with people who marry for far less reason than this," she'd said. "But of course, Kathryn, it's *your* life. You should do what you think is best *for you*, no matter who else might benefit."

And Kathryn hadn't been able to think of a good reason why *not* to marry the kindly old man when her mother had put it like that—especially given what she knew she would gain from it. It would cost her so very little. All *she* had to sacrifice was a couple of years. Not her whole life, as her mother had done, and for far less in return. Though Rose certainly hadn't objected when Gianni's money had allowed Kathryn to buy her a cottage in the sweet Yorkshire village of her choice, and then provide her with live-in care.

She never thanked you, either, a little voice pointed out, deep inside her.

But she felt ungrateful and small even thinking such things. Many women wouldn't have had a baby on their own, with the father adamantly out of the picture. Rose had never faltered.

Which meant Kathryn could do no less—no matter the provocation.

It was time she stopped worrying about Luca Castelli and what he thought about her, and got to work.

One blue-and-gold California day rolled into the next, filled with meetings and vineyard tours and endless business dinners, and Luca found himself more disgruntled than he should have been by the fact Kathryn was…good at the job. More than good, in fact, in the odd role she had to play. Far better at it than the assistant she'd displaced, though he hated to admit it. Marco had been an excellent administrative assistant, but had always been a little too conspicuously himself when out in the field trying to charm potential clients.

Kathryn, on the other hand—who Luca would have asserted could no more *blend* than the sun could rise in the west and was anything but charming besides—did it beautifully.

"No," he barked out one morning, when she'd walked into their shared breakfast room dressed in one of her usual work outfits, a skirt and heels and one of those soft blouses that made him unable to think of anything at all but the breasts pressed *just there* behind the silk.

Kathryn paused, her hand on the back of the nearest chair, her bearing that of slightly offended royalty. It put his teeth on edge.

"You can't wear that," he growled at her, feeling like some kind of sulky child, which was insupportable. He was not one of his nephews, having a tantrum. Why couldn't he control himself around this woman? "We are walking through the vines with one of the accounts today. They find the Castelli family on the verge of being too European for their tastes as is, so we must be certain to impress them with our homespun, regular-person charm."

"I don't think even you can convince someone you are either homespun or regular."

"I'm a chameleon," he said drily. And was uncomfortable with how that sat there on the sunny table like truth, when he hadn't meant it that way. *It's interesting that you're so determined to hide part of yourself away wherever you go*, she'd said, damn her. He scowled at her. "But I doubt you can say the same."

He was wrong. Kathryn turned and left the room and when she reappeared, she'd transformed herself. She wore jeans, a pair of boots and a soft, casual, long-sleeved shirt. She'd let her hair down to pool around her shoulders and had scrubbed the makeup from her face. She looked like a host of fantasies he hadn't realized he had. She looked like an advertisement for healthy Californian living. Like a dream come true.

The emissaries from this tricky account of theirs had agreed, hanging on Kathryn's every word and acting as if Luca was *her* assistant, a state of affairs that didn't annoy him as much as it should have done—because he got to trail behind her, admiring the curve of her bottom in faded denim.

And imagining what it would be like to throw her down in one of the tidy rows between the vines and taste all that sweet, soft skin and that mouth that was driving him to the brink of madness.

When they were finally alone again, having waved off the ebullient account managers who'd doubled their national order based entirely on the force of Kathryn's smile, he found himself watching her much too closely. As if he might pounce.

"I told you I could do the job," she said, and he wondered if she knew how fierce she sounded. "Any job."

"So you did."

"But don't worry, Luca," she said, and he had the sense she'd collected herself—remembered who they were. He hated that he felt it as a kind of loss—and it seemed to collect inside him with all the other things he hated about himself. "I won't let that get in the way of all my whoring around. I know you need that to feel better about yourself and, of course, my only aim is to please you."

He felt his jaw clench and every muscle in his body tense. But there was something about the way she stood there in the bright winter sun, her hands tucked into the back pockets of her jeans and the Sonoma wind toying with her dark hair. He had the strangest sense of tightness around his chest, as if there was a steel band clamping down on him.

He didn't know what to do with it. He didn't know how to handle it. Or her.

Or worst of all, himself.

"Why did you marry him?" he asked.

Her marvelous eyes were dove gray in all that too-blue California light, and she didn't look away from him.

"I don't see why it matters to you."

"And yet it does."

"I think you want there to be some kind of rationale,"

she said quietly. "Something you can point to that makes it all okay in your head. Because otherwise you're just a man who has grabbed his father's widow. Twice."

"Is there one, then? A rationale? Were you a street urchin he saved? Did you personally support a threatened orphanage and his money saved a host of children from eviction?"

She smiled at him, and it wasn't her usual smile. It wasn't that serene, bulletproof smile she trotted out for work and had used on him at least a thousand times in the past three weeks alone. This one hurt. It was sad and it was reflected in her eyes, and he didn't understand what was happening here.

What had already happened, if he was honest with himself.

Luca decided honesty was overrated. But it was too late. She was speaking.

"No," she said. "I married him because I wanted to marry him. He was rich and I was struggling through my degree and some personal issues, and he told me he could make all my troubles go away. I liked that. I wanted that." His mouth twisted, but her smile only deepened, and still it hurt. "Is that what you wanted to hear?"

"It doesn't surprise me."

"What do you think marriage is, Luca?" she asked, and she tilted her head slightly to one side.

He was mesmerized by it, by *her*, and it occurred to him that they'd never actually *talked* before. It had been all insults and glares, that scene in the library or in the hallway between their rooms, what he still thought was just another rehearsed story on the plane. She shook her hair back from her face and he wanted to do that for her. He wanted to touch her, he realized, more than he could recall ever wanting anything else.

And nothing had ever been more impossible.

"Not the transaction it was for you," he said, aware that his voice was too raw, too rough. It gave him away. "Not a bit of cold calculation with a monetized end."

But Kathryn only continued to smile at him in that same way, as if *he* made her sad. As if he was *doing something* to her. That tight band around his chest seemed to pull even tauter. It pinched.

"Who are you to judge?" she asked softly, and it was more of a slap, perhaps, because it lacked heat or accusation. She simply asked. "We were happy with our arrangement. We fulfilled the promises we made to each other."

He couldn't take it. He moved toward her, aware but not caring that they were standing out in front of the château where anyone could see them, and he took her face between his hands. This would be so much easier if she weren't so pretty, he told himself—if she was a little more plastic and a whole lot less polished.

If she didn't short-circuit every bit of control he'd ever had.

"Tell me more about how happy you were," he dared her, aware that he was furious. More than furious. "How perfect your marriage was—a union of two identical souls, yes?"

But she didn't back down. She didn't flush hot or look the least bit ashamed. Her hands came up and hooked around his wrists, but she didn't pull him away.

"Go on, then," Luca urged her, his voice an aching thing that simmered in the scant space between them. "Tell me how you fulfilled those promises to the old man. Were you contractually obligated to kneel before him and pleasure him a certain number of nights per week? Or was he past that point—did he have you tend to yourself while he watched? What promises did you keep, Kathryn?"

Something gleamed in that gaze of hers and turned her eyes a darker shade of gray, but she didn't jerk away from him.

"What amazes me about you," she whispered, "is how you think it's your right to ask these questions. You don't get to know what happened in my marriage. You can drive yourself crazy with all your dark imaginings, and I hope you do. You can whisper your filthy thoughts to anyone who will listen. It doesn't make them true, and it certainly doesn't require me to comment on them. If you want to believe that's what happened between me and your father, then go ahead. Believe it."

There was a resolve in her gaze Luca didn't like, and he didn't know what he might have done then, but down at the bottom of the château's long drive, a busload of wine tasters pulled in and started up the winding way toward them.

And he had no choice but to let her go.

Kathryn woke when the moonlight poured in her windows, making her blink in confusion at the clock. It was just before four in the morning, and that was, she realized after a moment or two of uncertainty, very definitely the moon and not the sun.

Her internal clock was still a mess, even after nearly a week in California, and she only had to lie there a little while before she accepted the reality that she was not going to fall back asleep. Not tonight.

She swung her feet over the side of the tall, canopied bed piled high with soft linens, and dressed quickly in the clothes she'd left draped over her chair, a simple pair of terry lounging trousers and a cashmere hooded top. She twisted her hair back out of her way, tying it in a knot at her nape. She wrapped a long merino wool sweater around her to cut the chill, and then she pushed open the glass doors that led out onto her balcony and stepped outside.

The moon was huge and so bright it lit up the whole of the valley and all Kathryn could see in all directions, pouring over the cypress trees and dancing over the gnarled rows of vines. Making the pockets of night where it didn't touch even darker, and turning the world a spectral silver. The breeze was high, whipping into her, just cold enough to feel like exhilaration.

She closed her eyes and leaned into it.

"Couldn't sleep?" asked a low male voice from far too close. "Perhaps it's your conscience."

Kathryn looked over, as slowly as possible, as a counterpoint to the sudden clatter of her heart. She'd forgotten that the balconies of these rooms all ran together here at the far end of the château, despite half walls between the rooms that were little more than decorative gestures toward privacy and did nothing to conceal her from Luca. Nothing at all.

He was sprawled on one of the soft loungers, wearing nothing but a pair of exercise trousers very low on his hips, as if he was impervious to the winter air around him.

And the moonlight crawled all over him. Sliding across that vast expanse of his chest, cavorting in the ridges and hollows, licking him and writhing over him, illuminating every inch of his shocking male beauty. And doing nothing at all to temper that stark expression on his face or that dark hunger in his eyes.

"Says the man who's clearly been out here awhile," Kathryn replied. Lightly. So very lightly. As if he was nothing to her. As if his voice did nothing to her. As if this was as unremarkable as having any other sort of meeting with him in the broad daylight, surrounded by other people.

But it was as if he knew exactly what she was trying to hide, or perhaps the moon showed him far too much, because he made it worse. He stood.

"What are you doing out here?" she asked.

"I have no idea," he said in a low voice, his gaze still on her. "Something I'm certain I'll regret. But that is nothing new."

The clatter of her heart became a deep bass drumming.

Luca raked back that thick fall of hair, the gesture as lazy as his hot eyes were not. Then he started toward her in that low, rolling gait that marked him as exactly the sort of predator she needed most to avoid.

Kathryn knew she shouldn't try to tough this out. She knew that there was no shame at all in simply turning tail and running, barring herself in her room against a man who looked at her with that much *intent*. But she couldn't bring herself to do it. She couldn't let him see how much he affected her. She couldn't let him know how he got to her. *She couldn't.*

More than that, she couldn't seem to move.

He walked over to the little half wall and then, his eyes never leaving hers, he simply swung himself over it with an offhanded show of male grace that made everything inside Kathryn clench tight. Then run hot, pooling low in her belly and making her think she might simply melt where she stood. Making her think that perhaps she already had.

Luca didn't stop. He walked straight to her and he sank his hands in her hair and he hauled her close to him. To that mouth of his, dangerous and impossible and lush. To his flashing dark eyes that saw too much and condemned too deeply.

"What are you doing?" she asked again.

But her voice was a whisper, not a protest, and he knew it. She could tell by the way his fingers sank deeper into her hair, holding her that much more immobile.

"Sleepwalking, I think," he told her in that low voice of his that wound around inside her, making her burn. "It's a terrible habit. Worse than alcohol. There's no telling what I'll do in the middle of the night and then forget come morning."

"Luca—"

"I'll show you what I mean."

His voice was little more than a growl.

And then he slid his mouth over hers.

CHAPTER SIX

KATHRYN TOLD HERSELF it was a dream.

The moonlight. This man.

It was a dream, that was all, and so it didn't matter if she simply opened to him. If she let him sweep her up his bare chest, cool to the touch but still so hard, like steel. If she made no sign of protest.

If all she did was kiss him back as hungrily and greedily as if she'd been the one to go to him.

And everything was heat. Fire. Need and longing made real in the silvery night.

His hands were big and hard, slipping from her hair to cradle her face, holding her where he wanted her.

And he plundered her mouth, using his lips and his teeth and that clever tongue of his, angling his jaw to take the kiss deeper, wilder.

She felt dizzy again—unmoored and lost—and was only dimly aware that he'd hauled her off the ground and up into his arms. She didn't care. It was a dream, so what did it matter if he was carrying her somewhere, his mouth still fused to hers? He was tall and so very strong, and the feel of him surrounding her made her shake and quiver deep inside.

He walked back through her door and straight to her

bed, laying her across the piled-high linens and following her down into the clutch of all that softness, and it was…astonishing. There was no other word for the press of him against her, so male and darkly perfect, so hard and *Luca*. There was no other way to describe that absurdly sculpted body rubbing all over hers.

Making her feel new. Like a strange creature, red-hot and molten, taking over the body she'd thought until this moment she knew so well.

This is only a dream, she told herself, and so she indulged herself.

He stroked his way deep into her mouth, tasting her deeply, and she met him. She ran her fingers through that thick dark hair of his, crisp and warm to her touch. She traced the magnificent line of his wide, muscled back down to his narrow hips, then worked her way back up those *ridges* on his abdomen that she could admit, here in this dream where nothing counted, fascinated her to the point of distraction.

Beyond that point, perhaps.

He tore his mouth from hers even as his hands moved. He propped himself up on one forearm and smoothed his other hand over her cashmere top, pausing at the top and then tugging—and it was a measure of how dazed she was that she didn't comprehend what he was doing until he'd unzipped her and the cool air teased over her bare breasts.

And she was panting as if she was running. As if she'd been running for miles.

Luca muttered something in Italian that washed over her like a caress, and then he bent his head and took one nipple she hadn't realized had pebbled into a hard point deep into his mouth.

Kathryn heard a noise that could not possibly have been her, so high-pitched and keening, bouncing back from the canopy above them, the ornate ceiling. She felt the dark current of his laughter shake through him and into her, making his shoulders move beneath her hands and shudder against her breasts. The sheer physicality of that stunned her, and then he simply sucked on her, that rich tugging setting off an explosion inside her. It seared its way through her, like a lightning bolt from his mouth straight down the center of her body to kick between her legs.

Hard and something like beautiful, all at once.

And Kathryn didn't know what to do. There was too *much* of him, everywhere. All over her, pressing her down with him into the embrace of her soft, soft mattress, making her wish this mad dream could go on and on forever.

He made a low, greedy sound that she recognized somehow, in a deep feminine place inside her she'd never known was there, and thrilled to at once. She dug her hands in his hair, but not to guide him—only to anchor herself as he smoothed his wicked palm down over her exposed belly, pausing to test the indentation of her navel, then dipping even lower to slip beneath the waistband of her soft trousers.

Kathryn opened her mouth to speak, to say *something*— to *do* something—

But Luca knew exactly what he was about. He didn't pause. He simply slid his hand down, so hot and hard, and then held the core of her, molten and hot and swollen with need, in his palm.

She made a noise, and he laughed again. He used the faint edge of his teeth against her nipple and made that lightning bolt roar through her again, wider and hotter and far more dangerous, and then he ground the heel of his hand against the place she ached most.

And Kathryn disappeared. She went up in a column of flame that tore her apart. She lost herself, shattering into too many pieces to count. She shook and she shook, bucking against him and unable to stop or hold on or do anything but survive the explosion—and when she finally came back to earth it was with a giant thud and a heartbeat so hard against her ribs that it hurt.

It *hurt*.

There was no pretending *that* was a dream.

Luca's hand was still down her trousers, tracing lazy patterns in her wet heat, and he'd propped himself up next to her while he did it. Watching her. Learning her. And Kathryn found she couldn't quite breathe. Something he made that much worse when he shifted from watching his own hand play with her, letting his gaze slam into hers.

His eyes were dark. So very dark. There was something powerful and supremely knowing in the way he looked at her then, and she shuddered again, as if she couldn't keep herself from falling apart. As if now he needed only to look at her to make her crack wide-open.

"Luca…" But she didn't sound like herself. She didn't recognize that small, profoundly needy voice that came out of her own mouth.

And she had no idea what to say.

He murmured something else in Italian, a low string of syllables that danced over her the way he did as he moved down the bed, hooking his fingers in the waistband of her trousers and yanking them down over her hips. He peeled them down her legs and tossed them aside, and Kathryn was shaking. She couldn't stop shaking.

And she was still so hot. So needy. Helpless, somehow, in the face of all that yearning and that intense look on his beautiful face.

"Luca," she said again, forcing herself to speak because this wasn't a dream, and reality was coming at her as hard as if the canopy had collapsed above her, bringing the whole of the château down with it.

"I have to taste you," he growled at her, his voice thicker and rougher than she'd ever heard it before, and that, too, slicked through her like lightning. Then he said something in Italian, and that, somehow, was worse. Or better.

"I don't think..." she tried to say.

"Good. Don't think."

He moved to take her hips in his hands, then settled himself between her legs as if he belonged there. He wedged her thighs open with his sculpted shoulders, and then he made a growling sort of sound that made a wave of goose bumps crash over the whole of her body.

"Bellissima," he murmured, directly into the heart of her need.

And then he simply licked his way straight into her core.

She tasted sweet and hot, the richest cream and all woman, and Luca drank deep.

Kathryn went stiff beneath him, shuddering anew, her hands tugging at him as if she couldn't decide whether to pull him closer or shove him away.

He took her over. He licked and he hummed, throwing her straight back into that fire, until she was rolling her hips to get closer to his mouth, begging him with her body.

He was so hard he thought it might kill him.

He found his way to the hot little center of her and sucked, hard.

And Kathryn made a low sound, long and wild. Then she was bucking against him, her hoarse cry rebounding off the walls, shattering beneath him all over again, and if he had ever seen anything better in all his life, he couldn't recall it.

Luca waited her out. She sobbed something incomprehensible and he liked that. He liked it too much.

He knelt up, letting his gaze trace over her as she lay sprawled there before him, more beautiful than he could have imagined—and the truth was, he'd imagined this very thing far more often than he was comfortable admitting, even to himself.

Her breasts were the perfect small handfuls, tipped in rose, and the center of her femininity was slick and hot. The taste of her poured through him like fire, arousal and need, the spice of a woman and her own particular sweetness besides.

And even here, open and shuddering, splayed out before him, there was something about her. A certain innocence, however impossible that seemed, that made him that much harder—the need in him taking on a near vicious edge.

He shoved his hair back from his face and looked around, wondering where she kept her condoms. Because surely she had some. Or perhaps she dealt with birth control a different way entirely, which meant he could—

And Luca froze then.

Because if Kathryn was on birth control, that would have been to keep herself from getting pregnant *with his father.* To keep herself from giving birth to a child that would have been Luca's own sibling.

Disgust and self-loathing hit him like a blow. Like an attack. He felt dazed.

How could he have forgotten who she was? How could he have let this happen?

You didn't let *this happen, you fool*, he growled at himself. *You did this all yourself.*

Kathryn was a spider at best, and now he knew exactly how sweet her web was, and he was ruined. *Ruined.*

Damn her.

He pushed back, levering himself off the bed and letting the chill of the winter night, even here inside her bedroom, sink into him from his bare feet up. He hadn't been able to sleep. No surprise, given the direction of his thoughts and his knowledge that she'd slept *just there* on the other side of his wall.

He'd tortured himself with the temperature, bathing himself in the winter moon as if it had been a form of cold shower. He had no idea how long he'd been out there, fighting a pitched battle with an enemy that he knew wasn't Kathryn at all. It was him. It was this need in him, gripping him hard and mercilessly even now, making him want to forget all over again and lose himself in that sweet, dangerous oblivion between her thighs.

You are the worst kind of idiot, he told himself harshly.

He watched her come back to herself, flushed and satisfied and more beautiful than any woman should be.

And far more dangerously compelling than *this* woman should be, especially to him.

He hated himself.

He told himself he hated her more.

"Is this how you do it?" he asked, and his voice was as cold as the night outside. *"Stepmother?"*

Kathryn jerked against the pillows as if he'd thrown a bucket of cold water on her. She looked stunned for a moment, and Luca felt something snake through him, hot and low and much too black to bear. It felt a good deal like shame—but he refused to let that stop him.

His breath sawed out of his chest, and Kathryn didn't help things. She sat up slowly, as if she ached. As if she didn't understand what he'd done to her—what he was doing—and he hated that she could keep the act going even now. When he was still so hard it hurt, and worse, he knew how she tasted now. And she was rumpled and flushed from his hands and his mouth—yet looked at him with her gray eyes dark as if she couldn't comprehend how that had happened.

He gritted his teeth as she swallowed, so hard he heard it, and then tugged her clothing back into place. And his curse was that howling thing inside him that wanted to strip her down and worship her, glut himself in her, until this madness in him subsided. Until he could *think*.

"I'm touched by this performance," he told her, his voice a dark thing in the moonlit room. "Truly I am. You look nothing less than ravished and yet innocent besides, as if I didn't just make you come. Twice."

He watched the way she shivered. The way she pulled her longer sweater tighter around her as if it was made of chain mail and could fend him off. The way she didn't quite meet his gaze.

"As a matter of fact," she said, carefully, as if she wasn't sure of her own voice, "I'd prefer not to have this postmortem just now."

"I imagine you don't."

She swallowed again, and there was nothing but shadows in her eyes when she finally looked at him.

"You were sleepwalking," she said softly. "I was dreaming. This never happened."

"Yet it did," he gritted out at her. "I can still taste you."

She pulled her knees up beneath her and hugged them close, and he loathed himself. He did. She looked like a lost little girl, and he was still hard and furious, and beyond all of that, she was still his father's widow.

His father's widow.

"Why did you marry him?"

He didn't mean to ask that again. He didn't know why he had.

But this time, when she gazed back at him, her gray eyes were like storms.

"To torture you," she told him, her voice still hoarse, but something hard beneath it. "Is that what you want to hear?"

"I suspect that's not far from the truth, if likely not so personal."

She made a frustrated sort of noise and rolled off the bed—but kept her distance, he noticed, as she skirted around to its foot.

"I'm taking a bath," she said in a low tone. "I want to wipe this entire night off me." She looked at him over her shoulder. "Torture yourself all you want, Luca. But I'll thank you to do it somewhere else."

And this time when she walked away from him, Luca told himself he was glad of it. That it was better.

No matter that his body still wanted her.

But that was all the information he needed, surely. The things he wanted were always the things that destroyed him—his family being a case in point. That was why, so long ago now he could hardly remember anything else, he'd stopped allowing himself to want anything.

He would conquer this, too.

Kathryn decided to treat the entire situation as if it really had been a dream. Everyone had unfortunately detailed and potentially steamy dreams about coworkers sometimes, surely. The trick was acting as if it had only ever happened inside her head.

She told herself she could do that. Why not? Luca was the master at playing whatever role worked best for his purposes. She could do the same.

Though it was harder than she'd anticipated to walk into that breakfast room the way she'd done every other morning in California and act as if her body didn't flush into shivering awareness at the sight of him.

It was so unfair.

He was gorgeous and terrible, commanding his side of the table with that lazy authority of his that she felt as if his mouth against her center again, bold and insistent. He was dressed in one of his devastatingly perfect suits today, crisp and lethally masculine as if he hadn't been up half the night, and Kathryn forced herself to stand there with her usual serene smile on her face. She was determined to do her best to *look* as calm and unruffled as he did.

But there was no controlling that low, wild lick of pure fire that swept through her, curling itself into dark knots deep inside, then blooming into something greedy and consuming in her sex.

You are in so much trouble, a small voice whispered inside her.

Worse, she was sure he knew it. That he could *see* every last thing she tried to hide from him. When all she could see in him was that harsh light in his dark eyes and that dangerous look on his face.

"Don't loom there," he said, all silken threat and a kind of menace that made her pulse pick up. "Sit down. This is meant to be a breakfast meeting to outline my plans for the day, Kathryn." He waited for her to look at him. To meet that awful gaze of his that tore straight through her. "Not agony."

There was absolutely no reason that should make her feel as if she might swallow her tongue. Kathryn ordered herself to pull it together. She pulled out her graceful, high-backed chair and sat down, the same way she had every other morning on this endless trip that she worried would leave her a mere shell of herself before it was done.

Maybe it already had, she thought with a shiver she fought to repress when he did nothing more shocking than fill her cup with coffee, a rich, dark brew that she thought was the precise color of his furious eyes—

She needed to stop.

"Tonight will be a family event," Luca said in a controlled sort of way that made the fact of his temper a living thing, dancing there between them. All the more obvious because it was hidden. Controlled. Just as he always had been—except for last night. Kathryn had to conceal the shiver that moved through her then. "Rafael, Lily and I—and therefore you, as my personal shadow—are expected at another winery in Napa."

"The next valley over."

"Yes." He set the silver coffeepot down on the table between them with a hint of something like violence, if carefully restrained. "Your command of geography is impressive."

"As is your use of sarcasm."

"Careful, Kathryn." His voice seemed darker then. Deeper. Infinitely more dangerous. "I know too much about you now. Far too many secrets about what makes you…" He paused, and she flushed then. She couldn't help it, no matter that she saw that gleam of satisfaction in his dark gaze and hated the both of them. "Tick." He eyed her. "You should keep that in mind."

He meant sex. All of this was about sex, the last topic on earth she wanted to discuss—especially with him. But it shot through her anyway, flame and heat, like the word itself was a heavy stone plummeting from a great height. It hit bottom in that molten-hot place between her legs, where she could still feel him. Where no amount of soaking in that bath earlier had managed to wipe away the exquisite feel of his hands or his mouth. She felt branded. Marked.

Though she thought she'd rather die right where she sat than let him know it.

"I'm so glad you brought that up," she said crisply. "Obviously, what happened last night can never happen again. You are my late husband's son and my supervisor, not to mention the fact that you are anything but a fan of mine. I'm appalled that we got as carried away as we did."

"If you plan to clutch at your pearls, you should have worn some." Luca's voice sounded decadent then. Dark and rich, and with that lazy note to it besides, as if he was enjoying himself. "As it is, it's difficult to take anything you say seriously when I can see how hard your nipples are, Kathryn. I don't think the word you're looking for is *appalled*."

Kathryn would never know how she managed to keep herself from looking down at her own breasts then, where she could feel a traitorous tightening that suggested he was right. How she only stared back at him with a faintly pitying air instead.

"It's winter, Luca," she said, almost gently. "You're wearing a suit. I am not. Do you need me to explain how female biology works?"

And that impossibly golden smile of his flashed then, as beautiful and bright as it was totally unexpected.

"Do you?" he asked, and there was that same note in his voice that every part of her recognized, down into her bones. It took her a moment to place it.

I have to taste you, he'd growled at her last night before he'd done just that. In exactly this same way.

Kathryn went very still. Or he did. Or maybe it was the world that stopped for a long, taut moment, as if there was nothing but the pounding of her heart and that betraying *tightening* everywhere else. As if he really could see straight into her. As if he knew. As if, were she to give him the slightest signal, he'd simply sweep all the breakfast things off the table and haul her across it, setting his mouth to her the way he had in all that silvery moonlight.

How could she fear him and want him at the same time?

"Good morning."

Rafael's voice from the doorway cut through the tension between them as if he'd used one of the ceremonial swords that hung theatrically in the château's tasting room in another part of the winery.

Kathryn told herself it was a relief. That it was *relief* that coursed through her, syrupy and thick.

She swiveled to face him, entirely too aware that Luca did the same thing—entirely too aware of Luca, come to that.

Rafael's cool gaze moved between them. From Luca to Kathryn and then back, and Kathryn was suddenly certain that he knew. That he could *see* what had happened between them, that he could hear the echo of those impossible cries she'd made into the night, that she was marked bright red and obvious.

"Lily and I won't be coming with you tonight" was all he said, in that remote way of his that made him such an excellent CEO. "She's having some contractions, and it's better that she stay off her feet."

"Is she all right?" Kathryn asked, frowning. "Isn't it a little bit early?" And then she regretted it when two pairs of dark and speculative Castelli eyes fixed on her in a way she didn't like at all. She forced a smile. "I beg your pardon. Am I not allowed to ask now that I'm merely a Castelli Wine employee?"

"No," Luca said at once. "It makes me question your motives."

"You would do that anyway," she replied smoothly,

without looking at him. "As far as I can tell, it's your favorite pastime."

Rafael smiled, and Kathryn was certain she didn't like the way he did it. "Lily is fine, Kathryn. Thank you for asking. This is nothing particularly worrisome, but her doctor would prefer she put her feet up for a few days, and that means another work event would be too much."

He aimed that smile at his brother then, and it took on a sharper edge that even Kathryn could feel. She was aware of Luca stiffening at his place across the table.

And of Rafael, still there in the doorway, his gaze entirely too assessing. "But it looks as if you have things as well in hand as ever, brother. I leave it to you."

CHAPTER SEVEN

HALFWAY THROUGH THE formal dinner laid out with luxurious attention to detail in one of the Napa winery's private rooms up high on a hillside, every plate and glass and carefully arranged bit of food as choreographed as some refined ballet, Luca was so darkly furious he had no idea how he kept to his seat.

He told himself it wasn't fury. Or it shouldn't have been. That Kathryn was simply doing what she did, what she had always done and always would, and there was no point reacting to it at all—

But that didn't help. Every time her musical little laugh floated across the table, he tensed. Every time that silver-haired jackass to her left with the wandering hands touched her, he thought smoke might pour from his ears.

It was one thing to know that this was what she did. That she was no doubt lining up potential selections for her future wherever she went. He'd never expected anything less. Yet it turned out it was something else to witness her in action.

Particularly when he could still *feel* her. Still hear those cries in his ears. Still taste her, the hard nub of her nipple and that creamy heat below.

Damn her.

He had no memory of the conversations he must have engaged in with the people sitting on either side of him. When the eternal dinner ground to an end at last and he could finally get the hell away, he escorted Kathryn to their waiting car with a hand that was, he could admit, perhaps a little too insistent against the small of her back.

"Is this an attempt at chivalry or are you herding me?" she asked under her breath, that damned smile of hers still welded into place even outside, in the dark, where there was no one to see her but him.

He wanted to mess her up, Luca acknowledged. He wanted to dig his fingers beneath that facade of hers and see what she hid away underneath. He wanted far too much, and all of it wrong. And dangerous, besides.

He was not a man who had ever been interested in entanglements. But *tangled* was the very least of the things he felt around this woman.

Luca held the passenger door of the sleek limousine open as she climbed inside, nodding brusquely at their driver. Then he swung into the limo's hushed interior himself, making no particular attempt to keep to his own side of the wide backseat as he slammed the door shut behind him.

Kathryn was digging in her evening bag. She glanced at him as he came close, then froze.

"What's the matter?" she asked. The faintest frown etched itself between her eyes, where that fringe of hers nearly touched her eyes and drove him utterly crazy with that same sharp longing he was finding it harder and harder—impossible—to control. Just as he could no longer seem to control himself. "What happened?"

"You tell me."

He felt outsized and more than a little maddened. He sprawled there next to her, too close but not quite touching her. Not quite. His blood was pumping through him much too fast. His heart was trying to kick its way out of his chest. He was holding himself back by the smallest thread.

He wasn't sure how he was holding himself back at all.

Her frown deepened, which was at least better than that damned smile.

"I don't know, Luca. I thought that went well enough. I'm not sure what you wanted out of it, but it seems as if every vintner in two valleys is deeply impressed with your varietals. What more can you ask?"

For the first time in his life, Luca did not care the slightest bit about wine or the wine business or anything having to do with his damned vines or vintages or barrels or whatever else.

"I could ask that when we are conducting business, you manage to keep your mind on that," he seethed at her. He didn't even try to contain that tone of his or the simmering outrage in it. "And not on laying your trap for your next victim."

Her gray eyes chilled. "What are you talking about?"

"You weren't particularly subtle," he gritted at her as the car began to move, sweeping them out toward the main road and the mountains to the west. "Everyone at the table got to watch you hang all over that poor man and play your little games with him."

"And by *little games*, I assume you mean the work you and I were there to do? That I was doing while you sulked?"

"You spent a long time off in the bathroom before dessert," he continued, not caring that he could see the effect of his harsh tone in the way she shivered slightly. "What were you doing, I wonder? Your target also disappeared for a similar span of time. And God only knows what you were doing beneath the table where no one could see."

He'd thought of little else. He knew the meal he'd been served had been the finest Californian cuisine, a fusion of the state's rich bounty presented to perfection, and yet it had all been tasteless and pointless to him.

Kathryn shook her head, her lips pressing together. "This is ridiculous. Not to mention offensive in the extreme." Her gray eyes flashed. "Of course, that's your thing, isn't it? The more horrible, the better."

"And here's what I wonder." He shifted so he was closer to her, looming over her, his whole body humming with that darkness, that tension, that driving need he could neither understand nor control. This was what she did to him. She made him lose the tight control he'd always maintained over himself, his world, his life. Always. He found that the most unforgivable. Maybe that was what made him move his face that much closer to hers—so she could *feel* his fury in every word he spoke. "How does a noted whore for hire seal the deal? On your knees or on your back? Does it vary with each mark or do you stick to a set routine?"

He didn't see her move, and that told him more about the blind single-mindedness of that darkness in him than anything else. He felt her palm against his jaw, heard the *crack* of it fill the car's interior with the bright burst of the slap she delivered and he saw the fire and the fury in her dark gray eyes.

The pain came a moment later, sharp and swift.

"You're a vile little man," she threw at him, and he didn't disagree with her. But that was neither here nor there. "The only thing more disgusting than your imagination is the fact you think you can dump it out on me whenever you feel like it, like a toxic spill."

Luca laughed, a darker sound than the night outside the car or the way her breath came out in angry pants, and tested his jaw with his hand.

"That actually hurt." He shifted his gaze to hers, and eyed the way she sat there, clearly trembling with rage. "Is this where you play the outraged and offended virgin? I must tell you, Kathryn. You're not that accomplished an actress."

She paled. He thought she might keel over, or explode, but she pressed her lips together again instead. She lifted a hand, and he thought she might try to hit him once more—and the operative word was *try*—but she only put her palm to her neck. As if she wanted to control her own pulse. Or her own breath.

Or herself.

And he didn't know what to do with that notion that swept over him like heat, that she might find herself as out of control in the middle of this mess as he clearly was.

"If you hit me again," he told her softly, "I'll return the favor."

"You'll hit me?" Her eyes were grim in the dark. "I'm glad your father is dead, Luca. He would have been horrified by you."

He ignored the little flare of something a good deal like shame deep inside him then, even as it knotted itself in his gut.

"Let's be very clear about this," he said, and he was aware on a distant level that the fury that had been riding him all through dinner had eased. Not disappeared, but loosened its hold. He didn't ask himself why. "It will be a very cold day in hell before I worry myself over what my father, of all people, might have thought about anything I do. Much less what you think. That's the moral equivalent of taking lectures on good behavior from the devil himself." He eyed her in the close confines of the car's backseat, where he was still too much in her space, and it still wasn't enough. Not close enough. Not *enough*. "But I don't hit women. Not even when they've hit me first."

She had the grace to look faintly abashed at that, and her gaze dropped to her hand. She flexed her fingers out in front of her, and he wondered if her palm stung as much as his jaw did. The idea didn't make that heavy knot inside him loosen any.

He reached over and took her hand in his, and held on when she tried to jerk it out of his grasp. He ignored the little *huff* of air that escaped her lips, and smoothed his fingers over her palm as if he was tracing it. As if he wanted to rub the sting out.

As if he didn't know what the hell he wanted.

"Hit me again, Kathryn," he said in a low voice, looking at her hand instead of her face, "and I'll take that as an invitation to finish what we started last night. No matter how many old men you make dance to your tune at a dinner table. No matter who you're pretending to be tonight."

Her fingers curled as if she wanted to clench them into a fist.

"I'm not pretending to be anyone," she snapped at

him. "The only person playing a game here is you. And there will never be an invitation to finish anything. That was an aberration. A terrible, horrifying mistake. I have no idea why it happened and—"

"Don't you?"

He hadn't meant to ask that question, but once out, it seemed to hover there between them, threatening everything. Pounding in him so hard it became indistinguishable from his own heartbeat.

"No," she whispered, but her gray eyes were too large and too dark. Her pretty mouth trembled with the lie of it. And he could feel the tremor she fought to repress in that hand he held between his. "I have no idea what you're talking about. I never do."

And Luca smiled. Hard. "Let me give you some clarity."

He let go of her hand and reached for her, wrapping his hands around her waist and lifting her out of her seat and over his lap. He heard her breath desert her as he settled her against him, her legs to one side. Then he simply bent his head and took her mouth with his.

Once again, that maddening fire. Once again, that swift shock, lust and need, greed and hunger, burning him alive.

As hot and as wild as if they were still in her bed. As if they'd never left, never stopped.

And she didn't fight him. She didn't pretend. He felt her give in to this thing that pounded between them, felt the heady rush of her surrender.

She hooked her arms around his neck as if she couldn't control herself any more than he could, then she opened her mouth to him and kissed him back.

And Luca lost track of everything.

That he was trying to make a point. That they were in the back of a moving car. That she was the last woman on earth he should be touching at all, much less like this. That he absolutely should not be doing this.

He simply lost himself in the perfection of her mouth. The sweet heat of the way she kissed him and tangled her fingers in his hair. The weight of her slender body against his and the sheer desperation in the way they came together.

Again and again.

But it wasn't enough.

He groaned against her mouth, and she shifted against him as if he'd lit her on fire, the curve of her hip coming up hard against his aching sex.

And Luca stopped pretending he had any control where this woman was concerned. Or at all.

He shifted her on top of him, swinging her around to straddle him. He shoved the dress she wore up and out of his way, settling her down astride his lap, and he almost lost it when she gasped into his mouth as the softest part of her came up flush against his hardness.

He could feel her shudder all around him, or maybe that was him, as lost in this insanity as she was.

There was no control. There was no hint of it. And the truly scary part of that was how little Luca cared that it was gone.

There was nothing but his hands buried in her hair again and his mouth against hers, feasting on her. Ravishing her. He could feel her wet heat against him and rolled himself into it, aware that only the fabric of his trousers and the insubstantial panties she wore separated them. He let the slick, hot glory of it build.

There was nothing but her taste, an addictive wildness against his tongue. She surrounded him, more beautiful with her dress at her waist and her hair half-falling down from its elegant little knot than any other woman he'd ever seen.

Than anything at all.

And Luca found himself muttering things he knew better than to say out loud, even if he was speaking in Italian.

"Tu sei mia," he told her. *You are mine.* He didn't know where that had come from, what the hell he was doing. Why he meant such things down deep in his bones, when he shouldn't. When he couldn't.

But he found he didn't much care then. He filled his hands with the taut curves of her bottom and guided her against him in an unapologetically carnal rhythm, until she tilted her head back and moaned.

So he did it even harder, watching her face go slack as she rocked against him, driving him crazy, making him so hard and ready for her it bordered on pain. He moved his hand from her gorgeous bottom, sliding it around to find the heat of her with his fingers through the barrier of those soft panties.

"Look at me, Kathryn," he ordered her, his voice little more than a growl.

She obeyed. And her eyes were wide and gray. Slicked hot with desire. Her lips were parted, and her cheeks were flushed. Luca felt something shift inside him, a sharp and uncompromising tilt. He couldn't name it, though there was no pretending he didn't feel it. He only knew that he was no longer the same man he'd been even five minutes before.

There was only Kathryn, arched above him, straining against him, her beautiful eyes locked on to his.

And there is this, he thought, sliding his hands into her panties and slicking his way through the molten wildfire of her sweet core to find the neediest part of her. Then he pressed down, hard and sure, and watched her hurtle over the side of the world.

She bucked against him as her pleasure tumbled through her, making greedy little noises that were almost his undoing, her fingers digging hard into his shoulders, her head thrown back and her lovely back arched like a bow.

And everything shifted again, but this time, all the hunger and greed and sense in his body surged straight to his sex.

Luca needed to be inside her. Right now.

She was still shaking, still astride him. She was still panting as she tipped forward until she could rest her forehead against his shoulder. And now he could feel her harsh little breaths as well as hear them, and somehow, that made everything hotter.

Closer. Crazier. Better.

He reached between them, amazed to find his hand was unsteady as he pulled himself from his trousers at last, so aching and so hard. Kathryn was limp now, still shuddering and gasping, and he simply pulled her panties to one side and lined himself up with her entrance, the scalding heat of her nearly enough to make him lose it right there.

He thought he swore in Italian, or perhaps it was a prayer. She was slick and hot, and he didn't care where else she'd been or with whom. He didn't care why. He didn't care about anything but the way she fit in his arms, his lap.

He didn't care about anything but this.

It had been two years of sheer torment with this woman; he could admit that now, when the truth seemed so obvious at last. He'd wanted her from the moment he'd first laid eyes on her. Perhaps he would always want her. But that wasn't something Luca wanted to think about. Not now when she was everything he'd ever wanted, poised there above him, hot and wet and nearly his.

Nearly.

He moved his hands to her hips to hold her right where he wanted her. He tucked his mouth against her neck, where he could taste her, salt and need.

And then finally, finally, he thrust his way home.

It hurt.

God, did it hurt.

Kathryn felt something tear, felt a shriek of agony sear through her like a burn, and then there was nothing but the hugeness of him. Deep, deep inside her. So deep she found she couldn't breathe, couldn't think, couldn't do anything but freeze there over him, that harsh thrust of his possession like a throbbing brand within her.

Luca swore.

Then again, in both Italian and English, and she scrunched up her face so she wouldn't cry and kept it buried in the crook of his shoulder as if she could hide from this. As if that might make the shuddering, aching heaviness go away.

But it didn't work.

"Look at me," he said, his voice hoarse. "Kathryn. Sit up."

"I don't want to."

He was still buried deep inside her, though he didn't

move. Then the car bumped over a dip in the road and thrust him deeper into her, and she felt the way he braced himself. Heard the small exhalation he made, as if this was no easier for him than it was for her. And that heavy sharpness radiated out from where the length of him was still inside her, making even her breasts feel stung with it.

As if the whole of her body was one giant *ache*.

"Sit up, *cucciola mia*," he said, in a voice she'd never heard him use before, something far warmer and indulgent than any she associated with him. He nudged her with his jaw. "Now, please."

And it seemed the hardest thing she'd ever done, to ease herself back, knowing he could see the panic and the pain and the leftover heat all over her face. To *feel him* lodged *inside* her as she carefully shifted position. To look into his dark eyes, so close to hers, aware that he knew things about her now she hadn't wanted to share.

Too many things.

It had all happened too fast. She'd been lost in another bone-deep, impossible shattering, torn apart into a million little pieces and unable to breathe, and then it had been too late.

Too late, she thought again.

She wasn't sure what that thing was that crept over her, deep in her chest and her gut, a raw sort of hollow. She was terribly afraid it might be a sob.

Luca reached up and smoothed her hair back from her still-flushed face. She squirmed against that thick, hard intrusion that connected them so intimately, and he only watched her do it. He didn't move—though she thought that steel line of his jaw hardened.

"Why didn't you tell me?" he asked, his voice the

quietest she'd ever heard it, and she didn't know what to make of that. She didn't know how to feel.

She moved her hips and didn't understand how people did this, or *why*, when there was no comfortable position and too much of that heavy, aching heat. "I didn't think you'd notice."

"Kathryn," he said, that low voice at odds, somehow, with the very nearly tender way his thumbs brushed over her temples, and her name in his mouth a kind of poetry that made that hollow thing inside her seem to hum. "You went from pleasure to pain in an instant. How could I not notice that?"

She shifted again, still trying to find a way to sit on his lap when he was *inside her*, and this time his eyes darkened. She caught her breath.

The car bumped again and this time, the sensations that spun out from that involuntary thrust were more of a deep spark than anything sharp or painful. The ache inside her…changed. The spark seemed to light it up, infusing it with something else besides the pain. She shifted experimentally, then tugged her bottom lip between her teeth when that *something else* bloomed into something better, and watched that slow hunger burn in his dark eyes.

She felt an answering echo of it in her, as if the heaviness and the stretched ache were connected to all that delicious heat she thought of as his, that she could feel easing back into her the longer they sat like this.

"I wasn't aware that it would matter to you whether or not you hurt me," she said, without meaning to speak.

Luca's hands moved to cup her cheeks, and his dark

eyes met hers, nearly grim in the shadows of this car slipping through the California night.

"It matters," he said gruffly. "You should have told me."

And that hollow thing inside her swelled, crashing over her like a terrible tide. She didn't know what it was. She only felt the sting of tears in her eyes and the throb of something far heavier in her chest.

And Luca deep inside her, hot and still.

"Tell you?" she whispered, because her voice had deserted her. "How could I tell you? You don't just think I'm a whore, Luca. You *know* it. You've never had the slightest doubt."

"Kathryn."

"You wouldn't have believed me." She only realized that her tears had spilled out when he wiped them away with his thumbs, more gentle with her than made any sense. "You would have laughed in my face."

He didn't deny that, though his gaze darkened even further.

He pulled her face to his and kissed her, and it was almost too much. The thrust of him deep inside her body and the impossible sweetness of his lips on hers. It made her brain short out. It made that great rawness inside her glow.

"Ah, *cucciola mia*," he murmured, pulling back from her mouth, still holding her face in his hands—almost as if he found her somehow precious. "I'm not laughing now."

And then he began to move.

CHAPTER EIGHT

KATHRYN TENSED, BUT Luca only pulled out slowly and then pressed back in, far more gently this time.

It didn't hurt. It felt…strange, but that was better than the pain.

"Breathe," he told her, in that bossy way of his that shouldn't have made something ignite inside her. But she did it anyway.

She pulled in a deep breath and let it out, and still he moved inside her. Lazy. Relaxed. An easy sort of rocking.

Slowly, almost despite herself, Kathryn began to anticipate him. She met him when he thrust in, moving her hips in a way that made a low, shimmering thing dance inside her.

His mouth curved, and she thought that later—much later—she would have to examine why it was that it made her flush with so much pleasure.

He maintained that same lazy pace, and let his hands wander where they pleased. He smoothed his way up her back. He tested the thrust of her breasts through the dress that was still bunched around her waist. He reached beneath it and drew patterns on the soft skin of her belly, on the outsides of her thighs.

Kathryn found herself moving more, rolling her hips and testing the depth of his stroke. *This* dragged the center of her against him, and it made everything inside her wind up tight. *That* made a sweet shudder work its way up her spine. She tried different movements, wriggling against him and rocking into him, and he let her, only that heavy-lidded heat in his dark eyes and the faint flush high on his cheekbones a hint that he felt the same fire she did.

And slowly, surely, inevitably, she forgot that anything had ever hurt her. There was nothing but the glide, the pull. The bright heat that expanded the deeper he went into her and the more she met each thrust.

There was a coiling thing inside her, huge and terrifying, and Kathryn didn't know which she wanted more—to hide from it or throw herself straight into its center. And in any case, it didn't matter. Because Luca let out a delicious little laugh as if he knew exactly what she felt, and took control.

He pulled her hips flush with his. He took her mouth in a deep, dark, endless kiss. And he began to move within her in earnest, each slick thrust making that coil wind tighter, making it bigger and wilder and that much more intense.

And she couldn't. She couldn't—

"You can," he said against her mouth, and she realized she'd said that out loud. "You will."

And he shifted beneath her, then ran his clever fingers down to the place they were joined, and rubbed.

The next time he thrust inside her, she imploded. A brilliant, impossible shattering that rolled out from the place where he maintained that demanding pace, tearing her soul from her body and her limbs apart.

She heard him groan out her name, his mouth against her neck, and then he toppled right over that same cliff beside her.

And for a very long time, that was all there was.

When Kathryn came back to herself, she was still slumped against him and still astride him, and the car was slowing to make its final turn into the Castelli vineyard.

She pushed herself back up to a sitting position and climbed off Luca at the same time, feeling the loss of that length of him inside her like a blow. It made her feel even more awkward as she struggled to wriggle her dress back into place. Even more...off center.

He didn't speak. She didn't dare look at him. She heard him zip himself up, and then there was the long drive up from the road to the château to endure in the same heavy silence. Kathryn felt too many things, thought too many things, all of them battering at her like a thousand desperate winds, but she couldn't let herself do that here. Not while he was still beside her, so male and so hard, and now something entirely different than what he'd been even an hour before.

She didn't want to change. She didn't want the shift. She didn't understand how she'd simply...surrendered to him when she was twenty-five years old and hadn't felt the slightest urge to give herself to anyone in all her years.

"You're much too pretty," her mother had told her when she was barely thirteen, with a frown that told Kathryn that this was not a positive thing. "Mind you don't let it make you lazy. *Pretty* is nothing more than a prison sentence. Best you remember that before you let it turn your head."

And she'd tried. She'd buried herself in her studies. She'd run from the slightest hint of male interest or even friendships with girls who had any kind of active social lives, lest she be tempted into joining in. She'd done everything she could think of to prove to her mother that her looks weren't a weakness, that she could take advantage of the gifts Rose had given her with all her scrimping and saving and hard work.

But Rose had never been convinced.

"They'll trap you if they can," she'd told Kathryn again and again throughout her teenage years. "Tell you it's love. There's no such thing, my girl. There are only men who will leave you and babies who need raising once they're gone. A pretty thing like you will be easy pickings."

And Kathryn had resolved that whatever else she was, she wouldn't be *that*.

Even at university she'd been good at holding herself apart, keeping herself safe. She didn't want boyfriends or even supposed male friends who might think they could get to her that way, when her defenses were down. She avoided any scenario that might lead to lowered inhibitions or the slightest hint of danger. No pubs with her classmates. No parties. She'd kept herself in her own little tower, locked safely away, where nothing and no one could ever touch her or ruin her or make her a disappointment to her mother, who had given up so much to make her life possible.

All this time, she thought now, as the limo pulled up to the château's grand entrance, and Rose had been right. It really was a slippery slope, and Kathryn had plummeted straight down it and crashed at the bottom. One single car ride with a man who despised her, and she'd lost a lifetime of her moral high ground, her entire self-definition. She'd become exactly what Luca had always accused her of being, what Rose had always darkly intimated she'd become one day whether she liked it or not.

The whole world was different. *She* was different. And she didn't have the slightest idea how to come to terms with any of it, or what it meant.

The driver opened the door, and Kathryn climbed out too quickly, shocked when she felt twinges in all sorts of unfamiliar places. She might have toppled to the ground, but Luca was there, taking her arm as if he'd anticipated this. Holding her steady.

Though he still didn't say a word.

Kathryn pulled her arm out of his grasp, aware that he let her do it, and felt a rush of sheer, hot embarrassment wash over her. She couldn't read that expression on his face, making him look like granite in the light that beamed out from the château's windows and the moon high above. She couldn't imagine what she must look like—wrinkled and rumpled, used and altered, like a walking neon advertisement for what she'd just done. Was it written on her face? Would the whole world be able to *see* what had happened right there—what she'd done? What she'd let him do?

The notion made her panic.

She all but ran up the steps and threw open the door, relieved that there was no sign of anyone around as she hurtled herself inside the château's ornate entry hall like a missile.

It's fine, she told herself, though she didn't believe it. Though she could hear the drumming panic in her own head. *Everything is perfectly fine.*

She made herself slow down. She was aware of Luca just behind her, a solid wall of regret at her heels, but she told herself to ignore it. To pretend he wasn't there. She forced herself to walk, not run. She headed up the stairs and then down the hall that led to the family wing. She made her way all the way to the far end of the château, and then finally, *finally*, she could see the door to her own room. She couldn't wait to close herself inside and…breathe.

She would take another very long bath. She would scrub all of this away. She would curl herself up into a tiny little ball, and she would not permit herself to cry.

She would not.

Luca said her name when she'd finally reached her door, when she had her hand out to grab the handle and was *this close*—

And Kathryn didn't want this. She didn't want whatever cutting, eviscerating, gut punch of a thing he was about to say. Whatever new and inventive way he'd come up with to call her a whore and make her feel like one.

But she wanted him to know how fragile she was even less, so she turned around and faced him.

He stood much too close, his dark eyes glittering, an expression she couldn't place on his beautiful face. She wished he wasn't so gorgeous, that he didn't make her ache. She imagined that might make it easier—might make that tugging thing near her heart dissipate more quickly.

She should say something; she knew she should. But she couldn't seem to make her mouth work.

"Where are you going, *cucciola mia*?" he asked softly.

She hated him, she told herself. The only thing worse

than his insults was this. That softness she couldn't understand at all.

"I don't know what that means. I don't speak any Italian."

His mouth moved into that curve again, and his dark eyes were much too intense. He reached over and tucked a strand of her hair behind her ear, and Kathryn knew he could feel the way that made her shudder. And her breath catch.

"I suppose it means *my pet*, more or less," Luca said, as if he hadn't considered it until that moment.

And the true betrayal was the warmth that spread through her at that, as if it was that laugh of his, bottled up, pure liquid sunshine starting deep inside her. Because he was dangerous enough when he was hateful. Kathryn thought that this other side of him—what she might have called *affectionate* had they been other people—might actually kill her.

Her throat felt swollen. Scratchy. Because of the noises she'd made in that car that she couldn't let herself think about? Or because of that brand-new rawness lodged inside her now? She didn't know. But she forced herself to speak anyway. "I don't want to be your pet."

That curve of his mouth deepened. "I don't know that it's up to you."

Kathryn felt restless. Edgy. As if she might burst. Or scream. Or simply crumple to the ground—and he seemed perfectly content to stand there forever, seeing things in her face she was quite certain she'd prefer to hide.

She scowled at him. "I don't know what you want from me."

This time, when he reached out, he took her shoulders in his hands and tugged her into his arms, and when he wrapped his arms around her, she melted. God help her, but she simply…fell into him. All that heat and strength, enveloping her like some kind of benediction.

"Come," he said quietly, letting her go. "I'll show you."

Kathryn knew what she needed to do. What her mother would expect her to do. One slip was bad enough. One terrible mistake. There was still time to save herself. There was still the possibility that she could call tonight a lost battle and go on to win the war, surely. She needed only to pull away from him, step inside her room and lock him out, so she could set about the Herculean task of putting herself back together.

But she couldn't make herself do it.

And when Luca opened the door to his bedroom and held out his hand as if he knew exactly what battles she was fighting and, more than that, how to win them, Kathryn ignored the great riot and tumult that shook inside her, and took it.

Luca didn't know how to make sense of any of this.

And that lost look in her too-dark gray eyes, something too close to broken, was too much for him. He had a thousand questions he didn't ask. A thousand more stacked behind them. He had the sense that there was something lying in wait for him, just over his shoulder or perhaps deep inside him, that he didn't care to examine.

Not tonight, when he'd discovered that she was precisely as innocent as she'd sometimes appeared.

It didn't matter how or why. Even the subject of her marriage to his father could wait.

What mattered—what beat in him like a darkening pulse that only got louder and more insistent with every breath—was that whatever else happened, whatever games she played or was playing even now, whatever the hell was going on here in all this California moonlight, she was his.

His.

Luca didn't wish to question himself on that. On why that surge of sheer possession seared through him, as if she'd branded him somehow with the unexpected gift of her innocence. He only knew that she was his. Only his.

And Luca wasn't done with her. Not even close.

She put her hand in his and let him lead her into his rooms, and there was no particular reason that should feel like trumpets blaring, drums pounding, a whole damned parade. But it did.

It should horrify him, he knew, that he had so little control where this woman was concerned—but tonight he couldn't bring himself to care.

He took his time.

He stood her at the foot of the great platform bed and undressed her slowly, not letting her help. He slid her shoes from her feet. He found the hidden side zipper on the bodice of her dress and eased it down, then tugged the whole of it up and over her head. He unhooked the bra she wore and pulled it from her arms, letting it fall to the floor with the rest.

When she stood before him in nothing but those panties he'd shoved out of his way in the car and that uncertain look on her face that he thought might kill him, Luca took a moment to ease his fingers through her hair. He pulled out what remained of that upswept knot she'd worn to dinner. He stroked his hands through the thick, straight strands, comforting them both.

And only when she let out a long breath he didn't think she knew she'd been holding did he finish undressing her, easing her panties down over her hips and then over the length of her perfectly formed legs.

Luca let himself look at her for a long time, indulging that possessive streak he'd never known he had. Because he'd never felt anything like it before tonight. He shrugged out of his jacket and kicked off his shoes. Still he gazed at her, letting her exquisite beauty imprint itself deep inside him. Every part of her was lovely, so astonishingly perfect that something moved in him at the sight, equal parts need and alarm.

He swept her up into his arms, enjoying the tiny noise she made, and then he carried her into the bathroom suite. He set her down next to the tub and ran the water, tossing in a handful of bath salts as it began to fill.

"Are we taking a bath?" Her voice cracked and she flushed, and Luca understood that this was a Kathryn he'd never seen before, this unsteady, uncertain creature who suddenly seemed much younger and far more breakable to him.

Or this has always been Kathryn, a voice in him suggested, more sharply than was strictly comfortable. *And you have been nothing but an ass.*

He shoved that aside, ruthlessly. There would be time enough to address the great mess of things that waited for him with the dawn.

Tonight was about this. Tonight was about her.

Instead of answering her, he stripped, watching her color rise the more he revealed. He was fascinated. Mesmerized by that spread of color, from her cheeks down her neck, to turn even her chest a pale pink, a shade or two lighter than the rose of her upturned nipples.

He wanted to feast on her. All of her.

When they were both naked he urged her into the hot water, settling her in front of him and between his legs with her back to him. He took the heavy mass of her thick dark hair in his hands and carefully made a new knot of it, high on the top of her head, and then wrapped his arms around her and held her there against him.

He didn't let himself think about anything. Just the sheer perfection of her body against his. The silken slide of the salted water, making her skin a smooth caress against his. He waited as she relaxed in increments against him, as she softened and, eventually, sighed. And only then did he begin to wash her.

He took his time. He touched her everywhere. He put his hands on every inch of her skin, saving that slippery heat between her legs for last, and a hard sort of satisfaction gripped him when she let out a hungry little moan at his touch.

Only when he'd made sure she was utterly boneless did he finish, standing her up and toweling her off, then carrying her back into the bedroom to put her in his bed at last. Her gaze never left him, wide and nearly green, and he'd learned her tonight. He knew what that faint quiver in her body meant. How she flushed when he crawled over her, a bright red on top of the pink she'd turned in the heat of the bath.

And when he was fully stretched out above her, skin to skin, he learned her all over again.

With his hands, his mouth. His tongue and his teeth. He explored her. She'd given him something he could hardly get his head around, could barely understand, and this was how he expressed his gratitude. His wonder. All those tangled things inside him that he knew better than to look at too closely. He worked them out against her lovely body, inch by perfect inch.

She arched up beneath him and he feasted on her breasts. She rocked against him and he held her down, tracing every muscle and every smooth curve, making her his. Making every last part of her inarguably his.

And this time, when he surged inside her, she was soft and shaking and ready for him.

She cried out his name.

Luca set a more demanding pace, gathering her beneath him, lost in the sleek glory of her hips against his. He built her up high. He made her sob. And then he threw her straight off that cliff and into bliss.

Once, then again.

And only then, when she was shattered twice over, her eyes slate green and filled with him and nothing else, did he follow her over that edge.

CHAPTER NINE

IT WAS NOT until the following morning—after Luca had woken up to discover that none of the previous night had been one of the remarkably detailed dreams he'd had about Kathryn over the past couple of years, because she was still there, sprawled out beside him and wholly irresistible—that he allowed himself to think about what the inescapable fact of her innocence meant.

First, he'd rolled over, instantly awake and aware and as hard for her as if he'd never had her. She'd come awake a moment later, and he'd watched her eyes go from sleepy to pleased to wary in the course of a few blinks.

He'd found he hadn't cared much for *wary*.

So he'd pinned her hands above her head and settled himself between her thighs. He'd expressed his feelings on her tender breasts until she'd been gasping and arching beneath him, and then he'd driven himself home once again, losing himself in all her molten sweetness.

And he'd found the sound of her gasping his name as she convulsed around him far, far preferable to any wariness.

He managed to control himself in the shower they shared—but barely—and maybe the fact that doing so was so much harder than it should have been kicked his brain back into gear.

Kathryn was dressing, her head bent and a certain set expression on her face that he didn't like. He stood in the doorway to the bathroom with only a towel wrapped around his hips and watched her, aware that he should not be feeling any of the things that stampeded through him then. He knew that expression she wore. He usually liked it when the women he bedded showed him that particular blankness, because it meant they planned to walk away from him with no fuss. And quickly.

He didn't want her to walk away.

He wanted her right here, and he didn't care how crazy that was. How insane this entire situation was. That no one but him—that no one, *especially* him—would ever believe that *Saint Kate* had been a virgin until now.

"Kathryn." She didn't precisely jolt when she heard her name, but that wariness was back in her gaze when she lifted it to his. "Why did you marry him?"

She pressed her lips together in that way of hers that he should not find so fascinating. She tugged her bra into place and then bent to pick up her crumpled dress, frowning at it in a way that made something in the vicinity of his heart clench. Luca didn't speak. He swept up his own discarded shirt and prowled over to her, watching the way her eyes widened as he approached. Her lips parted slightly, as if she needed more air, and he couldn't pretend he didn't like that.

He liked entirely too much. Her lush little body, packaged in that lacy bra and matching panties that highlighted parts of her he could never obsess about *enough*. The faint marks from his mouth, his unshaven jaw. He was a primitive creature, he understood then, though he'd never thought of himself in those terms before. When it came to Kathryn, he was nothing short of a beast.

Luca liked his mark on her. He liked it hard and deep, so much it very nearly hurt.

He settled his dress shirt around her shoulders, then tugged her arms through. And then he took his time buttoning it up, fashioning her a dress that was much too big for her frame, but was in its way another mark. Another brand.

The beast within him roared its approval.

"Are you going to answer me?" he asked in a low voice as he rolled up one cuff, then the other, to keep the sleeves from hanging nearly to her knees.

She swallowed, and he saw that her eyes had changed color again, to that slate green that meant she was aroused. *Good*, he thought. He didn't imagine he'd ever be anything but aroused in her presence again. He wasn't sure he ever had been anything else, come to that.

But she blinked it away and took in a shuddering sort of breath.

"He said he could help," she said.

She moved away from him, and the sight of her in his shirt did things to Luca that he couldn't explain. He didn't want to explain them. They simply settled inside him, like light.

"Why did you need help?"

Kathryn worried her lower lip with her teeth, which he felt like her mouth against his sex, but he held himself in check.

"My mother was single when she had me," she said, and Luca blinked. He didn't know what he'd expected, but it wasn't that. Something so…mundane. "She'd never expected or even wanted to have a baby at all, but there she was, pregnant. Her partner made it clear he couldn't be bothered, and in case she'd any doubts about that, moved out of the country straightaway, so no one could expect him to contribute in any way to the life of a child he didn't want."

"He sounds charming."

Kathryn smiled, very slightly. "I wouldn't know. We've never met."

Luca watched as she moved to the bed and climbed onto the mattress, settling herself near the foot with her legs crossed beneath her and his shirt billowing around her slender form. It only made her look that much more fragile.

And made him want to protect her, somehow—even against this story she was telling him.

"My mother had huge dreams," she said after a moment. "She'd worked so hard to get where she was. She wanted a whole, rich life, and what she got instead was a daughter to raise right when she really could have made something of herself."

Something in the way she said that scraped at him. Luca frowned. "Surely raising a child is merely a different rich life. Not the lack of one altogether."

Kathryn's gaze met his for a moment then dropped.

"She'd worked so hard to succeed in finance, but couldn't keep up with the hours required once she had me. And once she left the job she loved, at an investment bank, she couldn't afford child care, so she had to manage it all on her own." She threaded her hands together in front of her. "All of my memories of her were of her working. She usually had more than one job, in fact, so I wouldn't want for anything. She wasn't too proud to do the things others refused to do. She cleaned houses on her hands and knees, anything to make my life better, and despite all of that, I was a terrible disappointment."

Luca had the sense that if he disputed this story, if he questioned it at all—and he couldn't understand why there was that thing in him that insisted this was a story that needed disputing when until hours ago he'd been Kathryn's biggest critic—she would stop talking. It was something in the set of her mouth, the line of her jaw. The stormy gray color of her eyes. So he said nothing. He merely exchanged his towel for a pair of exercise trousers and then crossed his arms over his chest. He waited.

Kathryn let out a breath that was more like a sigh.

"She wanted me to be an investment banker, too. That was always her preference, because she could teach me everything I needed to know and because her experience meant she could direct me."

"I believe that is called living through one's child. Not the best form of parenting, I think."

She frowned at him. "Not in this case. I could never get my head around the math. My mother tried to tutor me herself, but it was a waste of time. I can't think the way she can. My brain simply won't work the way hers does."

"My brain does not work the way my brother's does," Luca pointed out mildly, "and yet we've muddled along, running a rather successful company together for some time."

"That's different." Kathryn lifted a shoulder then dropped it. "I nearly killed myself getting a First in economics. I spent hours and hours torturing myself with the coursework. But I did it. Then I went on to an MBA course because that was what my mother thought was the best path toward the brightest future." She blew out a breath that made her fringe dance above her brow. "But the MBA was beyond torture. I was used to putting the hours in, but it wasn't enough. No matter what I did, it wasn't enough."

She shook her head, frowning down at her hands, and Luca had never wanted to touch another person more than he did then. She looked too small and something like defeated, and it lodged in his chest like a bullet.

It occurred to him that he'd never seen her look like this. That she'd fought him every step of the way, if sometimes only with a straight spine and a head held high. But *defeat* was not a word he'd ever associated with her before.

He found he hated it.

Kathryn met his gaze again then. "And that was when I met your father."

He shifted position and realized he was holding himself back as much as anything else. As if he didn't know what he might do if he stopped—as if he still had that little control, when it still involved Kathryn yet wasn't about sex. He couldn't say he much enjoyed the sensation.

But one great mess at a time, he thought darkly.

"Ah, yes," he said. "In that mythic waiting room, the birthplace of your epic friendship. The only friendship the old man ever had, as far as I am aware."

"You asked me to tell you this story," she pointed out. "You keep asking."

Luca couldn't trust himself to speak, one more novel

experience where this woman was concerned—and one he knew he would have to think about later. He inclined his head, silently bidding her to continue.

"It happened just as I told you," Kathryn said, her gaze reproving. "We started talking. Your father was charming. Funny."

Luca snorted. "Old."

"Maybe everyone is not as ageist as you are," she snapped at him.

He raked his hand through his hair then, annoyed and frustrated in equal measure.

"It is time for the truth, *cucciola mia*," he said then, roughly.

He moved before he knew he meant to, crossing over to place himself directly in front of her, at the foot of the high bed. She tilted up that chin of hers, as if she expected him to take a swing, and Luca was obviously deeply perverse, that such a thing should excite him. Or maybe it was simply that he liked it when she fought. When she stood up for herself, even against him. When she was nothing remotely like *defeated*.

"I'm telling you the truth. I can't help it if it's not the truth you want to hear." She eyed him, as if his proximity bothered her. Luca hoped it did. It would make them even. "I think we've already established that you have a history of believing what you want to believe, no matter what the actual truth might be."

He felt his mouth curve in acknowledgment. "But this is not a question of innocence. This is a question of how a young woman meets a much older man in a medical facility, so she could have no fantasy that there was anything virile about him at all, and decides to marry him anyway. I have no doubt that he proposed to you. That was what he did, always. But what made you agree?"

Kathryn held his gaze, and Luca didn't move. He didn't even blink, aware somehow that she was making a momentous decision. And he needed it to be the right one. *He needed it*—and he wasn't sure he wanted to investigate why that need was so intense. After a long while, she let out a sigh.

"My mother has crippling arthritis," Kathryn explained. "When it flares up she can hardly move. It had become very difficult for her to take care of herself." She shook her head, more as if she was shaking off a wave of emotion than negating anything. "I should have been there to help her, but between the classes for my degree and all the studying I had to do to barely keep up, I couldn't even do that well. I lived with her, which was one thing, but it was all beginning to feel a lot like drowning." She sucked in a breath. "But when my mother came out of her appointment, she recognized your father at a glance. One thing led to another, and we all went out for a meal."

Luca waited.

"Your father is very easy to talk to, actually."

"That was not a common sentiment."

"My mother told him everything. My struggles with my degree. Her battle with her arthritis. He was very kind." Her gray eyes grew distant, and he thought she tipped her chin up that much farther. "And at the end of the evening, he asked if he could see me—just me—again."

"This is where I think I need some clarification," Luca murmured. "Did you date a great deal?"

"I didn't date at all," she retorted, and he almost didn't

recognize that fierce thing that soared in him at that, possessiveness mixed with a kind of triumph.

"But you dated my father."

For the first time she looked uncomfortable. "I didn't necessarily want to *date* him," she said softly. "But he'd been so nice, and so sweet, and I didn't see the harm in having another dinner with him. I thought I was doing a good deed."

"What did your mother think?"

She didn't quite flinch. But he saw the tiny, abortive movement she made, and his eyes narrowed.

"She's always worried that I had more looks than sense," Kathryn said quietly. "Which I'm afraid I proved to her through my failures with my studies."

"A first-class degree is, by definition, not any kind of failure."

"I had to work ten times as hard as she did, and I still only did it by my teeth," she said with a dismissive wave of one hand. "But when we met your father, it seemed a perfect opportunity to stop worrying about the brains part and let the looks do some good for a change."

"What," Luca asked through his teeth, "does that mean?"

"It meant we both knew he liked the look of me," Kathryn said, with an edge to her voice. She sat up straighter on the bed. "And he was just as funny and kind and charming when I went out with him alone. Still, when he asked me to marry him on the third date, I laughed."

Her gaze had gone fierce. Protective, Luca thought.

"He told me that he knew he was a foolish old man, vain and silly, to think a young girl like me would want to shackle herself to a man like him. He knew he didn't have much time left. He assured me that all he wanted was companionship, because he didn't have any of the rest of it in him any longer. He told me I was the most beautiful thing he'd seen in years, and he couldn't think of a better way to go than to have me holding his hand."

"He flattered you."

"He *needed* me," she snapped. "He was old and scared and lonely. He told me that he had sons he wasn't close to and no particular reason to imagine that might change. He didn't want to die alone, Luca. I didn't think that made him a monster."

He felt as if he was nailed to the floor beneath him. As if he'd turned to stone.

"And this is why you married him? Out of pity? Out of the goodness of your heart? To save an old man from loneliness? You are a saint, indeed." Her breath hissed from her mouth. Luca kept going. "But he was a very wealthy man, Kathryn, and he did not traffic much in saints or pity. He didn't have to. He could have bought himself a fleet of nurses to keep him company, if company was what he wanted in his final days. So I'll ask you again. Why did he buy you?"

"He didn't buy me, Luca," she threw at him, sounding as furious as she did vulnerable. "He saved me."

Kathryn wanted to snatch the words back the moment she said them.

They hung there in the air between them, the glare of them enough to cast the rest of the room and even Luca in shadow.

She didn't know what she expected him to do, but it wasn't to simply stand there and gaze back at her, with all of his intensity focused hard on her, in a way she understood differently today.

The truth was, she understood a whole lot of things differently today.

Her own body. His body. The things he could *do* with both. What that look in his dark eyes meant—and more, what it had always meant, all these years, though she hadn't had a clue. Where it had always been leading them, this mad thing between them that not even the night they'd spent together had eased at all.

But she'd never said that out loud before, that little truth about her marriage. She wasn't entirely sure why she had now.

"Go on, then," Luca rumbled at her when it seemed whole ages had passed. When she'd died a thousand deaths, each one of them more disloyal than the last. "Explain that to me."

He stood there like some kind of ancient god of judgment, sculpted and remote, with his arms crossed and that mouth of his in a stern line. And it didn't seem to matter that he'd had that mouth on parts of her body she'd had no idea could be that sensitive. That he knew her now in a way no one else ever had. That he was the only person on the earth who had ever been *inside* her. It all made her dizzy.

And it didn't change the fact that he stared down at her as if he was hewn from rock. Or that compulsion she didn't understand that worked inside her, that wanted to give him anything he asked for, anything at all.

Anything. Even this.

"My mother was thrilled," she said, her voice scratchy, as if her own surrender choked her on its way down. "She got a cottage and her own live-in nurses out of the deal, so she never needs to work again."

Her mother had been something a bit more complicated than simply *thrilled*, Kathryn thought, though she didn't know how to explain that to this man. She didn't quite know how to think about it herself. All these years later.

"Being the wife of a man like Gianni Castelli is a full-time job," Rose had said imperiously, sitting at the kitchen table in their grotty old flat with the real-estate listings spread out before her. She'd had no doubt that Kathryn would accept Gianni's proposal. It hadn't even been a discussion. "It will require study and application, of course, should you want to make it into a career."

"A career?" Kathryn hadn't understood. "He's not well, Mum. He's not likely to last five years."

"You need to view this as an internship, my girl. A stepping stone to bigger and better things." Rose had eyed her up and down then shaken her head. "You're pretty enough, there's no denying it. And while you haven't proved to be as smart as we hoped, I'd imagine you can succeed in *this* arena anyway. The only figure you'll need to know is the size of your allowance."

"Mum," she'd said then, uncertainly. "I'm just not sure…"

"You listen to me, Kathryn," Rose had said, and she hadn't raised her voice. She hadn't needed to raise her voice, not when she used that withering tone. "I sacrificed everything for you. I worked myself into this state. And what would we have done if Gianni Castelli hadn't happened along and gone ass over teakettle for that face of yours? You need to capitalize on that." She'd sniffed. "For my sake, if nothing else. The truth is you've proved yourself unequal to the task of a career in finance. How will we pay the bills without this marriage?"

"But..." She'd felt all the usual things she always had when Rose spoke like this. Shame. Guilt. Despair that she was so deficient. Anguish that she couldn't live up to her mother's expectations. And that sliver of something else, something stubborn and forlorn, that didn't quite understand why nothing she did, no matter how hard she worked, was ever good enough. "It isn't *we*, Mum. It's me. I have to marry a man I don't love—"

"You must be having a laugh." Though the look on Rose's face had indicated there was precious little to laugh about. "Love? This isn't a fairy story, Kathryn. This is about duty and responsibility." She'd brandished her hands in the air, her gnarled and swollen knuckles. "Look at what I did to myself to do right by you. Look at how I ruined myself and threw away everything that ever mattered to me. It's between you and your conscience how you want to repay me."

And put that way, Kathryn hadn't had a choice.

"It sounds as if your mother got the better part of the bargain," Luca said quietly, snapping her back into the present.

"She got what she deserved after all she did for me," Kathryn said stoutly. "And I certainly couldn't give it to her. Thanks to your father, she can live out the rest of her days in peace. She's earned that."

There was a certain tightness to Luca's expression that suggested he didn't agree, and she tensed, instantly on the defensive, but he didn't pursue it. He cocked his head slightly to one side.

"And what did you earn?" he asked. "How did saving your mother save you?"

"I got to quit my MBA course," she said in a rush, and she felt the heat of that admission wash over her like some kind of flu. "I walked away and I never had to go back, and it didn't matter that we were out of the tuition money. The whole slate was wiped clean. All that struggle, all those years of never living up to expectations, gone in an instant and forgiven completely, simply because your father wanted to marry me."

And maybe, just maybe, she'd enjoyed a little holiday from her subservience to her mother's wishes. Maybe she'd liked having someone treat her like some kind of prize for a change.

"Kathryn," Luca said, his voice so gentle it made her shiver, "you must know—"

But she didn't want to hear whatever it was he was going to say. She didn't want whatever devastation that was lurking there in his dark eyes, lit now with something very much like compassion.

She lurched forward instead, coming up on her knees before him and throwing out her hands to catch herself against the wall of his chest. He didn't so much as rock on his feet with the impact. He simply studied her.

"Listen to me," Kathryn said, aware that she sounded desperate. "You can think whatever you like about your father's intentions. But to me, he was a dream come true. You don't have to like that," she said hurriedly when the edges of his mouth turned down, "but it's the truth. It's a fact."

And she was so close to him then. Touching him again. Her palms were propped against the sculpted perfection of his pectoral muscles, and that delirious heat of his poured into her, making her flush all over again.

But this fever she recognized.

Kathryn didn't want to talk about her marriage. She didn't want to talk about their complicated families. She didn't know what that dark thing was that lurked there in the way he was looking at her then, and she didn't want to know.

She did the only thing she knew to do. The only thing that made sense.

She tipped herself forward and pressed her mouth to his.

And it felt artless and silly, nothing like the way he'd kissed her—and for a shuddering moment that felt like forever he merely stood there, as if he was stunned—but then he moved. He took the back of her head in his palm and he opened his mouth, driving into hers and taking complete and delicious control.

He kissed her and he kissed her. He kissed her until she was wound around him, pressing herself against him, desperate and wild—because now she knew. Now she knew what else there was. Where else they could go.

All the magical things he could do.

But Luca pulled away, still curving that big hand of his over the back of her head, his dark eyes glittering.

"Did you do that to distract me?" he asked, his voice gruff. His breath not entirely steady—which made a whole different fire ignite within her.

"Yes," she said. Her mouth felt swollen again. And even though she wore his shirt and it covered more of her than some of her own clothes, she felt stripped bare. Naked and vulnerable and wide-open to him in every way.

"Is that the only reason?" If possible, his voice was even rougher.

Kathryn shifted on her knees. She slid her hands up,

over his jaw, holding his face between her palms, the way he'd done before to her. And she was so close that she could feel that shake in him, low and deep. So close she could feel that he was unsteady, too.

It made her feel as if she was made of light. As if she was filled with power.

"You might have noticed that I like kissing you, Luca," she said, and her voice was solemn. Because somehow everything between them had shifted, and there was something much too serious in his eyes. "You're my first."

"Your first in bed."

She waited, still holding him. She saw the exact moment he understood. The very second it crashed through him, leaving him stunned. And then something far darker, hungrier and indescribably male, lit him up. It made his dark eyes gleam. It made him tighten his grip.

"Cucciola mia," he murmured, his mouth against her lips, "we might kill each other."

And then he bore her back down to the bed and showed her exactly what he meant.

CHAPTER TEN

A WEEK LATER they concluded their business in California and flew back to Italy with Rafael, Lily and a private nurse for Lily and her unborn baby in tow.

Luca could have done without the crowd.

It had been a week of abject torture, having claimed Kathryn in private yet having to act as if nothing had changed between them in public. That she was the assistant he hadn't wanted, and he the Castelli who had always hated her the most. Luca had found that his much-vaunted control had deserted him almost entirely, making him uneasy about where this madness was leading him—but he couldn't stop.

Any moment of privacy they had, he exulted in her. Cars. Alcoves. Out walking the property. He kept waiting for this grip she had on him to ease, for the wildfire only she had ever stirred in him like this to abate—but it still hadn't. If anything, it grew stronger. Every day brighter and hotter than the day before.

It would be different once they were back in Rome, he told himself. There would be no sneaking around to avoid his brother, or at least, far less of that kind of thing. With no element of the forbidden, he was certain the hunger would ease. It always did. He was not the kind of man who formed attachments, and he knew better to want things he couldn't have. He'd learned that as a child, and he'd never forgotten it.

In truth, it had never been an issue before.

But first they had to make it to Rome, and separate themselves from his brother and Lily, who would be flying on to the family seat in the Dolomites. Several hours into their nighttime flight, only Rafael and Luca remained awake in the lounge area of the jet, the others having long since headed to the jet's stately guest rooms.

Rafael was talking about their next steps as a company and how best to capitalize on the goodwill they'd sown about the accounts in the wake of the annual ball. Luca, meanwhile, had spent longer than he cared to admit imagining Kathryn spread out against the pillows just down the plane's narrow hall, her long dark hair—

"Kathryn," Rafael said, intoning her name as if he could read Luca's dirty mind.

Luca eyed his brother across the width of the lounge and maintained his infinitely lazy position, stretched out on one of the couches like some kind of *dauphin*.

"Yes," he said. "Kathryn. My personal assistant, in fulfillment of our beloved patriarch's will. I haven't complained, have I?"

"You have not," his brother agreed. He looked so stern and austere as he sat there, his bearing far more dignified than Luca's had ever been. "That is what concerns me."

Luca forced a laugh he didn't feel. "I am nothing if not adaptable. And obedient."

"But that is the point." Rafael raised his brows. "You are neither one of those things, despite the great joy it gives you to pretend otherwise."

"You are mistaken, brother. I am nothing but a jumped-up playboy with excellent staff, all of whom are well paid to cover for my incompetence. The tabloids have decreed it, therefore it must be true."

Rafael said nothing for a moment that dragged on too long. Luca found himself clenching his jaw and forced himself to stop.

"I expected you to run her off within the week."

Luca shrugged. "She proved somewhat more tenacious than anticipated."

Rafael considered him. "She was also a surprising asset these past two weeks. The accounts adored her. I suspect half of them raced to the tabloids to submit their own *Saint Kate* stories within hours of meeting her." He stretched his legs out before him. "Needless to say, this has put a rather positive spin on things. I had more business associates than I can count commend me—us—on our magnanimity in hiring her. She might as well be the mascot of the company."

Luca didn't remember moving, but there he was, sitting up and glaring at his older brother.

"This is a temporary situation," he said, his voice clipped. "We agreed on that."

"Maybe we should reconsider." Rafael shrugged when Luca continued to glare at him. "If using Saint Kate boosts our profile, I don't see why we *wouldn't* use her as long as possible."

"Perhaps," Luca said coolly, "the lady no longer wishes to be used. It's possible she had her fill of it during her commercial transaction of a marriage. Maybe all she wants to do is her job."

That was, of course, a huge mistake. He knew it the moment he spoke without thinking—as it was the first time he could remember doing so to a family member since he was a child.

Rafael blinked. "I don't care what she wants, as long as it benefits the company," he said in a low voice.

"The company," Luca muttered, again without thinking. Almost as if he couldn't control himself at all. "Always the company."

He didn't much care for the way his brother looked at him then.

"Have our objectives changed without my knowledge, Luca?" Rafael let that sit there for a moment, and the expression on his face was far too shrewd for Luca's peace of mind. "Have yours?"

It was not until she was safely barricaded in her little Italian flat that Kathryn really breathed.

And moments after that first, deep, full-bodied breath, she simply sank down on the soft carpet in her cozy lounge, as if the knees that had somehow carried her all the way through her trip to California and the long flight back were no longer up to the task. As if everything that had happened in the past two weeks finally caught up with her.

With a wallop.

She found herself looking around her flat, the morning light streaming in from the high windows that had sold her on the place, as if she'd never seen it before. It was hard to imagine the person she'd been when she'd left here. The person she'd left behind her in Sonoma somewhere.

How could her whole world change so quickly?

Her marriage to Gianni had been a change, certainly, but it had been a change of circumstances, not of who she was inside. She had merely swapped one set of duties and obligations for another, and the truth was, she'd found caring for Gianni infinitely more pleasant than statistics. Or tending to her difficult mother, if she was brutally honest with herself.

This was different. *She* was different.

And she had no idea if she needed to set about putting herself back together somehow, or if she needed to figure out a way to simply accept who she'd become. Whoever the hell that was.

Kathryn breathed in, deep. Then out again. She did it a few more times, and then she climbed back to her feet and decided that a cup of tea was all the answer she needed just now. Everything else would wait.

She was just finishing that same cup, sitting out on her small balcony with her view over the red-tipped Roman rooftops that made her heart sing a little in her chest, when she heard the banging on her front door.

Luca, she thought at once. Because who else could it be?

And the fact that her heart echoed that pounding told her more than she needed to know about those feelings that the tea hadn't suppressed at all.

She considered not answering it—but dismissed that thought in an instant. This was Luca. It wasn't as if he'd simply shrug and wander off.

Kathryn padded to the door in her bare feet and swung it open, not at all surprised to find him braced there against the doorjamb, one arm over his head and a scowl on his face.

"Where did you go?" he demanded.

"Home," she replied. "Obviously."

He ignored that. "Why did you race off like that? I looked around and you'd disappeared."

She didn't want to let him inside her flat, and she couldn't have said why. She crossed her arms over her chest and stood in the doorway instead.

"I came home," she said, very distinctly. "You told me I didn't have to go into work today. Has something changed?"

Something ignited in those dark eyes of his, and he pushed himself off the doorjamb. Technically, he'd moved back, and yet he still seemed to fill the doorway. The narrow hallway behind him. The whole of her flat he hadn't even entered.

"What do you think is happening here, Kathryn?" he asked softly.

She refused to show him her uncertainty. That had been situational, she assured herself. She'd lost her virginity to this man, and he was a very demanding, very detail-oriented lover. Anyone would have trouble finding her footing after that kind of combination.

But she was standing just fine now.

"What's happening is that after a long, two-week business trip, my boss is standing at my door," she said crisply. "If you don't have an assignment for me, I think you should leave."

She expected his temper, braced herself for it. Luca looked astounded for a beat, but then, impossibly, he laughed. And it was that same delighted, beautiful laugh of his that rivaled the Italian scenery itself and did far worse things to her poor heart. It made her scowl at him, so determined was she to ward him off. To keep that laughter from sinking in deep beneath her skin.

But it was like fighting off sunlight. No matter what she wanted, no matter what she did, it filled her.

"Come here, *cucciola mia*," he said when the laughter faded away.

He crooked his finger at her, and she wanted to bite him. He was a foot away at most. He was already too close.

"I'm right here," she told him. "I don't need to come any closer, and I'm not your pet."

"That's where you're wrong," he said in that dark voice of his that made need roll through her like a terrible thirst. "Come, Kathryn. Put that mouth on me. It will feel much better than using it as a battering ram when I can see you don't mean it."

"I do."

"You do not," he corrected her. He moved toward her then, advancing on her with that intense gleam in his dark gaze that she knew now was hunger. And the remains of that laughter that made him seem even more beautiful than he already was. "You're afraid."

"I most certainly am not," she said, but then she couldn't move any farther.

He'd backed her up into her flat and straight into the wall of the small foyer, and she hadn't even noticed. She swallowed, hard.

"I'm not afraid," she told him, very distinctly. "But I need some time to clear my head."

"Why?"

"I don't have to justify how I spend my free time to you."

"You don't. But you could spend it beneath me, driving us both insane with the way you move those hips of yours. You can see why I'd agitate for that option."

Her jaw worked, but no words came out. Luca grinned.

"We can't just...have sex all the time," she protested, but even she could hear that her voice was weak. Reedy.

This time that marvelous laughter stayed in his eyes, making them gleam gold and shiver straight through her.

"Why ever not?"

"Sex is a weakness," she told him, very seriously, the words coming from some part of her she hadn't known was there. "A weapon."

"That sounds like the ravings of someone who isn't very good at it, *cucciola mia*, and therefore doesn't enjoy it," he said with another laugh, obviously unaware that he'd just dismissed one of her mother's favorite sayings so easily. "A description that does not fit you at all."

She didn't know what expression she wore then, but his hard face softened, and he pulled her against him as if she was a fragile little thing, made of spun glass. He smoothed her hair back from her face, as she'd already discovered he loved to do. And when he gazed down at her there was something so bright in his eyes that it made her shake.

And her heart broke open inside her, telling her things she didn't want to accept. Making her feel things she'd never thought she'd feel for anyone, and certainly not for him. But she might have been a virgin before she'd met Luca, and she might have been completely untouched until he'd handled that, too, but she wasn't an idiot.

Only an idiot would tell Luca Castelli she was falling in love with him, she scolded herself. *He doesn't want to know.*

"I can't think around you," she whispered, though she knew she shouldn't. That it was far too close to a truth even she wanted to pretend wasn't real. "Sex only makes it worse."

She felt his chest move against her as if he was laughing, though he didn't make a sound. Slowly, slowly, his perfect mouth curved.

"I know," he said, and he ran his hands down the length of her spine, then over the curves of her bottom, pulling her flush against him. "Sex makes everything terrible."

He was hot and hard against her belly, and she thought he knew the precise moment when she simply... melted. Kathryn thought he always knew.

Luca smiled then. "But then it makes it much, much better."

And when he set about proving it, Kathryn surrendered.

Because she wanted him more than she wanted to resist him.

And she thought he knew that, too.

Some ten days after their return from California, Luca paused at his office door after finishing a round of calls to the States and frowned. It was late in the evening, and his staff had long since departed for the day—all except Kathryn.

She sat at her desk in the open space outside his office, where she was meant to act as his guard and first line of support, furiously typing—which didn't make any sense. He hadn't given her any work that needed finishing at this hour.

"You should have left hours ago," he said, and the beast that still paced inside him when it came to her growled in approval when she jolted at the sound of his voice, then melted into a smile. "Didn't I mention something about swimming naked beneath the stars? That happens upstairs, Kathryn. Away from the computer."

"I have to finish this," she said, her fingers flying over the keys. "Then we can stargaze all you like."

"It's the naked part that interests me, *cucciola mia*. The stars are a ploy. You may not have noticed this, but we're in the middle of the city."

She wrinkled her nose at him, which he found tugged at him in ways that he wasn't entirely comfortable exploring, but she typed on. He moved to stand behind her, smoothing his hands over her shoulders and tugging gently on the end of her fashionably sleek ponytail. She sighed happily enough, but she didn't stop, and he read over her shoulder.

And this time, he scowled. "This is Marco's report. He told me he'd have it in to me tomorrow morning."

"And so he will," Kathryn said, her voice even. "Just as soon as I finish it."

Luca pulled her chair back from the desk, forcing her to stop, then swiveled it around so he could look her in the eyes. Hers were gray and far too calm when they met his.

"You are not Marco's assistant," he told her, perhaps more harshly than necessary. "You are mine."

Kathryn was far more than that, though Luca knew he didn't have the words to tell her that. She was that pounding in his heart. She was that heat that never left him. And all of that was wrapped up in those cool gray eyes, that serene little smile, the entire package that was Kathryn. *His*.

"Perhaps you're unaware that it's part of your assistant's job to pretty up all the reports that make it to your desk," Kathryn said mildly.

"It is not."

"How strange," she murmured. "I have been assured by no less than six different members of the team that it is."

Of course she'd been told that—and who knew what else? He'd essentially declared open season on her when he'd brought her on board. How had he managed to forget that? But of course, he knew how. Because all he thought about was getting his hands on her—and she never, ever complained. She smiled instead.

He shoved his hair back with an impatient hand. "I will speak to them."

"No," she countered, "you will not."

"They cannot continue to abuse you in this fashion."

She leaned back in her chair and crossed her arms. "You can't interfere. It will work itself out."

"This is not a cause worth martyring yourself for," he told her. "I put this target on your back. I'll take it off."

"And if you do that, you might as well shoot me yourself," she said, with an edge to her voice. "I don't need you to give me special treatment. Everyone knows you were forced to hire me. You stepping in now will only make it worse."

"Kathryn—"

"I told you I'd be good at this and I am," she said, her voice low and her chin high. "My work speaks for itself. It will win over your team, and if it doesn't, doing all the work they don't want to do means I'll know their jobs as well as mine. It all only helps me."

"You don't need any help."

"I couldn't do the job I trained my whole life to do,"

she threw at him fiercely. And he knew she meant the job her mother had wanted for her. "This is my chance. I'm not going to waste it, and I'm not going to let you save me, either. I'll succeed or fail on my own."

He stared down at her, a kind of battle inside him that he didn't understand. Maybe he didn't want to understand it. Maybe what was shaking through him was so outside his experience, understanding the truth of it might break him in two.

"You let my father save you once," he said quietly.

She didn't flinch from that. She held his gaze, though he could feel the way it burned, and hers was solemn.

"And now I want to save myself," she said with soft determination. "And I want you to let me."

CHAPTER ELEVEN

ANOTHER WEEK EASED BY, then another, and Luca was forced to face the fact that his driving need for Kathryn wasn't going anywhere.

He'd spent more time with her than any other woman he'd ever been with. She worked with him. She traveled with him. She slept with him. He would have imagined that such familiarity could only breed the swiftest contempt, but Kathryn was a revelation. Daily. She fascinated him, from her cool competence in the office that even his staff had been forced to heed to her uninhibited delight in all they did together in bed.

It was too perfect. Too good. And he had learned the hard way that there was no such thing as "too good to be true." There was only paying for it.

His childhood had taught him well.

He remembered it all too vividly, the various ways he'd acted out in the vain hope of getting his father's attention. The commotion he'd caused. The precious objects he'd broken. The tantrums, the running away, the back talk. All so someone who was actually related to him would show him that they'd cared about him—but that had never happened.

And Luca was no longer an abandoned boy. He'd

long since forgiven his brother, who had handled their family situation in the best way he'd known how—and had then embroiled himself in a mad relationship with Lily. His mother had killed herself—he didn't care that the hospital had claimed it had been an accident, he'd never doubted what she'd done—rather than face the children she'd made. And Gianni had never paid the slightest attention to Luca. His heir apparent had been one thing, but Luca had merely been the forgotten spare.

He didn't know how to believe in the possibility that Kathryn could truly want him. That she'd chosen him to work with. That all of this wasn't a giant ploy.

"What reaction are you looking for?" one of his stepmothers had asked him years ago, when Luca had broken all the dishes at dinner one night. Gianni had merely exited the room, as if Luca was an animal far beneath his notice. His stepmother had remained, brittle and cold.

"I hate you," Luca had shouted at her, with all the fury in his ten-year-old heart.

"No one hates you," she'd replied, her gaze bland on his. "No one cares either way. The sooner you recognize that, the happier you'll be."

He'd never forgotten it. And he'd never begged for attention again.

Today was a lazy Sunday that hinted of spring. He breathed it in, hard. He'd woken Kathryn in his usual fashion while it was still dark, left her quivering in his bed and had gone out for a long run around his beautiful city while it was still shaking off the last of the night before. He ran through piazzas that were famed for their crowds, past famous fountains and monuments, all deserted this early in the day, as if Rome was entirely his.

He was waiting for the other shoe to drop and crush him where he stood. He told himself he expected it, so it couldn't possibly be too bad. Even if he couldn't quite imagine what that might be. He ran faster. Harder.

It was his favorite time to run, these early mornings that were all his. He usually took his time, doing lazy loops through places usually too packed to navigate. But he found that today, knowing Kathryn waited in his penthouse for his return, he ran even faster on his way back home.

She wasn't on the first level of the penthouse when he returned, as she often was, usually making coffee or putting together something to eat in his kitchen. He climbed the spiral stairs from his vast living area up to his rooftop bedroom, expecting to find her still sprawled in his bed. But that was empty, too, the duvet tossed back and the pillows still dented.

Luca peered out through the windows and saw her on the farthest part of the roof, her back to him, her eyes on the city laid out at her feet. He took a quick detour into his bathroom, showering off his run, then pulled on the pair of trousers he'd left at the foot of the bed before he went outside.

She didn't turn as he closed the great glass door behind him, or even when he skirted the pool. She stayed as she was, her back perhaps *too* straight, he thought, as he drew close.

"I hope you're not thinking of jumping," he said as he came up behind her. "I would not find that amusing at all." Kathryn didn't respond, not even when he came to stand beside her at the balustrade. She looked pale. Almost…scared, he would have said, if she'd been anyone else. If that made any sense. "Has something happened?"

She swallowed, and he saw she was hugging herself, wrapped up tight in one of the draped sweaters she preferred, as if she needed armor. Slowly, much too slowly, she turned to face him.

"I don't know how to tell you this," she said, and even her voice didn't sound like hers.

Her eyes were dark gray, the darkest he'd ever seen them. Her lovely mouth was pressed into a vulnerable line. And when Luca reached out to touch her face, she jerked away.

"I suggest you do it fast," he said, frowning, as something cold washed over him.

She looked lost for a moment. Then she seemed to collect herself.

"After you left," she said, still in that strangely disembodied voice, as if she was speaking to him from a great distance, "I was sick."

"Then, what are you doing out here?" he demanded, a protective impulse he hadn't known he possessed roaring inside him. "Come. We'll put you back in bed."

"I've had this strange stomach thing for a while now," she told him, not moving at all. "It comes and goes. I thought maybe it was anxiety." He waited. Sheer misery washed over her face, and she pressed her lips together, hard, as if she was holding back a sob. "But today something else occurred to me. So I went to the supermarket and I got a test. And I had my answer in an instant."

Luca felt as if he'd been frozen solid where he stood.

He was aware of everything. The breeze with its

hints of spring that danced between them and toyed with her hair. The way the old gold of the sun made the city gleam all around them. The clatter of traffic in the distance and bells ringing out on the wind.

And the thing she was about to say, that made all of this—all he'd felt and all that had happened since that night in the car in California—a lie. A scam. That other shoe he'd been expecting all this time, kicking him straight in the face. The ultimate act of a creature who had deceived him completely, snowed him utterly. Made him believe he could be a different man. Made him imagine for an instant that he could live a different life. Made him forget all the truths he knew about this one.

But he had always known better. He had never given up his control, not ever, until her. He had never begged for anyone's attention. He had never wanted a damned thing.

And this was why.

Luca thought what he would find most unforgivable when the dust cleared was that even now, even in this sharp, unbearable instant when he understood exactly how expertly he'd been played for a fool, he would have given anything at all for her to say something else.

Anything else.

Anything that would allow him to keep pretending he could be this other, softer version of himself—

But that was not his fate.

And she was an illusion.

He should have known that from the start.

Even then, he hoped. God, how he hoped.

"Luca," she said, his name in her mouth like a blow. The final betrayal in a war he hadn't realized she'd been fighting all this while. A war he understood, at last, he'd lost the moment he'd stopped viewing her as his enemy, when she'd never been anything but. *Never*. And that meant he would hurt her in any way he could. In every way. "I'm pregnant."

Kathryn found she was clenching her hands together in front of her, and she couldn't seem to stop it, no matter how revealing that was. No matter that the man she'd fallen in love with despite herself had gone so still he could have been part of the stone wall that surrounded his rooftop terrace. Just another Roman statue, and about as approachable.

She didn't know what she expected. Luca to grow pale. To shout. To keel over or stagger about dramatically. To react in some over-the-top and awful way, as she'd imagined he would and had braced herself against—because she'd spent a deeply unpleasant hour or so since she'd taken that test imagining all the various horrible ways Luca might take this news, and panicking about each and every one of them in turn.

He did none of those things.

Instead, he stared.

His gaze dropped from her face to her belly, where he should know perfectly well there would be no sign of anything. Not this soon. It took him a long time to drag that dark gaze of his back up. He stared at her far past the point where it could be considered anything but aggressive, while a muscle clenched in his lean jaw, and every nerve in Kathryn's body tied itself into a painful knot.

And yet when Luca finally spoke, his voice was something like lazy. Ripe with disinterest and bland insult.

She recognized that voice instantly. She'd forgotten how much she hated it.

"You have the necessary paperwork, I assume, to support this claim."

Kathryn blinked. "Paperwork? I took a pregnancy test. It's a...stick, not paper."

Luca's dark eyes gleamed, and not in a nice way.

"Kathryn, please," he said, with a little laugh that was like sandpaper against her skin. "Surely you cannot imagine that you are the first woman to share my bed and then decide she'd quite like to nurse at the Castelli teat for the rest of her life." He shrugged. Horribly. "I like sex, as you have discovered, and in these things there is always risk. I would never dismiss a paternity claim out of hand." His dark gaze hurt as it bored into her. "But I do insist that it be proved beyond any doubt."

She realized her hands had balled into fists. "Do you have a great many accidental children, then?"

"I have none, in fact," Luca said viciously. As if he meant it to be a blow. "Such is the perfidy of the average woman."

"You mean the average woman you choose to sleep with," Kathryn threw at him, because she couldn't seem to help herself. When he'd left this morning to go on his run she'd been toying with the idea of telling him how she felt, because it was so huge, so overwhelming, she didn't think she could keep it to herself. Now she rather thought she'd prefer to die. "Maybe the common denominator is less their treachery and more you."

He eyed her from his place a foot or so away with that same searing fury and simmering dislike that had always made her feel...restless before. When she hadn't known him. When she hadn't understood what that thing was between them.

Now it simply made her feel sick.

"I will assemble the usual team of lawyers and doctors," Luca said, sounding deeply bored. "I'll inform them you'll be in tomorrow for the typical workup." Despite that tone, there wasn't a trace of boredom in the searing fury of those dark eyes of his. Not the faintest hint. "Does that suit your schedule? You'll have a great deal of free time, if that helps. My father's will means I can't fire you, but I think you'll find you'll work better as a distant telecommuter from here on out."

"I…" Kathryn shook her head again, refusing to succumb to the wave of dizziness that buffeted her. She shouldn't have been surprised by this, either. When had she ever had the upper hand with Luca? Why had she foolishly held out some kernel of hope that he'd react better? She hadn't realized *how much* she'd been holding on to that hope until now, she realized. When he'd crushed it. "But…"

"I'm sorry if this does not live up to your fantasies of melodrama, *Stepmother*," he said, his voice like steel and that word as harsh as if he'd backhanded her with it. Kathryn fell back a step as if he really had. "You should be aware that eighty percent of the women who make these claims do not return for the appointment that would prove them liars. The other twenty percent must imagine that I'm kidding when I say I'll run these tests. I'm not. Which will you be, I wonder?"

Kathryn felt off balance and worse, something like half hollow, half sick. And beyond that, she had the sickening sense that this had all happened before. Not to her, but because of her. Her own mother had been forced to have a conversation just like this one. Kathryn, too, had been an accident. She found she couldn't get her head around that—it was too much déjà vu to take in at once.

But one thing was perfectly clear. She'd failed her mother. Again. And this time, in the one way she knew Rose could never forgive. That was fair enough. Kathryn was quite sure she'd never forgive herself, either.

"Luca," she said, and she didn't care that her voice shook, that her eyes were blurry with tears, "you don't have to do this."

He laughed. The derisive note in it scraped at her, as she supposed it was meant to do. "Your acting skills are impressive, Kathryn. Maybe far more impressive than I realized."

Her teeth ached. She realized she was gritting them. "You know perfectly well I was a virgin."

"I know that's what you wanted me to think," he threw back at her, his tone mild and unperturbed, though his eyes blazed. "But who can say what is true and what is one more bit of theater from one such as you? A DNA test is far more straightforward."

She shook her head at him, furious with herself that she was so susceptible to him. Furious that he always won. *Always.*

Furious that despite everything, she'd forgotten that deep down, this man hated her. Everything else was sex. The truth was that Luca had always hated her and always would. And they'd made a child out of that. Out of her profound stupidity in the face of the one temptation she hadn't denied herself.

It only takes one mistake, her mother had always told her.

And Kathryn had made it. But that didn't mean she

had to make another one. She'd told Luca she wanted to save herself. Now she had someone else to think about, and the best thing she could do for her baby was keep it the hell away from Luca Castelli and all that hate that burned in him like coals and never, ever went out.

It didn't matter that she thought she loved him. Maybe she did. But what mattered was what kind of life she could provide for the baby she carried. That swept over her with all the grace and conviction of a plan, as if this hadn't been a mistake at all. As if she'd made this decision instead of having it thrust upon her.

Kathryn supposed it didn't matter either way. None of this mattered. Someday her child would tell the story of his or her father with a shrug, just as Kathryn did, and the world would go right on turning.

Her broken heart didn't matter to anyone. It never had.

She cleared her throat and got on with it. "Let me make this simple, then," she said, pleased her voice sounded, if not quite even, like hers again. "I quit. I'll contact Rafael and let him know I'd prefer the bulk sum your father left me, and you'll never see me again. Are you happy now?"

If possible, his gaze got darker. More intense. The blast of his temper scorched her, the fire of it crowding her as if it had eaten the whole of Rome alive, the flames licking over her skin. She braced herself as if she expected him to haul off and hit her, because his gorgeously elegant fingers curled up into fists right there at his sides—

But he didn't hit her. Of course he didn't hit her.

That would have been easier to bear.

Instead, Luca reached over, curled a hard hand around her neck and hauled her mouth to his.

He tasted like sin and redemption, fury and betrayal, and Kathryn was a fool.

An inexcusable fool, but she couldn't stop kissing him back. Even if this was the last time.

Or especially because it was the last time.

He angled his jaw, taking her mouth as if he owned her, and the burn of it flooded through her. He hauled her even closer, so her breasts were crushed against his chest, and she arched into him despite herself.

Her heart kicked at her, a wild and desperate drumming.

He sank his hands into her hair and he devoured her, kissing her again and again. Until she was pliant against him. Until she was kissing him back with the same wildfire, the same mindless need.

And only then did he let her go.

"Luca..." she whispered.

But his face twisted with dislike and disillusion, and something so harsh it made her stomach ache.

"Get out," he told her, in a stranger's pitiless voice that rocked through her like a terrible hurricane, destroying everything in its path. She knew she'd bear the mark of it forever, her own, secret scar. "And, Kathryn..."

She waited, unable to see through the misery that clouded her eyes. Aware that she was trembling, and not sure she'd ever stop. The look he gave her ripped her apart, but when he spoke, his voice was arctic.

"Don't come back here. Ever."

Three days later, Luca was seething his way through a meeting in his conference room when every mobile phone in his office blew up with texts and calls.

His particularly.

He grimly ignored it, gesturing for the man in front of him to continue his presentation. But as the meeting droned on, he saw entirely too much activity on the other side of the glass. His mobile kept buzzing.

And finally, his senior PR person came and stood at the door with an expression on her face that boded nothing but ill.

"Excuse me," Luca said. "It appears I am needed."

He swiped his mobile from the tabletop and stepped out into the office, scowling at Isabella.

"What is it?"

"Ah, well." She actually backed away from him. "The tabloids. I think you'd better look."

He refused to think her name, even though it burst through him then like a song. He felt that like another betrayal. His mobile vibrated in his hand, but he didn't glance at it. Not with every person in his office trying so hard not to stare at him.

He made his way toward his office, past her empty desk that he hadn't been able to make himself fill yet because she'd ruined him, she truly had, and he closed himself inside.

He went to his computer to find his inbox full. Gritting his teeth, he clicked on the links that so many people had helpfully sent him. And there it was.

SAINT KATE IN SEX ROMP WITH GIANNI'S PLAYBOY SON!
SAINT KATE UPGRADES FROM FATHER TO SON!
SAINT KATE STEPMAMA DRAMA!

And underneath the shrieking headlines were the pictures. Kathryn on his roof. More to the point, Luca on his roof with her, half-naked, kissing her as if his life depended on it. As if she hadn't just revealed herself as the traitorous, mercenary bitch she was. As if that wasn't a scene of desperation and betrayal, and nothing more.

Next to him, his mobile buzzed again, this time with a text from Rafael.

Fix it, it read.

It was succinct and to the point, and did nothing at all to soothe the raging thing inside Luca that was too angry, too ferocious to be a simple beast. This thing wanted blood. This thing wanted payback.

This time, he vowed, he wouldn't rest until he'd destroyed her, too.

CHAPTER TWELVE

KATHRYN NOTICED THE sleek black luxury car, entirely too flashy for the quiet English country lane it blocked, the moment she came around the bend on her walk back from the shops.

It had been twelve days since she'd dragged herself out of Rome and back to England. Twelve days since she'd gotten on the next flight back home. She'd never been so pleased to return to her native Yorkshire in all her life. The wolds and the country lanes. The clouds and the green. The redbrick houses that lined this small village, just over five miles outside Hull's city center.

Even her prickly mother, she told herself, was a vast improvement over anyone named Castelli.

She slowed her pace as she drew closer to the car, parked as it was at a sharp angle directly in front of the cottage. Her carrier bag *thwacked* against her thigh. High above, plump clouds scudded across the winter sky, some thick with rain, some as wispy as cotton.

And then Luca threw open the low-slung driver's door and climbed out, unfolding himself onto her remote little lane like a nightmare come to life.

A nightmare, she told herself firmly, as her heart squeezed tight in her chest. *Definitely a nightmare.*

She couldn't pretend she was entirely surprised. She'd seen all the papers. So had everyone else in this tiny little village—and most of England, for that matter. To say nothing of all the world.

Kathryn had told herself that if she could weather a tabloid storm in a village this small, she could do anything. Including having a second generation of illegitimate children, like her mother before her. She'd imagined that when her pregnancy eventually became impossible to conceal, it would seem unworthy of comment in comparison.

"It's like you to give up, isn't it?" her mother had sniffed when Kathryn had made it home. "I think we both know that's your father's blood in you. Making you as weak as he was."

There'd been no point replying to that. Or to the far more unkind things Rose had said when the tabloids had splashed those pictures everywhere.

She'd decided that was all fine, too. She could stomp around in the chilly Yorkshire lanes wrapped up in concealing coats and heavy boots and pretend she was invisible, until she wasn't.

Luca, by contrast, looked lethal. Not invisible at all. He wore a pair of casual trousers and a shirt that would have looked unremarkable on any of the men Kathryn had just seen down on the high street, but this was Luca. He somehow looked as powerful, as darkly ruthless, as he had when he'd been wearing a bespoke suit. His hair was in its usual tousled state that somehow softened the austere male beauty of his hard face, making him that much more stunning. And no matter that he was scowling at her.

The difference was that today Kathryn didn't give a toss. He couldn't break what was already broken.

What he'd stomped into pieces himself on that rooftop far away.

"Oh, lovely," she said coolly as she drew closer. She didn't smile at him, not even a forced rendition of one, and she told herself it was a bit sad that felt like a rebellion. "Does this mean it's my turn to fling horrid accusations at your head and shred your character at will? I've been saving up insults, just in case."

"You took your turn in the tabloids," he bit out. "So here I am, and no matter that it took me over a week to track you down to this godforsaken place. What do you want?"

Kathryn blinked. "I don't want anything. I might have liked some compassion when I told you some startling news, but that ship sailed."

"What game is this?" His voice was soft, but Kathryn could hear the thunder in it. It rolled off him like electricity and deep into her, setting off a different set of explosions. "What can you possibly hope to win?"

Kathryn shifted her weight back on her heels and studied him, shoving her hands deep into her coat pockets as she did. He looked...unhinged, she thought. She'd never seen that wild look in Luca's dark eyes, nor that tension that seemed to grip him.

Luca slammed the car door shut with more violence than was necessary, rocking the magnificent sports car where it sprawled there, as muscular and dangerous as he was. Kathryn thought he might reach for her then, and braced herself against it—but he only eyed her in that predatory way of his that made her blood feel spiked in her veins.

Then he leaned back against the car, crossing one boot over the other and his arms over his chest as if he was not only wholly at his ease, but also impervious to the Yorkshire winter wind that whipped down the lane in irregular bursts to shake the trees and slap at them. As if he would stand there forever if she didn't answer him.

"I don't want anything from you." Kathryn met his dark gaze and felt that same old heavy, edgy thing flip over deep inside her. Maybe she would always have this odd yearning, this bizarre hope that he might prove himself a different man. But he wasn't. And she didn't have to tolerate the way he spoke to her. "I told you that you're going to be a father. What you choose to do with that information is entirely up to you."

"And this independent stance has nothing to do with the fact that if I fail to claim this child you can try to pass it off as my father's, I'm sure." Luca's eyes blazed, though he still stood there as if he was relaxed. "And in so doing, potentially win yourself a conservatorship of one-third of the Castelli fortune my brother and I now share between us. That is quite the luxurious life you've plotted out for yourself, *Stepmother*. Let me guess. You spent your entire marriage trying to get pregnant, but failed. Then when my father died, you realized you had one shot left. Rafael has never had eyes for any woman but Lily, not even when he thought she was dead, which left me."

She wished she could run him over with his own ridiculous car.

"Right," she said in a flat voice. "You've figured me out. Except for the fact that I was a virgin, as you know very well."

"There are words for what you are," he retorted, in that hard-edged way that slapped at her the same way it had in Rome. "But I don't think *virgin* is one of them."

"Yes," she said, scathingly. "You saw to that."

"You can't lose, can you?" He was seething, she realized. So furious that the only thing containing him was the way he held himself there, so rigid and still. "If I do nothing, the way I would with any other woman who tried to claim I'd impregnated her, the world will assume the child is my father's. You've guaranteed yourself a payday for the rest of your mercenary little life."

Kathryn opened her mouth to throw something back at him, to defend herself somehow, but instead found herself swamped by a tide of heavy emotion, as deep and as dark as the North Sea. She tried to fight it off. She'd sworn to herself that this man would never see her cry again, that he didn't deserve it—

But it was no use.

It rushed over her. It betrayed her as surely as he had.

Entirely against her will, Kathryn sobbed.

All the things he'd called her over these past two years, and the past twelve days in particular. All those vicious lies in the paper. All the nasty things her mother had said to her about history repeating itself, but much dumber this time. And the way Luca had turned on her so completely. So certain she was every terrible thing she'd been called.

So certain that he'd called her some of them himself, this same man who had tended to her so gently that night in Sonoma. Held her against him and bathed her himself.

She sobbed and she sobbed.

"How could you?" she demanded, when she could

talk—or try—through the flood of tears. "You were there, Luca. You know perfectly well this baby is nobody's but yours!"

"Why?" he threw right back at her, and he wasn't standing there so languidly any longer. He didn't sound like himself, either. Not lazy or amused in the least. He moved toward her, wrapping his hands around her upper arms and pulling her face to his. "You held on to your virginity against all odds for twenty-five years, even made it through an entire marriage with it intact, then threw it away in the back of a car with a man who used to be your stepson? Why would anyone do that without an ulterior motive? How could it be anything but a plot?"

Kathryn shook with all the huge and unwieldy things inside her. She didn't know when she'd dropped the carrier bag. Or when she started pounding her fists against his impervious chest.

"Because I love you, you jackass!" she cried.

He closed his hands over her fists and held them away from him, and something in the expression on his beautiful face made her still. She stopped trying to hit him. She stopped fighting. All she could hear was her own ragged breathing, and everything else was that raw thing in his eyes.

And the foolishness in her, that still hurt when he did.

"Then, you are the only one who ever has," Luca said, matter-of-fact and quiet.

And it turned out a broken heart could break again, after all.

Luca felt outside himself. He let go of Kathryn's hands, and she wiped at her face. And he didn't understand how he could feel turned inside out, a stranger to himself, and still enjoy it when she straightened and fixed him with that fierce scowl of hers.

Had he really come here to hurt her? He'd been lying to himself. He understood that he'd have taken any excuse at all to hunt her down. Any reason in the world to see her again. Anything to shift this darkness off him—and only she could do that, though Luca couldn't think of a single reason in the world she'd want to do anything of the kind.

"That's ridiculous," she said crossly now. "Of course you're loved. The whole world loves you. You are beloved wherever you go."

"I am known. It's not the same thing."

"Your family—"

"Listen to me," Luca said, his voice darker than he meant it to be and far more urgent. "My father loved his money and his search for new wives. My mother loved her own illness. Rafael loves Lily. I decided early on that I wanted no part of any of that, because there was no room for me anyway. I wanted control, not love. I wanted to make sure nothing and no one could hurt me the way all of them either hurt others or were hurt themselves. Maybe the truth is I don't know how. It isn't in me."

Her scowl deepened. "Luca—"

"And then came you," he gritted out. "You got under my skin from the first. You spent two years married to my father and still, you drove me crazy. I've never met anyone who bothered me more."

"You've mentioned that. At length."

"But I couldn't stay away from you, Kathryn. I couldn't stop." He shook his head. "And then, when I touched you, I didn't want to stop. I thought that maybe I'd finally found the thing that brought down every other member of my family. I thought maybe I could be different." He blew out a breath. "Then you betrayed me, and I knew."

Her gray eyes were dark and solemn. "You knew what?"

"That it's no more than what I deserve," he said harshly. "I don't blame you for wanting to do this on your own. You shouldn't want me, Kathryn, and you certainly shouldn't want me near any child. What would I teach it? To be like me?"

"Stop," she commanded him.

"I'll support you in any way you want me to," he said gruffly. "But I won't be surprised if you think that's a terrible idea."

Kathryn stared at him for a long moment, then made a low, hard sort of noise. She surged forward, wrapping her arms around him. And he couldn't seem to keep himself from folding his own over her, to keep her there.

"My mother lives her whole life in the past, Luca," she whispered fiercely. "Nothing is ever good enough for her, certainly not me." She reached over and took his hand then dragged it to her still-flat belly. "But this baby won't live like that. This baby will be loved. It already is."

He shook his head. "You're both better off without me."

"Luca," she whispered, her voice just as ferocious, "I love you. That isn't going to go away, no matter what you do."

"I don't know what that is," he threw at her. "You should pay attention. I'm a terrible man, Kathryn. Terrible enough to let you take me back, because I want you too much. Terrible enough to keep you when I know I should let you go. What would you call that if not crazy?"

"Love, you idiot," she told him, tears falling down her cheeks again. "I'd call it love."

Luca reached over then and cupped her face between his hands, drawing her closer. Drawing her in, where he'd never thought he'd have her again. Where he would do his best to earn her.

"I think," he said, right there against that mouth of hers, "that you're going to have to show me what you mean. And it might take a while."

And he could feel her smile, right there against his own, and it was like coming home.

"I have a lifetime," she told him.

Which, Luca decided as she pressed her mouth to his at last, was a very good start.

The second time she married a Castelli, it was a bright June day with an achingly beautiful English summer sky arched blue and impossible above them that no one had to tell Kathryn was its own miracle.

She was beginning to depend on miracles.

Kathryn hid her pregnancy, early in its second trimester, behind the grand white dress she hadn't worn to her first wedding. The bells rang out, and the hordes that Luca had insisted upon inviting packed the village church and spilled out into the lane. It was a far cry from the quick trip to the registry office that had comprised her first set of wedding vows.

The paparazzi had hounded them after those pictures, after Luca had come to Yorkshire and they'd worked things out between them. That hounding had taken on the edge of hysteria when Luca had only shrugged one day at the usual set of shouted questions and announced that he and Kathryn Castelli, yes, the widow of his father formerly known as Saint Kate, were engaged.

They'd been back in Rome by then, tucked away in the penthouse he'd insisted she live in with him, and she'd taken it upon herself to warm up a little bit. She'd started with flowers. Lots and lots of flowers. Acrobatic and colorful, splashing warmth and cheer throughout the stark, steel and crisp-lined space.

"How many flowers are too many?" he'd asked the other day, turning in a circle in the center of the massive space.

"They're a metaphor," she'd replied tartly, typing on her tablet. "The more color in this flat, the more love in your cold, cold heart."

"Then, you'd better call the florist and have more delivered," he'd told her, that simmering look in his dark eyes that still made her own heart flip in her chest. "I feel almost empty."

Then he'd showed her how much of a lie that was, right there on the sleek sofa.

"You haven't asked me to marry you, I note," she'd pointed out after the engagement announcement had spilled all over the papers.

"I'm getting around to it," Luca had said, watching her arrange another dramatic bouquet. He'd been cooking dinner, something Kathryn would have said was entirely beneath him.

"Just as you were getting around to telling me you were a gourmet cook?" she'd asked.

"I am a man of intense mystery and many facets,

cucciola mia," he'd told her. "And I cannot eat in restaurants every night of my life."

"This has nothing to do with you and your control issues, I'm sure," she'd replied, and then laughed so hard it had made her ache when he'd thrown a handful of chopped nuts at her.

The paparazzi had carried on chasing them around Rome, until the day Luca had actually paused while out on one of his runs and had answered one of their salacious, impertinent questions.

"How can you live with yourself now that you've seduced your father's wife?" the man had shouted at him.

Luca had smiled. That glorious smile.

"Have you seen her?" he'd asked. "I live with myself just fine."

Kathryn had only rolled her eyes at that one. She'd been far more concerned that she be able to continue working, and to do the things she wanted to do in the company. And she hadn't been above winning that argument by using the heavy artillery.

When she'd finished with Luca, he'd laughed and told her he'd give her anything if she knelt before him just like that and did all of it over again, her mouth and her hands, every day.

"All I want is my own marketing campaign," she'd told him. "This is merely a side benefit."

"Keep this up," he'd replied lazily, "and I'll give you the whole damned company."

She won the respect of most of her coworkers eventually. And the ones who couldn't handle her presence in the office stopped mattering to her and usually stopped working there, too. The day Luca smiled at her across the conference room table after a presentation she'd slaved over and called her brilliant was all that mattered.

Because she'd been right. This was what she'd been meant to do.

Luca had been the one to book the church and take care of all the wedding details.

"You could participate, *cucciola mia*," he'd said once, on a trip to Australia to tour the Barossa Valley. "It's your wedding, too, I hesitate to remind you."

"Wedding?" she'd asked mildly. "What wedding? No one has proposed to me. How could there be a wedding?"

He'd only grinned.

Rose, of course, had been her usual vicious self. But on one of her visits to the little cottage in Yorkshire, Kathryn had abruptly cut her off when she'd started to spew her usual venom.

"You sacrificed for me, Mum," she'd said, holding her mother's gaze so there could be no mistake. "I can never thank you enough for that. That's what mothers do. And I did my best to do my part, too." She'd waved her hands at the cottage where they'd stood. "You'll never want for anything again. I'll always take care of you."

"Aren't you high and mighty now that you've lain with not one but two—"

"Careful," Luca had warned from his position in the far doorway, where he liked to stand while she visited her mother—like her very own emotional bodyguard. "Very, very careful, please."

And Kathryn had understood that it was Luca who had given her the strength to do this at last. To understand that she didn't have to suffer through her mother's rages and nastiness. That she didn't have to participate in this dysfunction. Luca loved her. He wanted to marry her. They were having a baby, and most of the time they were happy together.

She had nothing to prove to anyone, least of all to this angry, bitter woman who should have loved her most.

"If you can't learn to keep a civil tongue in your head, you'll never see your grandchild," Kathryn had told her. "I might choose to subject myself to this out of obligation and devotion, but I'll never let you tear into my baby the way you do me." Rose had sputtered about threats. "That's a promise, Mum. Not a threat. The choice is yours."

And then later, Luca had held her tight and hadn't judged her at all for crying over the childhood she'd never had with Rose.

Kathryn thought she could do no less for him.

She'd gone out of her way to make sure that they spent as much time with Raphael and Lily as possible, because they were the future of the Castelli family, not the grim past that Luca had already survived. She'd come to understand that no matter how lovely Gianni had been to her, he'd been a neglectful father to Luca. But Luca and Rafael were brothers, and they owned the company together, and they loved each other. That was what mattered now.

They'd gone up shortly after Lily had given birth to little baby Bruno, another dark-eyed, dark-haired Castelli male, and stayed at the old manor house for a few days to marinate in the new shape of their family.

"I hate it here," Luca had told her when she'd woken one night to find him standing by the window instead of in bed. "I've always hated it here."

He'd told her of his lonely childhood, of all the ways he'd tried to get his family's attention. Of all those sad years where he'd been left to his own devices, or the tender mercies of the staff, or the frustrations of his stepmothers.

"You're not a child any longer," she'd told him, rolling out of the bed to go to him. She'd sneaked her arms around him and pressed her cheek to his back. "This house is what you make it. It's only a house."

"It always seemed like a curse."

"You can break the curse," she'd promised him. "All you have to do is love me."

"That, *cucciola mia*, is no trouble at all."

And they'd broken more than a few curses that night, driving each other blissfully mad in that great big bed.

In the morning they'd gathered in the library with Rafael and Lily and the small boys, all of them bursting with pride over the new addition. This was the new version of the Castellis, Kathryn had thought. Not the stiff, formal way things had been the first time she'd come here with Gianni. No furious, horrible Luca. None of that pounding confusion because she'd been with the wrong man.

Nothing but love. So much love, in so many forms.

"Are you truly marrying in June?" Lily had asked as they'd sat together on one of the sofas, watching Rafael hold his brand-new son, that Castelli smile of his lighting up the whole of Northern Italy. "That's only a month away."

"Luca is planning a huge wedding to someone," Kathryn had replied with a laugh. "But he has yet to ask anyone in particular, as far as I know. It's very mysterious."

"About that," Luca had said.

She'd looked up to find him standing before her, the whole world in his dark eyes. Then he'd dropped to his knees, and she'd clapped her hands over her mouth. Kathryn had heard Lily's gasp from the sofa beside her, and had sensed more than seen the way Raphael had turned that smile of his their way.

"I love you," Luca had said. "I want to give you the world. I want this baby and I want you, Kathryn, *cucciola mia*, to be my wife and the mother of my children and the best thing in my life, forever. Will you marry me?"

"I don't know," she'd said, looping her arms around his neck and smiling at him with everything she was. "I've grown so fond of you calling me Stepmother. How can I give that up?"

"You won't regret it," he'd promised her, his hard mouth curving and so much light in his dark eyes. "I have far better names for you."

"I love you," she'd whispered. "I think I always have."

"You are the love of my life," he'd said as he'd tugged her hand down from his neck and slipped a ring onto her finger, where it sparkled so brightly it made her feel dazzled. Or perhaps that was him. "You are the reason I know that such things exist. You are my heart, Kathryn."

"Yes," she'd whispered, tears flowing freely down her cheeks. "Always yes, Luca. Always."

And she married him with his brother at his side and her new sister-in-law at hers, because family was what mattered. Their family. The one they'd made, taking what they needed from what they'd been given and leaving the rest behind, where it belonged.

"This life is too beautiful," she told Luca that night,

their first night together as husband and wife. "How can it ever get better than this?"

Four months later, they found out together, when Kathryn gave birth to a marvelous little creature the Castelli family hadn't seen in generations.

A little girl.

"Hold on tight, *cucciola mia*," Luca told her as they sat together on their first night as their own little nuclear family at last.

He held their perfect daughter in his arms, his dark eyes filled with love and light and the whole of their future, right there within reach.

Theirs for the taking, Kathryn thought happily. Theirs, always.

Luca's smile then was big enough to light up the night. "It's only going to get better from here."

And it did.

* * * * *

EXPECTING HER ENEMY'S HEIR

PIPPA ROSCOE

For Michelle,
who knew exactly what I meant when I said,
'And he kept the land because...'
Working with people who understand you is a dream,
but being friends with them is a gift.
Loves ya!

CHAPTER ONE

TODAY WAS THE DAY.

Amelia Seymore peered through the window at the dark grey clouds on the horizon, while early morning joggers and cyclists risked life and limb in the narrow juncture between the bus and the pavement. The start, stop of the number 176 as it crawled north across the bridge was making her nauseous, but it was the smell of damp wool and deodorant that forced her from the bus a stop early, gasping for fresh air. Or at least as fresh as you got in Central London during peak commuter hours. Amelia shook her head trying to regain the focus and sense of stability she had a reputation for. Maybe she was coming down with something.

Get yourself together, she ordered herself firmly. Nothing could distract her or knock her off course. Today had been ten years in the making, but it wasn't the long hours, sleepless nights or the punishingly hard work that steeled her. It was the memory of her father's face the last time they had spoken. The look in his eyes as he had turned away from her, his shaking hand reaching for the bottle of whisky on his desk. *That* was the reason she and her sister, Issy, were doing this. That was why she *had* to succeed today.

Scanning the four-lane road, and too impatient to wait

at the lights, Amelia skipped behind a cyclist and in front of a police car. Waving an awkward 'oops' at the cops, she arrived in front of a building considered to be the brightest addition to the crown jewels of the London skyline. While the Shard glittered like a diamond and the Gherkin shone emerald green, the imposing rose-hued building that housed Rossi Industries had been affectionately nicknamed The Ruby and was considered the perfect edifice for the two devastatingly handsome property tycoons who owned it.

Amelia craned her neck to look up at the impressive head office of the international conglomerate that inspired both awe and anger in her. Every single day for the last two years she had made this same walk, knowing that she was entering the lair of the two men that had destroyed her family. And every single day she had promised herself and her sister that they would have their revenge.

Vengeance hadn't come naturally to Amelia. And it certainly hadn't been immediate. She and her sister had been fifteen and thirteen, respectively, when they had first seen Alessandro and Gianni Rossi. Not that they'd known who they were back then. No, they had simply been two young men who had interrupted a Sunday roast to speak with their father. And in one conversation, the Rossi cousins had stolen their father's company out from under him and decimated everything that she and her sister had ever known.

Cold fury tripped down her spine as she retrieved the ID swipe card that proclaimed her Project Manager for Rossi Industries and entered the building. Amelia smiled at the security guard in spite of the memories that held her stomach in a vice, passing through the barriers to the bank of lifts that would take her to the sixty-fourth floor.

As she waited in the deserted lobby for the lift to arrive, she counted down the floors as if it were a ticking bomb the Rossis had no idea of and she *relished* that today would be the day their world shattered, just as hers and Issy's had. And then it wouldn't matter if she had nearly thrown it all away in one night, just over a month ago...

We shouldn't be doing this.

Amelia clenched her teeth, trying to ignore the way the rough, gravelly voice rubbed against her skin even now and once again desire wrapped around a part of her she'd never known she had. A desire that hit her like a tsunami, drawing her beneath the surface and snaring her in the undertow.

I... I want to.

With those three words she had betrayed her family, her sister, *herself.*

No!

She wouldn't let that one night, that one *mistake*, ruin everything she and Issy had worked so hard for. Yes, she had spent one illicit night with her boss—her enemy—Alessandro Rossi. But it didn't change anything. She just had to ignore the cascade of erotic memories that haunted her. Because no matter what had happened six weeks ago in Hong Kong, it in no way justified or excused what Alessandro and Gianni had done ten years ago to her family. And because of that, today was the day that the Rossi cousins would fall.

Alessandro looked out of the floor-to-ceiling window of his penthouse office to see London stretched out below him like a supplicant. Power. It ran through his veins, not just because of his immeasurable wealth, or the considerable achievements he and his cousin had accomplished in the years since they claimed control of their first business. It might have once belonged to another, but it had flourished into an empire under the Rossi name. No, the power came from the knowledge that the first meeting of his very busy day would green light a deal that promised to send shock waves through the business world.

The Rossi name was already renowned, but this deal would see it written in the history books. In years to come, there might even be two young upstarts who would read of the Rossi name and success and think—*that's what I want to be*.

Alessandro caught the grim smile on the face of his reflection and nodded. How would his father feel when he saw it? When he heard that Alessandro and Gianni had achieved success beyond his wildest dreams...but not under the name of the men who had fathered them. *No*. The first chance he and Gianni got, they legally changed their names, desperate to erase the stain of their fathers in a way that they would feel to the core of their blackened souls. They had chosen Rossi to honour their *nonna*—the only member of their family who had truly shown them kindness.

My blood runs in your veins, boy. And it will run in your children's and your children's children's.

But his father's warning was irrelevant. The blood line would end with him. He would make sure of it.

Not that Alessandro indulged in self-sabotage. Rossi Industries was his life, consuming all his time and energy. Where his father sought to destroy and strangle the last breath from the vineyards he overworked, or the wife he had constantly abused, Alessandro was determined to leave the world better than it had been; *that* was his legacy.

His watch beeped with a fifteen-minute alert for the morning's meeting. It really was bad timing that it coincided with Gianni's one and utterly immoveable holiday of the year. But, he reminded himself, the Aurora deal had been vetted by his cousin, everyone on the board, by his most trusted advisors, and the project manager he trusted far more quickly than was deserved after just two years of service.

Amelia Seymore.

Alessandro straightened the knot in his tie, checking the button behind it, but in his mind he was undoing the button and yanking the tie from his neck as he watched that same woman looking at him, breathless want filling her words.

I... I want you.

Are you sure, Amelia? Because—

Just tonight. Just now. But we will never speak of it. Ever.

He'd been so desperate for another taste of her lips he'd have agreed to anything. *Cristo*, if she'd known how much power she'd wielded in that moment, she could have had him on his knees begging to give her everything he owned. Embarrassment crept up his neck in angry red patches.

He flexed his hand, the memory of her naked thigh beneath his palm taunting him, leading him deeper into the one night—the *only* night—he'd crossed a line both professionally and personally. A line that was as much a taboo as it was utterly wrong. Shame, thick, heavy and ugly, crawled across his skin. He wasn't *that man*—he didn't sleep with his staff. Only apparently he was.

We will never speak of it.

A knock cut through the memory of Amelia's edict and he returned to the seat behind his desk, hiding the near constant state of arousal he'd been in since he and Amelia Seymore had returned from the successful deal in Hong Kong six weeks ago.

'Come.'

His secretary entered the room two strides and stopped, having learned quickly that he liked his space.

'There are no changes to the schedule for today. Asimov has checked into his hotel and he and his people will be here for the eleven a.m. briefing. Lunch is booked at Alain Ducasse at The Dorchester and Gianni called to say, "Don't mess it up."'

'He said "mess"?' Alessandro queried.

'I'm paraphrasing.'

Alessandro held back the smirk at what his cousin would have really said. Raised as close as brothers, their knowledge of each other's thoughts was only one of the reasons for their immense success.

'And the nine a.m. meeting?' he asked his secretary.

'The room is set up, the audio and visuals have been tested by IT, Ms Seymore is already in the room and has given me a spare presentation pack for you to view now, if you'd like.'

'That won't be necessary.'

And it really wouldn't. If Amelia Seymore said that she'd do something, she did it. She assessed projects, met with clients, ran projections, assessed workflows and got it done. She was nearly as exacting as himself. Which was why he'd entrusted the Aurora project to her.

Not because they had shared one utterly incendiary and completely forbidden night together, but because she was excellent at her job, always early, always correct and always had the right answer. She could have been made purposefully for him.

'Sir?'

If only she didn't distract him in ways that no other person had ever done.

'Repeat the question?' he forced himself to ask, as distasteful as he found it.

'Would you like your coffee in here, or down at the meeting?'

'Here.' Clearly, he needed to gather himself.

As members of her team filtered into the glass-walled meeting room, Amelia lined up the presentation packs with the notebooks and pens she'd asked Housekeeping to provide. Alessandro was particular, he liked things neat and exact.

And he'd liked the way she'd sounded when—

Red slashes heated her cheeks and a light sweat broke out across her shoulders. She slammed the door shut on her memories, trying to ground herself in the moment. Stepping back from the large boardroom table, she caught sight of the sketch of the building that might have changed the face of inner-city apartment living across the world, had the Rossi cousins not built their empire on the back of her father's broken soul. Really, Alessandro and Gianni had brought this on themselves.

For ten years *this* was what she and Issy had planned for. The stars had aligned in a way that had seemed almost preordained. After two years of project after project, Amelia's position within RI was unquestionable. And because of that, the most important project the Rossis had ever undertaken was in her hands, just as Gianni's annual holiday broached the horizon. Everyone knew that together Alessandro and Gianni were undefeatable. But separated? It was the only time there was a chink in their legendary armour. A chink that Amelia and her sister would use to bring them to their knees.

Issy had spent years turning herself into the perfect distraction for the legendary playboy with his own hashtag #TheHotRossi. Yesterday, an Issy styled perfectly to Gianni's tastes had flown to the Caribbean with the sole purpose of luring him onto a boat and keeping him away from Alessandro while the final decision on Aurora deal was made. And with Gianni safely out of contact, Amelia could now commit the greatest act of industrial sabotage ever recorded, ensuring that the Rossis' world was left as obliterated as hers and her sister's had been.

We're doing the right thing, aren't we?

The question Issy had asked before she left for the airport yesterday had poked and prodded at Amelia's conscience. Not because Amelia didn't absolutely know that they were doing the right thing, because she *did*. But in order to set their plan in motion, she had been forced to lie to her sister. Something she'd never thought she'd ever do.

Years before, when they had first started their quest for vengeance, they had made a pact. *No revenge without proof of corruption.* From even the beginning they had refused to become the very monsters they hunted. And, of course, Amelia had agreed. Because there *would* be a paper trail. There *would* be evidence of countless corrupt deals and ruined businesses Alessandro and Gianni had left in their wake on their journey to becoming a globally recognised name in property development. But in two years she'd found...*nothing*. Nothing other than what had been done to their father.

Panic had begun to nip at her heels. What if she could never give Issy the justice she'd promised her? What if everything they'd sacrificed to achieve their revenge was for nothing? While normal teenage girls had been going to parties and clubs, Issy and Amelia Seymore had planned and plotted. Amelia had forced herself through every business course and language module possible to make herself the perfect future employee for Rossi Industries. And her sister? Issy had trawled through the online world, researching every inch of their enemies' lives. No corporate press release, business deal, tweet or social media post was left unseen. They had spent *years* on their mission, forsaking so much of their teenage and young adult years.

But then had come the business trip to Hong Kong; her third major project with Rossi Industries and one she and her team had invested months of work on. Alessandro wasn't supposed to have flown out for the meeting himself. It was highly unusual, but she hadn't let it put her off her stride. She'd nailed the presentation, and the strong relationship she'd built with the client had earned them not only the commission but a personal invitation for her and Alessandro to dine with Kai Choi. It would have been a grave insult to refuse, so while her team members had returned to London, she and Alessandro had remained in Hong Kong.

Even now she was shocked by how thrilled she'd been to land the deal. Amelia's job was supposed to be a ruse. A means to an end. But instead, the dizzying excitement she'd felt had been reflected in the eyes of the very man whose opinion should matter least. Eyes that had turned excitement into heat after holding her gaze for just a little too long. Her heart jerked in her chest, as if it were tied to the memory of the moment that the line between them had been shattered.

A shattering that had forced her to do something she had never intended. She couldn't wait to find proof any more. The guilt, tension, the *desire* she still felt for a man who had destroyed her family was pulling her apart from the inside, spinning her further away from the control that she was known for. Amelia's plans were beginning to unravel, her command of the situation slipping from her fingers like sand.

So, she had done the unthinkable.

Amelia had told her sister that she'd found proof of their corruption and, in doing so, set in motion the takedown of the Rossi cousins. It was a lie that would take Issy's trust—the beautiful, delicate but utterly unbreakable thing that it was—and break it. Amelia had betrayed the one person who had been her constant companion since the death of their father and the emotional and physical retreat of their mother. Issy, who was bright and lovely and always, unfailingly, *good*. Just the thought of it chipped away at the crack that had formed in her heart, even as she told herself that she had done it for the right reason. The Rossis *needed* punishing.

Thomas Seymore had died by their hands as surely as if they'd killed him themselves. The demons sent by Alessandro and Gianni had haunted their father until he had finally drunk himself into an early grave—never recovering from the damage done to his reputation or status. And their mother? She had never been the same. Leaving their friends, their school, their social circle, losing her husband, declaring bankruptcy had broken something in the once vibrant Jane Seymore and no matter what Amelia and Issy had done, their mother had never come back to them.

'I hope Gianni comes back soon. I hate meetings when it's just Alessandro.'

'He's such a ballbreaker.'

'At least by the end of this meeting we'll know which company the project will partner with. The back and forth has been going on for months.'

For the first time that morning, the erratic beat of Amelia's heart settled because this was it. At the end of this meeting, she would guide Rossi Industries to partner with the wrong company and seal their fate. She would deliver Issy the revenge that Amelia had promised her ten years before and finally, *finally*, they would be done with this; she would walk away and never look back.

The room went quiet and she looked up to see Alessandro take his seat at the head of the table. When everyone was sitting up, backs straight, silent and waiting, he nodded for Amelia to begin what would be the last deal Rossi Industries ever undertook.

Today was the day.

Alessandro turned a page on the printout Amelia had provided the team. She was articulate and concise—nothing was wasted. Even the image she presented was considered; elegant but subtle, nothing intrusive, almost nothing memorable. He imagined she'd rehearsed the presentation over and over again. He would have, in her position. She stood to the left of the large screen displaying the two companies vying for partnership on this once-in-a-lifetime opportunity, the gentle glow of the screen making her nothing more than a silhouette.

Just as she had been against the gauzy curtain of the hotel room in Hong Kong when he'd reached for the tie holding her wrap dress together and pulled. The dress had sighed open to reveal perfection. The black-lace-underwear-embellished skin that drew his hand like a magnet. The slide of his palm over the smooth planes set off a wave of restlessness that crested over her body, her breasts heaving with each inhalation and when he reached for her, his own body trembled.

'And this is the problem we have,' Amelia claimed to the room, bringing him back to the present with a start he managed to disguise by reaching for his coffee, when caffeine was patently the last thing he needed.

He tuned out her words, remembering the first time he'd encountered her. His attention had snagged on her name, linking her to a moment in time that Alessandro refused to dwell on. Her file had revealed an impressive academic record, a notable drive, and enthusiastic references. She had interviewed well and he was sure that she would excel in her role, just like all of RI's other employees. And it should have ended there. But...

She had ignored him.

And that was unusual. It wasn't arrogance talking, but experience. Over the years, Alessandro had attracted as much attention as his charming playboy cousin, Gianni. He simply chose not to indulge. Alessandro had no desire to entertain anyone with expectations of a *more* he had absolutely no interest in pursuing. Which had earned him the nickname 'The Monk'. Despite this, it hadn't escaped Alessandro's notice that the looks he owed to an impressive combination of genes attracted a certain amount of attention, wanted or not. Yet, Amelia Seymore had treated him with the same cool impartiality as she did every other colleague in the building. It might not have made her close friends with her colleagues, but her talent and efficiency were undeniable, and she impressed her managers and team alike.

Her hair—rich admittedly, with reds and chestnuts and hints of golds—was always up, efficient in a bun, or plait, or some kind of twist that Alessandro was sure defied the laws of gravity. He shouldn't know that when it was down, it reached just below her shoulder blades, curled with the curve of her breast and curtained over nipples that were a fascinating shade of pink.

Her features were small, equally proportioned to ensure that nothing stood out, except that they *all* stood out. Lips of the palest pink that were neither lush, nor dramatically shaped into a bow, but that had explored his body with a ravenous fascination that had driven him to the edge of his control. The arch of a mahogany eyebrow framed her face in perfect symmetry with the line of a jaw that had fitted perfectly in the palm of his hand, concealing a pulse point behind her ear that flushed when she became aroused.

An arousal that when he had lain between her thighs, her body trembling beneath his touch, the wet heat welcoming him, calling to him, enticing him to taste, to tease, to—

Cristo.

He cleared his throat and the entire boardroom looked up at him. Amelia pinned him with a gaze that showed nothing but professionalism—and yet he still felt her censure. A flick of his hand and she continued.

'It is clear that this decision is one of utmost importance and will shape the face of not only the project, but the future of this company.'

He needed better control over himself. Control that Amelia seemed to have mastered.

She had been true to her word. Absolutely nothing had changed. It was almost as if it had never happened. Which was absolutely for the best, he assured himself. Once this meeting was done, and the choice of partnership had been decided, he would have nothing further to do with Amelia Seymore other than as a name on paperwork pertaining to the project. There would be no need for any kind of interaction other than that, which, Alessandro decided firmly, was most definitely a good thing.

As Amelia began wrapping up the presentation, a sense of eager expectation filled the room. Her team wanted to get this decision made and move on, but they had no idea of the true consequences that would follow which company was chosen.

Everything about the presentation had been created to seem as if she was offering them a choice between Chapel Developments and Firstview Ltd. If Rossi Industries partnered with Chapel Developments, then it would be the most successful partnership in the property development world working on a venture that was as daring as it was creatively ingenious. But if they chose to partner with Firstview Ltd, then every hope and dream in this room would turn into a nightmare. Firstview didn't have the infrastructure or the financial backing to support the project to fruition. Of course, Amelia had worked incredibly hard to ensure that wasn't evident in the least, but a partnership would be the ruin of them all.

She looked at Alessandro's leadership team—she could see it in their eyes. Respect, understanding, eagerness and more than just a little avarice. This deal could make them billionaires in their own right. And it turned her stomach. Greed, the same greed that had destroyed her family. The nausea hit her hard again, throwing her momentarily. As if needing to see the one person her vengeance hung on, she looked up to find Alessandro's gaze firmly on hers. Waves of unnatural fire arced across her body, short-circuiting her brain for just a nanosecond—and she remembered. Remembered the crushing endlessness of the orgasm he had given her, flooding her body with a rush she'd never experienced, one that had threatened to undo everything she'd known, everything she'd sacrificed. And in the crushing aftermath of that wave, she found her voice.

'My suggestion is that Firstview is the only possible way forward to achieve the desired outcome.'

And with that one sentence, she started the process of destroying one of the biggest property companies in the world—ensuring that finally, ten years after Alessandro and Gianni had taken everything from Amelia and her sister, they would know how it felt for their world to crumble.

CHAPTER TWO

SOMETHING WAS WRONG, but Alessandro couldn't put his finger on what. The feeling had started around the time that Amelia wrapped up her presentation that morning, successfully getting one hundred per cent agreement on her partnership proposal for the Aurora project.

He checked his watch. The day had all but disappeared. If he left now, he might be able to make it back in time to hit the gym, grab dinner and check over the Aurora contracts for whatever it was his subconscious was snagging on. In the ten years since he and Gianni had taken the Englishman's business and turned it into an empire, Alessandro had learned to trust his gut. And his gut was telling him that something was wrong.

Alessandro was tempted to call Gianni. He'd messaged him earlier about the decision to move ahead with Firstview Ltd, but his cousin's yearly holiday was sacrosanct and Alessandro disliked the idea of disrupting it. Outside the twelve days Gianni spent each year in the Caribbean, he worked as if the Devil himself held the reins and he deserved the break. Alessandro switched off his computer, grabbed his jacket, turned off the lights in his office and made his way towards the elevator that ran through the centre of the building.

Designed by Rob Weller, the Rossis' preferred architect, the atrium that extended through the entire building was a marvel. Built five years ago, Rossi Industries rented out the lower floors to various businesses, a newspaper and a TV studio. But the upper levels were used solely by RI and had been created with meticulous eye for detail and consideration for the needs and well-being of his staff.

The dynamic open-plan design made the most of the natural light brought into the building through lightly tinted windows. Rose on the outside but not on the inside, the light worked with the white accents to create a bright, easy space in which to be. Social spaces were balanced with work areas, with healthcare facilities, staff restaurant, a gym, and a landscaped terrace and café on the wraparound balcony. The roof garden was accessible by only his and Gianni's offices on the penthouse floor, but was often used as a space for company events.

Alessandro was proud of what they had achieved. Pleased to know that Rossi Industries was a company that looked after its staff, never wanting them to push themselves to the brink, always knowing that the health of his staff was first and foremost to him.

I don't care how tired you are. There is more work to be done.

Refusing to shy away from the vicious childhood memory of his father's demands, Alessandro embraced it. Happy to know that he had walked away from his childhood refusing to be cowed by the mean-spirited, violent man. Everything he'd done was to ensure that he was nothing like Saverio Vizzini.

When the lift arrived, he faced the 'back', which displayed all the floors and staff areas of Rossi Industries. With the evening pouring into the building, the few lights bouncing off glass meeting rooms and breakout areas sparkled like stars in the night sky. Housekeeping staff would turn off any forgotten lights but one in particular caught his eye, and he'd pressed the corresponding floor's button before he knew it.

For one brief moment he wavered. Told himself not to get out of the lift. To continue on to the parking level and leave. He wondered, later, what might have happened if he had. Whether things would have been different and whether he'd have wanted them to be. In the end it didn't much matter. Things had been set in motion long before that day, and Alessandro doubted that he'd have managed to escape them.

They'd done it. Amelia had sent Issy a message to let her know that Rossi Industries had taken the bait, that Alessandro's and Gianni's destruction was all but assured. Not that the end of Alessandro and Gianni would be immediate. No, her plan of vengeance hadn't been as simple as a swift, painless death.

Just like what had happened to her father, to her mother and the lives she and her sister had known, the destruction of Rossi Industries would take months, perhaps even as long as a year if Firstview managed to hide their ineptitude better than she thought they might. But Amelia would be long gone by then. She would be offered 'a job that she couldn't refuse' and she would leave, without even seeing out her notice. There was, of course, no dream job. Amelia Seymore would simply disappear into thin air.

All she needed to do now was wait out the next few days while the contracts with Firstview Ltd were signed, then Issy could leave Gianni in the Caribbean and return to the UK and the sisters could celebrate.

But Amelia didn't feel like celebrating. Instead she was effectively emptying her desk. Not so that anyone would notice, because she'd need to continue to work here for the next few days, she rationalised. But when the time came, it would probably be best if she was able to make a quick exit. A *very* quick exit.

He would be so angry.

It didn't matter, she told herself firmly, resenting the way that even a small part of her worried about Alessandro. Guilt throbbed in her heart, knowing that her immediate concern should be her sister, not a man who had caused such irreparable damage to her family.

She had just switched her computer off when the hairs on the back of her neck lifted and her heart beat a little too late and a little too hard. *He* was there. She didn't have to turn around to look. She *knew* it. Unbidden, his words from that night ran through her mind like raindrops.

If this is only for one night, then I would give you everything you could ever want for. You only need to ask. So ask me, cara. *Ask, and I will make it so.*

She'd asked for things she'd never even dreamed of in a moment of unbridled desperate desire and he'd done them and more.

'Amelia?'

She couldn't face him, not yet. Not when she had to bite her lip to stop herself from crying out in need, in want. Instead, she did the only thing she was capable of and nodded. Inexplicably, her eyes felt damp.

Was she crying? For *him* or for herself?

Enough!

She pasted a bright smile on her face and turned to meet him.

'Mr Rossi. What can I do for you?'

Something flashed in his eyes, hot, angry even, but it was gone in less than one of her frantic heartbeats. She thought she saw him look to her neck—where he had pressed open-mouthed kisses before drowning her in a pleasure she never knew existed, before he had taken possession of her body and—

'What are you still doing here?' Alessandro asked.

'Just finishing a few things. I was just…leaving,' she said, realising that he was too. Now she was going to be stuck in a lift with him for the entire journey down to the ground floor. 'You?' she asked, inanely because… well. What really was there to say to a man she had slept with and was on the brink of completely and utterly destroying?

'On my way out,' he replied, his features almost too guarded, as if he knew exactly how silly this conversation was.

Neither of them moved. Instead, the silence spun a cocoon around them, the air thickened by heated looks and unsteady breaths. Her desire pawed at her when she noticed his hand flex by his thigh. A hand that had caressed her skin, had delved between her legs, had pulled her harder and deeper against his open mouth.

Could he hear the thud of her heart? The way that her breath caught in her throat? His gaze flickered between her lips and her eyes before he turned away, her heart aching and angry and wanting and she didn't know any more. If only he weren't so *handsome*.

His body was angled proprietorially towards her and she felt crowded even though there were nearly two feet between them. The powerful cords of his neck stood out as he reached up to fuss with his tie knot, the deep tan of his skin rich and evocative next to the starched white origami-like fold of his collar. A stubble Amelia was half convinced that he hated was already visible across his jawline and neck, and she was haunted by the memory of how it had felt beneath her fingertips, how it had sounded as she'd explored every single inch of him that night.

The broad shoulders she'd gripped, the lush thick raven-dark hair she'd fisted in her hands as he'd thrust into her. Amelia hated to think that she had been brought so low by good looks, but what else could it have been? The man had utterly destroyed her family and she had all but begged him to ruin her too as she had gripped the edge of the table in his hotel suite. She'd spread her legs wider, to make room for him between them, her body welcoming the hard angles of his hips. The brush of his arousal at her core had sent a gasp through her body...

Amelia slammed the door shut on a memory she should have buried so deep she could never find it again. The only way she'd survived the last six weeks was knowing that they'd never speak of what had happened in Hong Kong. Keeping it tucked away behind a pane of impenetrable glass was the only thing that had kept her sane.

'Shall we?' she asked, assuming the emotionally indifferent tone she had worn for two years, as if she didn't feel torn apart by the weight of desire and the need for a vengeance that had begun to taste bitter in the last few months.

Amelia's breezy tone ate at Alessandro. There he was feeling as if his life had been upended by this innocuous English girl, and she was utterly unaffected by the most sensuous night of his life. Perhaps somewhere in the recent years of his *'Monkdom'*, he had developed perversions. The thought horrified him so much that for a shocking moment, he stilled, causing a flash of concern to pass across Amelia's features.

'Are you—?'

He turned on his heel and stalked back towards the lifts. He should never have stopped on her floor. Once again he wrestled with that sense of frustrated desire and shame. Resisting the urge to pull at his collar, he reminded himself that he had taken advantage of a junior member of staff and he deserved every ounce of inner turmoil that he was currently struggling with.

Crossing the floor, he recognised that it had been rude to cut her off mid-sentence but had he not, he might have—*God forbid*—actually answered her question and admitted that no, he wasn't okay in the slightest and was, in fact, being driven out of his mind with a need for her that felt unnatural.

'Maybe I should take the stairs,' he said as they reached the lift, realising that he probably shouldn't be taking the lift with her.

A slight frown across her brow appeared to question the sense in walking down *sixty-four* flights of stairs. And now he couldn't ignore the fact that he'd just volunteered to do precisely that in order to avoid spending the minute and a half journey with her in the lift.

She blinked at him, shutters over an unfathomable gaze, and turned to face the elevator doors. 'If you like,' she said.

Her response had him grinding his teeth and he was about to leave when the lift arrived, the doors sliding open, and now there was no escape. Leaving would be the height of stupidity, showing the exact extent of how much her presence affected him *beyond* what he had already revealed.

He gestured for her to enter before him and he caught her glancing at his hand before she stepped into the lift. As she turned to look out into the centre of the building he saw the delicate blush at the pulse point behind her ear, his gaze snagging on the way her shirt had come open beneath the pull of the strap of her bag on her shoulder.

Heat crawled across his shoulders, making Alessandro want to yank at the collar of his shirt. She wasn't as unaffected as she appeared and just the thought of that enflamed *everything*. This time, instead of staying in the lift he should damn well get out. Alessandro closed his eyes but instead of blessed darkness he saw her straddled across his lap, taking him deep within her, riding a sensuous wave that consumed them both. The doors closed behind him and the lurch in his gut had nothing to do with the gentle descent.

'Congratulations,' he forced out through numb lips.

For a moment, he thought he saw guilt flash in the golden green depths of eyes that he had once, inconceivably, thought unnoteworthy. But he must have been projecting, because the guilt was his burden to bear.

'Thank you,' Amelia said before biting her lip and turning her attention back to the floors flying past the glass windows.

'Are you celebrating?' he asked.

Minchione! Clearly, she didn't want to speak to him and no wonder. The burning shame of self-loathing now heated his internal body temperature rather than arousal and he was unusually thankful for it.

'No, my sister is…'

Amelia swallowed her words, wishing she could have bitten off her own tongue. 'Away,' she concluded, aware that Alessandro was waiting for her to finish her sentence. Oh, God, this was her punishment. To be stuck in a small enclosed space with the man she'd just ruined—the man that, in spite of everything, she still wanted with a desperation that left her breathless.

Enemy, enemy, enemy!

'What was that?' Alessandro asked, bending slightly as if to listen more closely.

Instinctively she jerked away from him and instantly regretted it. From the tic in his jaw, Alessandro hadn't missed it. His hands fisted by his thighs and oh, God, what was wrong with her? Why was that so sexy?

She had become a stranger to herself in the last six weeks. Ever since she had secured the deal in Hong Kong, something had changed. Because how could she recognise the woman who would sleep with the man that destroyed her family? How could she have betrayed everything she and her sister had worked towards? How could she have weighed one night of pleasure with a childhood of misery and chosen *him*?

Once again a wetness pressed against the backs of her eyes. Not here. And not now! She just needed to get out of this lift and away from Alessandro Rossi. She could have her breakdown when she was home.

Count to ten, darling, and it will be fine.

But the words she'd whispered to her sister through their teenage years didn't work this time. It wouldn't be fine. Issy was off in the Caribbean somewhere, having kidnapped Gianni Rossi, and she was lusting after a man who was the Devil incarnate.

She hadn't expected it to feel like this. Wasn't she supposed to feel victorious? Wasn't it supposed to be amazing, this feeling? Vengeance almost guaranteed, it should have been the crowning achievement of all she'd ever wanted. But she didn't. Instead she felt...*guilty*. She felt sick. And shivery. And no, she hadn't come down with a cold. But...something was *wrong*.

'If this is...' he said, and trailed off, awkwardness looking strange on Alessandro's handsome features. She'd never seen him like this. In the boardroom he was powerful, determined...confidence didn't even factor, it was something beyond that. A supreme self-belief. And the night they'd shared in Hong Kong? A shiver ran the length of her spine. He'd unlocked fantasies that night she'd never even known she'd had. 'If you want to speak to HR... I think we should speak to HR.'

Her head snapped up out of the desire-dazed fog. She almost laughed. She *wanted* to, absurdly. In three days' time, their one night in Hong Kong would be the least of his problems. She would be gone and Alessandro Rossi would never see her again, no matter how hard he might look.

'I don't know what you think we would need to speak to HR about,' she said, purposefully keeping her face blank.

He frowned, his eyes, usually so clear, clouded and confused, she almost didn't like to see it.

'Hong Kong,' he said, as if trying to find a tether to hold onto in the conversation that was clearly difficult.

'Hong Kong was a roaring success. We finalised the deal with Kai Choi, went for dinner with him and his team to celebrate, and then I returned to my hotel room and you returned to yours. I'm not exactly sure why we would need to share that with HR.'

'So, nothing happened?'

'Nothing happened.' It couldn't have. Because she couldn't have been that person. Shame and guilt—and the traces of a desire so heavy it still ran in her veins—made her just a little dizzy.

Alessandro nearly reached out a hand to Amelia as she swayed a little. But she flickered an angry gaze at where his hand twitched and he stopped himself just in time.

Because, of course, grabbing her right now, putting his hands on her was an excellent *idea.*

Alessandro was really beginning to dislike his inner voice, though he could hardly argue with being called a fool. He opened his mouth to object to Amelia's statement. Because there was something inherently wrong about her denying that night had happened. Denying that what they'd shared had happened. Because it had.

Unlike Gianni, Alessandro stayed out of the limelight. His photograph was never in the newspapers, his name only appearing in print if linked to his cousin. He was not instantly recognisable to the person on the street, and were they ever asked if they knew of him, their answer would be 'Alessandro who?' His privacy was a closely guarded thing, so Alessandro could perhaps forgive Amelia for thinking that he did this kind of thing all the time. Not with staff—no, she had at least, thankfully, acknowledged that it was unusual for both of them.

But beyond that, the last time he had shared a bed with someone had been… He tried to think back. Years? Certainly more than two. He was incredibly discerning in his choice of partners, in what attracted him, which was why he had been so shocked to find that Amelia, the perfect employee, who on the surface could have defined English 'plainness', had grabbed his attention and yanked on it, leading him into a night that had proved as unforgettable as it was indescribable.

So he was about to reply, to refute her statement, to tell her that he knew it wasn't just him affected by that night, that he wanted more, to tell her all of the most asinine things that it had never once occurred to him to say to another human being before now, when the doors to the lift opened and Amelia practically ran out into the foyer.

'Amelia,' he called after her as she hurried towards the exit, no longer caring who saw or heard him.

'See you tomorrow, Mr Rossi,' she called over her shoulder without looking back.

He stood, in the centre of the atrium, watching her leave through the main entrance to The Ruby and thought, *yes*. He *would* see her tomorrow. And this time, he'd not let her run away, because he hadn't missed the way that her breath had caught, that her pulse had flickered, and her skin had crested pink with desire. It wasn't just him in this madness. It couldn't be.

He was brought back to earth by a ringtone reserved exclusively for his cousin and could only imagine what Gianni would say when he confessed his sin of sleeping with a junior member of staff. Their lawyers would have a field day.

'Gianni, how—?'

'Andro, listen, I don't have much time.'

'Okay, but what's the—?'

'Amelia Seymore,' Gianni interrupted. 'She's Thomas Seymore's daughter.'

'What?' Alessandro demanded. 'I can't hear you properly.' He *couldn't* have heard Gianni properly. It was just the crackle on the line.

'Listen to me, Amelia Seymore is a traitor. She's been…spy this whole time. She's…with her sister to destroy us.'

'Amelia Seymore?' Alessandro repeated like an idiot, the line was so bad, but he knew if he wanted to he could read between the crackle.

'Yes! Seymore. The…project is compromised.'

'Which project?' he demanded, but he realised Gianni hadn't heard his question.

'And listen, she claims to have found some kind of proof of corruption against us.'

'Corruption? What corruption?' The line was getting even worse. Frustration and incredulity were vying to escape the tight fist he had on his emotions.

'I don't know, but…the messages I read, Amelia… found evidence of corruption… I'm in the Caribbean with her sister. I'll…and stop her communicating with anyone and causing any more damage. Can you deal with Amelia? This needs to be nipped in the bud and damage limitation undertaken immediately.'

'Consider it done,' Alessandro growled darkly.

'I maybe out of reach for a while, but I'll try and get a message to you when I know what's going on.'

'Likewise. Speak soon, cousin.'

When Alessandro ended the call, his jaw was clenched so tight it had started to ache. He was *still* standing in the centre of the atrium, *still* looking at where he had last seen Amelia.

She was Thomas Seymore's daughter, come to destroy them?

He scoffed, surely not. Amelia? Capable of sabotage? No. The thought was so strong that he gestured with his hand, cutting through the empty air. But then a montage flickered through his mind. Amelia hesitant, guilty, conflicted, angry...

My sister is away...

And suddenly it all started to make sense. Fury found its way into his veins and travelled throughout his body in a single pump of his heart. *Cristo*, he could have laughed at himself. He'd been so stupid. Taken in by the oldest of ruses. He shook his head in disgust. And he'd more than simply let her. He'd asked her for it, *begged* her to let him sign his own ruination. But it wasn't just his own—it was his cousin's, it was his company, his staff...

No!

Gianni had warned him in time. Alessandro still had a chance to turn things around. He spun on his heel and, instead of going home to his apartment, he went back up to his office and started to plan. Thomas Seymore's daughters had no idea what they had started and he and Gianni would make damn sure they would live to regret the day they messed with the Rossi cousins.

CHAPTER THREE

HANDS BRACED AGAINST the sink, Amelia stared at herself in the mirror the next morning. Accusations and sleeplessness had drawn dark slashes beneath her eyes and she looked unnaturally pale, even considering the harsh bathroom lighting.

You can do this, she told herself sternly. *It's two measly days. Alessandro will be in meetings for most, if not all, of that time.* All she had to do was play nice with her team for two days. All she had to do was smile.

All she had to do was let go of the sink.

She released the death grip she'd had on the porcelain and with one last glare at herself in the mirror, she grabbed her jacket and bag and let herself out of the small flat she shared with her sister in Brockley. The broken lift and the unusual heatwave made the stairwell unbearable and she emerged onto the pavement already hot, sweaty and out of sorts. That was why she came to a stop and simply stared at the sight that met her, genuinely unsure whether it was real or not.

Alessandro was leaning against a sleek black vehicle that to call a car would probably be some kind of insult. Hands fisted deep in his pockets and eyes hidden behind aviator sunglasses that screamed money, he exuded a lazy sexuality that should have come with a health warning.

But there was also something else. Something that put her senses on alert.

It was a slow roll of emotion, building to a crescendo as sharp as any sudden fright and she had to press her hand over her heart to keep it in place. She forced herself to take a deep breath, wishing it were still because of the fright, but honestly, the sight of Alessandro made her sex *ache*. A pulse flared across her body, a chain reaction that touched from sense to sense until her whole body practically trembled with want.

'You scared me,' she accused, trying to catch her breath as she searched for a reason why Alessandro Rossi would be waiting on a South London street, for *her*.

Could he know?

No, she dismissed. There was absolutely no way that he could have discovered Firstview's inadequacies already, especially as it had taken her months.

'My sincere apologies, Ms Seymore. I'm afraid we are quite short on time.'

'Time? For what?' Amelia asked, closing the distance between them. There was an unusual tension in the way Alessandro held himself. Dark glasses might have hidden eyes from her, but she sensed that she was under the very intense microscope of his focus.

'We've just received news of an important business proposal and with the Aurora project all wrapped up, you're the only project lead that I can spare.'

Only Alessandro would wrap up one deal the night before and start a new one before coffee the next morning. 'My team needs briefing and there are a few things…' She might not understand what was going on, but, whatever it was, she knew she couldn't spend any more time with him in such close proximity. 'Is there not someone else who could—?'

'I'm afraid not. You are the only person it can be.'

'But—'

'Ms Seymore, is there a problem?' His words were like a leash, yanking her back into place.

'No. Of course not,' she replied as she stepped forward to meet him beside the car. And he still didn't move. Now that she was this close, she could see that he hadn't shaved and the stubble from last night was now a dark swathe across his jaw. A muscle flexed at the hollow just beneath the dark line and she felt the tension thicken between them, building until finally he stepped aside to open the door, gesturing for her to get in.

'Where are we going?' she asked as the car pulled into the road, attracting more than a few stares from neighbours who were understandably shocked to see such an expensive car in the area.

'Not too far.'

He passed her a file, explaining that it was a brief he needed her to read ahead of the meeting. Frowning, she scanned the opening documents outlining a prospective client they were considering. There were nearly fifty pages here and an anxious heat crawled across her shoulders.

Amelia was finding it hard to focus, not just from the motion of the car and trying to read, but the awareness of Alessandro himself. Arm propped up against the window, chin rested in his palm, his gaze glued on some invisible point in the distance.

Concentrate. It was just one meeting and then she'd be back with her team and done for the day before she knew it.

Only, rather than turning off the South Circular into London, they continued to head out east.

'It's a very important deal, Amelia. I'd really like to get it right,' he warned, as if noticing that she was distracted.

'Of course.'

She turned back to the pages and lost herself in what could be an exciting new deal for Rossi Industries. Scanning the projections, the highly sought-after location of the land for sale and the cultural interest in the surrounding area, she could see how it would come together. It would be incredible. Partnering with Chalendar Enterprises was clever and would save Rossi Industries time overall, the two businesses having worked together before.

And even though Amelia wouldn't be there to see it happen, she was already identifying which team members would be best, what areas might be problematic and how to navigate them. In her absence they would probably give the project to Brent Bennet, but he often made mistakes on the contracts. She should give Legal a heads up…only she wouldn't. Because she would be long gone by the time that happened. The car slowed to a stop and she looked out of the window to see tarmac.

'Alessandro, where is this meeting?'

Alessandro said nothing, opening the door of the car and getting out onto the runway of a private airfield just outside London. He said nothing because a worryingly large part of him wanted to shout and rage and yell. But now wasn't the time for that. There was too much at stake.

He held the door to the car open for her and hated the way that, no matter how the shocking discovery of her true identity had blown his world apart, his body hadn't got the memo, and the soft scent of jasmine that rose from her skin as she passed in front of him hardened his arousal as much as his anger.

The betrayal of it. Of her. He would deal with that later, but for now his one focus, his only goal, was to find out what she had done and stop it before the rot could take hold. His plan was simple—isolate, interrogate and eliminate.

No one other than her father, Thomas Seymore, had managed to pull the wool over their eyes so successfully. Alessandro choked back a bitter laugh. He and Gianni had, naively, believed that they had learned their lesson that one and only time. Clearly, they were mistaken.

And to think she had the gall not to even change her surname. It had been staring him in the face the whole time and what had he done? Smiled at her, thanked her, and asked her for more.

'Sir?'

'*Sì?*' he snapped and Lucinda, a member of his air crew who had been with RI for nearly six years, flinched a little. 'My apologies. Truly, Lucinda,' he said, warning himself to keep his cool.

His emotions swung like a giant pendulum, back and forth between the weight of the past and the future of his company.

He watched Amelia settle into a large cream leather seat, fasten the safety belt and look out of the window. She seemed a little disconcerted but he knew, now, just how good an actress she really was.

'Coffee, Mr Rossi?'

'*Grazie mille*, Lucinda,' he replied sincerely, taking the espresso over to a seat on the opposite side of the cabin.

He just needed to get to Villa Vittoria. It might have been a refuge for him and Gianni for the past ten years, but there was also a deep irony in taking Amelia Seymore back to the scene of the crime. He refused to think of it as kidnap, even though his conscience contorted itself in order not to do so. He was simply taking her to a place where he intended to cut her off from any possible forms of communication until he could identify just how badly she had sabotaged his company and the hundreds of thousands of people he employed globally. It was the only solution he had been able to come up with in the twelve hours since he had received the call from Gianni.

When they were safely at the villa, all hell could break loose. He just had to get her there first without her realising what was happening. It was why he'd given her the file, to distract her and keep her from asking too many questions.

'How long has Lexicon been looking to develop the land?' Amelia asked, flicking back and forth between a few pages. Unease gripped his stomach, empty aside from the coffee he'd all but inhaled. He'd not had long to put together the fake file—in half an hour he'd brought together a mishmash of four old, and failed, pitches. But he could play this game better than anyone, he thought, subtly rolling his shoulders. The Seymore sisters had messed with the wrong billionaires.

'A while,' he replied, knowing that she had been seeking a specific answer. A perverse part of him delighted in withholding it, wanting to needle, to irritate, to annoy. It was a small petty victory, but he could not lose sight of the greater picture. Because so much more than his ego depended on him rooting out the damage she had done and putting an end to it immediately.

'We will soon be taking off, so if your safety belts are fastened?' Lucinda asked, smiling when they had both nodded to affirm that they were. 'Lovely. Flight time should be just under two hours—winds are in our favour and the journey should be smooth sailing.'

With that she retreated before Amelia could get a word out of the partly opened mouth. That delectable, betraying mouth.

I think we should speak to HR.

He couldn't believe the words he'd uttered. Lust-ridden fool. Perhaps that had been her plan after all. To seduce him and—no. Her refusal to speak to HR, her insistence that they never speak of it, her behaviour since Hong Kong, it didn't make sense if that was her plan.

That he had been foolish enough to open the door to any kind of impropriety in the first place was his very own cross to bear. Self-disgust and acceptance—they burned with enough heat to bring pinpricks of sweat to the back of his neck. Alessandro would take whatever punishment he deserved for his transgression. But the sisters' text messages had claimed to have identified proof of corruption.

Impossibile.

Even the word 'corruption' left a bitter taste in his mouth. It was an outrage that this younger Seymore was trying to claim that against them. The audacity of it was simply incomprehensible and while he could concede that there was a certain ingenuity to their plan of attack, it was this—this supposed evidence of corruption—that betrayed the sheer magnitude of their stupidity.

It was simple. Once he had the information he needed, he would ensure that neither he nor his cousin would hear the name Seymore ever again.

* * *

Amelia was feeling really quite uncomfortable by the time they disembarked the plane and got into the limousine waiting for them. She had enough sense to know that any more questions would be met with either silence or derision, which had kept her pretty much quiet no matter how strange the situation was becoming. She pressed a hand to her stomach, and although she desperately wanted to turn up the air conditioning in the back section of the sleek vehicle, the thought of attracting Alessandro's attention was worse.

Italy. They were in Italy.

And even though they had left London comparatively early, the travel and time difference meant that it was now midday and Amelia was hot. Everything felt a little damp and stifling. The air between them was thick and heavy, and she had to work hard to calm her breathing.

She had never got over the way that the Rossis travelled continents as if by the click of their fingers. When she'd interviewed for her position, Amelia had known international travel would be expected, which was why she'd not been able to lie about her name. A copy of her passport was held on file by Rossi Industries and she was expected to carry proof of identification with her at all times.

But as she gazed out of the window, trying to ease the roil in her stomach, the sight of cypress trees in the distance struck her with such a wave of familiarity. The sound of little girls laughing and the scent of sunscreen rose up around her. A warm dry heat hit her skin, turning it rosy in her mind, and the taste of lemon sorbet made her mouth water.

Amelia hadn't been back to Italy since her and Issy's lives had changed for ever. But for just a moment, Amelia wanted to bask in her memories. Her parents enjoying a lazy afternoon beside an azure blue pool in a sprawling villa on the far edges of Capri. Her father's cream linen shorts and brown sandals displaying pale English skin and the mosquito bites their mother used to tease him about. Jane Seymore's smile when she looked at her husband as they had lunch looking out across a stunning sea punctuated by jagged rocky outcrops. Issy's terrible aim as she threw beach balls at her while she was trying—and failing—to get a tan.

She had forgotten it. The last family holiday they'd had before the Rossis had ripped apart everything they'd known, and her heart filled with an old ache she hadn't allowed herself to feel since she and Issy had chosen vengeance.

She felt, rather than saw, Alessandro's attention fix on her. The touch of it so different from the heated *yearning* from the past few weeks that it brought her out of her memories. Now it felt cool and tasted like anger and Amelia began to fear that just maybe he *had* discovered who she was.

Italy, Lexicon, the deal. It could almost have been purpose built for her. She spoke fluent Italian—one of the three languages she had studied in order to embellish her résumé for Rossi Industries. The land—it was similar to a deal RI had rejected about two months before she'd interviewed for her position—a deal Issy had researched to help Amelia with her interview. The sudden change in Alessandro's temperament—she'd seen him under huge amounts of pressure before, right down to the last beats on several billion-dollar deals, and he'd never been *cold*. Clipped, harsh, demanding and exacting to the point of brutal? Absolutely. But there was a heat, drive, a momentum that swept you up and made you want to meet those standards, made you want to be with him in that success. It was…attractive, *alluring*.

Stop!

There was no way that Alessandro could have discovered anything wrong with the deal and she had covered her tracks too well in the company to have been identified as Thomas's daughter. But, oh, God, what if something had happened to Issy? What if Gianni had—?

Her swift gasp of shock drew not just Alessandro's focus, but his gaze.

'Ms Seymore, is something wrong?'

His words, full of grit and gravel, shifted her pulse into a higher gear.

'No, Mr Rossi,' she replied through bloodless lips. She had to know. Picking up the file beside her, she scanned the documents and looked at the memo date from Lexicon to Rossi Industries. Second of June. She managed to stop her hands fisting before the crumpled paper could betray her discovery. It would be highly unlikely to near inconceivable for anyone in Italy to have sent a work memo on *Festa Della Republica*. Italy's Republic Day was a fiercely celebrated bank holiday on which *no one*—bar first responders—worked.

'You put the documents together yourself?'

He nodded, his gaze inscrutable.

Oh, God. He knew who she was.

Amelia Seymore was in serious trouble. And if she was, so was her sister.

* * *

Alessandro knew there was a risk that something in the documents could tip Amelia off, but with such little time he'd had no choice. And now, as the limousine made the last twists and turns towards the only place in the world he could have brought her, did it really matter if she knew that she had been found out? Because that had been the only conclusion to draw from the shocked gasp she'd tried to hide.

And in interesting contrast to that momentary betrayal of emotions, the woman beside him seemed unduly calm. He could almost be impressed by her. *Almost*. He looked out of the window before he did something stupid like look at her again.

The opening move of the game had been made. He had brought her into his domain and if she hadn't already, then soon she would realise the reality of her situation. That she was completely and utterly at his mercy.

The thought detonated such a riot of emotions, it infuriated him that Amelia Seymore could be so...*calm*.

The electronic gates at Villa Vittoria parted smoothly and the driver took the fork in the road that would lead to Alessandro's half of the dramatic oval-shaped compound. The other would have taken them to Gianni's half of the unique estate. With near enough two hundred and fifty acres across the entire property the estate was worth more than ten million euros. But it was what lay at the heart of the compound that made it priceless to Alessandro and Gianni.

As the car took the road that swept alongside a large area of land that looked to the world like a pretty wildflower meadow, it was so much more to Alessandro. To him and Gianni, it was what could have utterly broken them, but instead it had become the thing that defined them.

Poppies, cornflowers, daisies and violets covered the stretch of land that Alessandro and Gianni had bought after years of secretly saving every single penny they could. Scrimping and sacrifice had garnered enough money to make the initial purchase, and a savage loan with near-insurmountable interest rates from a highly unscrupulous money lender was to cover the build that would have been their first property.

Would have. Had it not been for Thomas Seymore.

Thomas Seymore had seen Alessandro and Gianni, two eighteen-year-olds with hope in their eyes and barely enough money in their pockets, and considered them easy targets for his villainy. He had been wrong to underestimate them. And he had paid the price.

And now, it seemed, he had to teach the daughter exactly the same lesson.

So be it.

The car pulled up alongside his half of the estate that bracketed one side of the land that had been sold to them illegally. Oh, they could have tried to sell it on, offloading it onto another poor unsuspecting bastard, perhaps even pay off a surveyor as Seymore had, to ensure that the buyer didn't discover until it was too late that the land was unfit for development. But instead, they'd kept it. As a reminder, not to ever forget the sting of that betrayal, a reminder of just how far they had come. Slowly, but surely, they had bought the land surrounding the little parcel Seymore had sold them and they had eventually turned it into Villa Vittoria, their home and their refuge.

Beside him, Amelia opened the door of the limousine and stepped out, her gaze scanning the impressive vista before her with something like awe. He exited the vehicle and, with a knock on the roof, the driver departed, leaving just the two of them standing on the sandy driveway facing off against each other.

'Why am I here?' Amelia demanded, only a slight tremble in her voice.

'To face the consequences of your actions, *cara*,' he growled in warning.

'Funny.' The word sliced out through tightly clenched teeth. The paleness of her skin serving to highlight the slashes of anger painting her cheeks red. 'I was about to say the same to you.'

CHAPTER FOUR

Despite her fiery response, the sun heated Amelia's skin to the point of discomfort and her mouth was dryer than a desert. During Issy's online investigations, she had found mention of the estate that the Rossi cousins shared, but there were no photographs or plans anywhere online. From the scarce descriptions her sister had been able to cobble together though, it could only be where Amelia was now.

Alessandro had discovered who she was and brought her onto his territory—a move calculated to cause her the maximum amount of disturbance. He clearly thought she was at his mercy. But he had also, clearly, underestimated her.

This was her mess and she had to fix it. Her first priority was to make sure that her sister was okay. The last message she'd had from Issy was a picture she'd sent yesterday of her in a luxurious room on the yacht she'd obtained to lure Gianni Rossi away from contact. Everything in her wanted to grab her phone and call Issy immediately. But she had to play this carefully. Once she knew that her sister was okay, Amelia would identify exactly what it was that he knew, what he *thought* he knew, and what damage she could still do. She just needed to get him talking.

And the best way to do that? Make him think he was the one in control.

She looked around. In the distance she caught sight of a wall that ran the length of the estate from what she could tell. On the far side of the large wildflower meadow was a villa—similar in design to the buildings behind her, but with slight differences. She narrowed her gaze, recognising Gianni's flair for the dramatic in contrast to the starker, more serious lines of property that suited Alessandro's personality. But she was surprised that he had chosen to bring her to such a private place—his *home*.

She shaded her gaze from the midday sun and craned her neck to look up at Alessandro, who had, once again, chosen to hide behind his sunglasses. *Coward.* He gestured behind her to a small stone pathway leading away from the main building. Fighting him on such a small thing would be foolish. She was going to have to be very careful and very clever.

They turned their back on the drive and skirted the edge of the main building. Large trees provided blessed relief from the Italian sun and in the near distance she spied what could only be their destination—a low-slung building beside an azure-blue pool. Floor-to-ceiling gently tinted windows wrapped around the structure, making it one of the most lavish pool houses she'd ever seen.

Only the best for the Rossis, her sister's voice reminded her.

From here Amelia could just make out a large open-plan kitchenette and lounge to one side and a glass-fronted shower with a half-wall that presumably hid a toilet. Her eyes returned to the shower, where butter-coloured marble stood stark against powerful lines of dark granite. It suited Alessandro to perfection. She could just imagine him hauling himself from the pool, stripping out of his costume and prowling straight into the shower and—

'Is there a problem?' Alessandro asked with faux civility.

She had stopped walking. At some point in the midst of her daydream she had actually stopped walking. She *had* to get better control over herself.

'You mean aside from the fact that you have, to all intents and purposes, kidnapped me and I am now trapped in a foreign country with no money or clothes?'

He notched his head to one side. 'You have your phone?'

'Yes, of course I...'

He held out his hand.

'No. Absolutely not,' she said, punctuating it with a shake of her head.

'No one will help you, *cara*. You are mine until I find out exactly what you've done and how you can fix it, before I remove you from my and my cousin's lives for good.'

'I still think I'll be keeping hold of it,' she said as she pushed past him and continued towards the pool house, hastily pressing the call button for her sister. In her peripheral vision she saw him take out his phone and press a button. Instantly the signal bars on her phone disappeared. What the—?

He had a signal jammer?

'You actually blocked the phone signal?' she demanded.

'Of course. You are a threat and you need to be contained.' Despite his words, his tone was painfully civilised and that, Amelia knew, was when Alessandro was at his most dangerous.

Panic nipped at her pulse, but she ignored it as they reached the pool house, the glass door frame sliding back as if ready for their arrival.

'Would you like some lunch? I had my staff prepare something,' he said as he walked towards the clean, simply designed kitchen.

If he had staff, then…

'*Before* I gave them all the rest of the week off,' he added, as if reading her mind.

A week? Just how long did he plan on keeping her here?

'Oh, I get a meal before you start the interrogation, then?' she threw at him.

'If you like,' he said with a shrug as if he cared little if she ate or starved to death.

She picked at her thumbnail, struggling to play it cool while her mind conjured all manner of scenarios Issy might be going through. She couldn't take it any more. Concern for Issy eclipsed everything.

'I'll not say another word until I know if my sister is okay.'

Alessandro bit back a curse. She was a traitor. A spy. She had done who knew what damage to his company and yet still every single inch of her shone with defiance, the burning heat in her eyes curling around him like a flame. Taunting him. Daring him.

And for the first time in his life, he was at risk of losing his legendary cool. He'd kept himself in check ever since his father had first used his fists on him, determined never ever to become anything like the monster who had provided half of his DNA.

He turned away from her before he did something he'd regret—something that had none of the violence of his father and all of the passion of a lust-filled youth. What kind of spell had she cast upon him? He placed the plates his staff had put together on the table and retrieved a bottle of wine from the fridge. At her raised eyebrow, he simply stared at her.

'I'm less concerned about your sister, and more worried about what she is doing to my cousin.'

Amelia opened her mouth as if to say something but snapped it shut. She was apparently planning to stick to her word not to say anything until she heard from her sister.

Amelia and Isabelle—sisters and daughters of Thomas Seymore. He searched Amelia's face for signs of the tall, thin British man who had sold them a worthless plot of land all those years ago. He couldn't quite see it. Where her father had been lean and long, his features sharp and harsh, Amelia was petite, softer, *sweeter*. Looks that were clearly deceiving.

He frowned. Perhaps he should have kept an eye on the Seymore family. But he'd thought the business done with the moment he and Gianni visited the old man to let him know that his company was not his own any more. After that, Alessandro had cared only about the harsh lesson they'd learned at the hands of a selfish, corrupt, rich Englishman.

He took out his phone and pressed the button to lift the signal blocker. The technology had been installed as part of the electronic security system designed by Thiakos Securities, one of the best in the business.

'Call her,' he said, with a careless shrug.

Before he'd finished speaking Amelia had her phone pressed to her ear.

Alessandro poured himself a glass of wine as she turned her back on him.

It was no great loss to let her speak to her sister—if anything it would hopefully loosen her tongue enough to talk. *Then* he would uncover just what it was she had sabotaged. Of course, the most logical target would have been the Aurora project. But it could have been anything she'd worked on in the last two years. And that was a lot of projects. Because she'd been so *good* at her job.

He watched a drip of condensation glide from the lip of the water jug and down over the shoulder and remembered chasing a bead of her sweat with his tongue, her cries in his ears and her skin hot and flushed beneath him. It had fallen into the wide valley between her breasts but he'd became distracted by a taut rosy nipple. He'd palmed both breasts as he thrust deeper into her, licking up the salt from her skin and—

The slam of her phone against the table yanked his attention back to the present, his gaze clashing with her mute anger. He pulled at the collar of his shirt and rolled his shoulders.

'No answer?'

She simply glared at him and, for the first time since Gianni had called him the night before, he almost laughed. Here they were, dealing with the highest stakes possible, and she was playing a child's game of silence.

Sighing in frustration, he dialled Gianni's number and listened as a recorded message informed him that the number he was trying to reach was unavailable. Irritation mixed with a touch of concern, he called again even knowing it wouldn't produce a different outcome. Frowning, he tried to reach the captain of Gianni's yacht.

A brief conversation revealed that Gianni and Amelia's sister had just been let off the ship.

'Satisfied?' he asked, hanging up the phone, knowing Amelia had followed the conversation in Italian.

The swift, single shake of her head was expected. If he were in her shoes, he doubted he would have been either. He brought up the search engine on his mobile and searched for #TheHotRossi. The hashtag the press had given Gianni usually made him smile, but not today.

Choosing the images tab, he scrolled through pictures of his sharp-cheekboned, chiselled-jawed cousin and found what he was looking for. A model with her thumbs hooked—supposedly seductively—in the waistband of her bikini had failed to realise that the photographer's gaze had shifted over her shoulder to the couple at the end of a jetty. Gianni's yacht was backing away from St Lovells, the small Caribbean private island owned by Alessandro's cousin, but it was the couple that drew the eye. Long blonde hair had been caught by the wind, a face similar to Amelia's, but different too, staring up at Gianni with so much intensity the photograph felt intrusive.

Unsure what to make of it, he nevertheless slid the phone back across the table to Amelia.

'It was time-stamped less than an hour ago.'

Amelia scrutinised the picture. 'I want to talk to her.'

'I'm sure you do. I've a few things I'd like to say to her myself.'

'You will stay away from her, you beast.'

Alessandro laughed. 'Beast?' he demanded, but it was

his eyes that taunted her, reminding her that it wasn't what she'd called him in Hong Kong.

Amelia looked away, needing to hide her illogical reaction. This constant push and pull between them was making her nauseous. Wasn't it why she'd been forced to lie to her sister and tell Issy that she had proof of their corruption? She'd just wanted it all over. The vengeance, the lies, the pretence. Fighting Alessandro, fighting herself. It had been so exhausting and so *hard*.

'You needn't worry about your sister. Gianni is, despite popular opinion, a gentleman.'

'Yes,' she said. 'By all accounts, he's most definitely the nicer of the two of you.'

Alessandro glared at her from across the table. She'd meant what she said though. From all of Issy's research it was clear that, where Alessandro ran cold, Gianni ran a passionate hot, full of charm he used as indiscriminately as he did freely. And a huge part of all of Amelia's plans had been to ensure that her sister would be safe no matter what.

It had always been Alessandro that was the wild card.

She poured herself a glass of water, hastily making and discarding various plans and options. She didn't feel physically threatened in the slightest and she didn't think for one minute that Alessandro would lay a finger on her.

But he had. In Hong Kong. There, he'd touched, teased, delved with those fingers, bringing her to orgasm again and again and—

She thumped the empty glass of water she'd consumed in one go down on the table. Alessandro watched her with steady eyes as she refilled it, not caring that she looked rattled, she was thirsty and she would drink all the water she needed.

She squared her shoulders, placed her hands in her lap and composed herself. She'd always known that discovery was a possibility. She'd rehearsed this moment over and over in her mind—what she'd say, how she'd answer whatever questions she could imagine him asking. In some ways it was a relief to finally be here and get it over with. 'Interrogate away, Mr Rossi,' she said with a dismissive sweep of her hand.

'What did you do?' His words were clipped, his tone uncompromising.

'You might have to be a little more specific than that, Mr Rossi,' she said, leaning back in her chair, unconsciously trying to put just a little more distance between them. As if he'd noticed, he leaned forward, erasing her momentary reprieve.

'You have done something to damage Rossi Industries.'

She held his gaze, trying to ignore the muscle flaring at his jaw like a warning beacon.

'Well?'

'I believe that was a statement, not a question,' she replied. The flash of anger, a gold lightning strike, was expected but the rumbling thunder of disdain cut her to the quick. Gritting her teeth, she stared at a point just below his chin. The tie of his knot was slightly skewed, as if he'd pulled at it and then tried to twist it back into place.

'According to your sister, you claim to have found proof of corruption.'

Her adrenaline spiked, sending a scattering of stings to nerve endings all over her body.

'But as we both know that is simply neither true nor possible, so there is only one logical conclusion. You have lied; to your sister—maybe even to yourself. An act that is desperate and dangerous and I don't like either of those things. So I ask again, *Amelia*. What. Did. You. Do?'

Stubborn and mutinous, Amelia refused to answer his question. Refused to meet his eye. Refused to engage. But she couldn't deny that everything he said was true. She had lied to her sister, to herself. She *was* desperate and it *had* been dangerous. But if she told him now then it would all have been for nothing.

'You are playing a very dangerous game.'

And finally, she couldn't hold it back any more. 'With rules *you* wrote, ten years ago,' she accused, the words dripping with bitterness and resentment.

'Frankly, Ms Seymore, I don't care. I don't care what you think happened ten years ago, what you think your father did or did not deserve, or what happened to him or you after that.'

Outrage lashed at her soul, in a silent cry of pure injustice. It howled and raged in her chest, wanting out, wanting to cause as much hurt as had been done to her and her sister.

'What I care about is the nearly hundred thousand employees in Rossi Industries and the countless associated businesses that would be negatively impacted by your temper tantrum.'

She gasped. 'Temper—'

'And honestly? It is inconceivable that you and your sister are playing a petty game of revenge for a man who was more corrupt than anyone I know. And given the number of billionaires, businessmen and politicians, that's really saying something.'

He was breathing hard, but not as hard as Amelia. The blood had drained from her face, leaving her worryingly pale, but the sheer force of his anger was still riding him hard. So he missed the genuine disbelief and confusion shadowing her gaze before it was shuttered.

No, all he saw was misplaced outrage and indignation. How dared she? The little fool had put so much at risk he was incandescent with anger.

'You can spare me your lies, Alessandro, there's no gallery here to play to.'

'Lies? *You* talk to *me* of lies?' he accused as he saw his barb hitting home.

'I did what I had to,' Amelia replied, unable this time to meet his gaze.

'With no thought to the consequence of your actions?'

'Why should I have? What more can you do to me? You've already taken *everything*.'

Refusing to let her words needle into his conscience, he pressed on.

'Amelia—I wasn't speaking of you. The consequences of any kind of sabotage will put hundreds if not thousands of jobs on the line, the ramifications for their families could be devastating. Didn't you think of them?'

'No!' she cried, the first real sense of emotion breaking through the façade that she had held in place for two years. 'No. I didn't. I was thinking of my father, who you *broke*. I was thinking of the way he lost not only his business, but his house and his friends and his social standing. It destroyed him.'

He hardened himself against the emotion bringing tears to her eyes that she was too proud to shed. Her loyalty, passion, her love for her father might have been alien emotions to him, but even he would have to have been a rock not to be moved by her. He looked away, out to the edge of the pool and beyond to the piece of land that Thomas Seymore had sold them.

Land that was so unstable it would never have supported the foundations needed for any kind of housing or development. Thomas Seymore's deception had set them back years and thousands of euros and had been a both brutal and harsh lesson. They had nearly broken themselves, working every single hour they could to buy, fix and flip a much cheaper property nearly a hundred miles away from where he now sat with Amelia. He and Gianni had clawed their way, property by property, deal by deal to the point where they had been able to finally mount a hostile takeover of Seymore's own business.

'I remember it, you know. The day you came to our house.'

Alessandro turned his gaze back to Amelia. But there was no indignation in her tone this time, it wasn't strong with conviction. It was the voice of a daughter who had heard things said about her father that she shouldn't have.

'I remember what you said to him.'

The single thread of shame woven into that whole encounter began to unravel deep within him. Alessandro hadn't taken pleasure from that day—in fact it had been precisely that point that had brought him back from the edge of a cliff he'd been far too close to. In that moment, he'd never been more like his own father and Alessandro had sworn never to be that man again.

'Don't,' he said, before she could repeat the words he and his cousin had said that day.

The look she gave him shamed him anew.

'You might not have made him drink, but you put the bottle in his hand. You might not have put him in the ground, but you dug that hole, Alessandro. You and Gianni.'

Angry at the truth of her words, at the events that he had unknowingly started, Alessandro lashed out.

'Amelia, you might be a lot of things, but you're not stupid. Didn't you ever wonder why it was so easy for two twenty-year-olds to take over your father's business? Did you ever think that we shouldn't have been able to do it?'

'Why should I?' she demanded with the blind loyalty of a child. 'He was my father!'

Perhaps it was the differences in their upbringing. Perhaps he might have been the same had he had a father with even an ounce of love in him. But he hadn't, so he couldn't conceive of her naivety. He shook his head, intensely disliking that he was going to have to destroy Thomas Seymore all over again.

'You might not have the proof of *our* corruption,' he said to her, pushing back to stand. 'But you should know that I kept everything about our dealings with your father.'

He walked over to the corner of the living room and retrieved an old faded brown folder from a side cabinet. He returned and placed it in front of her on the table.

She looked up at him, her eyes betraying the first glimpse of doubt he'd seen in her. His conscience told him not to do this. But it was already done.

'Proof of corruption indeed,' he said, looking out to the wildflower meadow. 'How fitting.'

And he left, knowing that she would read the contents of that folder. She wouldn't be able not to. As the sun began to fall, he paced around the large swimming pool, his gaze returning far too often to the female form bent over the table, turning page after page. With her experience at his company, he knew she would easily interpret the sale documents, evaluations, the different surveys. He'd even left the paperwork for the loan in there—he didn't care if she read that. He had no shame about how desperate they had been to agree to the punishing repayment rate, nor how hard they'd worked to pay it back, seeing it only as proof of how far they had come. Their plans, their hopes and dreams...*everything* was in that folder.

He heard the scrape of her chair against the floor and turned. She pinned him with such a look his heart lurched. Or at least he thought it had. Then, as the papers in Amelia's hands scattered, he realised it was her—and he was running before she hit the floor.

CHAPTER FIVE

HER HEART HURT. That was the first thing she noticed. Not the dull pain in her head that kept her eyes closed, or the hot agony in her shoulder that forced her onto her side. It was the ache radiating out from her heart and soul, confusing her momentarily until she remembered.

She turned to bury her face in a pillow so plush and silky soft she wanted to climb into it. A breath left her lips in a shudder and she curled in on herself like a child. But that only made her think of her father. The father she had looked up to, even as he sank deeper and deeper and further and further into a bottle. Even as he ignored his daughters' pleas and his wife's desperation—a wife who would then choose to follow him into a drug-induced oblivion after his death.

In the aftermath of their neglect, Amelia had stepped in to pick up the pieces. To make sure that Issy had a meal to eat after school, did her homework on time. That clothes were washed and bills were paid. She'd had to wrestle money for food from their mother before she could spend it on whatever drug she could find to fill the hole left by her husband's death. And in those horrible early years it had only been the idea of retribution against the Rossis that had kept her and Issy going. It had been her suggestion—their plan of vengeance—and they had clung to it like a lifeline. But she couldn't hide from the truth any more. Page after page in that horrible file had peeled back the scales from her eyes and she had seen. Seen more than she'd ever wanted to.

It had *never* crossed her mind that her father had been corrupt. Never. By the time Thomas Seymore lost his company she had been only fifteen years old. She'd been to his office only twice, his talk of work so boring when her life was full of the exclusive private school she and Issy had attended, piano lessons, ballet, the occasional horse-riding lesson. Until it had been snatched away from her, she had lived a life of blissful ignorance, never truly understanding the depth of her privilege. And when it had been snatched away? She'd known exactly who had been responsible. The two men who had visited with her father that Sunday afternoon.

Just like every week, Issy had prepared the vegetables while she'd made the Yorkshire pudding. The small glass of wine they'd been allowed with the meal had tasted rich and decadent and naughty. And when it had been interrupted, Amelia and Issy had listened at the doorway to their father's office, giggling at the handsome Italian men meeting so importantly with their father. Until the conversation had become harsh and angry.

You are done, old man. Finished. You will never work in this industry again. And if you even think to try, we will make sure that you will regret it.

Everything you thought you had—it's ours now and there is not a thing you can do about it. Any pathetic attempt to crawl back into this industry will be met with swift and significant reprisal. Know that and choose not to test us.

When they had left, Thomas Seymore had looked up

to find the eyes of his wife and children on him, having heard the entire exchange. For a man whose pride and standing was everything, the two youths Alessandro and Gianni had been had struck their mark.

Only now, lying there cocooned in luxury once again, the words took on a different meaning—and rather than sheer hatred towards Alessandro and Gianni, Amelia now tossed and turned in the wake their accusations and taunts left behind them. Instead of arrogance and venomous poison, she heard the quake of injustice. Her father had conned them into buying land he knew they'd never be able to build on. He'd not simply seen them as soft targets, he'd purposefully set out to bribe an official to make it happen. How many other times had he done something like that? How many other people had he scammed and conned?

And... *Oh, God. Firstview. The Aurora project. Issy!*

A sob rose to her lips and she tried to cover her mouth with her hand.

'Amelia...'

Her sob turned into a cry of alarm. She hadn't realised she wasn't alone and the thought that Alessandro had witnessed her pain made her feel vulnerable and exposed in a way she'd never experienced before.

'I'm sorry... It's okay, *you're* okay,' Alessandro said, his tone unusually gentle and careful.

She inhaled a shaky breath and turned to find him sitting in a chair in the corner of a room she didn't recognise. He looked...terrible. His shirt was undone at the collar, sleeves rolled back and there wasn't an inch of clothing that wasn't creased or crumpled in some way. The stubble she remembered had morphed into something much more substantial—the beard lending him even more of a forbidding appearance.

'Where am I?' she asked, trying to sit up. Hand out in a gesture for her to stop, he took a breath—nearly as shaken as her own.

'In my home.'

'Not the pool house?'

He shook his head once.

Taking a quick assessment, she realised she was no longer in the business suit she'd worn before. She shot him a look full of accusation and the hand he'd held out shot up in surrender.

'Not me,' he said simply.

'Then who?' she growled.

'My doctor.'

She frowned. She remembered standing from the table, the shock loosening her fingers on the file, the paper dropping and a look of alarm so stark in his eyes that she felt genuinely scared but she didn't know what for and then…

'I fainted,' she remembered. 'You called a doctor?'

'Of course,' he replied, outraged by her surprise—as if she'd accused him of breaking the Geneva Convention. She swallowed, her throat painfully dry. Alessandro must have noticed as he stood from the chair and brought her a glass of water. She had to crane her neck to look up at him, and he stared at a spot beside her on the bed as if not wanting to make eye contact. 'Can you…?'

She nodded, levering herself up against the headboard. She took the glass from his hands, careful not to make contact. She didn't know if that might send her back into a faint.

A knock on the door drew her attention to a little old man with deeply tanned skin and a shock of white hair.

'Ahh, you are awake. Marvellous,' he pronounced, as if she knew exactly who he was and why he would think it was marvellous. 'Alessandro, if you would?' The old man gestured for him to leave and Amelia held her breath. This was her chance! She needed to get out of here.

Once Alessandro left, she took a breath and turned to the old man. 'I've been kidnapped. I'm being held against my will,' she whispered urgently.

'I know, dear,' he said, sitting on the bed beside her, picking up her hand and patting it gently. 'Alessandro explained everything.'

'Wait, what?' she asked, confused by a response that was entirely the opposite of what she'd been expecting.

'He really is quite lovely, when you get to know him.'

'Alessandro? Lovely?' she asked, truly bewildered.

'Yes, well. You know, aside from...*that*,' the old man said, apparently reluctant to use the word kidnap. 'Now. I need to talk to you about some tests we would like to run to find out why you might have fainted.'

Alessandro sat in the early morning sun, with his head in his hands and his mind completely blank. Instead of the dawn chorus of birds, or the chatter of cicadas, a high-pitched buzz rang in his ears. He'd been awake for nearly forty-eight hours now, having only really caught the odd hour or so the night before as he sat vigil by Amelia's beside. He hadn't reached her in time. She'd hit the floor with an alarming thud, the sound of which would haunt him for the rest of his life.

He'd called Dr Moretti before moving her and only when the man had agreed to come straight away had he allowed himself to breathe. He'd picked her up and carried her straight to this room. Moretti had arrived in under twenty minutes—but the damage had been done.

Alessandro had been plunged right back into a nightmare from his childhood and the horror of waiting for the doctor to come for his mother, lying bruised, bloodied and broken on her bed. His father's gaze had been full of anger, resentment and indignation, but the whites of his eyes had held only fear. Fear that he'd finally gone too far.

A cold sweat and tremors had racked his body so much so that Moretti had tried to assess him first, but Alessandro had thrown him off in favour of Amelia. Only when the man had started making his assessment had Alessandro begun to calm down.

For a while at least.

Because then had come the questions—about her medical history, any allergies, intolerances, how long since she'd last eaten, was she on any medication. Thankfully he had access to her medical file on his work computer and he'd shared it with Moretti. Having read it, the doctor had declared that, as there was no immediate life-threatening urgency, any further diagnosis could wait until she woke.

Alessandro had been tempted to argue but his mouth had been quicker than his brain. 'What tests?'

'Oh, the usual. FBC, LFT, U and E, glucose, HCG.'

The first he'd recognised from reruns of medical dramas he'd catch late night on TV when he couldn't sleep. But HCG?

'Yes. HCG levels will let us know if she's pregnant,' Moretti had blithely declared.

And that was when Alessandro's mind had gone blank

and the doctor had put two and two together much quicker than he and Amelia might have.

It wasn't possible. They had used protection. Every. Single. Time.

Because Alessandro would never have taken such a risk. Never. Alessandro had made a promise to his father—his direct bloodline would end with him. And he'd meant it. He had absolutely no intention of forcing such a heritage on any other poor bastard. What Gianni chose to do was on him. But Alessandro? No, he had been clear about this since the very night that Amelia's collapse had reminded him of; he would never have a child.

He scoffed, laughing bitterly at himself. He'd always thought of it as his decision, as if his will alone were enough to make it so. Now he could see that the sheer arrogance of such a thought was shockingly naïve and ignorant. Because if she *was* pregnant, if there *was* a baby, Alessandro knew that whatever happened from here on out was up to her.

A woman who had hidden her true identity, snuck into Rossi Industries like a spy, determined to prove them corrupt, and, when that hadn't happened, had sabotaged them. And from the little he did know about Amelia? She was excellent. Quick, intelligent, focused, determined. Without a shadow of a doubt, if she had intended destruction, it was assured. And he still had absolutely no clue what she'd done. He had a team of people searching through everything she'd touched, but that could take too long.

He shook his head. Was that really important? They needed to deal with one thing at a time. And first—

Dr Moretti came out into the small courtyard, eyes

bright as always. 'It is a beautiful day,' he announced unnecessarily.

Alessandro resisted the urge to growl. The old man had always been kind. Had always been there when his mother or Gianni's mother had needed him, the mean, vicious streak shared by the two Vizzini brothers. An image formed in his mind of the two bitter old men, slowly drinking their vineyard into insignificance. The pure glee in his father's eyes that his direct bloodline might continue made his throat thick with acrid bile.

'Come sta?'

'Tired, thirsty, a little confused, but she's better than you from the look of things,' the doctor replied in quick-fire Italian. 'She's asking for you.'

Alessandro swallowed. His heart began to race, his pulse pounding in his ears.

'Take a breath, Alessandro, or *you'll* faint this time.'

He nodded and drew quick and deep, holding it there for a few seconds before controlling the release. And then readied himself for whatever was to come. Even if that meant he was tied for the rest of his life to a woman he could never trust and who could probably never trust him.

Amelia shook her head back and forth. This couldn't be happening.

'I'm on the pill,' she said, looking up at the doctor.

'And I used a condom,' Alessandro said, also staring at the poor man as if delivering the news of Amelia's pregnancy made it his fault.

'I had a period,' Amelia said, her lips numb with shock. 'I didn't... Oh, God, I've been taking the pill all this time...' The sudden and shocking fear that she might have somehow already hurt the little bundle of cells trying desperately to grow into a tiny human was horrible.

'Please...' Dr Moretti said in a way that clearly requested some calm from the other two adults in the room. 'Firstly, there is no evidence to suggest that continuing to take the hormonal contraception harms a pregnancy. Secondly, no contraception is one hundred per cent assured. It seems this is an instance of...' He looked between Amelia and Alessandro as if trying to gauge the appropriate word, and decided it didn't need clarifying. 'It is possible that, for some women, periods continue throughout the entire pregnancy. You will want to monitor this with your own doctor when you get home.'

Home. A flat she shared with her sister. A sister still hell-bent on vengeance against her baby's father and his cousin. Oh, God, Rossi Industries. Firstview. She pressed her fingers to her mouth, trying to keep the swell of nausea down. It was all too much.

'Water biscuits. My wife swore by them through all four of her pregnancies.'

She glanced up at the doctor and then to Alessandro, who looked as pale and shocked as she felt.

Moretti, realising that there was clearly much to be discussed, announced that he would let himself out and left the two of them alone in a room that suddenly felt stifling. She needed air. She decided that she wanted to get up at exactly the time that Alessandro collapsed back into the chair she had woken to find him in that morning, only a few hours ago when the world had been completely different.

When she wasn't carrying her enemy's baby. Only, wasn't *she* the enemy?

She bit back a groan. It was all so confusing. She lifted

the sheet back and swung her legs out, her feet hitting the cold floor with a slap, yanking Alessandro's attention back to her. Or more specifically her legs. Slashes of red appeared across cheekbones that could cut glass, and she looked away, clenching her teeth against the shocking wave of responding arousal she felt at the sheer *heat* in his eyes.

She might have been able to blame a lot of what had happened in the past six weeks on the hormones, she now realised, but not what had initially driven her into the arms of this enigmatic, powerful and, most definitely, dangerous Italian.

By the time she looked back up, Alessandro had found something intensely interesting out of the window to look at.

'Where are you going?' he asked, his voice thick and rough.

'I'd like some air,' she replied, fighting another wave of nausea that had more to do with guilt than her pregnancy.

The large Alessandro-sized T-shirt hung from her small frame, beneath which was—thankfully—her underwear. The hemline hit her high on her thigh but she decided that modesty and propriety were the least of her and Alessandro's problems.

She stood, testing her strength, and was happy to find that she wasn't as weak as she'd feared. She got to the door of the room, the burning touch of Alessandro's gaze on her the entire time, and realised she didn't know where to go.

'A little help?' she asked, ruefully.

A hand appeared at her elbow and she jerked away from it. 'Not that kind of help. How do I get out of here?' She stood aside to let him pass and lead the way. Beams of sunlight flooded the hallway and she realised she didn't know what time it was.

'How long was I out?'

'The entire night,' Alessandro replied.

She frowned. 'And you?'

'I stayed with you.'

Instinctively she reached out to take his wrist, pulling him round and dropping his hand the moment he looked at where they touched—as if he wasn't sure whether to push her away or hold on.

'Have you slept at all in the last two days?'

He laughed, a single punch of bitterness and incredulity. 'That matters to you?'

Yes, it did, she was surprised to find. Without the line her vendetta had drawn between them, the feelings she'd tried to deny were creeping in. But, clearly, he wouldn't have believed her if she'd admitted as much. Instead, she bit her lip to prevent any further stupidity from escaping and when he turned back to lead her out of the house, she followed in silence.

Step by step, very quickly, Amelia was realising just how dire her situation truly was. As someone whose job was to make assessments, identify problems and present solutions in order to achieve the greatest success, she was under no illusions about her current predicament.

She had nothing—no savings, no inheritance, no security. After their father had passed, they had finally been able to declare bankruptcy, Thomas Seymore's pride refusing to countenance such a necessary but drastic move while alive. Nine years on, Amelia lived in a one-bedroom flat with her sister in South East London. The majority of her—admittedly impressive—salary from Rossi Industries went to pay for her mother's stay at the rehab centre in South America from her very first pay cheque. What wasn't eaten up by rent had gone into the props Issy had needed to grab the attention of the notoriously extravagant Gianni Rossi. Issy had contributed what she could from her salary as an auxiliary nurse at the children's hospital, when she wasn't spending hours online hunting down every single little bit of information she could get on the Rossi cousins. *Everything* the two girls had done had been streamlined to ensure that as much time and finances as possible could be poured into a vendetta she had instigated. And it had all been for nothing.

Because Alessandro and Gianni had done nothing wrong. There had never been any corruption on their parts. They were completely innocent and she had sabotaged the business owned by the soon-to-be father of her child.

As Alessandro opened a door, she rushed out into the courtyard taking huge gulps of much-needed fresh air. Because if their unborn child were going to have any hopes at a better life than either of its parents, then she would need Alessandro Rossi's help. And she had absolutely no idea if he would give it to her.

Alessandro watched Amelia, hands braced against her thighs, bent at the waist, taking giant breaths of the cool morning air. Gone was the perfectly poised controlled employee who had impressed, not just her manager, his board, but himself with her quick, smart, intelligent and controlled approach to the projects. Gone, too, was the passionate, sensual woman with a desire that eclipsed common sense in a way that was only matched by his own.

But all he could think, all he could hear in his head

on a loop, was *you're pregnant*. He felt strangely numb, recognising dimly that the shock of it had robbed him of any sense. He was going to be a father.

But the images that word threw at him were not the kind of loving, doting parent that inspired the kind of loyalty that had driven Amelia to attempt revenge. They were the kind that brought him out in a cold sweat.

He hated that in front of him was a woman in quite obvious emotional turmoil and all he could feel was panic. He looked away as Amelia pulled herself up straight and felt her gaze on him, even though he wished for the world to be anywhere but here in that moment.

'I can't…imagine what you must think of me.'

'I'm trying very hard not to form an opinion right now, because I don't have all the facts and I don't like jumping to conclusions,' he announced while his molars groaned under the intense pressure of his tightened jaw. It wasn't a lie; he was very close to an edge she had driven him to.

'This… I…' She shook her head, words coming hard for both of them, clearly. She took a deep breath, as if she knew that this was important. To him, to her, he didn't know any more, but he couldn't help but admire the strength she drew on to stand before him under the weight of his scrutiny—a scrutiny that had buckled many a lesser person.

'This wasn't part of the plan. Sleeping with you, or the baby.'

His heart pounded in his chest. Her declaration tapped into a question he'd struggled with from the very first moment Gianni had called him. Did he believe her? He studied her, head held high, back straight, shoulders drawn down. She looked like a soldier facing a firing squad, who had spoken her final words. She met and held his gaze, the pale green orbs so open it was as if she'd flung back the shutters and was asking him to look deep within her. Instead, he looked away and missed the slash of hurt that nearly rocked her on her feet.

'It's yours.'

Cristo. That he hadn't even considered any other possibility showed just how powerful a spell she had cast on him. He nodded to convey his understanding but still couldn't look at her. He went to pull at his collar, to relieve the tightness around his throat, only to find that it was already open. Intensely disliking that she might have caught the sign of his discomfort, he moved his hand to the back of his neck, his fingers brushing against the cold sweat that was gathering there with alarming frequency whenever Amelia was near.

Think it through. Be rational, he ordered himself. He had used a condom and even if she had lied about being on contraception, the chances were slim that pregnancy could have been a secured outcome. And after two years at his company, he might not know her—the *real* her— but she couldn't hide the way she thought. He'd seen it in the choices she made, how she approached and assessed a project, the solutions she offered to problems. And at the very least he knew that she would never have created a plan around a possible pregnancy resulting from one single night with him, that couldn't have been guaranteed in itself.

'So Hong Kong was...' he asked, wanting to know.

She shook her head and looked away, a blush rising to her cheeks and the gentle shrug of her shoulder, the fine bones there marked by his oversized T-shirt. It appeared she was as unable to explain that night as he was.

When she looked back at him, she was squinting up

at him, the early morning Tuscan sun turning her brown hair into burnished gold, her pale skin into a sunburst as if even the morning were conspiring against him.

'What now?' she asked.

That was a very good question.

CHAPTER SIX

AMELIA FOUND THE KITCHEN. It was bigger than her flat in Brockley and it made her heart thud. The countertops looked like—and most probably were—marble. She and Issy had money growing up. *Before.* But nothing like this. This was…unfathomable.

She ran her fingers across the cool slabs of white, shot through with grey. It would have looked clinical had it not been for the deep brown wooden floorboards and the copper fixtures. There was a large twenty-seater table between the counter and the floor-to-ceiling windows that wrapped around the entire ground floor of the villa's main building. Having worked out the coffee machine and made herself a decaffeinated espresso, she had been too uncomfortable to sit at the table. The thought of Alessandro sitting here to eat, all by himself, it just… it had made her heart ache in a way she tried to ignore.

He had retired to finally get some sleep, but the warning he'd left her with still sounded in her ears.

Do not think of trying to leave, Amelia.

Oh, she wanted to. She wanted to run. Wished she could click her fingers and be back in Brockley with her sister. Which had just made her worry about Issy. What was she doing now? Was she with Gianni? Was she okay?

Feeling a little unbalanced, she made her way to the sunken seating area facing a fireplace—the mixture of modern and new creating a sense of old comfort that was so lovely she couldn't help but sink into the lush leather. Leaning back, she felt something poke into her hip. Turning, she saw her handbag, and inside she found her phone.

It had signal! Alessandro must have forgotten to turn the signal jammer back on. Without thinking, her fingers had hit call on Issy's number. And then she hung up before it could connect.

What would she tell her sister about her pregnancy? How would she explain herself? How could she ever apologise enough for lying to her and setting them on a path of revenge that was so wholly misdirected?

The questions piled up one after the other, making her head swim. It was her fault they were in this mess, but she couldn't afford to wallow in self-pity. She needed to know if Issy was okay, so she hit the call button again. Her heart dropped when an automated response told her the phone was not in use. Unease swept through her, but she reminded herself that Alessandro and Gianni were not the monsters they had thought they were. And while Issy was impulsive and chaotic in the most adorable way, there was only so much trouble she could get herself into.

No. At this point, Amelia really needed to think about the trouble *she* was in. But trouble felt like the wrong word. Because she couldn't use that word and think of the child growing within her.

It had surprised her, really. It had been like the swell of a wave, starting slowly at first but growing larger and larger until it became an unstoppable feeling, gathering momentum and washing aside everything in its path. This immoveable force had whispered into her heart and soul and she had felt utterly and irrevocably changed by it.

She wanted this baby.

It was a knowing, settling deep into her very being—standing out in stark contrast to Alessandro's feelings.

Because she hadn't missed the way he had looked at her. Hadn't missed the accusation in his gaze, or the sense of something deeper, swelling beneath it all like a monster from the deep. He didn't want this, but for some reason she was sure that it had nothing to do with her attempts to sabotage Rossi Industries. And an ache began to form in her chest. She rubbed at her sternum, wondering whether the decaf coffee was to blame, but really she knew. She knew that it was because of what she had seen in Alessandro's gaze. Fear and alarm.

And on some level, she could understand. A child was a huge responsibility. One that would not only change her life but connect her to Alessandro for ever. It would be all consuming with, or without, his help and it would change the very essence of who she was.

But it could also be a beautiful thing, her heart whispered. One she wanted so much she could scarcely bear to hope for it. A child that she would love and never reject, never subjugate to her own needs. A child that would have so much more of a chance than she and Issy ever had.

Guilt swirled heavily in her stomach. Issy had lost so much, sacrificed so much for a vendetta that she had instigated. Had her mother known? That their father had been corrupt? That he had sold land knowing it wasn't fit for development? That he had conned people—people who had put everything they had into their plans? People like Alessandro and Gianni. So much had been lost to her father's greed. Who would she and Issy have become had they not spent ten years on this path of vengeance? Where would they be now?

Free.

The thought came unbidden to her mind and for such a soft word it hit her with the force of a truck, rocking her to her core.

Standing in the doorway, he saw her sway. The phone he'd seen her use to make a call—probably to her sister—hung listlessly from her fingers. He fought against every instinct he had to go to her. Earlier that morning, he might have. But he'd managed at least four hours' sleep and now he was thinking more clearly.

This woman had committed an act of sabotage against his business. Her motivation mattered little. She had done something to Rossi Industries and before he could even think about her pregnancy, he needed to know what she'd done. Only once that was resolved, could they talk about…

His gaze landed on her stomach, knowing that there would not be any signs of the baby she carried for at least another three months. Instead of letting his thoughts linger there, he took in the rest of her. She was dressed in the clothes he'd put out for her before he'd retreated to his room. Despite the way she had rolled the waistband of the trousers, they still hung a little low on her hips.

He probably could have raided Gianni's compound, fairly sure that there would be some women's clothing left behind by one of his lovers, but the thought of dressing Amelia in another woman's clothes made him faintly nauseous. Instead, he'd found a shirt from years ago, before he'd filled out into the broad shoulders he was now used to. Still large on her, she'd twisted the edges of the shirt into a knot and somehow looked carelessly fashionable.

Desirable.

No. In his mind a hand slashed through his thoughts, sending them scattering. Enough. Ever since the phone call from Gianni, he had been on the back foot. With so much at stake, he needed to take control of the situation.

'Amelia,' he said, calling her attention to him. When she came out of her thoughts, her gaze cleared enough to look at where he was gesturing to the table. She returned her phone to her bag and left it on the sofa, slowly making her way to a table she eyed with discomfort.

'Would you prefer to talk elsewhere?' he asked, not out of consideration for her feelings, he told himself, but more for curiosity.

'What, for Interrogation Take Two?' she asked, a forced lightness to her tone attempting to take the sting out of her words as she sat on the opposite side of the table. He eyed her coffee cup with a suspicion that must have been obvious because she defensively explained that it was decaf.

He sat down and rolled his shoulders, trying not to pull at the collar of the shirt he had dressed in. Earlier it had made him feel in control, but now that Amelia was dressed more casually, it felt almost puritanical and obvious. As if he were trying too hard to maintain a boundary between them that had already been obliterated.

'Obviously the...' baby '...*pregnancy* changes a lot. But I need to know what you did,' he said.

Her eyes flared, guilty slashes painting the paleness of her cheeks a glowing red, and his stomach dropped.

'It's the Aurora project,' she confessed. 'I'm sorry, if I'd known—'

'Just that? Or are there any other projects that are at risk?' he interrupted, his thoughts scrambling to damage limitation. The instinct to call his CFO was riding him hard, but he didn't know if there was more.

'No. Just Aurora.'

He nodded once. 'Is it salvageable?' he asked, a buzz ringing in his ears. It had been a project he'd spent years on. One that would be visible from his father and uncle's vineyard, it was meant to be not only Rossi Industries' crowning glory, but the final twist of the knife in his father and uncle's back.

She bit her lip. Neither lush nor pouty, her mouth shouldn't have been cause for any kind of fascination— but still he noticed the way the top lip line was more straight than curved, the bottom lip marginally fuller than its partner, exposed by the straight white teeth pinning and blooming the soft pink flesh—

Dio mio, he needed to get a grip.

'Have the contracts been signed?' she asked, shoving him back into the conversation at hand.

Before he'd caught the few hours of sleep he'd needed, he'd managed to get a message out to his staff to stop any paperwork going through at all on any project. It had caused absolute chaos, but clearly it had been worth it.

'Have they?' she asked in the face of his silence.

He was tempted to let her stew, but that seemed almost petty now.

'No.'

She breathed a huge sigh of relief, her head falling into her hands, before she swept the hair back from her face and he caught a glimpse of the woman he had worked beside for two years.

She nodded as if to herself. 'It's Firstview. They don't have the capability to see the project through.'

'We would have picked that up,' he said, dismissing her statement.

'I made sure you didn't.'

He scoffed.

She raised an eyebrow and he got worried.

'How?' he demanded.

'They hid it well enough, but I knew what to look for and I erased or covered the things they hadn't managed to hide.'

'You falsified documents?'

'Yes.'

He shook his head in disbelief. They would never have found it. She could have got away with it, and the damage to the Aurora project—the knock-on effect for not only that project's contracts, but their finance repayments, the partnerships, their reputation—it could have bankrupted them. He struggled to fight back the wave of poisonous anger.

'Does anyone else in the company know? Do you have anyone else in the company working with you?'

'No and no,' she replied clearly and without hesitation.

'You did all this on your own?'

'Mostly,' she admitted with some reluctance.

'Your sister,' he realised. 'And what does she have to do with it?'

'She was to distract Gianni and keep him away until the Aurora project contracts are signed. We knew that were the two of you together it was likely you'd uncover something to bring our plan crashing down.' Amelia looked away, unable to meet his gaze.

'Issy doesn't know,' she confessed, guilt and shame eating at her. 'Anything she does…it's…she's innocent.'

Alessandro looked down on her, disgust pouring from him, and it was nothing she didn't deserve.

'Why?'

Amelia could have pretended to misunderstand his question. Remind him she was getting vengeance for her father, but that wasn't what he was asking. Alessandro valued loyalty above all else, it was clear from his work ethics and his relationship with Gianni. She had shamed herself by lying to her sister and involving her in the first place and Alessandro wanted to know why.

A jagged breath tore through her lungs. Could she admit to him that *he* was the reason? That ever since whatever madness had taken over them in Hong Kong, she'd not been able to sleep without dreaming of him? That she'd walk through The Ruby in London, her skin a hair's breadth from fire every single day because she might round a corner and see him? That her heart was constantly running too fast or too slow, depending on whether she had a meeting with him? That after ten years of wanting his destruction, all she wanted was his touch?

She was about to answer but he cut her off with a huff of bitterness. 'Would it even matter if you did answer? I have no idea which Amelia I'd get.'

A frown cracked through the mask she was trying to hastily adopt but his quick gaze snagged on it.

'The perfect employee? The traitor?' he clarified unnecessarily.

But he was wrong. Issy was the one who had adopted a persona, who had made herself into exactly what Gianni liked—half starving herself into a smaller physique, wearing heels for his desired height, dying her hair to his preferred blonde. But Amelia? She had been herself. She hadn't had to change at all because she'd enjoyed her work. Deep down, she could admit to herself that she'd even been thrilled by it. The cut and thrust of it. The success of projects was *her* success. The pleasure she took from impressing the powerful figures in Rossi Industries. No. Deep down, one of the most painful regrets would be that she would actually miss it when she was no longer there.

'The seducer?' Alessandro's question burst through her thoughts.

'No.' The denial rose to her lips before she could call it back. She deserved his scepticism, but their child deserved more. Their baby that was little more than a few cells held together by hope and possibility. A hope that seemed to pour from her soul in an endless stream. 'No,' she repeated, this time with more strength and meeting the storm in his eyes. 'I told you before, that was nothing to do with the plan.'

'And you expect me to believe that?' he all but spat.

'Frankly, I don't expect you to believe anything that comes out of my mouth ever again,' she admitted and seemed to have shocked him. 'But you have a situation that only *I* can resolve.'

Alessandro went deadly still, his eyes going from stormy to horrified before passing to shock, sending her headlong into an ocean of emotion that she hadn't expected.

'No!' she exclaimed, her hands flying to her abdomen as if to physically protect their child. 'No,' she said, pushing away from the table, the chair screeching against the floor painfully. She walked along the window line to the far end of the table, looking out at the meadow. She knew that there were many options out there and that this wasn't a decision that should be made lightly. But she also knew the truth of her heart, so she turned back to Alessandro and said, 'I'm sorry if I hadn't made that clear but I'm keeping the baby. Whether you're a part of their life or not, I am having this baby.'

He stared at her, his gaze again unfathomable, his silence absolute. It was as if he were giving her all the rope he could in the hope that she might somehow hang herself with it.

'I meant Aurora. I can save Aurora. I *want* to. Please let me help?'

Instead of relief she saw disbelief and it angered her, even though she knew it was deserved.

'I think I'll handle it from here on out,' he replied, his words dripping with disdain.

'Well, good luck with that,' she replied, sarcastically.

'What's that supposed to mean?' he demanded, leaning back into his chair, even though instinctively she knew that he wanted to close the distance, to crowd her, dominate, and Amelia bit back a curse. Why did that set her pulse racing? Why did that determined look flare between her legs and make her ache with want?

She blinked and the moment was gone. While her heart rate settled to something as close to normal as possible, she gathered herself to answer his question.

'You've only two options now. You give up the project or find another partner. Chapel Developments won't touch you—their CEO doesn't like to be considered second best. And yes, you could have another team at RI look through the project to see if they can find an alternative, but you don't have time. The quotes, the projections, the contracts are all time sensitive. With the cost of materials changing near daily, you've got a month, at most, and that's being generous. And you have no one that could vet an alternative partner and do the groundwork to build a relationship that could support the partnership in that time.'

'No one other than you,' he said, zeroing in on her point.

'I know this project inside out. I know the players... and I know the substitutes.'

'You have someone in mind.'

'I do.'

'Who?'

She stared at him as he waited for an answer. This was her only bargaining chip. This was her only chance to make a deal that would force him to listen to what she had to say. To what she *needed* to say. This was the one and only time she would get to set the tone for her future, for their child's future, and if she got it wrong, it would be disastrous for them all.

Dio, she was good. Glorious even. She had been made for the cut and thrust of the boardroom, of his world. Her mind was sharp, her intellect quick, and her confidence? He might not be quite sure about who she was half the time but no, that wasn't fake at all. He was turned on. Not by her body, but by *her* and he hated it. Hated how dangerous and traitorous this woman truly was.

'I will tell you, but I want something in exchange.'

He shouldn't have been surprised, but he was still somehow insulted and disappointed at the same time.

'How much?' He pushed the words through teeth he'd ground together.

She blinked as if shocked by his words and he begrudgingly had to admit, she was a very good actress. But she was an actress that was also going to be the mother of his child. The reminder cut through him like a knife.

'How much what?' she asked through pale lips.

'Money? How much money do you want?'

The shutters came down and for a moment he thought that he might have it wrong. She turned around and looked out at the meadow her father had sold him all those years ago. She probably didn't even know that it was that particular plot of land and perversely he wanted to keep that from her.

She looked away, her words spoken to him over her shoulder. 'I don't want money. I wanted a…détente.'

'You want to make peace, while holding back the fix to a problem *you* created?' he demanded, wondering at the brass balls on the woman he'd got pregnant.

'I wanted for us to try to start again without all this,' she said, weaving a hand back and forth between them before shrugging her slender shoulders. 'I wanted us to be able to have a conversation about what we're going to do about our child, without wanting to tear each other raw.' There was a helplessness in her eyes that he couldn't deny—fake or not, and he was leaning towards the latter. 'I wanted us to find a way forward that wasn't destroyed by the past, but I can see now that's impossible.'

Her breath caught, the old linen shirt she wore stretched across her chest, and he dragged his eyes away before he could be distracted by her again.

Our child.

Alessandro had done everything he could to honour the promise he'd made his father—he'd been so determined that his direct bloodline would end with him, that he'd never—not even once—allowed for any other possibility. He'd been happy with that. Welcomed it even.

But his child was growing within Amelia Seymore. A real child and deep within him something turned—years and years of determination and belief were twisting and morphing beneath the weight of something else. His child was here and no matter how he'd thought he'd feel in that moment, and he was feeling a lot, it *wasn't* horror. It *wasn't* anger, or disappointment. As scary as it was, it felt something like hope. The hope that maybe he could do better, be better, than his own father. That he could provide his child with more than he'd ever had, with a better life than he'd ever imagined for himself. And now that determination to end his bloodline seemed petty in comparison to the feeling of protectiveness pouring through him with the power of a tsunami.

He looked back to where Amelia stood, shoulders slumped in defeat, breath almost painfully slow in comparison to what it had been only moments ago.

'You want peace? You want to start again?'

Amelia turned, her eyes filled with such hope—hope that was worryingly close to the way she had looked up at him that night in Hong Kong, as if she were half afraid that he'd say no to their one night and half afraid that he'd say yes. Just as it had that night, her gaze had cleared and a truth had come pouring into her gaze.

'Yes.'

Could he do it? Start afresh with her?

He *had* to. She was carrying his child. Their child. And no, he would never trust her. That bond had been broken irrevocably. But that didn't mean they couldn't at the least be cordial. Whatever happened, he would ensure that his child grew up in a world nothing like his own childhood. He would do whatever it took.

'Who?' he demanded, forcing to push through the exchange, because his first goal was to make sure that Rossi Industries didn't fall because the mother of his child had sabotaged it.

'I don't think you're going to like it.'

'There's a lot that I don't like at the moment. This will be the least of it, I'd imagine.'

She had the grace to look away.

'Who?' he demanded again.

'Sofia Obeid.'

He pinched the bridge of his nose. 'Amelia,' he said, not knowing whether he was cursing her or begging her.

'I know what you think of her,' she said, her hands gesturing for patience or peace, he wasn't sure which. 'But hers is the only company with the capital to help see Aurora to fruition within the timeline and without incurring incredibly painful financial penalties.'

He glared up at her, frustration and intense irritation coursing through him. Sofia Obeid had a reputation for being incredibly difficult and impossible to work with. Not that RI would know as she had refused to take a meeting or even a phone call from the Rossi cousins before now.

'What makes you think you can get a meeting with her?'

'Because I can,' she replied simply.

He scowled as he took in the way the sun streamed in the window and slipped through the linen shirt to outline the subtle curves of the woman not only carrying his child, but who had clearly been sent to test him to his very limits.

'Please. I want a chance to fix this, but I also want a chance to start again,' she said, courage and something like hope shining in her eyes. 'A chance for our child to have more than we did.'

And he was helpless to refuse. 'Okay. But before we do anything, we need to get you some clothes of your own.'

CHAPTER SEVEN

ALESSANDRO WOULD USUALLY have driven himself, but he needed all his wits around him with Amelia present, so had reached out to the driver he kept on staff. In the distance he could see their destination, the city of Orvieto, sitting on a large stretch of rock rising dramatically and almost vertically from the surrounding landscape.

While they were out, his staff would air the main part of the house and fill the kitchen with whatever they might need for the next week and disappear as if they'd never been there. No matter what she said about wanting to rectify her sabotage, Alessandro wanted to keep the people Amelia interacted with to a minimum. He still couldn't be sure that she was telling him the truth.

Liar.

He refused to acknowledge his conscience's taunt. He disliked that her desire to make amends had softened his response to her, but her solution? He pressed a closed fist lightly against his mouth. Sofia Obeid. Of all the people that Amelia could have offered up as a new partner on the Aurora project, why did it have to be the one woman who had refused until now to give them even the time of day? Alessandro and Gianni had considered and discarded her before the start of the project because of that. Amelia wasn't wrong—she was their best option, and if

Amelia could get Obeid to sit down with them then who was he to argue?

Alessandro wanted to speak to Gianni. But he'd tried his mobile again last night and couldn't get through. Deep down, Alessandro knew that he could have tried to reach him on St Lovells, Gianni's private island, but what would he have said? That he'd not only opened them up to sabotage, but he'd managed to get their enemy pregnant? He didn't need to speak to Gianni about the project because he knew what his cousin would say. *Do what you need to do. And get it done.* Alessandro didn't need Gianni's permission—he needed absolution.

Amelia sat in the car beside him, picking at the bed of her thumbnail, and he wanted nothing more than to slap her hands apart and tell her to stop. Because the sign of deep worry made him feel like a monster. Because...his mother had used to do the same exact thing, each night while she waited for his father to come in from the vineyards. But he was nothing like his father and she was nothing like his mother. Amelia Seymore was hardly an innocent in all this.

Her mobile phone beeped and he resisted the urge to try and check the screen in case it was a message from her sister. Instead he looked out of the window as they drew closer to the city famous for the defensive walls built from the same rock on which it sat, the stunningly beautiful duomo with its striking white and green façade, and some reasonably decent wine. Certainly, better than anything his father and uncle had produced on their vineyards.

I don't care if your fingers are bleeding or your back hurts. You will not stop until these grapes are harvested, do you hear me, boy?

'Alessandro? Did you hear me?' Amelia's soft voice punctuated the hold his memory had on him and he turned to look at her. A shadow passed across her face before she turned back to her phone. 'Sofia has agreed to meet. But the window is tight. She says she is considering a similar proposition—'

Alessandro scoffed. 'Doubtful. There is nothing remotely similar out there to Aurora.'

Amelia nodded in agreement. 'She's willing to meet us in Marrakesh tomorrow, but she has warned us not to get our hopes up.'

'Playing hard to get?'

'Most definitely. She's interested but cautious. Historically her company has partnered with those with a longer track record than RI.'

'What makes you think this will work?' he asked, genuinely curious.

'Because she will respect who you are and what you have done,' she replied.

'Why? You didn't?' he said, his tone darker than he'd intended. He hated losing his legendary control around her. Her compliment—intended or not—had grated, but not as much as the way she simply took his harsh retort as her due. Feeling disconcertingly mean, he was about to apologise when their driver pulled to a stop at the pedestrian area within Orvieto's walls.

Instinctively after exiting the car, he came around the vehicle to open the door for Amelia. She was back in the clothes she'd travelled to Italy in and, despite the slight creases, she looked composed and collected. The way she had looked to him for the two years before Hong Kong. Because after? After Hong Kong, all he'd seen was lust and want and need.

Shaking off the thought, he saw her eyes soften as she looked into the old town in Orvieto.

'What?' he asked, curious to see the city through her eyes.

She gazed up at him, the answer on the tip of her tongue, but looked away as she answered him in a small voice. 'We talked about coming here—my family—when I was younger.'

He tried to temper the anger that rose in him at the mention of her family—of her father. What was it about this woman that pushed buttons that had lain dormant for years? She cleared her throat as if aware of the impact of her words and slowly made her way towards the open square in the heart of Orvieto. He watched her go, letting her rebuild her armour piece by piece—because he *wasn't* a monster.

Catching up with her a few moments later, he gestured with his head towards the shopping district where Gucci sat next to Ferragamo, Dolce and Gabbana rubbed shoulders with Tom Ford.

Her steps slowed, pulling his attention back to her.

'Something wrong?' he asked, his patience wearing thin.

'I can't... These shops...' She stared at them with an expression that somehow merged shame and embarrassment. 'I can't afford them,' she concluded on a whisper.

Fury etched his body into hard lines. He closed the distance between them in a stride, letting loose only a fraction of the anger that was almost constantly simmering beneath the surface whenever she was near.

'What game are you playing now?' he demanded.

Confusion blew her eyes wide open. 'I don't know what you mean—'

Outrage poured through him. He'd given her the détente she'd asked for, he was trusting her with so damn much and she was *still* trying to pull the wool over his eyes. 'I know exactly how much I pay my staff, so don't try the "poor me" pity act,' he forced out through clenched teeth.

Amelia took a step back from the overpowering wave of his frustration. Nostrils flaring and breathing hard, Alessandro looked pushed beyond an edge she'd never even seen him close to and that she had done this to such a powerful man filled her with shame, but also with an anger to match his own.

So instead of backing down, she stepped forward, stealing back some of that righteous indignation that had fuelled her for years.

'Yes, you pay your staff very well, Alessandro, but how many of your staff have student loans to pay off?' She jabbed an angry finger at him that he stared at in outrage. 'How many of your staff have to pay not only for their own needs but those of their sisters?' She stepped into him again, losing some of the control that restraint had given her. 'How many of your staff have to pay for their mother's rehab facility in South America? How many of your staff had to be a parent to their own mother and father when they were just fifteen years old?'

The shock in his gaze cut through her fury and she realised what she'd just revealed. She pulled back her hand, covering her mouth and shaking, and turned away. She heard the approach of two tourists so she crossed the cobbled street to lose herself in a shop window displaying an inconceivable amount of fridge magnets.

She forced herself to calm down—it wasn't just her

any more that she had to think of. But the venom in his tone—the anger. They would *never* get past it. How on earth was she supposed to raise a child with a man who hated her?

How do you even know he wants to?

'I didn't...' His voice behind her was thick and rough, like the crunch of gravel. He cleared his throat. 'I didn't know.'

'Isn't that the point?' she asked, feeling helpless. 'I believe you said that you didn't want to know or care.'

He had the good grace to look about as shamed as she'd seen him—which extended to the clench of a jaw she wanted to soothe, and the fisting of his palms she wanted to release. Seeing him anything other than determined and powerful felt wrong somehow, as if she'd caught a glimpse of a vulnerability that few saw.

He took a breath—for patience or strength, she couldn't tell—and it emerged from his lips on a sigh that she felt gently against the nape of her neck.

'Are you hungry?' he asked, his tone an awkward shade of gentle.

She nodded and let him guide her away from the shop window, down the cobbled street, and towards a little café with seats overlooking the city walls and down into the stunning patchwork quilt of fields interspersed by the tall, thin cypress trees that made it look so different from England.

She ignored the exchange of Italian between Alessandro and the manager, who seemed desperately eager to find them only the best table in the café. She ignored it because she was numb.

Because she realised what she had been doing—that she had been trying to distract herself from the fact that she was having a baby with a man who hated her. That she was about to have a child that would look to her to show them how to be, how to behave, how to see the world and how to love. And she didn't want that child raised in anger or arguments. She didn't want that child raised in struggle, or instability, as she and Issy had been.

Alessandro appeared at her side, and she let him guide her by the arm to the small, white-cloth-covered table. She took a seat as the waiter poured ice-cold water into their glasses and disappeared. Not once had Alessandro looked at her since they arrived.

'We can't keep at each other like this.'

'No, we can't,' he agreed.

Amelia looked at her hands, at the bitten skin around her thumb, knowing that it was a sign of distress and worry. Their baby deserved more than this. She wanted Alessandro to understand her. She needed him to know where she came from and what had pushed her to do what she had done. Only then might they have a chance to move on from the hurts of the past.

'I... After my father lost the business,' she explained, 'he wouldn't work for anyone else. He was a proud man, but no longer had the capital or will to start over. Whatever income he had went into pretending that we hadn't lost everything, for a while at least. My parents spent more money in those first months than I think they had when they'd had the financial security to do so.'

'That is unforgivable.'

She might deep down agree, but there was still a large part of her that wanted to defend her parents, wanted—needed—to see them as the victims. Because if they hadn't been, then how could they have allowed what happened next?

'It wasn't long before we were forced to sell the house. To downsize. We moved to a different area in London, to a different school where Issy and I didn't fit in. Without his money and largess, the people Dad had thought of as friends soon lost interest. Mum became bitter and Dad became mean. His drinking got out of hand and the physical and financial toll was irreparable.

'I tried to keep the worst of it from Issy, but by that point she was old enough to see what was going on. It's a miracle that she didn't veer off the rails and rebel.'

Alessandro was beginning to suspect it was less to do with miracles and more to do with Amelia and the strength she had to keep what was left of her family together. 'And your mother?' he couldn't help but ask.

For the first time since he'd known her Amelia actually looked defeated. 'She never recovered. She loved him so much, but she had also loved that lifestyle and without either she just gave up. She started leaning on anything that would help her escape the reality of her new life.'

Her words shattered something old and brittle deep within him, resonating with the exact frequency he had felt himself. He knew what it was like to be let down by not just one but two parents and while he would never, *ever*, blame his mother, nor would he forgive her her betrayal. Because if she had kept her word, then the world would be a very different place right now. He opened his mouth to say something, to try and reassure Amelia as he'd never been quite able to reassure himself, but she continued.

'It was…difficult, trying to make sure Issy and I had what we needed. But we made it happen.'

Amelia left a lot unsaid, but he could imagine her

struggle had been incredibly hard, fighting her mother at every turn. He could see how she had become the head of the family and how, just in the way she described it, she had done so without question or complaint. Perhaps it hadn't even occurred to her that she shouldn't have had to. And against his will he felt guilt. Guilt over his involvement that had left two children so vulnerable.

'And we had you.'

Her words surprised him.

'You and Gianni became a focus for us. Became something that drew us together and drove us forward. Our need to avenge our father gave us strength even in the darkest of times. While our mother wallowed, we used our thirst for revenge to get us up in the morning and keep us going. And while I am truly sorry for what I have done to Rossi Industries, I…we…needed it.'

In her eyes, he saw only truth and he couldn't stop the understanding blooming in his chest. He knew how strong that drive and purpose could be, the power it could provide, but he still struggled with what could have happened to Rossi Industries and the thousands of people employed there.

'Is that why you thought we were corrupt?' he asked.

She bit her lip before answering. 'I needed you to be. Because I needed to blame someone—anyone—that wasn't the two people who were supposed to be…my parents, my guides, my role models.'

Once again, her words and his childhood began to fold together and he wasn't sure how to feel about it. He sighed and gave up the urge to fight the sympathetic feelings trying to emerge.

'I understand. If I'd had someone to blame for my parents' misdeeds, I would have,' he admitted. Something flared in her gaze. Surprise, shock...that indefinable thing that had sparked one night in Hong Kong and had yet to blow out.

Connection.

Alessandro batted the errant thought away, instead focusing on the fact that she had given him something, and he felt the unaccountable need to meet her in kind. But could he do it? Gianni was the only other person on the planet who knew where they came from, the rest of the world believing that the Rossi cousins were placed on this earth as fully formed, financially powerful property gods.

'This wasn't supposed to happen,' he admitted, opening his hand to the skies.

'You and me, or me and...'

'Both?' he admitted, even as a fist twisted his gut and something close to pain roared in his body to take the words back, as if it were sacrilege to say such a thing to the woman carrying his child. He could see that his words had struck her just as hard and hastened to explain, even when speaking of his childhood was the last thing he'd ever willingly talk about.

'My father was...*is*...he *still* is...a despicable man. He is mean, violent, prejudiced, ignorant and vile in the worst ways. And he doesn't have an alcohol addiction to excuse it.' His voice was rough, scratched out from hatred and hurt. 'Gianni and I grew up on a vineyard in Umbria. I am assuming you know this?'

Amelia nodded. 'You and Gianni have never tried to hide your beginnings. And even if you had, Issy would have found it.'

'I'm beginning to think we might have employed the wrong Seymore,' he said, genuinely impressed by the accurate and detailed research Isabelle Seymore had seemed to gather. He was momentarily distracted by the slight curve of Amelia's lip, her pride in her sister something he respected and understood.

'No, we're not ashamed of our humble beginnings, but we don't like to think on it much. It wasn't a nice place to grow up for either Gianni or myself. We certainly don't talk about it.'

'Then why are you talking about it now?'

'Because you need to understand where I'm coming from as much as I needed to understand you.'

She nodded, slowly, that connection again becoming stronger between them.

'Vizzini Vineyards produces a really quite disappointing Sangiovese. My father and his brother have neither the patience nor the interest to produce anything but. The ground is hard and barely fertile, and my father and uncle too stubborn, too mean and too lazy to do anything about it.

'But every day they go out there and ravage the land and vines as if they might actually one day produce something that would be half decent and make them rich beyond their wildest dreams.

'It will never happen,' Alessandro stated adamantly. 'But that didn't stop them from forcing Gianni and me to work ourselves to the bone.' He huffed out a bitter laugh. 'You want to know why we're so successful? Yes, we're hungry for it, yes, we're determined, but what puts us above everyone else? We were born breaking ourselves; it's in our blood, not by nature, but by nurture. Our only saving grace was our *nonna*. She was the only person that could still the hand of my father and his brother. She was devastated by her sons' abuse and helped us as much as she could, protecting our mothers and us. It is why we chose her maiden name as our surname.'

***

His eyes softened, making him look so utterly different from the man that ruled boardrooms with an unquestionable authority and conviction, that seared ineptitude away with a single look. This was a youth who had loved and hurt, who was soft and warm. Gianni and Alessandro could have easily each taken their own mother's maiden name. But they had chosen someone who had loved and tried to protect them, they had chosen something that bonded them together as a family, perhaps even closer than brothers, despite only being cousins.

But then his face darkened, as if a cloud had covered the sun.

'She passed when Gianni and I were eight years old.'

His loss was so palpable that Amelia wanted to reach for him, but he had waded too far into the waters of his memories.

'After that, there was nothing holding my father and uncle back. They treated us little better than slaves, working the fields and the machinery during the day, and being their punching bags at night.'

'What about your mother? Gianni's mother?' she asked, unconsciously echoing his earlier question to her.

Alessandro looked away. 'Mine was unable to help,' he said, the simple words concealing so, so very much. 'And Gianni's story is his own.' He shook off her question and turned back to the table.

'My father used to say, "The Vizzini name is all that matters." He was obsessed with it. Every single day, he would say, "It will live on for generations to come." And I promised him, the day that I left, that the Vizzini name, the blood in his veins…it would end with me. It is—*was*—the only vengeance I could take against him.'

He said it looking deep into her eyes, opening himself to her so that she would understand, that she would know the truth—the depth of his promise. And she did. She knew the power of such a promise. Her heart ached for the boy he had been but it also ached for the child they had made together and the future that she had barely hoped for that was beginning to disappear like sand on the wind.

'But now that promise doesn't matter,' he dismissed. Eyes that had been so expressive moments before, so free with their emotions, shuttered, the barrier falling between them with shocking speed and ferocity. 'The child will never even hear of the Vizzini name if I have my way.' There was a determination that she had never seen from Alessandro darkening his words to a level that sounded almost threatening, but not. Amelia realised that it was more like an oath or a promise.

'I need you to hear this and know this.' He pinned her with a steady gaze that she couldn't look away from. 'Our child will not want for anything. *Everything* I have is theirs. I don't know what the future holds for us, but no matter what—our child will be protected from anything it is in my power to protect them from.'

Amelia's heart pounded in her chest. The vehemence in his words, his promise, wrapped tightly around her, but rather than suffocating, it was comforting. A fear that she hadn't realised she'd had eased. Yes, she'd known that she could find a way to provide for herself and her child alone if she'd needed to. Issy would have helped without question. But Issy—bright, beautiful Issy—deserved more, she deserved not to be held back by family vendettas or obligations.

But what did his promise mean for her? Did he want to raise their child together? Did he want more? The thought of sharing a family with Alessandro, of sharing that responsibility, of working together to care for their child without fighting, bickering or mistrust… That was something that lived in a fantasy tied deeply to one night in Hong Kong that she couldn't yet bring herself to name.

She knew Alessandro was still angry, and he clearly didn't trust her, both of which he had a right to. But Alessandro was also a man who loved his grandmother, who was loyal to his cousin beyond all else. She knew and appreciated the tenets he lived by. She knew *him*. He was a good man.

That was why she'd been forced to lie to Issy, who would never have embarked on their plan unless Amelia had promised her proof of that corruption. Because Amelia had known, even then, that there was no proof. That this strong, powerful, proud and determined Italian would never have done such a thing. So she had launched them into their vendetta in a bid to be free of a man she was hopelessly and irrevocably falling for. She bit her teeth together to force back her feelings again.

Because wanting a man who would protect her the way he had promised to protect their child—the way no one had ever promised to protect *her*—was a hope too far. Willing back the wet heat pressing against her eyes, she could at least hope for something smaller. If she could help him save the Aurora deal, she could hope for a place to start at least.

CHAPTER EIGHT

AS THE PLANE banked into a hard turn, steeply angling the private jet, Alessandro felt his stomach drop. He looked across the cabin to where Amelia accepted a glass of orange juice from the air steward with a smile that did things to him. He'd checked with Dr Moretti three times that it was safe for Amelia to fly at this stage of her pregnancy. The concern he felt for her, the *possessiveness*, had shocked him. For years he'd been determined to ensure that his father's blood ended with him.

But now? Now that Amelia was carrying his child, when his mind wandered it went to a place where there was a dark-haired child wrapped safely in their mother's arms, where there was an uncle who looked like Gianni who would spoil that child rotten, where there was a bond between him and a woman he had never imagined for himself that looked very much like Amelia Seymore.

But when he opened his eyes, there was a company he needed to save from damage done by that very same woman. He had meant what he said to Amelia the day before. That he would give their child whatever they needed, but...

I want a chance.

He cast another gaze to where Amelia sat poring over documents at the table. He'd spent half the night reading the same material the Aurora team had sent over while they'd been in Orvieto. They had returned to Villa Vittoria after a shopping trip that had been less than easy. Apparently offering to pay for it hadn't made things better, only worse. The only thing that had forced her through the doors of the clothing store where Amelia had bought everything she needed was the prospect of meeting with Sofia Obeid in three-day-old clothes.

They had been nearly done when the shop assistant guided Amelia to the lingerie section.

Monk indeed.

Lace, straps, belts, hooks, bows, ribbons, ties... *Cavolo*. It wasn't as if his fevered imagination needed any more to think about. There hadn't been a single night since Hong Kong when he hadn't woken up in a cold sweat relieving none of the fire of want and need in his body. And last night had been the worst yet. As if the knowledge that she was carrying his child had suddenly made everything so much more intense.

He looked out of the window cutting off any curiosity as to what she was wearing under the cream silk shirt that should be conservatively respectable had he not seen the lithe body beneath it. *Cristo*, what madness was this? And why—all of a sudden—was he fascinated by little buttons? A row of them at each wrist and another row at the nape of her neck leading all the way down the back of her top to where it tucked into a pair of wide, high-waisted navy trousers.

Sophisticated. Attractive.

They made her look confident. He hadn't realised how much he'd missed seeing her like that, until that very moment. That he was making her less somehow stirred his conscience and reminded him of things he never wanted to think on.

He cleared his throat. 'Talk me through the meeting.'

He knew the plan but he needed something to focus on that wasn't Amelia, their child and their future. Especially when all it made him do was think about his past.

A villa had been booked at the hotel where Obeid had suggested they meet. Harrak Marrakech was a fourteenth-century palace set amongst twenty-eight acres of orchards that opened out towards a view of the snow-capped Atlas Mountains. Comprised of deluxe villas, each with private pools, gardens, a private chef and personal staff on hand twenty-four hours a day, it was a very impressive hotel, even to Alessandro who, amongst the sprawling property empire, owned several of his own with Gianni.

While the car took them from the airport to the hotel, Amelia talked him through the changes she'd made to the pitch document in order to cater specifically for Obeid. He agreed with most of the changes, made a few tweaks, and left her to make the required amendments, trying to ignore the fact that this was beginning to feel very much like the trip to Hong Kong.

'She will expect you to do the talking, and she may be offended that Gianni isn't there with you, at the meeting,' Amelia warned as she got out of the car and waited for him to join her. His gaze caught on features he'd once thought plain, which he now knew beneath their subtlety to be exquisite.

He nodded in response to Amelia's statement, knowing that the world was used to the Rossi cousins being two halves of the same whole. Dammit, *he* was used to it. But he had to keep a lid on the irritation lashing at him, needling him, if he had a hope to claw any success back on this project.

He looked up at the building that had quaintly been called a villa and even though he had some of the most impressive buildings in the world under his company name, *this* was incredible.

'Is...is this okay? Sofia would expect you to stay in the most expensive accommodation. Anything less would be either insult or—'

'Weakness,' Alessandro concluded, agreeing with her choice of villa.

A uniformed staff member opened the door to their villa and beckoned them in. A second staff member waited in the marble hallway with two trays, one with glasses of champagne, cool, refreshing orange juice, or water, and the other with dainty pastries, bright with sprinklings of either paprika or pistachio, salty or sweet.

He thanked the staff, listening with one ear as their private concierge informed them of the suite's amenities, while the majority of his attention was spent taking in what could only be described as paradise. He felt Amelia's wary gaze on him like a tentative caress, and in a blinding moment of clarity he realised, that was it. *That* was what was irritating him so much.

There had been no hesitation in Hong Kong, there had been no timidity, nothing held back at all. She had met him touch for touch, taste for taste, thrust for—

'That will be all,' he said, cutting off the staff mid-sentence, knowing that he sounded insufferably rude, but he was being driven to distraction from wanting something that he couldn't allow himself to have. Before he could do any further damage, he turned on his heel and disappeared into his room.

* * *

Amelia looked out at the incredible view of the Atlas Mountains, more perfect than any picture. In the garden, a long narrow pool led towards an ornamental arch to reveal the majestic snow-capped peaks in the distance. This was a luxury like she had never known or seen before.

The villa alone had more rooms, bathrooms, and living areas than she could conceive of and that didn't take into consideration the subterranean pool and steam room. She looked over her shoulder at the dark wood table polished so that it was almost a mirror, sprawled with paperwork, charts, workflows, and research on Sofia Obeid. But what she really saw was the heated look in Alessandro's eyes after he dismissed the staff.

She had seen the face of the man she had spent a night with in Hong Kong. The man who had broken through every single barrier she had wedged between them, the man who made her want to give everything up for just one of his touches, one of his kisses.

She laughed quietly at herself. Back in Italy she had thought she only wanted, and had only negotiated for, a fresh start. But she couldn't afford any more lies. Not to others, or herself. She wanted more. A yearning in her heart, so deep, that only peeling back the layers of her desire for vengeance had revealed it, exposing that raw need to the air.

She wanted *him*.

She wanted to feel alive in the same way that she had that night in Hong Kong. She wanted him to look at her the way that he had that night. Not with anger, or distrust, but something like wonder. As if he'd been as surprised as she, that it was happening, that it was possible to feel that way... It had created an addiction in her. It was the only way to explain it. This constant craving coursing through her veins, travelling throughout her entire body, enslaving it to a need that felt unquenchable.

Focus.

She had to focus. It was imperative that this meeting was successful, that the damage that hung above Rossi Industries like the sword of Damocles—a sword *she* had put there—was removed. Only then would she be able to meet Alessandro on a level playing field. But in some ways, she also wanted to delay that moment. Because she could feel it on the horizon; building between them, getting bigger and bigger and harder to ignore. A storm, a reckoning, that she both wanted and feared.

Alessandro appeared in the arched doorway on the opposite side of the exquisitely decorated living area. If he was trying to hide his thoughts, he'd failed because she could easily read the intensely erotic images in his mind. Goosebumps broke out across her skin. Every single line of his body was drawn with tension, and more. The more that called to that secret place within her. A place that he had imprinted himself on, making sure that she would never be able to think of another man in the same way.

Amelia clenched her hands, his gaze drawn to the movement, and as he took a step forward she instinctively took a step back—halting him mid-stride. He'd opened his mouth as if to speak, when the villa phone's ringtone sliced the air between them.

Blindly she reached for the handset built into the wall beside her and listened to the voice on the other end.

'Yes... Absolutely... We look forward to seeing you soon.'

She placed the handset into the cradle on the wall and

looked up to find Alessandro staring studiously out of the window.

'Sofia Obeid is on her way.'

He nodded without sparing her a glance.

Get your damn head on straight, right now, or you're going to lose everything you and Gianni have worked so damned hard for.

Amelia instructed the private staff to provide refreshments and drinks in the shaded courtyard in the villa's garden. Covered by a pergola dripping with extravagant fuchsia blossom and rich green leaves, the courtyard edged a pool that reflected the mountains in the distance. It should have been peaceful, serene even, but Alessandro was on edge—a feeling he disliked intensely. Inviting Sofia Obeid into the villa felt personal, invasive. Again, that protective instinct rose in him, surprising in its intensity, wanting to keep this place, and Amelia, to himself. And it shook him to his core.

Presently she was fussing over the table in a way that reminded him of the day she had helped to pitch for Firstview, the day she had tried to sabotage his company. And he was trusting her to save it? This could just as easily be another trap. He pushed the thought away, searching for a calm that was far from natural, but successful nevertheless.

He grounded himself in facts, in the presentation, in the confidence that it was a sterling project that would be more than just a roaring success. In the belief that Obeid would see this and partner with them—even if it was a partnership born from desperation rather than choice.

Amelia looked up as if she'd felt the change in him. Awareness flashed in her golden green gaze, before she looked away. They heard the knock on the door, the villa's staff greeting their visitor, and Alessandro turned to welcome what would either be their salvation or damnation.

Sofia Obeid was a very attractive woman. Six feet of sheer elegance and beauty did nothing to distract from the lethal intelligence in her sharp gaze. Despite her reputation for being impossible to work with, Alessandro could at least appreciate her exacting standards. And though there had been whispers of impropriety, Amelia had assured and reassured him that she had found not one single ounce of evidence pointing to the truth of it. And given how ruthlessly she had investigated him, Alessandro was almost sure that that was what they were—whispers.

'Ms Obeid. Thank you for meeting with us. I know that it was both short notice and inconvenient for you.'

Her eyes narrowed momentarily, as if she was surprised that he was so openly acknowledging his need for her visit.

She hates obsequiousness with a passion. Be simple, be honest, be direct, Amelia's coaching whispered into his mind.

Sofia nodded once, glanced at Amelia, who bowed her head in a way that surprised Alessandro, but seemed to satisfy Sofia.

'Would you care to sit?' he asked, gesturing to the table.

'Thank you,' Sofia replied in a precise English accent that spoke of her years of private schooling in Britain.

She sat in the middle seat, gesturing for him and Amelia to take the chairs either side of her.

'Where is the other one?' she asked when they were all seated at the table.

'The other—?'

'The *Hot* Rossi?'

Alessandro just about managed not to choke on the coffee he'd just taken a sip of. The unconcealed disdain of Sofia's tone making his cousin's moniker somehow amusing. He was about to come up with a lie, when a warning flashed in Amelia's gaze. A warning Sofia might or might not have seen.

'He is in the Caribbean.'

'You expect me to take this business deal seriously while one half of Rossi Industries suns himself and his ego on a beach, presumably—if reports are true—surrounded by as many women as he can get his hands on?'

'I do. My cousin might—' he saw the flash of scepticism in Sofia's gaze '—*does* have a reputation, but he works harder than anyone else I know. He earns his one holiday a year, each and every other day in the office. And as you—and the world—have noted, we are effectively one and the same. If I speak, it is for the both of us, unquestionably. And I promise you, if he could be here, he would. It is not a reflection on how much we value your time and input here.'

Sofia looked between Alessandro and Amelia, and it was only because a part of him was trained almost exclusively on Amelia at all times that he noticed an imperceptible nod from Amelia that seemed to give Sofia some kind of reassurance.

Warning bells sounded in his mind, loud and impossible to ignore. Something was going on. He didn't know what yet, and he couldn't work out why, but he didn't like it at all. So while he gave Sofia the pitch he knew by heart, his mind tried to calculate all possible angles that could be played here. But he kept running up against one.

Amelia. If anyone needed this deal to go ahead as

much as he did, it was her. He couldn't see what was in it for her to sabotage this.

'What happened to the original partner?'

'It was discovered that they didn't have the capability to see the project through,' he replied, holding Sofia's enigmatic gaze.

Obeid raised the wing of a midnight-black eyebrow in surprise. 'That is either incompetent or inept.'

Alessandro kept his mouth shut, refusing to dignify her statement with a response.

'I heard you were hours away from signing,' she pressed again.

'We were,' he admitted. 'But I'm not the only one at this table who has backed out of their obligations at the last minute,' he said, his tone cracked like a whip, lashing out at yet another betrayal.

Obeid simply held his gaze. A lesser person might have flinched. Instead, what he read in Sofia's blue-black eyes was only impatience. As if she'd been surprised it had taken them this long to get to this part of the conversation.

'Good. We are done playing polite, then?' she asked, her cut-glass tone unflinching.

In the corner of his eye, he saw that Amelia looked away from the table.

'I don't believe you would have ever approached me unless you had absolutely no other option.'

'This is true,' he replied, his tone level now that hostilities were almost open on the table. 'But that doesn't mean I don't have a choice.'

'Explain.'

His stomach ground down at the thought of it, but he knew that Gianni would agree with him. They had lived too long with someone else's foot on their necks to ever allow themselves, or Rossi Industries, to be in that same position again.

'My choice. Partner with you, or drop the project altogether.'

But they would lose millions, a voice screamed in Amelia's head. *Not to mention the damage done to their reputation.*

No, no, no, no, no. Her pulse fluttered at a frantic speed and she looked to Sofia, who was considering Alessandro's words.

'And the money you have already invested in the project? Not to mention the irrevocable damage to your illustrious reputation?'

'Are nothing in comparison to our integrity,' Alessandro replied resolutely. Something twisted in her heart. This was the Alessandro that she had been with in Hong Kong. Integrity, loyalty, pride. She'd been confused by it, torn between the belief that he was corrupt and the instinctive knowledge that he wasn't. Amelia drew in a shaky breath and held it, appreciating the significance his words would have for Sofia.

'I know something of that, Mr Rossi,' Sofia replied. 'Some reputations are earned, some are not. Some are fabricated by bitterness, jealousy and lies and some are simply misunderstandings. If you want to move ahead as partners, I would like that.' She caught a flash of surprise in the tightening across Alessandro's shoulders, but his face betrayed nothing. 'My assistant has sent Ms Seymore several direct references of previous partnerships who are happy to speak to you plainly and truthfully about their experience working with my company.'

Sofia rose from the table, and though Alessandro

rose to bid her farewell, he stayed at the table as Amelia walked her from the villa.

It was just the shade of the interior that broke a cool sweat between her shoulder blades, Amelia told herself. The meeting was a success, she had to hold onto that.

Sofia turned just before reaching the front door. 'He knows,' the other woman warned her.

Amelia nodded. 'I know,' she replied, heart see-sawing painfully. She'd known the risk before arranging the meeting. 'He's not stupid.'

Something close to sympathy shone in Sofia's gaze. 'This is a dangerous game, Lia. I hope you know what you're doing.'

Amelia nodded, the warning an echo of the one Alessandro had given her only days earlier. But neither had recognised that the game had already been played and lost, she and Alessandro just hadn't admitted it yet.

She closed the door behind a woman who had once been her closest school friend ten years ago, and turned to find Alessandro staring at her from the end of the hallway, anger, bitterness and something else in his gaze that was quickly eaten up by the darkness.

'You are right about one thing. I'm not stupid,' he said, before turning on his heel and disappearing. And her heart dropped.

Despite that, she raced after him, desperate to explain before any more damage could be done. She reached the courtyard to find him pacing back and forth, all of the emotions he'd kept contained during the meeting finally unleashed in movement that reminded her of a caged panther.

'Alessandro—'

'But I am though, aren't I?' he demanded, his nostrils flaring at deep, quick breaths heaving his chest.

'Are what?'

'A fool!' he roared. 'A fool you have played not once, but twice. *Cristo.*' He cradled his head in his hands. 'How could I have ever trusted you?'

His words stung like a whip against her back. 'You can't, and you won't. Which is why it didn't matter,' she said, the truth almost too painful to bare.

Her response jerked his head from his hands. 'It didn't matter?' he demanded.

'No. All that mattered was that the meeting was a success. Sofia is—*was*—an old friend. We lost touch after I was forced to change schools. When I realised I needed to fix the Firstview problem, I reached out to her. She's been mistreated badly by…well. That's her story to tell. Safe to say, her reputation is unjust. Her only condition to meeting with a rich, Italian business titan who would never have considered lowering himself to meet with an Arabic businesswoman with a bad reputation was that I keep my existing relationship with her a secret.'

Her words were like barbs and she could see that they had struck home. Amelia knew what it was like to have to prove herself in a male-dominated world, and she couldn't even begin to imagine how hard it must be for Sofia. The dark shadows in her old friend's eyes were enough broad strokes to suggest that her road had been a hard one. But Amelia wouldn't let Alessandro throw this deal away because he was too stubborn to see the wondrous possibility of its success.

'That is unfair,' he said of her last words.

'But true. You are not the only one who has something at stake with this deal. This will be the making of her company—a chance to rise above rumour and prejudice. You will get to move ahead and achieve the success you forecasted for this project.

'And what will you get?' he demanded, the expectation of her betrayal vibrant in his gaze.

She could lie to him, but Amelia was so tired, and, unable to fight it any more, she confessed the truth. 'More. I'd wanted more between us.'

CHAPTER NINE

More? his internal voice roared. *She wanted more?*

'By lying?' he demanded incredulously.

'You can't have it both ways, Alessandro,' she replied. 'I undid the damage that I had done with the Firstview deal. You didn't set rules as to how I did it.' She looked up at him, her eyes wide with stubborn-willed refusal to back down. 'And it wasn't a lie,' she ground out through clenched teeth.

She was a magnificent madness in his veins. They stood, toe to toe, breathing heavy and hard and hot and all he could think of was how much he wanted to take her mouth with his, to plunder the complex essence of Amelia Seymore.

'I have done all that I can do,' she said. 'The decision is now yours.'

For a moment, he wasn't sure whether she was talking about the deal or the unspoken thing that practically throbbed in the air between them. Anger, resentment, need and want thrashed in his chest, twisting and turning, desperate to get out.

As if she sensed it, her pupils flared beneath the heat of his attention, the flutter in her neck flickering in a way that made him want to see if he could feel it beneath the pad of his thumb. Feel that she was as affected as him, know the truth of it in her body—a body that couldn't lie or betray him.

He forced himself to turn away and missed the flash of hurt that throbbed in Amelia's eyes.

You can't, and you won't. Which is why it didn't matter.

Her words taunted him as he stalked from the villa. Because she was right. He couldn't trust her, wouldn't. He punched Gianni's number into his phone, unsurprised but annoyed when he was told that it was still out of reach.

At the very least, he should have felt satisfied. With Obeid the project could go ahead if he and Gianni wanted it to. He should have felt relief, he should have felt victorious. So why was guilt slashing wounds into his chest at the memory of Amelia's words, of her accusation that he'd never trust her?

Because you want to.

The startling realisation pulled him up short.

He wanted to believe her, just as he'd wanted to believe his mother when she'd promised she'd take them away from his father and uncle.

And he'd never wanted anything more in his entire life. His father and uncle had become so much worse after their mother passed away that they had driven Gianni's mother from the house leaving Gianni behind. Alessandro's mother was all they'd had left but when Saverio had come in from the fields there was only so much Alessandro had been able to do to distract his father from his anger towards his mother. His desperation had been almost suffocating as he'd pleaded with her to take them away after one particularly brutal night.

We'll leave. I'll come for you and we'll leave.

Gianni and he had stayed up all night, whispering reassurances and making plans through the minutes and hours, neither wanting to give up hope that Aurora Vizzini would come to take them away. Even as dawn had crested over the vineyards, and they'd rubbed sleep and sadness from their eyes, knowing that Alessandro's mother had lied, the worst of it had been the hope; the desperate hope he'd had, the need to believe his mother when she had said that she would take them away, that they would be safe.

Nothing was spoken about that night ever again, not with his mother and not with Gianni. And sometimes, in the dead of night, he drove himself to distraction wondering if his mother's promise had even happened.

But Amelia was different, an inner voice taunted him. Her first concern, when he'd brought her to Italy, was her sister. The protective instinct and determination in her so clear and obvious he almost couldn't believe it. Truth had been the only note he'd heard when she'd told him of her childhood. And he'd read between the lines to see deeper, to *know* that she would do anything to protect her family. That she had sacrificed for her family, for what she thought was right. And she'd done it again when she'd agreed to lie to him for Obeid, putting Rossi Industries above her own needs, above *him*. Because she had known what that concealment would do to him.

But that anger—that constant simmering presence beneath his surface whenever she was near—lashed out. So much his life had changed in the space of just days. Or, he wondered, had the change started all those weeks ago in Hong Kong? When success, respect and admiration had led them down a path he'd never thought he'd take? One wrong move had completely undone the entire chessboard of his life. A move he was fighting hard not to repeat.

I'd wanted more between us.
The decision is now yours.

His mind hurt from working out all the angles, exhausted from days of too little sleep and entirely too much adrenaline. It had weakened his resolve and all he wanted, all he needed, was a taste of her to quench the maddening thirst for her.

He looked up to find himself back at the villa, his steps unconsciously bringing him back to where he needed to be. He found Amelia pacing in the living area.

Worry had etched lines across her features, a few wisps of hair had loosened from where it had been pinned back, but shutters came down on her concern as she turned to stand tall and proud beneath the storm of his gaze, determined to meet him head-on. No. Amelia Seymore might have lost her battle, but she wouldn't let herself be cowed.

And he hated how much that turned him on. He'd thought he'd recognised it, the fight. He'd thought that was what fed the burning lava hot in his veins, he'd thought anger was what had locked his chest in a vice ever since he'd left her at the villa hours before. He'd thought fury was what had driven him here.

But he'd been wrong.

In that one moment, he realised that it wasn't she who had fooled him. No. He had fooled *himself.* Because the only thing that was riding him now, and riding him hard, was the sheer desperation to feel her touch, to taste her once again, to feel her wrapped around him as she screamed his name.

He closed the distance between them in two short strides, gathering her into his arms, and claimed her mouth with an undeniable and unyielding possession.

A gasp that sounded like surrender and felt like fire engulfed his soul. *Mine*. And in a single heartbeat, her name etched itself irrevocably deep within him.

Every single defence she'd thought she had against him crumbled the moment his lips met hers. A summer storm, fierce and furious, answering every single one of her unspoken prayers—and then as quickly as he had come for her, he tore his mouth from hers.

'*Cristo,*' he said, his forehead pressed against hers, his chest heaving with their shared breath. 'Please,' he all but begged, 'send me away. Tell me you don't want this.'

'I can't,' she replied, closing her eyes against the sheer intensity of all that she wanted and all that she feared she would never have. But she wouldn't, couldn't hide from this any more. Opening her eyes, she looked deep into his gaze, saw the storm that threatened on the horizon and faced it. 'Because I do want this.'

'Then we're both damned.'

He claimed her lips with such possession for a moment she lost herself. She was his creature—one of pure sensation, responding only to his touch, his taste. The tongue taking her mouth teased her heart, the hands pulling her to him left fingerprints on her soul. And for the briefest moments she surrendered to it, luxuriating in the shocking intensity of his desire, before her own became too much to ignore.

Leaning into his kiss, her hands flew to his chest, fingers fisting the superfine cotton of his shirt and pulling him into her, deepening a kiss she'd already opened herself up to. She felt as much as heard the growl build from Alessandro, raising the hairs at her nape not from fear of him, but fear that she might not be rid of this feeling, this sensual high that fizzed and popped and burst through her body. She wanted to call it madness, but beneath it, beneath the intoxicating fever of his touch, it was the sanest she'd felt since Hong Kong. Because while her heartbeat raged out of control, he soothed her soul.

'Amelia.' He said her name like a plea—as if he too had finally found that same sense of peace. But as he pulled away from her, she followed him, unwilling—unable—to break the connection. Her lips found his and he groaned into the kiss in a way that melted her body against him.

Rising to her tiptoes, she pressed herself to the length of his body, desperate to feel the steely outline of toned and taut male heat against her. Heat flashed over her from the evidence of his arousal, coalescing deep in her throbbing sex.

Despite the ferocity of his kiss, he was being gentle with her, his touches light, his hold careful and it only frustrated her, making her want more. Because she knew what it was like when Alessandro Rossi lost himself in his desire and that, *that*, was what had kept her heart racing when she'd known he was near, *that* was what had filled her dreams with such eroticism she'd ached when awake. *That* was what she wanted now.

Reluctantly she pulled back from the kiss, studying the scorching heat of his gaze—a heat wrapped in chains. He wanted this as much as she did but he was holding himself back. She could almost read the thoughts in his eyes, the warring conflict of should they, shouldn't they.

The words she'd said to Alessandro that night in Hong Kong rose to her lips, a symmetry and irony to it that made her heart hurt a little.

'Just tonight. Just now. But we will never speak of it. Ever.'

Before she'd even finished the sentence, Alessandro had closed the distance between them, crowding her body in the most delicious of ways.

'Amelia, what we do now, here? We *will* speak of it.' The authority in his tone sent shivers of arousal across her skin, tightening her nipples, throbbing between her legs. 'We will acknowledge it. It will not be ignored. Not again. Do you understand?'

The sting of his admonishment dissolved beneath a tide of need so acute, so powerful, she trembled. The pure possession in his gaze, his refusal to ignore this thing between them...it was everything she'd ever wanted.

'Do you want this?' he demanded, and she saw chains holding his desire back begin to snap beneath the heat of their mutual need. She knew what he was asking, knew that it was about more than this one moment, than this night...it was more than the question he'd asked only moments ago.

'Yes. I do,' she replied as he searched her gaze and she opened herself to him, hoping that he saw the truth of her words, of her heart. 'But I want *you*. Not some careful, half touch. So I'm asking, do *you* want this?'

Surprise flared in the rich depths of his gaze. As if he'd thought he'd hidden his feelings better. And she was relieved when he didn't simply dismiss her question, but considered it as seriously as she had. This was the line they would draw—before and after. She knew it as she knew her next breath. And it had to be crossed now or never.

'Yes, I do,' he replied, the last chain of his restraint breaking in his gaze.

Relief sagged through her, but she had no time to dwell on it because that touch that had been gentle was suddenly a brand against her skin. He gathered her in his arms, lifting her up against him. Instinctively she wrapped her legs around his hips so as not to fall—not that she would have. The moment she was in his arms she felt safer than she could ever remember.

He kissed her as he walked them from the living room, the erotic play of his tongue against hers a promise of what was to come when they reached their destination. The arm braced beneath her thighs a tease of where she wanted him to touch her. Her breath caught in her lungs as his other hand wrapped around her hair and gently angled her head back to give him access to her neck as he pressed open-mouthed kisses across her collarbone and down between the v of her breasts, through the oyster satin of her shirt.

Her taut nipples punched at the silk and he covered them with the damp heat of his mouth. Her head fell back on its own, pleasure bursting through her as he reached the bed and laid her gently down on it.

The afternoon had given way to dusk, and still the soft honeyed rays of the sun streamed through white linen curtains. It was the exact opposite to Hong Kong and Alessandro was glad. He refused to allow this moment to be shrouded in darkness or secrecy. He wanted the light, wanted reality; undeniable, unhidden reality.

He wanted to see every single inch of her as he brought her to climax, he wanted to feel it and know it was real. A blush rose to Amelia's cheeks in response to the thoughts she could read in his gaze, he realised. And he bared himself and his desires to her as he reached up to undo the buttons on his shirt one by one.

She bit her lips, watching his hands lower down his body, hungry and heavy. Without taking her eyes from him, she reached behind her to undo one of those tantalising little buttons and drew the shirt over her head. He had reached the last of his shirt buttons as she did so. They both discarded their tops at the same time, eyes for nothing but each other.

He stood, frozen still at the sight of her lace-covered breasts, and when she leaned back on her elbows, his arousal shoved painfully against his trousers. The look in her eyes was pure want. His mouth ran dry and, spellbound, he climbed onto the bed, unable to resist the lure of her.

Instinct took over, powerful and primal and intense. He gently tugged at her ankle, pulling her down the bed as he rose to meet her, covering her body with his, and the sigh he bit back turned into a groan of sheer desire. He slipped an arm beneath her, gathering her to him as he feasted on the smooth planes of her chest and the wide v between her perfect breasts. With one hand he pulled at the lace cup of her bra, exposing her nipple, taut and tempting. He took her breast into his mouth, gorging on pleasure and teasing cries of delight from Amelia.

Her hands flew to his head, fisting in his hair, pulling, pushing as if she wasn't sure whether she wanted more or less of the delicious torment. 'Alessandro...'

'Tell me what you want, *amato*,' he said, desperate to bring her pleasure. 'Tell me what you want and you shall have it.'

She arched, as he turned his attention to her other breast, tugging the lace down and feasting on her flesh.

There hadn't been so many words between them in Hong Kong. The shocking intensity of their passion like a sudden firestorm, burning to extremes before burning out. But here? Now? This would be different. This would be no quick thing, he silently promised them both.

'Your desires are safe with me,' he said, pulling back so that she could see the truth of his words. 'Your needs are safe with me. *You* are safe with me.'

The flare of her pupils reminded him of a solar eclipse. Desire blotting out rationality and restraint. 'Put your hands on me,' she said, her tone husky with arousal and need.

'As you wish.'

He found the fastening of her trousers, flicking the button and making quick work of the zip. She shivered as his palm slipped beneath the cotton fabric and caressed the curve of her backside. She cried out as his fingers delved beneath the lace of her panties into the delicate soft wet heat of her.

In a single breath he was more aroused than he'd ever been in his life, and even then, holding back from what he wanted was shockingly easy in order to give her more.

He wanted this, her pleasure. He wanted to see starbursts in her eyes, not confusion, doubt or worry. He wanted to see what he had seen in Hong Kong. Feel what he had felt there. A gasp fell from her lips and he wanted to taste it, taste the surrender to all that was passion and sensuality on her lips. His heart pounded against his ribcage as she shifted in his arms, her eyes becoming soft and unfocused as his fingers circled her clitoris, sweeping around the soft delicate flesh and returning again and again to a sensual torment that teased them both in equal measure.

He studied every part of her face, the way that she bit her lower lip trying and failing to contain her responses, responses that were like a drug to him. *He* did this to her, *he* gave her this. A flush stained her cheeks and crept up her neck, her eyes closed then opened, unseeing, lost in sensation and sensual frustration as her orgasm danced just out of her reach.

In seconds, he had pulled at her trousers, slipped them from beneath her and removed them from her legs. Carefully caressing his way back, his hand pressed her thighs apart gently and he lowered himself between her legs. The heat of her gaze on him seared his soul, and as he parted her to him he felt her flinch. 'You are safe with me,' he promised again, as he gave into his need for the most intimate of kisses.

Her learned her song then, the cadence of her pleasure—in the cries and moans and pleas that filled the air. His heartbeat pounded the rhythm, the sound of his blood roaring in his veins the base line, and above it all rose a melody so sweet he'd never tire of hearing it, and when her orgasm crested, the crescendo was so powerful, he felt changed by it.

He gentled her with soft touches and words as she came back down—as affected by her pleasure as she had been. But when her eyes found his, focused, intent and full of need for more, his body answered without a thought.

He kissed her with the desperation of a dying man, as if this were the last thing he would do with his life. His body, hot and feverish for her touch, relished the way her hands skated across his skin, fingers soothing and then gripping his shoulders, biceps, flanks—as if she wanted to explore every inch of him.

Alessandro pulled away reluctantly to remove his trousers, his gaze not leaving hers once. Automatically he reached for his wallet and withdrew a condom from it and stopped to look at it in his hands. His mind utterly blank because...because...she was already pregnant.

Never, not once in his entire life, had he had sex without protection. Never had he been skin to skin with anyone and, looking up, he saw the same thought reflected in Amelia's eyes.

The realisation of how important this moment was nudged its way through the haze of Amelia's climax. For a man who had sworn never to have children, she imagined the question about whether to use protection or not would be as alien to him as it was to her. But she was pregnant already and the desire to feel him—to be with him—without a barrier between them suddenly became more than just a want. It was a need that she couldn't explain. Carefully she reached out to take the condom from his fingers and placed it on the side table.

He looked at her, studying her intently, and she opened herself up to him—laying herself bare to his silent inquisition. She wanted this and she trusted him. And in that moment, she saw that trust reflected back at her.

The bonds holding Alessandro back shattered and her heart soared to see the ferocious desire riding her hard reflected in his gaze. He leaned across the bed and thrust her into a realm of infinite pleasure with his kiss, the press of his body against hers igniting a hunger she feared would never be sated.

She wrapped her arms around him and held on tight, half afraid that he'd leave, as if already she could feel him slipping through her fingers. But the thought disappeared as he bent his head to her chest and claimed her breast as if it were already his.

Pleasure arrowed through her to the heart of her sex and when his deft fingers gently pressed her legs apart and delved into that exact same place, she couldn't contain the cry of sheer want that left her lips.

He gently pushed her legs aside to make space for himself and she trembled when she felt the jut of his erection against her sex. Both Amelia's and Alessandro's eyes drifted shut from the shared pleasure of the moment, luxuriating in the sensations that were new to them both, until neither could resist the lure of what was to come.

Slowly, Alessandro pushed into her, her muscles tightening, flexing, drawing him further into her. Amelia tried to capture the feeling with words, but nothing stuck, flitting away on a tide of sheer sensation and connection. They were both trembling with the force of their pleasure, with the shock of it, the surprise. It twisted something deep in Amelia, turned it, opening it into something beautiful. He filled her so perfectly that she felt as if they had been made for each other, as if finally something was beginning to make sense for her and her journey.

And then, when she thought she couldn't take any more feeling, he began to withdraw and she cried out at the loss. A rueful smile pulled at Alessandro's lips and in Italian he rained down praises and promises as he pushed into her again, and again, and again. The erotically slow strokes he teased them with seemed endless to her, launching her into that strange infinite place, until it seemed even Alessandro Rossi couldn't take it any more.

As his movements became quicker, his thrusts more powerful, their connection became more tangible. Sweat beaded his brow, her neck, between her shoulder blades, and down his chest, the air became hot with cries and moans and pants and pleas.

Harder and harder and higher and higher he drove her to the pinnacle of her climax until finally, just when she thought she couldn't take any more, Alessandro thrust them over the edge into an abyss of nothing but sheer pleasure.

CHAPTER TEN

IT TOOK A while for Amelia to realise she wasn't asleep any more. Nestled into the curve of Alessandro's huge frame, with his arm clamped over her waist, it had felt like an impossible dream. In Hong Kong, she'd not allowed herself to sleep. She'd stolen from the hotel room while Alessandro had been in the bathroom, unable to face the consequences of her actions...until those consequences had come looking for her.

But here, there was no chance of her sneaking out of bed. Alessandro's arm was a weight holding her in place and he, apparently, slept like the dead. It was such a normal everyday thing to know about him that it made her smile, and burrow deeper into his embrace, close her eyes and fall back asleep.

When Amelia woke, she was alone. The heat, the safety, the promise of the night before—noticeably absent. Alessandro was in the bathroom and she wondered if she'd conjured the comparison with Hong Kong into reality. Should she leave? Should she stay? Would he emerge from the bathroom with a smile, a frown, or that purposefully blank look that meant he was waiting to take his lead from her?

This was the father of her child and she didn't know. Hurt swirled with guilt. It wasn't good enough. She had to do better, *they* had to do better. Now that her sabotage had been undone, she had to turn her attention to them. Because if she did want the security he offered and the relationship her child deserved, then she had to feel more than…than…discomfort and awkwardness. She looked at her ringless finger and wondered if perhaps it might for ever be bare now. A ring promising her to Alessandro far too much to ever dream of, let alone hope for.

I want a chance.

She knew that Alessandro would keep their agreement, but it was what she did with that chance that mattered now. For the sake of their child, they needed to get to know each other, outside the boardroom and the bedroom. She just had to figure out how.

She slipped from the silken sheets of his bed, returned to her room, and took a shower, thinking about how she could achieve what she wanted. She rolled her shoulders beneath the spray of the powerful jets and felt his palm trace the length of her spine. She soaped her skin and felt his open-mouthed kisses and the pleasant ache between her thighs from where she had gripped him, urged him, held him deep within her. But despite the pleasure he had given her last night, the satisfaction, her body craved him again. It was a drumbeat just beneath her skin, always, constant, somehow slipping into time with her pulse. Reluctantly she pulled her thoughts back to the idea beginning to form in her mind. It was a little…*simple* but she believed that it would be effective.

By the time Alessandro emerged from the hotel suite room Amelia had dismissed the staff to give them some privacy, and was waiting for him at the table. He was dressed as if ready for the office, as always, and still as desperately handsome as he had been the night before.

Any hope that their shared passion might have somehow taken the edge off her desire for him was dashed, instantly and irrevocably.

His gaze flickered from her to the table and confusion pulled at his brow. He was probably wondering why there were bits of torn paper in a glass jar. She nudged the steaming shot of espresso she had made him and steeled herself. She was about to explain when—

'I've offered Obeid the Aurora project and she has agreed.'

Amelia's mouth shut with a snap. It was as she'd expected, but she couldn't help but feel hurt at being excluded.

'The team in London will push on with it from here.'

She stiffened, realising the implications of his words.

What did you think would happen, Amelia? That he'd keep you on the project?

'You will no longer—'

'I understand,' she interrupted him, curt in her desire to not hear him say it. For two years working for Alessandro had been a ruse. But it also hadn't been. She'd enjoyed the work she'd done there. She'd been good at it too. But right now? She had more important things to worry about.

He studied her acceptance with something like scepticism that only proved her point.

'Will you sit?' she asked, pushing aside the small bruise forming on her heart.

'We should be getting back to the jet.'

She clenched her teeth together, fighting the impulse to reveal just how affected she was by his dismissal. He might be the boss, but he seemed to have forgotten that she had never been a mere underling who jumped at his every whim. He caught her gaze, held it, testing the strength of her will and, clearly finding it unbending, he took the chair opposite her.

There was an air of impatience about him and it was this, this power struggle, this discord that they had to get over.

'I am pregnant,' she stated.

'Sì?' he replied, his confusion evident.

'The threat hanging over the Aurora project and Rossi Industries has been neutralised.'

Begrudgingly, it seemed, he acknowledged that statement with a curt nod. *'Sì.'*

'But you don't trust me. You want me. I know that,' she said, a blush rising to her cheeks as she maintained control of the conversation. 'But you don't, we don't... *know* each other.'

His gaze flickered to the jar on the table that contained lots of little folds of paper.

'Yet,' she hurried to clarify. 'We don't know each other yet.' Amelia took a breath. 'You've said that you will protect our child financially and, I'm sure, well beyond that. But our child will need more than just financial support and physical security.'

It was something that she had learned the moment that both those things had been ripped away from her and her sister. Using that memory to give her strength, she asked, 'What about their emotional needs? In those precious first few months and years, and then later on in life? And where will we live? Will we even live together?' she asked, seeing his eyes flare in response to her last question. 'I want...to do this *with* you. I don't want to tell you about my first scan after the fact, or first steps or first anything. I want you to be there with us, I want… I want to share it with you.'

And it wasn't just for her child, Amelia realised as her heart quivered in her chest, waiting for his response. For years she had taken the reins, looked after her sister, taken care of her mother, made the hard decisions and had the difficult arguments and still, despite that, she wanted to give him part of this and it terrified her. Because if she learned to rely on him, if she learned to lean on him and he walked away? It would break her heart permanently.

But she couldn't let fear deter her and she pressed on. 'I don't know how long Issy and Gianni will be away, but when my sister comes back, I want to share this news with the happiness that it deserves. I want to be able to tell her what my future and our child's future is going to look like in the next few months. There is nothing that can be done about the Aurora project now for at least another week. And I want… I'm *hoping* that you will give us that time for us to learn enough about each other to see if this might work? To see if we can be more. To see if…you can trust me.'

Alessandro couldn't pretend that he hadn't seen the sincerity and the need behind her questions. She had laid herself more open here than in what they had shared last night. And her hopes fed almost directly into his daydreams, fantasies that were becoming more like wishes with each moment he shared with her. Wishes that had gold bands and diamond rings that shocked as much as scared him.

But he couldn't pretend that he didn't feel a sense of panic, a sense of being rushed that made him anxious, as if his hand was being forced before he'd had time to think things through properly himself.

He thought about what she'd said about Gianni and her sister. The moment he'd finished his call with Sofia he'd sent word to St Lovells, ensuring that his cousin would at least know that the project had been saved and there was now no longer any threat to Rossi Industries. But hadn't he avoided speaking directly to Gianni because he had no idea how to explain to the man closer to him than any brother what was happening with Amelia?

No matter what he felt, though, the last thing he would allow was for his child to grow up amongst frigid cordiality or burning mistrust and resentment. He and Amelia *did* need to work together to find a way through it all for the sake of their child.

'What are you suggesting?' he asked, curious as to how what she was hoping for fitted into the folded pieces of paper in the jar.

'I have written out a number of things we can do together.'

Dios mio. 'Amelia. Is this the romantic version of team-building exercises?'

He instantly wished he could call the errant thought back, until Amelia's surprised laugh fell between them, lightening the mood and brightening her eyes in the most incredible way. 'It is the solution to a problem,' she forced out through her smile.

Reluctant to lose the moment, he eyed the folded paper suspiciously and continued to play the grouch. 'Fine, but if you expect me to fall back with my eyes closed and trust that you'll catch me—'

This time the laughter that erupted from Amelia was

fresh and wild like the flowers on the meadow between his and Gianni's estates.

'You'd crush me,' she replied, after successfully swallowing her laugh.

He couldn't help the responding pull at the corner of his lips, or the way that it captured Amelia's gaze.

'I would,' he agreed and, somehow, they were no longer talking about trust exercises. Shaking the erotic thoughts from his increasingly dirty mind, he took a sip of the espresso, only mildly cooler since it had been made. She knew how he liked his coffee. Black and scalding. He refused to acknowledge it, but it meant something to him. 'Okay,' he said, taking a deep breath. 'But,' he said, bargaining, 'I reserve the right to veto.'

She considered his offer. 'You can have *one*,' she countered.

He narrowed his eyes, assessing her as an opposing player in this game she had created.

'If I do this, then you will do the same ones that I pick,' he demanded.

This time she narrowed her eyes as—he imagined—she remembered whatever it was she had written on those little pieces of paper. He held his breath, despite believing that she wouldn't have asked him to do anything that she wouldn't do herself.

'Okay,' she agreed.

Something eased in his chest. 'Then let's play,' he said, reaching towards the jar.

Amelia's hand shot out to halt him, drawing his eyes to hers. He would feel the punch to his gut for days.

'It's not a game,' she said quietly.

He just about managed to stop the flinch that pulled at his body. She was right and he knew it. There needed to be trust. They needed to find some kind of accord, because he couldn't, wouldn't let his child grow up in an environment that remotely resembled the one he had been born into. He would make sure that their child had better.

'I know, Amelia,' he promised.

You are safe with me.

His words from last night echoed into his mind, his vow one that he had meant and one that he wouldn't break.

'So, I just…' He dipped his hand into the jar and riffled around inside as he'd seen children do at the local village fete his father and uncle had tried to sell their horrible wine at.

The thanks in her eyes was painful to bear—that it was for such a small thing. Had he really been acting like such a monster? Swallowing, he pulled out a tear of paper and unfolded it. There in looping handwriting that belonged to Amelia was not what he had expected to read. He had been prepared for a checklist—dinner out, a film maybe. Even an art gallery.

He should have known better.

'Are they all like this?'

She nodded, watching him carefully.

'And you will also do these?' he reminded her.

'I will do every one that you do,' she said.

He placed the piece of torn paper on the table, smoothing it flat with his fingers as if the sudden slap of pain raised by this simple request hadn't caught him by surprise.

Take me somewhere from your childhood.

He cleared his throat. *Cristo.*

'Veto,' he said, not caring what weakness it revealed in him. He would never take her anywhere near his childhood. She nodded, looking sad but not surprised. Instead, she passed him the jar. He pulled another tear of paper, trying hard not to tense up from fear of what this one might say, and opened it.

Show me something you're proud of.

And he soon realised just how clever she really was. There was no doubt that after even just a few of these that sense of connection he'd felt from the very first would be strengthened. At least, he could readily acknowledge, his child would have a mother who would fight for them and fight hard, no matter the cost.

'Okay,' he said, sliding back his chair. 'Let's go.'

Amelia was only a little surprised to be heading back to Italy. Part of her had imagined that they would be on their way to London, to The Ruby that was the heart of his and Gianni's company or any of the other incredible buildings Rossi Industries had developed across the globe. But instead, they touched down at the same private airfield they had left the day before, the relatively short flight time between Italy and Morocco still a wonder to her.

Alessandro had been tight-lipped from the moment that he unfolded the first piece of paper. She'd caught sight of the one he'd vetoed and, although she understood why, it had still hurt to be shut out from such a huge part of what made him *him*.

And she was *so* drawn to him, she forced herself to acknowledge now. Handsome, powerful, brooding, absolutely and unquestionably. But it was the flashes of fallibility that sank claws into her, the lightness that he kept well hidden beneath that serious exterior—the way that, despite all his authority and power, he could still get flustered by her, that he could still be amusingly petulant. Beneath all the layers of hurt and damage done by his parents and her father, she could see glimpses of the boy he might have been and she grieved the loss of that boy with such intensity it shocked her to the core.

Amelia could understand the damage, hurt and fear that had led Alessandro to make that promise years ago. But in denying himself a future family, someone to love and be loved by, he had shrunk the people around him to one or two and she wanted more—not for her child and herself, but *him*. She wanted more for Alessandro than what he had allowed himself.

Rather than the sleek black car she expected, a small Prussian blue old MG convertible two-seater sparkled in the sunlight on the runway. She frowned and cast her gaze back to the staff carrying their luggage.

'Don't worry, *tesoro*. Our belongings will be taken back to the villa. We're just taking a detour along the way.'

The term of endearment was almost carelessly thrown her way, as if it hadn't been one of the words he'd whispered over and over and over again to her last night as they'd made love. She wouldn't, couldn't regret it. It had been the most magical experience of her life so far, but she knew that it would make it so much more difficult if this plan—the plan for her child's future happiness—went awry.

He opened the door for her, his chivalry ingrained in a way that felt natural and touching.

'Where are we going?' she couldn't help but ask.

'You'll see. For now, just enjoy the ride,' he said, slipping his sunglasses on, putting the car into gear and letting the engine loose in a roar that sent vibrations through her body. She laughed and the smile across Alessandro's features took another bite out of her heart.

An hour later, they pulled up to a residential street on the outskirts of a small town. It was pretty, but she wasn't quite sure what made it so particular to the billionaire beside her. He parked in a bay and got out of the car and, leaning against the silken surface, looked at a building on the opposite side of the road. It was the Italian equivalent of a two-up, two-down, Amelia thought as she realised that this was what he wanted to show her. A family came out of the door, the parents too distracted by their children to notice them by the car. Risking a glance at Alessandro, she saw a small smile pull at the corner of his lips as if happy to see the rambunctious family spilling from the house.

'When we realised we couldn't build on the land your father sold us, we were in trouble.' He shook his head, and cleared his throat. He didn't need to explain—she'd seen the terrible terms of the loan he and Gianni had taken to buy the land from her father, she knew how urgent the repayment schedule had been.

'We had to do something else and quickly. Renovating and reselling was our best option, so we started with this one. This house. We worked day and night, just the two of us, grit, determination, and a hell of a lot of luck. So many things could have gone wrong. But we did it. Renovated, decorated, sold and bought. We did it over and over and over again, flipping houses until we had enough capital to pay back the loan and start developing our own property. But this? This was the first house. This was the one that started what would one day be Rossi Industries.

'It's humble and I'm okay with that. But what I'm really proud of? Was that we got back up. We didn't let it break us. We got back up and we kept going, kept moving forward.'

His gaze, hidden behind his sunglasses, would have been full of vehemence but she didn't need to see it to feel it. She knew that need. That driving force pushing you back up, pushing you on, unable to break no matter what was thrown at you. Because he'd had Gianni and she'd had Issy and another thread was woven in place, binding them together, even if it was against their own will.

'Your turn,' Alessandro said, twisting the conversation away from himself and his past.

Amelia glanced at the café at the end of the road and he levered himself away from the car, offering his arm in a gesture that was supposed to be ironic, but, when she slipped her hand through the crook of his arm, was anything but.

When they sat at a table on the pavement shown to them by a waiter who barely spared them a glance he smiled, realising that he missed this. The simplicity of having a coffee and not needing to rush because of a meeting, or decision or…

Amelia was looking at him. He felt her gaze like a touch, a caress. Softer than he probably deserved and hotter than he expected. But when he caught it, and held it, a blush rose to her cheeks and memories of the night before crashed through his mind.

The waiter slapped down a bottle of water and impatiently demanded their orders. Amelia hid the choke of a laugh behind her hand as Alessandro ordered them coffee and a selection of pastries, sure that Amelia would be hungry by now.

'That's funny to you? People being rude to me?' he asked, amused by her reaction.

'I just wondered what your staff would think to have seen that interaction.'

'Why?'

'Well, they are…in awe of you. I doubt they'd even believe their eyes.'

He frowned. 'I don't…am I…?' He rarely stuttered, but the thought that his staff might be in any way intimidated by him was terrible.

As if sensing his thoughts, she reached across the table, her small fine hands cool despite the heat. 'No. You are an excellent boss. You can just be a little *stern*.'

He nodded, acknowledging the truth of it. He knew that. Stern was probably a good description. And when the waiter returned with their drinks and the pastries, he felt the shift in mood, as if she was gearing herself up to meet her part of the task she had set them.

She retrieved her phone, unlocked the screen and swiped it a few times as if searching for something on it. Then she passed it across the table to him where he saw a picture of Amelia with her arm around a beaming brunette, younger than her, but the connection between them unmistakable. Isabelle Seymore was holding a giant ice-cream sundae, the sisters cheek to cheek, the pure joy emanating from them infectious.

'Your sister?'

'Yes,' she said, smiling with such affection it was a physical presence. 'Taken on her eighteenth birthday.'

He frowned, searching Isabelle's features for the differences time had wrought between then and the recent picture of her with Gianni.

'I thought she was blonde.'

'Gianni doesn't like brunettes,' Amelia explained.

It was true. Gianni's tastes ran to blonde, tall, easy and quick—to leave, that was. But instinctively he knew that none of those descriptions would fit Isabelle Seymore.

'This is what you're most proud of?' he asked, distracted as to what her meaning was. Getting her sister to lure his cousin into a trap? Their plans for vengeance?

'My *sister*.' Amelia stressed the words as if reading his thoughts. 'My sister is what I'm most proud of. We weren't always close, not when we were younger.' She smiled ruefully. 'I'd imagine from the outside looking in, we were just two more rich girls spoiled silly for their entire lives. We bickered over unimportant things as if it were the end of the world and took everything, especially each other, for granted. But after... There were so many ways in which Issy could have taken a different path. A darker path. She was younger than me when our father's business collapsed. And in the year that followed both he and our mother battled their own demons. Bit by bit Mum lost herself to addiction and Dad lost his health, as you know.

'But there are so many ways a young woman can hurt without parental stability, so many ways that hurt can be twisted and turned into dangerous things—dangerous self-beliefs... There were so many ways in which she could have fallen off the rails and she didn't.'

'You didn't let her,' he guessed correctly.

'A little. But that doesn't take into account the fact that she is who she is—and that is a genuinely good person. She is an auxiliary nurse on a children's hospital ward. She is *good* in a selfless way that I admire and had absolutely nothing to do with. *She* nurtured that goodness, protected it, not once letting our parents' selfishness darken or break that.'

Just the way she spoke of her sister made him want to meet her. Different from Amelia, because there was a thread of darkness to Amelia. No, not darkness. Just… experience. Acceptance that bad things happened in life, bad things she'd seen and felt. Different from his own, but still present, and fundamentally entwined with him and his.

Because—now that the anger and sense of betrayal over the Aurora deal was dissipating—he could see just how much Amelia had needed to take on at such a young age. To care for her sister, herself and even her mother, that would have been a heavy burden to bear alone, with no real help.

Our only real concern, he remembered one of the senior management members saying of Amelia, *is that her self-sufficiency could lead to an isolation amongst her team members.* At the time, Alessandro hadn't been overly concerned, sure that she was just focusing too much on her projects. But now he wanted to curse the parents who had forced their daughter to grow up far too soon.

He wondered what would have happened to Amelia and her sister if they hadn't been set on the path of revenge that had consumed ten years of their lives. What their lives would have looked like, who they would have been. And then, he couldn't help but wonder what would have happened if Gianni hadn't called him with the news, if he hadn't been warned about Amelia. Not with him, or Rossi Industries, but for the two sisters who would have reached their goal.

'What did you plan to do after?' he asked.

'After?'

'Yes, if you were successful. If you'd brought RI to its knees. What were you going to do after?'

For the first time since he'd known Amelia she looked—blank, desperately trying to hide something behind that nothing expression.

'I don't know,' she whispered, and his heart broke just a little for the girl she had once been.

CHAPTER ELEVEN

AMELIA HAD FELT unsettled ever since the conversation at the café with Alessandro. She couldn't quite put her finger on it, but she couldn't deny that she was feeling out of sorts. Standing in front of the mirror in Alessandro's beautiful en suite in Villa Vittoria, she took in the changes since the day Alessandro found her outside her flat in Brockley.

Despite the subtle sense of unease, her skin was now sun-kissed with a gentle golden glow. Freckles that had only ever shown themselves in Italy had been sprinkled across her forearms and her nose, warming the paler complexion she was used to. Her cheeks, ever so slightly rounder, had taken on an almost permanent blush thanks to the passion that she shared with Alessandro during heady nights she could barely credit were real.

The day after visiting the café, Alessandro had picked another piece of paper from the jar.

Tell me something about yourself that no one else knows.

He could have chosen to speak of so much but secretly she'd been just a little relieved when, instead of delving into the harder conversations available to them, he'd confided that he didn't like cartoons. Obviously, she'd thought he was absurd, but he'd seemed equally bemused when in return she'd shared that she didn't like sandwiches that were cut the wrong way. He'd stared at her for a moment and then made her two sandwiches so that she could illustrate the diagonal cut versus the half cut. He shook his head, threw his hands up in the air and stalked off muttering about silly English sandwiches.

The next morning, Amelia woke to find Alessandro waiting for her with a smile. He held out one of the paper tasks, looking strangely excited.

Take me somewhere you've always wanted to go.

And she'd buried her laughter beneath the sheets because he'd looked so much like an impatient child that she'd half expected to end up in Disneyland. Instead, as the view from the jet's window morphed from stretches of sea into stretches of desert, she realised that they were in Egypt to visit the Pyramids of Giza. None of the pictures she'd seen had done them justice. The sheer size and sense of history was breathtaking, even in spite of the large groups of tourists around them, chatting happily away and taking pictures.

Alessandro had asked if she wanted a private tour, and she'd declined because she liked the way he was when he was surrounded by people. As if he could relax and disappear in the crowds, rather than adopt that aura of power needed when he was the sole focus. It surprised her how easily he was able to give over that control and that attention and go with the flow of the loud tour guide, and throughout it all she felt his gaze on her almost as much as she saw it on the pyramids.

The following day while making her a decaffeinated coffee, Alessandro asked if there was somewhere she'd always wanted to go. Amelia looked up at him, nestling her cup in the palm of her hand.

'Could we go to Capri?' she asked, yearning in her heart making her pulse a little erratic.

'Of course. If you want, we can take a drive down the Amalfi coast and a boat to cross the gulf of Naples. Or we could take a helicopter if you like?'

She thought back to the last holiday her family had taken together, before her father had given up and before addiction took over her mother. They'd taken a hot, sweaty and *scary* drive down from Naples along the Amalfi coast—her mother hiding her eyes from the oncoming drivers, she and Issy squealing in delight at the twists and turns, too young to know better. It made her smile despite the ache in her heart. 'Boat, I think. I'd really like to take the boat.'

'Are you going to make me stand in line at the ferry terminal with the other tourists?' His demand was full of mock outrage and she was beginning to suspect that he secretly enjoyed being so anonymous.

'Actually, this time I think I'd like it to be just the two of us.'

In what felt like the blink of an eye, Alessandro had whisked them down to Positano and hired the most beautiful little speedboat she'd ever seen. It was like something from an old black and white film. Silken mahogany glowed beneath the Italian sun, perfectly offset by the deep racing green paint, the boat's sleek lines so smooth she wanted to run her hands across it.

Alessandro took the helm with attractive confidence and welcomed her aboard as if she were some grand duchess and he a lowly captain. The playfulness between them was addictive and her heart began to stretch towards the hope that it could always be like this between them.

She closed her eyes, letting the sun's rays warm her, and simply enjoyed the tang of salt in the air, the spray of the water, the rocking of the boat as Alessandro navigated around the deep swells caused by other seafaring craft.

But as they drew closer to the beautiful island, beloved by the rich and famous and lowly tourists alike, a sense of panic began to chip away at her pulse. The waves felt harsh as they jolted her and the grey craggy rocks beneath the lush greenery of the coastline felt threatening. The heat became uncomfortable and she began to feel breathless.

'*Tesoro*, are you okay?'

Usually, the endearment would have warmed her, but it barely even registered as she began to shake her head.

'Is it the baby? Is—?'

'No, it's not the baby. But…can we go back? Can we just…?' She gripped onto the seat beneath her, knuckles white, desperate to hold on while her world swayed in a way that went far beyond the sea.

Her obvious distress caused Alessandro serious concern and he quickly sped them away from the paths of the large tourist ferries and any other vessels, slowing only where it was safe, and he moored them just off a craggy coastal inlet. Turning off the engine, he sat and wordlessly pulled her into his lap, not stopping to question her need for him.

Amelia wrapped her hands around his neck and clung

to him as he swept circles on her back, trying to sooth the jagged breaths.

'*Cara...*'

She buried her head in his neck, scared to explain her feelings.

'Whatever it is, Amelia, it will be okay.'

You are safe with me.

Remembered words enticed her to speak, encouraged her to share the feelings so strong they had overwhelmed her.

'How could they?' she whispered. 'How could they have left us like that?' she asked him, even then knowing it was not his place to answer. 'I'm so...angry,' she said, realising the truth of the feeling thundering through her veins. 'I'm furious,' she cried, her hands fisting against the fact that the two people in the world who should have protected her and her sister had been so utterly selfish.

'We lost so much,' she said as the tears dampened Alessandro's linen shirt and her heart buckled beneath the onslaught of her feelings. 'Not money, or houses or friends. We lost *them*.' And for the first time she opened the door to the room where she had locked all that anger and all that resentment—not at having to look after and care for her sister, but resentment of her parents' utter neglect. And as her hurts poured out into the sea around them, Amelia let herself be comforted by the man who had, only days before, been her enemy.

Alessandro whispered to her in Italian; words of comfort to the incredible woman in his arms, until the storm of emotions that had gripped her had passed enough for him to talk to her about it. He knew that fury, he knew how hard it was to keep it controlled—he struggled with that himself. But Amelia, it seemed, had not realised what she had been fighting, her revenge plan keeping her and her sister from realising who had hurt them the most.

In that moment Alessandro wanted to destroy Thomas Seymore all over again. But if he had the chance to do so all over again, would he have? Knowing what it had done to Amelia and Isabelle? He could not take it back, and he could not apologise for it either. It had been a fundamental part of what had made him and Gianni who they were today and he was not, and would not be, ashamed of the men they had become. But that didn't mean he couldn't recognise the damage that had been done to Amelia and Isabelle Seymore's lives by his and Gianni's own need for revenge.

The sigh building deep in his chest was tired and heavy with thoughts of the past, clashing with the hopes he knew Amelia had for the future. A hope to do and be better. And he wanted it. He wanted it so damn much it terrified him. Because he'd had that same look, that same hope, once before and when that hope had been betrayed it had taken him decades to recover. He didn't think he'd survive it again. As if noticing the edge of darkness to his thoughts, Amelia stiffened in his embrace, until he forced the thought from his mind. Determined, instead, to soothe her hurts in this moment.

'Amelia,' he said, pulling back so that she could read the truth of his words. 'I really am truly sorry for what happened to your family. That was never an outcome we intended.'

She nodded her head, but he could still see the upset in her eyes. An almost violent urge to conquer any hurt she faced, any pain, and remove it from her path rocked him to his core. Despite the shocking power of that emotion, he gently swept back a sleek chestnut tendril of hair from her face. 'I'm sorry that you struggled and I'm sorry that you didn't have people there to look after you and take care of you when you needed it most. I'm sorry you had to do so much on your own.'

As he said the words, his own heart turned—like a sunflower following the sun—as if his words were trying to heal a hurt of his own, as if they were just as relevant to his childhood as hers. And this time when tears flowed freely down her cheeks, he knew that they were good tears, healing tears, necessary, so that she could be freer than she had been before. He placed a gentle kiss on a watery smile, and a little laugh escaped her.

'You can't kiss me now, I'm all…gross from crying.'

And Alessandro barked out a laugh. 'Amelia, *cara*, you are many things, but gross is not and never will be one of them.'

'I have a feeling,' she replied ruefully, 'that the next seven months might test that statement.'

For a moment they were caught up in a shared smile, his gaze dropping to her stomach where their child was slowly growing. Amelia, bottom lip pinned by a flash of white teeth, reached for his hand slowly—as if giving him enough time to back away. He felt hypnotised, unable to move—unsure whether he wanted this or not, scared in a way that he only vaguely remembered from a very long time ago. He let her take his hand and she placed it over her abdomen.

Surely, he wouldn't be able to feel the flare of her stomach this early on in the pregnancy, but he imagined that he did. Imagined that in there was the best part of both him and Amelia. They stayed like that for a while, lost in thoughts and hopes and dreams of a future they both wanted too much to say, until the blare of a passenger ferry startled them apart, and they turned to find tourists waving and yelling their greetings across the stretch of water.

Alessandro smiled, to cover the disquiet the moment had brought him, and said instead, 'Shall we go home?'

Amelia would remember the next few days with the hazy glow of summer and heat and a softness that she hadn't encountered before—from Alessandro or anyone other than her sister, for that matter. Alessandro could be funny, she discovered, enjoying the way that she could tease his ego without denting it or provoking a retaliation. He'd made her laugh as he'd answered another paper task to tell her something about Gianni that no one else knew.

She'd not been able to hold back the tears of laughter as Alessandro described in great detail, and a not inconsiderate delight, the time Gianni had tried to 'frost' the tips of his hair with bleach, only to have to shave his head and wait for his hair to grow back.

In exchange she'd told Alessandro about the time that Issy had fallen off her 'Gianni diet', ordered four pizzas, ice cream, garlic bread and sides, then got so scared about what her evil gym instructor would say the next day, she'd been too upset to eat it all, and she'd taken the entire lot downstairs to their neighbour.

Alessandro surprised her again with his impressive cooking and the fact that he was a secret foodie was almost one of her favourite things about him. From the incredible ingredients in the fully stocked fridge, Alessandro would create dinners at an almost gourmet level. After which, they continued to explore the passion they had discovered in Morocco. Amelia's nights were full of a heady sensuality that left her breathless and wanting in the daylight. Slowly they learned each other's pleasures, indulging in pleasing and receiving in ways that she could never have imagined.

But that, Amelia would later recognise, was the end of that brief momentary paradise they had together. Because the evening they returned from an idyllic day in Umbria, Alessandro received a message from work that had him locked in his office until long past midnight. And when he'd come to their shared bed that night, tiptoeing and trying to be so quiet, she let him think she was still asleep because she didn't have the courage to ask him about it.

The following morning, he was gone from the bed before she woke. But by the time she came down for breakfast, she was surprised to find him waiting for her. When he saw her, he put his phone away and offered her the decaffeinated coffee he had made for her and a slip of torn paper and it didn't matter what the paper said, just that he was still willing to do the silly tasks she had hoped would bring them together.

They were barely twenty minutes' drive away from the estate when he received another call and he cursed.

'You can put it on speaker if you like?' she offered, hoping that way he might be able to continue driving. And maybe, even, that she'd discover what was wrong and see if she could help.

'No, it's okay,' he replied, not meeting her gaze and signalling to pull over.

He got out of the car and took the call, pacing up and down the side of a dusty road. She tried to catch some of the conversation in between the roar from passing cars but it was useless. And she felt...frustrated and cut out. Even if it wasn't the Aurora project, she had worked with him for two years—she was good at her job. She could help if he would let her, but he wouldn't.

'I'm sorry, I have to go back,' he announced when he returned to the car.

The sudden engine ignition and the sweep of the U-turn prevented any further response from her. Only it turned out that Alessandro hadn't meant back to the villa, but back to London. Without her.

He returned that evening and Amelia clung harder to him that night than she had done before, as if sensing that he was slipping through her fingers, just as she had begun to realise that she loved him. It hadn't been quick, or sudden, it hadn't hit her like a punch, or stolen her breath. It had grown, piece by piece, as she'd uncovered little bits of him, like precious stones on a beach, hidden beneath sand and sea.

The loyalty he had to Gianni, the integrity he'd had with his business and his staff, the standard he held himself to, and the drive and determination to succeed. Those had all made him admirable in her mind even as she'd tried to sabotage him. And the physical connection they'd had? The strength of it had overpowered her own mind—her own determination to hate him, to make him pay for what had been done to her family. But his concern and care for her when she had collapsed, and then when she had emotionally broken on the way to Capri, made her feel as if she was seeing the *real* Alessandro Rossi. The way that he made her coffee, made her favourite dishes, those things had built in her heart. He had considered her in a way that no one had ever done before and it made her realise what she would lose if he walked away from her.

She worried about him when he went to London again the next day. The entire time he was away, her focus was on him and what he was doing, what was going wrong to take so much of his focus. And she could hear it, the whispered warning in the back of her mind. That he was cutting her out because he didn't trust her. That she was relying on him too much. That restless feeling creeping up on her grated on raw nerves and pacing inside the villa wasn't helping. Instead, she looked out across the pool and knew where she wanted to go.

As she entered the pretty wildflower meadow she was greeted by the red thumbprints of poppies bobbing and weaving across the tall grasses, reminding her of the finger paintings that her sister would bring back from the children's ward. Soft smudges of purples and cornflower blue, crested on the waves of gentle colours that called to her and softened her fears.

She lost track of time, just enjoying the simplicity of being here, until she found a rocky outcrop that nudged at her memory. It wasn't far from the section of land that belonged to Gianni, but she had known it would be there somehow and it unsettled her. She looked around, mentally drawing the boundaries of the land she had traversed, and her pulse began to thud heavily in her heart.

She knew this land.

She had seen it in drawings, and paperwork and a folder that had her father's name on it. And the realisation horrified her because finally she knew what it meant. Not just for the past, but for her future.

CHAPTER TWELVE

IT WAS LATER than Alessandro had hoped, but finally they were beginning to make headway on the problems that had stalled the Aurora project. Sofia Obeid had been impressive and as dedicated as he had been throughout the tense renegotiation with their contractors. Bitterly, he had to agree with Obeid; it would have been much quicker if they'd had Amelia on board, but he had dismissed the suggestion without excuse. Because how could he tell Sofia why he had cut Amelia out, when he couldn't even explain it to himself? Still. What was done was done and all he wanted to do was sink into a soft bed, and find that blessed oblivion only Amelia could offer him.

It was dusk by the time he returned to the villa, the sun reluctantly loosening its grip on the day. But Amelia wasn't in the house. He searched the rooms, not yet worried until she saw that the sliding door to the garden was open.

He marched towards the pool, concern sweeping through him like a wave, images of Amelia fainting again, of being in trouble and out of his reach, flung through his mind like sea spray. He gathered his speed and couldn't resist the urge to call out. Her name echoed in the vast area of the sprawling estate and something twisted in him at how lonely and desolate it sounded.

He rounded the corner to find her standing at the edge of the wildflower meadow, relief cutting through him to reveal a thread of heated anger, now that fear was edging from his system.

'Didn't you hear me calling?' he demanded as he reached closer to where she stood.

She turned to pin him with a gaze that nearly stopped him in his tracks.

Accusations, hurt and anger simmered there and he felt as if he had stepped back in time, as if they belonged on the face of a woman who wasn't yet carrying his child. He looked between her and the field and realised that she knew, that somehow she had figured it out.

'This is the land my father sold you.'

He wanted to curse. He wanted to deny it. He'd known that this moment would come and yet he'd prayed it wouldn't. Finally he nodded, watching her warily, as if suddenly she had become a great threat to him. And she was. In some ways that was exactly what she was. Ever since Hong Kong, she had changed him, had him thinking things, feeling things, remembering things—none were welcome and none were wanted. *Cristo*, he should have been able to resolve the issues they'd had on the Aurora project with the click of his fingers, but no, it had taken three days, because of her.

'You kept it.'

'Yes.'

'Well, let's face it. You did more than just keep it,' she said, her tone heavy with a cynicism he didn't recognise in her.

He frowned.

'Really?' she demanded. 'You aren't that clueless,

Alessandro. You are self-aware enough to know what you were doing.'

The taunt cut deep. 'Of course I knew what I was doing. Gianni and I made the decision the moment we could afford to,' he bit out. 'We built our homes around that one moment of betrayal so that we would never forget. *Never.* So that we would know the value of our hard work, and know that the only people we could trust was ourselves.'

She shook her head as if horrified by his words. 'This is more than my father,' she said, needling out the truth from him against his will. 'This is deeper than that.'

He reached for her instinctively—and she pulled away. He fisted the outstretched hand that dropped to his side.

'I need to know,' she said, her words barely audible in the gentle buzz and flutter of night-time wildlife. In the dusk he saw her place a hand over where their child grew within her and Alessandro knew she was right.

'To know what?'

'If you are capable of forgiveness. If there is even the slightest bit of hope for our future. You wake up every morning and look out at *this*,' she said, gesturing to the field behind her. 'You force yourself to hold onto that bitterness, to that symbol of betrayal. Is this how you feel about your mother?' she asked, her words hitting him like bullets in the chest, her eyes shining like diamonds in the darkness, her tears for him hurting more than he could possibly say.

'She betrayed us.' He slashed his hand through the air as if cutting off any more conversation. 'I know she tried the best she could,' he forced out, his heart and his hurt at war as it always had been. 'I know that she loves me—and Gianni too. And I love her too. So much that it hurts. But she still betrayed us.'

***

'Alessandro,' Amelia said, shaking her head helplessly, not knowing what to say. 'What happened to you was devastating. It was so wrong and I am truly sorry,' she said, hoping that he would hear the sincerity in her words. Her heart broke for him, for the child he had never been allowed to be. But that hurt made her even more sure that what she was doing was right. 'You have never forgiven her?' she dared to ask.

His silence was a knife to her heart. And now it was breaking for her, as the flame of hope she'd nurtured in his absence had just been snuffed out.

'Will you ever forgive *me*?' she asked, refusing to be cowed by the question. Her words rang into the night, clear and true. And she saw it—in his eyes—the past, his pain, his demons, all rising in the shadows around him.

'Amelia, you are pushing this too far too fast,' he warned her. And he was right, because she *was* pushing this too fast—even as she knew she shouldn't, but she couldn't stop herself from throwing them towards an impossible conclusion. Because if she didn't, she would only watch him walk away from her again and again and again. She was never going to be enough for him, just as she hadn't been enough for either of her parents.

'Does it matter?' she asked.

'Yes,' he said, sincerely. 'It does. I need time. Please...'

But she couldn't give him that, she thought, even as she knew she was wrong to refuse him it. The idea of watching another person in her life give up on her was too much. She had given her heart to him and he was already shutting her out because he didn't trust her. It rocked her to be standing here in the proof of how adamantly he clung to his betrayals.

'You won't forgive me, will you?' she said, her heart shattering beneath his gaze. 'It's why you kept the problems with Aurora from me, because you can't trust me.'

It was as if he'd been turned to stone, her statement proved truer for it. The only reason she knew he was still alive was the breath sawing in and out of his chest.

'Yet you trust me with your child?' she asked, half terrified, her breath caught in her lungs, because if he didn't—

'Yes.'

The word burst from his lips and she knew, instinctively, that he was telling the truth. She was thankful for it, but it wasn't enough.

'I need more than that, and our child does too.' She needed to know that their child would be raised in love and support without bitter undercurrents that dragged unformed hearts under.

He flinched. She barely caught it in the shadows of a night descending relentlessly, as if time was—and had always been—running out for them. And he simply stared at her while their lives began to come apart at the seams. Everything she'd hoped for, wished for in the sweetest of dreams, was falling away and he was doing nothing to stop it.

'Say something, damn you,' she hurled at him.

'There is nothing left to say.' His voice was raw as if he'd struggled to say even that.

'Yes, there is,' she said, her voice now shaking with a hurt and devastation that was only just beginning. 'You lied to me, Alessandro. You told me that you would keep me safe, you would protect me. You cling so tightly to others' betrayal, but it's you. *You* are the one who betrayed me, this time, Alessandro. *You* are guilty of that.'

And with that, she stalked past him and returned to the house, every step dimming the hope that he might stop her until it was snuffed out completely with the message that dinged her phone.

The jet is at your disposal.

Amelia hadn't been surprised to find a car waiting for her by the time she came downstairs with her clothes all packed in her suitcase. She'd been tempted to leave the things he had bought for her in Orvieto behind, but stubborn and stupid were close enough and it was possible she would need the clothes before long.

She knew that Alessandro would give her whatever she needed. He would never turn his back on her or their child. There would be painful, difficult, stilted conversations to come, but all she needed, right now, was time, space and...*her sister*.

She wanted to go home. But as the private jet swept in the arc that would bring them down to the English runway, she knew that the flat she shared with her sister just wasn't it. Home was where the heart was and she had just left that in Italy in the keeping of a man who was so determined to protect himself, he might never understand the value of what she'd given him.

She was holding herself together with numb fingers and desperation when she received a text message, and then another and then another. Hope turned to ash the moment she caught her sister's name on the phone's screen and she hated herself for being disappointed that it wasn't Alessandro.

Are you okay?

I'm back.

Where are you?

I don't know, her mind cried in reply. Amelia didn't have a plan for this. And for the first time in her life she wanted to give up, to curl up in a ball, to howl her pain as her mother had, to lose herself as her father had. But she couldn't. She had a little life to protect and, as much as her fragile heart was fractured and breaking, she needed to get up. She needed to make a plan. She needed to be the strong one.

Issy's name flashed up on the screen a second before her phone started to ring. Evidently her sister was too impatient to wait any longer.

'Issy?'

'Oh, my God, Amelia. Oh, thank God. Are you okay? Where are you?'

Amelia struggled to respond, wanting to tell her, wanting to give her answers to her questions, wanting to explain so much more, wanting to beg for forgiveness for lying to her about the evidence of corruption, for putting her in jeopardy with Gianni, for ruining her childhood on some naïve and mistaken path of vengeance. But instead, all she was capable of saying was her sister's name, before a sob took over and the tears came and they wouldn't stop.

In some distant part of her mind she knew she was on the verge of hysteria, that she needed to stop, pull herself together, but she just couldn't. It wasn't just Alessandro, it was her mother, her father, it was all of it and she couldn't keep it in any more. It was pouring out of her and nothing would make it stop.

Then she felt hands come around her. Small hands, but strong arms and she looked up to find Issy staring at her, tears in her own eyes, and concern stark across her features.

'Lia, please. You're okay. It's okay, I promise. It will all be okay,' her younger sister said, smoothing damp tendrils of hair away from her hot wet face.

Amelia didn't even think to ask how Issy had found her on a private jet on a runway in England. She didn't think to feel shame or embarrassment about what the staff had witnessed or where they were. She just let her sister envelop her, let herself sink into her sister's loving embrace and let that feeling heal and soothe just enough to get through the next minute and the minute after.

'I'm so sorry, Issy. I'm so, so sorry.'

'Shh. You have nothing to be sorry for. Nothing,' her sister said with such vehemence, it nearly made Amelia smile.

As her jagged breathing slowed and eased, she looked up and saw Issy for the first time. The Caribbean had glazed her skin golden, the blonde of her hair actually suiting her. 'Issy, you look beautiful.'

'Thank you,' she said, a simple shoulder shrug accepting the compliment without deflection or dismissal and it was lovely to see. 'You, however, Lia, look bloody awful.'

Amelia barked out a laugh and something eased in her chest. 'Oh, Issy. I've made such a mess of things,' she said, the sadness returning as swiftly as the flutter of a bird's wings.

'Whatever it is, we will fix it,' Issy replied confidently, and Amelia relished the feeling of being comforted, of being cared for. Issy turned to look behind her at the man standing at the top of the cabin.

Amelia's heart lurched, the height and breadth so similar to Alessandro it had fooled her for a moment. But then she saw all the ways in which Gianni Rossi was different from his cousin, one of them being the sheer love she saw when he looked at her sister.

Something unspoken passed between them and Issy turned back to her and asked, 'Can you come with us? I want to take you home.'

And even though the word jarred, even though Amelia was sure her sister didn't mean back to the one-bedroom flat in Brockley, even though she nodded and let herself be gently taken from the cabin of the private jet, she knew that wherever she was going it wasn't home, because Alessandro wouldn't be there.

For the next few weeks Alessandro stayed at Villa Vittoria, taking complete control of the Aurora project. He saw every email, every message, every report—it all went through him. And he knew that he was behaving like a tyrant, but somehow it had become imperative that nothing go wrong on this project. That nothing caught him by surprise again.

Gianni had tried to talk to him when he'd returned from the Caribbean, but for the first time in his life Alessandro didn't want to talk to his cousin. Just seeing the happiness Gianni had found with Isabelle Seymore, of all people, was unbearable and he *hated* that he felt that way. Never had he been jealous or resentful of the cousin who was more like a brother to him, but Gianni's joy came too soon after the sheer shock of Amelia's departure from his life.

You're hiding. I understand that. But it can only last so long.

But Gianni was wrong. Alessandro could make it last as long as he needed it to. Technology allowed him to stay in Tuscany and only fly out when necessary for meetings in both Europe and on the African continent should Sofia Obeid need it.

If she had noticed anything different about his exchanges, she had said nothing. Nor had she mentioned Amelia once. Which, instead of soothing his curiosity, only made it worse as he wondered if they were in communication, wondered if they spoke regularly, or at all.

He was not that surprised when he received the first message from Amelia informing him of her obstetrician's details. Of the first appointment. Of the results of the first scan. He hated himself for answering each message with one-word answers, but he wasn't capable of more. Because he would trail off into explanations, or justifications or demands that she return to him, or pleas that she let him return to her. And he wasn't ready for that. He knew that. *Recognised* that. Because she'd been right. He was still stuck in the past, its grip a vice around his heart and soul holding him in a place where he was not worthy of a future with Amelia and his child. Not yet.

He knew what it looked like from the outside...that he'd abandoned everything, including the mother of his unborn child, but he had never—*would* never do that. He had sent Amelia access to an account just for her that was separate from an account for their child. He had sent her the paperwork that showed he had no access to that account, would not be able to see any expenditures or receive notifications, knowing that it was the least he could do.

The only person he saw, aside from Gianni or Sofia in the occasional meeting he attended, was his mother. As the weeks turned into months, he began to travel to Milan almost once a week. The first time he'd visited it had been intensely painful. He had been full of resentment, anger and hurt. He hadn't expected much, he hadn't even really expected to talk, but his mother had appeared relieved, as if she'd been waiting for this day to come. That time they had simply, and very awkwardly, made polite conversation. Aurora Vizzini hadn't questioned him, asked him why he was there, or pushed him beyond what he was capable of, which was probably for the best. If she had, he might have left and not come back.

On the third visit they'd argued, impatience getting the better of him, hurt taking over, but as he'd left, she'd told him that she loved him. On the fifth visit he'd told her about Amelia and on the seventh he finally asked why they hadn't left that night. Why—when he and Gianni had needed to leave so badly—had she stayed?

Sitting in the chair, she couldn't meet his gaze. 'The shame and guilt that I couldn't be strong enough for you and Gianni…it will never leave. The horror that I allowed that man to inflict upon you…' She trailed off, shadows haunting her gaze.

And that was when his hurt and anger welled up to the surface, only to be swept back down in a whirlpool of guilt and anguish. 'But what about what he inflicted upon you? I couldn't stop it, Mamma,' he said, his voice quiet, but as rough as if he'd been howling his pain for years. Hot damp heat pressed against his eyes. 'I couldn't stop him, Mamma,' he repeated uselessly.

'You were a child, Alessandro, of course you couldn't stop it.'

'But I wasn't always—I grew, I was—'

'No, *mio bambino*, it was not for you to protect me. I was…glad when he realised that he could no longer… behave the way he had done.'

The anger and frustration that Alessandro had felt, once he had become bigger than his father and the physical threats had lessened but the manipulations and constant mental abuse had increased. And still he'd been powerless to do anything until they'd been old enough to escape, to get out, find jobs and work to support themselves—to support her.

'I couldn't get us out sooner,' he replied, the hot, furious energy leaving him utterly drained, as if he'd run a marathon.

'You got us out,' his mother stated, her eyes full of vehemence, determined that he would see how much that meant to her. *It is more than I did,* came the silent conclusion. 'I am so sorry for what I was unable to do as your mother.'

He shook off her apologies and she snatched up his hand, her skin silky soft and paper thin, her age startling to him as if only moments ago she'd been a young woman at the mercy of her husband.

'You need to hear it, know it and believe it. I am sorry that I could not protect you.'

'And I am sorry for exactly the same thing,' he replied, all that anger, all that hot rage melting away beneath the realisation that it was never about betrayal. It was never about being let down or lied to…it was about the helplessness that he'd felt as a child that had stifled and terrified him.

All these years he'd thought that he'd got up and got out, all these years he'd taken pride in his determination and ability to succeed, to strive forward, move on, but he was still there. Amelia had been right. He was still locked in the past, in his body, unable to escape—because *he* was the trap he had made for himself. *His* were the chains that roped his body and his mind and his heart.

It's you. You are the one who betrayed me, this time, Alessandro. You *are guilty of that.*

And in that moment, he realised how truly he had messed things up and finally he broke. The invincible shields he'd drawn around himself shattered all at once, falling to the floor, leaving him vulnerable and weak. And this time he allowed his mother to wrap her arms around him and protect him.

CHAPTER THIRTEEN

Three months later...

AMELIA FOLDED HER jumper and placed it in the suitcase beside the bed in the spare room of Gianni's penthouse apartment in London as her sister, Issy, hovered anxiously in the corner. She couldn't help but feel the pull of a smile tugging at her lips, knowing that her sister wouldn't stay silent for long.

'Don't go,' she begged.

'Issy.' Amelia turned and smiled. 'It's not far.'

'It's the other side of the river!' Issy cried.

'It's fifteen minutes away,' Amelia said, setting free the gentle thread of laughter beneath her words. Issy's eyes, though, were full of concern—a concern that Amelia understood. When Issy had first found her, she had been utterly devastated. Full of heartache, not only for the future she had lost with Alessandro, but the past she had lost because of her parents.

The first month she had spent with the new and delightfully happy couple had been hard in many ways. The conversations that she'd had with Issy about their parents had been honest, difficult, but ultimately deeply healing. And they were conversations she wouldn't have had, had

Alessandro not initially allowed her to come into those feelings in a safe space.

She resisted the urge to check her phone. Usually, he was quick with his one-word responses to her messages about her obstetrics appointments, but uncharacteristically he hadn't messaged in reply to her last one.

'Are you sure you're ready? I mean, you can always stay here a little longer?'

'Don't you want the place to yourself with your new husband?' Amelia asked.

'God, yes, but, oh—I'm sorry!' Issy had a hand pressed to her mouth, clearly worried about what Amelia would think, but she needn't have worried.

'Never be sorry, Is! Never. I'm thrilled for you,' Amelia said, wrapping her arms around her little sister and holding on tight. 'Really. But it's time that I got used to doing this on my own.'

Understanding shone in her sister's eyes, before she heard Gianni calling for her below. With a quick kiss to her cheek, Issy left Amelia alone in the lovely room that had been a haven for her when she most needed it. Her heart turned in her chest as she wondered about Alessandro, worried about what haven he had gone to after she had returned to England.

Over and over again she had replayed their conversation in her mind, seeing at almost every turn where she had gone wrong, but been unable to stop herself from doing so. She despised herself for not being able to give him what he'd needed when he—who had rarely ever asked anything for himself—had asked for it. She'd wanted to, but she'd been so battered and bruised, having only just accepted the damage from her parents, it had not been within her power.

Amelia had found a female counsellor in North London in the second month, knowing that she had many things to work on in order not to make the same mistakes as her parents when it came to raising her child. She would accept whatever help in whatever form to provide her child with the best that she could possibly give, and that had—she reluctantly realised—included dipping into the account that Alessandro had provided for her.

She needed her own space to think and to be. Looking back now, the unease she had felt, the desperation that had driven her to force Alessandro's hand, what had shaped so much of those last days with him, had been fear. Fear that had teeth and claws from the neglect of her parents who had left her alone carrying a burden that was too much for a young teenager. But she wasn't that scared young teenager any more. She was an adult now, who relished the chance to care for her child, to accept that responsibility not as a burden but as a gift.

Now she could see that she wanted to share her life with Alessandro because she loved him, because she admired him, because he was exactly the kind of man her father had never been to his family—but most importantly Amelia knew that she didn't *need* him to be the parent she wanted to be and the woman she knew she already was.

Her heart hurt to recognise it, but her soul knew it was right. As right as her need to find the right way to truly apologise to him. But for the first time, where Alessandro was concerned, she didn't have a plan. A fix. Something that she could prepare for. Only…she knew that she wanted to apologise. Because for all her accusations of betrayal, she *was* the one who had let him down when he had needed her understanding the most.

* * *

Alessandro knocked on the door, unease painting thick strokes of ice across his back. When Gianni opened the door, he caught surprise, shock, hurt all flit across his cousin's gaze, before it was replaced with indifference—a look Alessandro had never thought to see on Gianni's face. But he could concede that it was the least he deserved.

Ever since Amelia had left Villa Vittoria, he'd been acting like a stranger. After the painful confrontation with his mother, Alessandro had completely retreated. He'd handed over control of the project to the team with final oversight going to Gianni and Sofia. He'd left Italy and its memories so that he could have the time and space to think clearly about what he wanted for his child, what he wanted for himself, and what he wanted for Amelia.

Looking back on it, he could see how badly the lie about Firstview had sat with Amelia. The shadows beneath her eyes, her behaviour stilted and pained, until the truth had come out. And then her fierce love and protection for her sister, her determination to make it right, her adamant protection of their child and her desperate desire to give their child more than they had…it overwhelmed him.

He didn't just lust after her, that wasn't the connection that had formed between them—as he'd tried to convince himself early on. It was *her*. He loved her. He was inspired by her, awed by her. She was greater than him in every way and he missed her so much it was as if part of him had gone. A part he'd never known existed.

'Are you waiting for an invitation?' Gianni demanded as he beckoned him into the London apartment he was now sharing with his new wife. Isabelle Seymore had taken Gianni's surname and was now Isabelle Rossi and Alessandro was still wrapping his head around how the two cousins had fallen so deeply in love with the daughters of their one-time enemy.

'You!'

The hurled accusation from the living room where a woman who resembled Amelia was pointing at him as if she had accused him of being the murderer in a country house crime drama.

'You!' she repeated.

'Yes, me,' Alessandro replied in the hope that acknowledging it might make her stop—his hands might have also gestured surrender.

This, he knew, he also deserved.

She glared at him and he knew he'd made a mistake.

'You think this is funny?' she demanded.

'There is nothing funny about it,' he replied truthfully and something in his tone must have made her stop, as she glanced uncertainly at Gianni who, he saw, shrugged.

'What do you want?' Isabelle asked, eyeing him with a considerable amount of suspicion.

'I want to know where Amelia is.'

Isabelle snorted and he thought he'd heard her say, *yeah, not likely*, but he couldn't be sure. He looked at Gianni.

'I need to see her.'

Gianni shook his head. 'You are my cousin—my blood. But she is my wife. You'll understand one day.'

'Not if no one tells me where Amelia is,' he all but growled, his frustration getting the better of him.

'You broke her heart,' Isabelle accused.

'I know,' Alessandro admitted.

'No. You don't. She is my sister and I will fight to the

death for her and her child,' she said fiercely and suddenly he saw it—the similarity between the siblings, the passion, the fire, the determination. 'You—' she stabbed a finger at him '—broke—' another stab '—her.'

'And I promise you that—if I get the chance—I will spend every single day for the rest of my life ensuring that it never happens again. I know that nothing I say will fix the damage that has been done, but she needs to know that it was *me*, not her.' His words burned and cracked as they came from his soul, but he needed to say them. '*I* caused the cracks that broke a strong, powerful, beautiful woman,' he said, thumping his chest. 'I need her to know that,' he said to Isabelle, his tone all but begging.

Something flickered across Isabelle's gaze and he felt the hairs stand on the back of his neck. He felt the pull of that connection that he only ever felt when Amelia was nearby. He turned, slowly, vaguely registering Gianni pulling his wife from the room, because all he saw was Amelia. Amelia glowing, eyes bright, cheeks flushed healthily and skin still wearing the faint bronze of Italy. Amelia so round with their child that it took his breath away.

'You're here?' Alessandro couldn't believe his eyes.

'Yes, I... I wanted to be with family,' she said, unable to meet his gaze.

He took a step forward, but the way that Amelia held herself made him stop. She looked as if she were trying to hold the pieces of herself together and he hated that he'd done this to her. But he bore it, because that was his due.

'You heard what I said to your sister?' he asked, his words sounding as if they'd been dragged across gravel.

Amelia nodded, sending a wave of chestnut rippling

down her back. Her hair was longer, richer, more vibrant than he remembered.

'It was not... I wanted to...' Alessandro bit back a curse. He'd planned what he'd wanted to say to her, how he wanted to start, and this was going horribly wrong. He wasn't prepared, but that didn't, couldn't matter. She deserved to know and hear the truth of his feelings and he needed to tell them. He took a breath—a deep one.

'You make me flustered,' he admitted, helplessly. 'And I don't get flustered. At least not any more. My mother tells me that it used to happen to me as a child when I desperately wanted something,' he said, ruefully, rubbing the back of his neck.

'*Tells* you?' Amelia asked, picking up on the tense he had used.

He nodded. 'We've been spending some time together,' he replied, noticing the way her hand had begun to sweep slow, soothing circles over her round belly. He wondered if she'd felt their baby kick.

'I went to see her. You were right—about so many things. But the first and most important one was how trapped I was by the past. How it coloured everything and made it impossible for me to move on, move forward with any kind of life, let alone one that I want more than my next breath.' He hoped that she could read the truth in his gaze—that it was a life with her that he was speaking of.

Amelia was standing by the large window looking out onto the street as if only partially listening to him, but he knew—he knew that all of her considerable focus was on him. He felt it like a touch—warm, comforting, hopeful.

'I realised that it was not her I was angry with,' he said, willingly offering Amelia the deepest of his truths, baring his soul to her, hoping that somehow he might be worthy of her, 'it was me.' Some of the shame he had spent years wrapped in still lingered, but he was working through that knowing that neither he nor his mother deserved to feel shame or anger any more.

Amelia turned to him at his words. 'Alessandro—' She reached for him and he went to her, but he also needed to finish. As if she had read the thought in his mind, she held her words back.

'There is much more work I need to do, she and I need to do, but all this time I thought that I had left the past behind me and you were right. I was chained by it. And had it not been for you I would never have seen that, never have realised it. No matter what happens after today, or in any of the days that follow, I want you to know that you have changed my life for the better because of who you are. And I love you.'

Amelia's heart quivered, little gentle shakes rippling throughout her body.

'I love you,' Alessandro said again, as if he knew that she needed to hear it. 'And I will never stop loving you.'

She reached a hand to the chair to hold herself up. 'And I know that I offered you the security you wanted with one hand, and took it away with the other—the security to know that you were safe and loved and trusted—and I will never forgive myself for that.'

Amelia wondered if his words were magic, summoning all the broken shards of herself, raising them from the ground and bringing them back together. She wanted desperately to speak, to share of herself in the same way that he was, but she held herself back because she knew that he needed to say this. They had time, she began to realise with an expansion of her heart. They could take this time not to rush.

'I understand,' Alessandro continued, 'if you choose to move forward on your own with our child. I would…' His words stumbling once again, letting her know how hard this was for him, how much he struggled with what he wanted and letting her go to have what she wanted. 'I would like to be involved in my child's life,' he said, her heart cracking, but not breaking, reforming anew rather than what it had been like before, reforming to make room for him, right beside the love she felt for their child. 'But I trust that you know what is best for our child,' Alessandro said, and even the thought of him retreating, of him removing himself from their lives, cut her to the quick.

Finally, as if on the brink of his retreat, she found the courage to move towards what she wanted with her whole entire being.

'Alessandro,' she said, closing the distance between them and taking his face in her hands. 'I'm so sorry,' she said. The surprise in his gaze would have been near funny if it weren't so sad. 'I'm so sorry,' she repeated uselessly. Months of planning what she would say and her heart simply beat too loudly for her to hear what she had hoped to have the chance to say.

'I was so scared. I saw you retreating into work, shutting me out, which,' she said, holding up her hand to stop him from explaining, 'I understand, utterly and completely. It was what you needed to do in that moment. How *could* you have included me after I nearly destroyed your company? But I used that to feed fears I barely knew I had. I panicked and just couldn't see how you would want to stay with me when…when even my parents hadn't. But I'm working on that, and on much more,' she said, wanting to share the decisions she had made in the last few months, wanting to share so much of *her* life with him, not just their child's.

'I love you,' she said, her words overwhelmed by the depth of her emotions. 'I love you—powerful, proud, driven and occasionally flustered, you. The you who is loyal, caring, protective and who wears that love for his family on his sleeve.' His eyes exploded with hope, starbursts alight with love and want and the infinity that she had thought she had found with him once before.

He took a sharp breath, as if shocked by her declaration, and gently pressed his forehead against hers as if in reverence.

'If you take me back, I promise you'll not regret it. I'll spend every single day proving myself worthy of you.' He pulled back enough to look her in the eye.

'If you take me back, I promise to spend each and every day showing you the love and family that you are worthy of a hundred times over,' she said with a vehemence that matched the man she loved.

Her lips found his, and everything she'd ever wanted was in that kiss. Love, reverence, security, and everything she wanted to give him, she desperately hoped he felt. But when she wrapped her arms around him to pull him against her, something poked into her ribs. Angling back, and reluctantly breaking the kiss, she pressed her hands to his chest.

'What is…?'

Alessandro reached into his jacket inner pocket, a flush riding his cheeks.

'I've been carrying this with me for the last two months,' he said, and although there were nerves in his gaze, there was a dizzying anticipation. He pulled a small blue velvet box from his jacket. 'After all the mistakes I made, there will never be a right time. I know that. But I had hoped to at least do this properly,' he explained as he lowered himself to one knee.

Her hands flew to her mouth, stifling the gasp that caught on a smile. He opened the box to reveal a ring so perfect it could have been made for her. It had small green sapphire stones around a perfect red ruby, and it reminded her of the wildflower meadow at the heart of Alessandro's home.

'Amelia Seymore, you are the better part of my world, the whole of my life, and the only future I could ever have. I love you in a way that makes me better, that makes me want to be better and that brings me hope every single day. Will you do me the greatest honour, and be my lover, my partner, my companion so that I can love you, protect you and be with you for the rest of my days?'

Tears gathered in her eyes, and she happily shed them to see the shining love in his gaze for her.

'Yes,' she said, nodding. 'Oh, yes, please,' she added, pulling him from the floor so that she could embrace him. 'I love you, Alessandro Rossi,' she said, before placing her lips across his, and finally, after what felt like years of searching, Amelia Seymore came *home*.

EPILOGUE

'*Cara*, please, you're doing it all wrong—*ouch*!' Alessandro exclaimed as his wife slapped his hand away from the meal she was trying to prepare. It wasn't the slapping hand that worried him, but the knife gripped in the other that he eyed warily.

'Mr Rossi. I have six years of experience when it comes to making our daughter's favourite meal. Would you care to argue the same?'

The look in his eyes plainly told her he could, but instead he said, 'I would care not to argue at all, Mrs Rossi, but if you insist, perhaps we can take this into the other room?' The innocent expression on his face was utterly obliterated by the heady desire pouring from his gaze.

His hand slipped around her back and pulled her as close to him as her eight-month baby bump would allow. As much as Amelia wanted to, and she really did, Issy and Gianni and their children were due over soon and so much still needed to be done.

It had been nearly six months since she'd last seen them, her current pregnancy had been a little difficult and had prevented her from flying over to the Caribbean Island Issy and Gianni spent half of the year on, and she was desperately looking forward to seeing her sister.

Amelia looked across the counter top to the large wooden table set for their entire family. She remembered once imagining Alessandro sitting at it all alone and it pleased her to know that she had never seen that come to reality. As her husband tried to distract her with kisses to her neck—his favourite place on her body, it seemed—she remembered with a full heart the Christmases, New Years, birthdays, and every celebration they could make, shared with family and laughter and love.

'They would understand,' he whispered seductively in her ear. 'They're worse than we are. At it like rabbits, as you English like to say.'

'Mamma, what are rabbits "at"?' their daughter, Hope, asked innocently from the other side of the kitchen counter appearing—as usual—from nowhere. Hope Rossi had inherited her parents' ferocious intelligence and her love of books from her paternal grandmother, if Aurora Vizzini's proclamation was anything to go by.

'Jumping. Running and jumping around the meadow,' Amelia replied without missing a beat while Alessandro choked on his shocked laugh.

'The one where we meet Uncle Gianni and Auntie Issy and Mia and Matteo for picnics when they're home?'

Amelia nodded. She wondered just how much her niece and nephew would have grown as Alessandro swept up their daughter in his arms and threw her into the air, catching her without even raising Amelia's blood pressure. He had kept true to the promise he had made, not only the day he proposed, but before then, in a café in Orvieto. He had kept them safe, he had given them everything they could have even wished for, let alone needed.

And she had never, in the days and years that followed,

questioned his love and unconditional support. She'd had it when she had chosen to work with Sofia Obeid, at first part time after her maternity leave and then full time as partner in Sofia's company. And she'd had it while she had explored her issues from her parents with the therapist. Sometimes she still felt the echoes of the past, as she knew Alessandro did, but the healing that had been done with Aurora, who was also set to arrive for his birthday meal shortly, was a beautiful thing to see.

'My love,' he said, gently moving her out of the way of the oven so he could check on the food. It turned out that Alessandro loved nothing more than providing for and feeding his family. A family that would grow again in just one month's time. 'Can you please sit down?' he asked, still concerned about how much she was doing at this stage of her pregnancy. She shot him a glare that had none of the anger of their early interactions and all the heat that had burned between them from the very beginning.

He could see that she was about to argue when Hope heard the chatter of her cousins and the laugh of her uncle and aunt coming from the garden and she was off like a shot, allowing Alessandro to steal a kiss from his beautiful wife. He remembered how he had once been shocked by the possessiveness that had made him fear he had lost his mind. Instead, he realised later, it had been his heart. And only once he'd accepted his love, and had that love returned, had he found a peace and sense of rightness that he had never imagined possible. That didn't mean that they hadn't argued or that there hadn't been hard times to overcome. But they had faced, and would continue to face, each and every challenge together, safe in the knowledge and assurance of their love.

No one looking at them from the outside would have ever believed that they had once been enemies. Enemies who had become lovers and then soulmates bound together for the rest of their days by a love that was true and everlasting.

* * * * *

AT THE RUTHLESS BILLIONAIRE'S COMMAND

CAROLE MORTIMER

With many thanks to all at Mills & Boon

PROLOGUE

'WHAT'S *HE* DOING HERE?' Lia couldn't take her eyes off the man standing back slightly on the other side of the open grave where her father's coffin would soon be laid to rest.

'Who—? Oh, God, no...'

Lia ignored her friend's gasp of dismay as her feet seemed to move of their own volition, taking her towards the dark and dangerous man whose image had consumed her days and haunted her nightmares for the past two weeks.

'Lia—no!'

She was barely aware of shaking off Cathy's attempt to restrain her, her attention focused on only one thing. One man.

Gregorio de la Cruz.

Eldest of the three de la Cruz brothers, he was tall, at a couple of inches over six feet. His slightly overlong dark hair was obviously professionally styled. His complexion was olive-toned. And his face was as harshly handsome as that of a conquistador.

Lia knew he was also as cold and merciless as one.

He was the utterly ruthless, thirty-six-year-old billionaire CEO of the de la Cruz family's worldwide business empire. A business empire this man had carved out for himself and his two brothers over the past twelve years by sheer ruthless willpower alone.

And he was the man responsible for driving Lia's father to such a state of desperation that he'd suffered a fatal heart attack two weeks ago.

The man Lia now hated with every particle of her being.

'How dare you come here?'

Gregorio de la Cruz's head snapped up and he looked at Lia with hooded eyes as black and soulless as she knew his heart to be.

'Miss Fairbanks—'

'I asked how you *dare* show your face here?' she hissed, hands clenched so tightly at her sides she could feel the sting of her nails cutting into the flesh of her palms.

'This is not the time—'

His only slightly accented words were cut off as one of Lia's hands swung up and made contact with the hardness of his chiselled cheek, leaving several smears of blood on his flesh from the small cuts in her palm.

'No!' He held up his hand to stop two dark-suited men who would have stepped forward in response to her attack. 'That is the second time you have slapped my face, Amelia. I will not allow it a third time.'

The second time?

Oh, goodness—yes. Her father had introduced them in a restaurant two months ago. They had both been dining with other people, but Lia had been totally aware of Gregorio de la Cruz's gaze on her, following that introduction. Even so, she had been surprised when she'd left the ladies' powder room partway through the evening to find him waiting for her outside in the hallway. She had been even more surprised when he'd told her how much he wanted her before kissing her.

That was the reason she had slapped his face the first time.

She had been engaged at the time—he had been introduced to her fiancé as well as her that evening—so he had stepped way over the line.

'Your father would not have wanted this.' He kept his voice low, no doubt so none of the other mourners gathered about the graveside would be able to hear his response to her attack.

Lia's eyes flashed with anger. 'And how the hell would you know what my father would have wanted when you don't—*didn't*—know the first thing about him? Except, of course, that he's dead!' she added vehemently.

Gregorio knew far more about Jacob Fairbanks than his daughter obviously did. 'I repeat—this is not the time for this conversation. We will talk again once you are in a calmer state of mind.'

'Where you're concerned that's never going to happen,' she assured him, her voice harsh with contempt.

Gregorio bit back his reply, aware that Amelia Fairbanks's aggression came from the intensity of her understandable grief at the recent loss of her father—a man Gregorio had respected and liked, although he doubted Jacob's daughter would believe that.

The newspapers had featured several photographs of Amelia since the start of the worldwide media frenzy after her father had died so suddenly two weeks ago, but having already met her—*desired her*—Gregorio knew none of the images had done her justice.

Her shoulder-length hair wasn't simply red, but shot through with highlights of gold and cinnamon. Her eyes weren't pale and indistinct, but a deep intense grey, with a ring of black about the iris. She was understandably pale, but that pallor didn't detract from the striking effect of her high cheekbones or the smooth magnolia of her skin. Long dark lashes framed those mesmerising grey eyes. Her nose was small and pert, and the fullness of her lips was a perfect bow above a pointed and determined chin.

She was small of stature, her figure slender, and the black dress she was wearing seemed to hang a little too loosely—as if she had recently lost weight. Which he could see she had.

Nevertheless, Amelia Fairbanks was an extremely beautiful woman.

And the sharp stab of desire he felt merely from looking at her and breathing in the heady spice of her perfume was totally inappropriate, considering the occasion.

'We will talk again, Miss Fairbanks.' His tone brooked no argument this time.

'I don't think so,' she said, scorning his certainty.

Oh, they *would* meet again. Gregorio would ensure that they did.

His gaze was guarded as he gave her a formal bow before turning on his heel to walk across the grass and get into the back of the black limousine waiting for him just outside the graveyard.

'Señor de la Cruz?'

Gregorio looked up blankly at Silvio, one of his two bodyguards, to see the other man holding out a handkerchief towards him.

'You have blood on your cheek. Hers, not your own,' Silvio explained economically as Gregorio gave him a questioning glance.

He took the handkerchief and rubbed it across his cheek before looking down at the blood that now stained the pristine white cotton.

Amelia Fairbanks's blood.

Gregorio distractedly put the bloodied handkerchief into the breast pocket of his jacket as he glanced across to where she stood beside a tall blonde woman at her father's graveside. Amelia looked very small and vulnerable, but her expression was nonetheless composed as she stepped forward to place a single red rose on top of the coffin.

Whether she wished it or not, he and Amelia Fairbanks would most definitely be meeting again.

Gregorio had wanted her for the past two months—he could wait a little longer before claiming her.

CHAPTER ONE

Two months later

'I NEVER REALISED I'd accumulated so much *stuff*.'

Lia groaned as she carried yet another huge cardboard box into her new apartment and placed it with the other dozen boxes stacked to one side of the tiny sitting room. The other half was full of furniture.

'I'm sure I don't need most of it. I definitely have no idea where I'm going to put it all.' She looked around the London apartment with its pocket-size sitting room/kitchen combined, one bedroom and one bathroom. It was a huge downsize from the three-storey Regency-style townhouse she had shared with her father.

Beggars couldn't be choosers. Not that Lia was exactly a beggar—she had a little money of her own, left to her by the mother—but the comfortable lifestyle she'd known for all of her twenty-five years no longer existed.

Every one of her father's assets had been frozen until the extent of his debts had been decided and paid by his executors—which would take months, if not years. Considering the dire financial situation her father had been in before his death, Lia doubted there would be anything left.

Their family home had been one of those assets, and although Lia could have continued to live there until everything was settled she hadn't wanted to. Not without her father. The business sharks were also circling, ready to snap up the assets of Fairbanks Industries as soon as the executors had decided when and how they were going to be sold off to pay the debts.

Lia had used her own money to pay her father's funeral expenses and the deposit on this apartment, plus the few bits of furniture she had deemed necessary to fill the tiny space. She hadn't been allowed to remove anything from the house except personal items.

She had resigned from all the charitable work that had taken up much of her time—with her father dead and his estate in limbo those charities no longer considered the name Fairbanks as being a boon to their cause!—and she'd looked for, and found, a job that paid actual wages. She needed to be able to earn enough at least to feed herself and continue paying the rent on this apartment.

She had taken charge of her own life, and it felt strangely good to have been able do so.

Cathy shrugged. 'You must have thought you needed it when you did the packing.'

She didn't add what both of them knew: a lot of the contents of these boxes weren't Lia's at all, but personal items of her father's she had packed and been allowed to bring from their home. Items that had no value but which had meant something to him, and which Lia couldn't bear to part with.

Lia had put all these boxes in storage for the past

two months, while she'd stayed with her best friend Cathy and her husband Rick. That had been balm to her battered emotions, but a situation Lia had known couldn't continue indefinitely. Hence her move now to this apartment.

She was over the absolute and numbing shock of finding her father in his study, slumped over his desk, dead from a massive heart attack the paramedics had assured her would have killed him almost instantly. Cold comfort when they'd been talking about the man Lia had loved with her whole heart.

In some ways she wished that previous numbness was still there. The loss of her father's presence in her life never went away, of course, but now a deeper, more crippling agony at the loss would suddenly hit her when she least expected it. Standing in the queue at the local supermarket. Walking in the park. Lying in a scented bubble bath.

The loss would hit her with the force of a truck, totally debilitating her until the worst of the grief had passed.

'Time for a glass of wine, methinks,' Cathy announced cheerfully. 'Any idea which one of these boxes you put the wine glasses in?' The tall blonde grimaced at the stack of unopened boxes.

'I'm space-challenged—not stupid!' Lia grinned as she went straight to the box marked 'Glassware', easily ripping off the sealing tape to take out two newspaper-wrapped glasses. 'Ta-da!' She held them up triumphantly.

Lia had no idea what she would have done without Cathy and Rick after her father died. The two women had been friends since attending the same boarding school from the age of thirteen, and Cathy was as close to her as the sister she had never had. Closer, if what she'd heard about sisterly rivalry was true.

Luckily Cathy worked as an estate agent, and was responsible for helping Lia find this affordable apartment. But, even so, there was only so much advantage she could take of Cathy's friendship.

'You should go home to your husband now,' she encouraged as the two of them sat on a couple of the boxes drinking their wine. 'Rick hasn't seen you all day.'

Rick Morton was one of the nicest men Lia had ever met—as much of a friend to her as Cathy was, especially this past two months. But the poor man must be longing to have his wife and his apartment to himself.

'Are you sure you're going to be okay?' Cathy frowned.

'Very,' Lia confirmed warmly.

Rick had been persuaded to go off and enjoy a football match with his friends that afternoon. A welcome break for him, it had also allowed the two women to move Lia into her new home. But there had to be a limit to how much and for how long Lia could intrude on the couple's marriage.

'I'm just going to unpack enough to be able to make the bed and cook myself something light to eat before I go to sleep.' Lia gave a tired yawn: it had been a long day. 'I don't just have a new apartment to organise, but a new job on Monday morning to prepare for too!'

Cathy slipped her arms into her jacket. 'You're going to do just fine.'

Lia knew that. After the past two months she had no doubt that she was capable of looking after herself. Nevertheless, she still had to fight down the butterflies that attacked her stomach whenever she thought of all the changes in her life since her father had...*died*. She still choked over that word—probably because she still couldn't believe he was gone.

And he wouldn't be if Gregorio de la Cruz hadn't withdrawn De la Cruz Industries' offer to buy out Fairbanks Industries. The lawyers might have presented that death knell to her father, but there was no doubt in Lia's mind that it was Gregorio de la Cruz who was responsible for the withdrawal of that offer.

Her father had watched the decline of his company for months and, knowing he was on the edge of bankruptcy, had decided he had no choice but to sell. Lia firmly believed it was the withdrawal of the De la Cruz offer that had been the final straw that had broken him and caused her father's heart attack.

Which was why all of Lia's anger and resentment was now focused on the man she held responsible.

Futile emotions when there was no way she would ever be able to hurt a man as powerful as Gregorio de la Cruz. Not only was he as rich as Croesus, but he was coldly aloof and totally unreachable.

The man had even been accompanied by two bodyguards at her father's funeral, for goodness' sake. They hadn't been able to prevent Lia from slapping him, though. Was that because Gregorio de la Cruz had *allowed* it? He had certainly indicated that the two men should back off when they would have gone into protection mode.

She was thankful it had been a private funeral, and that there had been no photographs taken of the encounter to appear in the newspapers the following day and stir up the media frenzy once again. There'd been enough speculation after her father's sudden death without adding to it with her personal attack on Gregorio de la Cruz.

Nevertheless she had found a certain satisfaction in slapping the Spaniard's austerely handsome face. Even more so at seeing *her* blood streaked across his tautly clenched cheek.

As the days, weeks and then months had passed, and Gregorio de la Cruz's chilling promise that they would talk again hadn't come to fruition, Lia had mostly been able to put the man out of her mind. Just as well, because she only had enough mental energy to concentrate on the things that needed her immediate attention. Such as packing up the house, with Cathy and Rick's help, and finding herself an apartment and a job.

But she had successfully done all those things now—including securing a job as a receptionist in one of London's leading hotels.

Having no wish to start answering awkward questions from a prospective employer or, even worse, become the recipient of sympathetic glances that just made her want to sit down and cry, Lia had applied for several jobs under the name Faulkner—her mother's maiden name.

Nevertheless, she had no doubt it was her years of being *the* Amelia Fairbanks that had given her the necessary poise to secure her job. The manager of the hotel had obviously liked her appearance and manner enough to give her a one-day trial. He had admitted afterwards to being impressed with her warmth and the unflappable manner with which she'd dealt with some of their more difficult clientele.

The poor man had no idea she was usually on the

other side of the reception desk, booking in to similar exclusive hotels all over the world.

So—new apartment, new job.

Cathy was right: she was going to be just fine.

But not if one of her new neighbours was going to ring her doorbell at nine o'clock at night, when she was soaking in a much-needed bath after having pushed herself to empty half a dozen of the boxes once she'd eaten a slice of toast.

It had to be one of her new neighbours, because Lia hadn't sent out new address cards to any of her friends yet. It was the next job she had to do—once she had unpacked completely and arranged her furniture ready for receiving visitors.

Not that she expected there to be too many of those. Amazing how many people she had thought were friends had turned out not to be so once she was no longer Amelia Fairbanks, daughter of wealthy businessman Jacob Fairbanks. Even David had broken their engagement.

But she refused to think about her ex-fiancé now!

Or ever again after the way David had deserted her when she'd needed him most.

Going to answer the door wrapped only in a bath towel was far from the ideal way to meet any of her new neighbours, but it would look even worse if Lia didn't bother to answer the door at all. It must be obvious she was in from the amount of noise she'd been making unpacking boxes and moving furniture around.

Impatient neighbours, Lia decided as the doorbell rang again before she'd even had chance to wrap the towel around herself.

She might be new to living in an apartment, but she

knew at least to look through the peephole in the door before opening it. Except she couldn't see anyone in the hallway—which meant they had to be standing out of view. Well, there was always the safety chain to prevent anyone from coming in if she didn't want them to. And she *didn't* want them to. She was nowhere near ready— or dressed!—to receive visitors.

The reason her visitor had been standing out of the view of the peephole became obvious the moment Lia opened the door and saw Gregorio de la Cruz standing in the hallway!

'I do not think so.' He placed his handmade Italian black leather shoe in the six-inch gap left by the door chain, effectively preventing Lia from slamming the door in his face.

'What are you doing here?' Lia demanded, her hands gripping the door so tightly her knuckles showed white as she stared at the tall Spaniard.

He was once again dressed in one of those dark bespoke tailored suits, with a pristine white shirt and a perfectly knotted dark grey silk tie. Along with that slightly tousled hair, he looked like a catwalk model.

'You seem to have asked me questions similar to that several times now,' he answered evenly. 'Perhaps in future it might be wise of you to anticipate seeing me where and when you least expect to do so.'

Lia didn't want to *'anticipate'* seeing this man anywhere. Least of all outside the door to her apartment. An apartment he shouldn't even know about when she had only moved in today.

Except he was the powerful Gregorio de la Cruz, and he could do just about anything he wanted to do.

Including, it seemed, finding out the address of Amelia Fairbanks's new apartment.

'Go to hell!' She attempted to close to door. Something that wasn't going to happen with that expensive leather shoe preventing her from doing so.

'What are you wearing? Or rather, not wearing...?'

Gregorio found himself totally distracted by the view he could see of Amelia's bare shoulders, where tiny droplets of water dampened her ivory skin, and what appeared to be a knee-length towel wrapped around the rest of her body. Her hair was loosely secured at her crown, with several loose tendrils curling against the slenderness of her nape.

'None of your damned business!' There was a flush to her cheeks. 'Go away, Mr de la Cruz, before I call the police and ask them to forcibly remove you.'

He arched a dark brow. 'For what reason?'

'Stalking. Harassment. Don't worry, I'll think of something suitable by the time they get here,' she threatened.

'I am not worried,' he assured her calmly. 'I merely wish to speak with you.'

'You have nothing to say that I want to hear.' She glared at him, her eyes a deep metallic grey, the black rings wide about the irises.

'You cannot possibly know that.'

'Oh, but I do.'

Gregorio was not known for his patience, but he had waited for two long and tedious months before seeking out this woman again. Two months during which he had hoped her emotions would not be quite so volatile. Obviously time had not lessened her resentment towards him. Or the blame she felt he deserved for her father's death at the age of only fifty-nine.

To say he had been shocked by Jacob Fairbanks's demise would be an understatement. Although it must have been a strain for the man—and his company—to have been under close scrutiny of the FSA financial regulators. They were still investigating, and all of Jacob Fairbanks's assets would remain frozen until their investigation was complete.

Gregorio had no doubt that it had been the withdrawal of De la Cruz Industries' offer to buy Fairbanks's company that had caused the FSA's investigation. But he would not be held responsible for the bad business decisions that had brought Jacob Fairbanks to the brink of bankruptcy. Or the man's fatal heart attack.

Except, it seemed, by Amelia Fairbanks...

'No bodyguards this evening?' she taunted. 'My, aren't you feeling brave? Facing a five-feet-two-inches-tall woman all on your own!'

Gregorio's mouth tightened at the jibe. 'Silvio and Raphael are waiting outside in the car.'

'Of course they are,' she scorned. 'Do you carry a panic button you can press, if necessary, and they'll come running?'

'You are being childish, Miss Fairbanks.'

'No, what I'm *being* is someone attempting to get rid of an unwanted visitor.' Her eyes flashed. 'Now, take your damned foot out of my doorway!'

His jaw tightened. 'We need to talk, Amelia.'

'No, we really don't. And Amelia was my grandmother,' she dismissed. 'My name is Lia. Not that I'm giving *you* permission to use it. Only my friends are allowed that privilege,' she added with a sneer.

Gregorio knew he was most certainly not one of those. And nor did *'Lia'* intend for him ever to become one.

It was unfortunate for her that Gregorio felt differently on the subject. He didn't only want to be Lia's friend, he had every intention of becoming her lover.

When his parents had died twelve years ago they had left their sons only a rundown vineyard in Spain. As the eldest of the three brothers, Gregorio had made it his priority to rebuild and expand, and now he and his brothers owned a vineyard to be proud of, as well as other businesses worldwide. He had done those things by single-mindedly knowing what he wanted and ensuring that he acquired it.

He had wanted Lia from the moment he'd first set eyes on her. He would not give up until he had her.

He almost smiled—but only almost—at the thought of her reaction if he were to state here and now that that was his intention. No, he knew to keep that to himself. For now.

'Nevertheless, the two of us need to talk. If you would care to open the door and put some clothes on…?'

'There are two things wrong with that demand.'

'It was a request—not a demand.'

She raised auburn brows. 'Coming from you, it was a demand. I don't *care* to open the door, *or* go and put some clothes on. And nor,' she continued when he would have spoken, 'as I've already said, do you have anything to say that I want to hear. Because of you my father is dead.' Tears glistened in those smoky grey eyes. 'Just leave, Mr de la Cruz, and take your guilty conscience with you.'

Gregorio's jaw clenched. 'I do not have a guilty conscience.'

'Silly me—of course you don't.' She eyed him scornfully. 'Men like you ruin people's lives every day, so what does it matter if a man had a heart attack and died because of you?'

'You are being melodramatic.'

'I'm stating the facts.'

'Men like me?' he queried softly.

'Rich and ruthless tyrants who trample over everyone and everything that gets in your way.'

'I was not always rich.'

'But you were always ruthless—still are!'

For the sake of his brothers and his own future, yes, he had become so. Had needed to be in a business world that would have eaten him up and spat him out again if not for that ruthlessness. But ruthless was the last thing he wanted to be where Lia was concerned.

He shook his head. 'You are not only being overly dramatic, but you are also totally incorrect in your accusations. In regard to your father or anyone else. As you would know if you would allow me to come in and talk to you.'

'Not going to happen.' She gave a firm shake of her head.

'I disagree.'

'Then be prepared to take the consequences.'

'Meaning?' Gregorio's lids narrowed.

'Meaning I'm being extremely restrained right now, but if you persist in this harassment I promise you I *will* take the appropriate legal steps to ensure you are made to stay away from me.'

He raised his brows. 'What legal steps?'

'A restraining order.'

Gregorio had never experienced this much frustrated anger with another person's stubbornness before. He was Gregorio de la Cruz, and for the past twelve years no one had dared to oppose him. Lia not only did so, but seemed to take delight in it.

He had never felt so much like strangling a woman and kissing her at the same time, either. 'Would you not have to engage the services of another lawyer in order to be able to do that?' he retaliated.

Colour blazed in her cheeks at his obvious reference to the fact that David Richardson was no longer her family lawyer *or* her fiancé.

'Bastard!'

Gregorio had regretted the taunt as soon as it had left his lips. At the same time as he couldn't take it back when he only spoke the truth. David Richardson had left this woman's life so fast after her father's death and Fairbanks Industries being put under investigation, Gregorio wouldn't be surprised if the other man hadn't suffered whiplash.

He took his wallet from the breast pocket of his jacket before removing a card from inside. 'This has my private cell phone number on it.' He held out the white gold-embossed business card to her. 'Call me when you are ready to hear what I have to say.'

Lia stared at the card as if it were a viper about to strike her. 'That would be *never*.'

'Take the card, Lia.'

'No.'

The Spaniard's jaw clenched as evidence of his frustration with her lack of co-operation. She doubted many people stood up to this arrogant man. He was far too accustomed to *telling* people what to do rather than asking.

Lia had acted as her father's hostess for years, so she had met high-powered, driven men like him before. Well…perhaps not *quite* like Gregorio de la Cruz, because he took arrogance to a whole new level. But she had met other men who believed no one should ever say no to them. Probably because no one ever had.

She had no problem whatsoever in saying no to Gregorio.

Lia didn't remember her mother, because she had died in a car crash when Lia had still been a baby. But for all Lia's life her father had been a constant—always there, always willing to listen and spend time with her. Their bond had been strong because of it. When her father had died Lia hadn't just lost her only parent but her best friend and confidante.

'I'm asking you to leave one last time, Mr de la Cruz.' She spoke flatly, sudden grief rolling over her, as heavy as it was exhausting.

Gregorio frowned at the way Lia's face had suddenly paled. 'Do you have anyone to take care of you?'

She blinked in an effort to ward off her exhaustion. Which in no way stopped her from continuing to fight him verbally. 'If I tell you that I'm alone are you going to offer to come in and make hot chocolate for me? Like my father did whenever I was worried or upset?'

'If that is what you wish.' He gave an abrupt inclination of his head.

'What I wish for I can't have,' she said dully.

Gregorio didn't need her to say that her wish was to have her father returned to her, because he could already see the truth of that in the devastation of her expression: the shadowed grey eyes, those pale cheeks, her lips trembling as she held back the tears.

'Is there anyone I can call to come and sit with you?'

'Such as...?'

Not her ex-fiancé, certainly. David Richardson could not have truly loved Lia, otherwise he would have remained at her side and helped her to weather the storm that had followed her father's death. Instead he had distanced himself from any scandal that might ensue once the investigation into Jacob Fairbanks's finances was complete.

Gregorio had no such qualms. He had no interest in the outcome of that investigation, nor in what other people might or might not choose to say about Lia or himself. His private life was most definitely off limits. He might not be in love with Lia but he certainly wanted her, and he would be pursuing that desire.

Lia appeared to be swaying now, and there was not a tinge of colour left in her face. She looked so fragile that a puff of wind might knock her off her bare feet.

What had she been doing when he'd arrived? She was obviously naked beneath the towel wrapped about her, but she claimed she was alone so she obviously wasn't entertaining a lover. The obvious explanation was that Lia had been taking a shower or a bath in order to wash away the dust of having moved in to her apartment today.

The loosely secured hair and the droplets of water that had now dried on the bareness of her shoulders would certainly seem to indicate as much.

'Take off the safety catch and let me in, Lia,' Gregorio instructed in his most dominating voice. It was a voice that defied anyone to disobey him.

She attempted a shake of her head, but even that looked as if it was too much effort. Her head seemed too heavy to be supported by the slenderness of her neck.

'I'm not sure I can,' she admitted weakly.

'Why not?'

'I... My fingers don't seem to be working.'

Gregorio stepped up close against the partially open door. 'Move your right hand slowly, then slide the catch along until it releases.' He held his breath as he waited to see if she would do as he asked.

'I don't want to.'

'But you will,' he encouraged firmly.

'I... It's... You...'

'Move your hand, Lia. That's it,' he encouraged gruffly as she hesitantly moved her hand towards the safety chain. 'Now, slide the lock along. Yes, just like that,' he approved softly. 'A little more—yes.'

Gregorio breathed softly as the safety chain fell free and he was able to push the door open. Not quickly or forcefully, but just enough to allow him to enter the apartment.

To be alone with Lia at last.

CHAPTER TWO

THE APARTMENT LOOKED to be in absolute chaos to Gregorio's gaze. There were boxes everywhere, and furniture stacked haphazardly in the tiny sitting room. The kitchen looked as if there had been an explosion of cooking utensils in its midst, and not a single surface was visible beneath pots and pans and cutlery.

Gregorio had never seen this side of moving to a new home before. The vineyard in Spain had belonged to his family for years, and the three de la Cruz brothers had grown up there. The rambling ranch-style house was full of family heirlooms as well as memories. And he had hired an interior designer to decorate and furnish the apartments he had acquired in New York and Hong Kong, as well as his houses in Paris and the Bahamas.

No wonder Lia was exhausted.

Lia managed to rouse herself slightly as she heard the finality of the closing of the door to her apartment. She wasn't completely sure how, but Gregorio de la Cruz was now standing inside her apartment, rather than outside in the hallway.

She remembered now... She had opened the door and let him in. Not because she'd wanted to but because she had felt *compelled* to. His voice, deep and mesmerising, had ordered her to unlatch the safety chain, and because she had been consumed by that black exhaustion she had done as he'd instructed.

He seemed taller and larger than ever in the confines of her untidy apartment. Taller, darker, and just plain dangerous. Like a huge jungle cat preparing to pounce on its unsuspecting prey.

The almost-black hair was in that tousled style again, and his face was set in harsh lines. His shoulders looked huge beneath the tailored suit, his chest defined and muscular, waist slender, hips and thighs powerfully muscular.

Lia could smell the aftershave he wore, easily recognising it as one that cost thousands of pounds an ounce. Even so there was a fine stubble on his chin, as if he was in need of his second shave of the day.

Her gaze moved quickly upwards and was instantly ensnared by glitteringly intense almost black eyes. 'I—'

'You need to sit down before you fall down.' Gregorio stepped across the room to remove several items from one of the armchairs before lightly grasping Lia's arm to support her until she was seated. 'Do you have any brandy?'

She somehow looked more fragile than ever seated in the chair.

'Wine,' she answered with a vague wave of her hand in the direction of the kitchen area.

Wine would not revive her as well as brandy, but it was still alcohol and better than nothing. Gregorio found a half full bottle of red wine on the breakfast bar, a used glass beside it. Predictably, it wasn't one of the de la Cruz vintages.

'Here.' Gregorio held the glass of wine in front of

her until she took it from him with slender fingers that shook slightly. 'Have you eaten anything today?'

'Um…' Her forehead creased as she gave the matter some thought. 'A bowl of cereal this morning and some toast this evening. I think…' she added doubtfully.

He scowled his displeasure before turning on his heel to stride through to the kitchen area. There was a loaf of bread on one of the units, a tub of butter and a carton of milk—and nothing else when he pulled open the fridge door and looked inside.

'You do not have any food.' He closed the fridge door in disgust.

'Maybe that's because I only moved in a few hours ago.'

Gregorio held back a smile at the return of her sarcasm. Evidence that Lia was feeling slightly better? He hoped so.

'Which begs the question—how did you know I'd moved in here today?' She eyed him suspiciously.

Gregorio had known about the apartment in the same way he'd known about everything Lia had done in the two months since her father's death. He was given daily reports on her movements by his head of security.

No doubt it was an intrusion into her personal life that Lia would take exception to if she knew about it. But it was Gregorio's belief that the Fairbanks's situation was not yet over, and until it was she would accept his protection whether she wanted it or not.

'Drink your wine,' he ordered dryly as he took his cell phone from his pocket.

'Look, Mr de la Cruz—'

'Gregorio. Or Rio, if you prefer,' he added huskily. 'That is what my family and close friends call me.'

'Of which I'm neither. Nor do I intend to be,' she added dismissively. 'What are you doing...?' She frowned as he made a call.

'I had intended inviting you out to dinner, but now that I see how tired you are I am ordering dinner to be delivered to us here instead.' Gregorio put the cell phone to his ear, his gaze remaining challengingly on Lia as he waited for the call to be picked up.

Lia was starting to wonder if she had fallen asleep in the bath and was having another nightmare. Because Gregorio de la Cruz couldn't *really* be in her apartment, ordering dinner for both of them. Could he?

He certainly seemed real enough. Tall, muscular, and bossy as hell.

It seemed surreal after the months of torment she had just suffered through. Because of *him*.

Being a little unfair there, Lia, a little voice taunted inside her head.

Gregorio wasn't responsible for the decline of her father's company, nor the ailing economy. He had also been perfectly at liberty to withdraw his interest in buying Fairbanks Industries if he had decided the company wasn't viable.

Lia *did* believe it was the withdrawal of that offer which had resulted in her father's company being put under investigation, though, and only weeks later in her father's heart attack and premature death.

She had to blame someone for all that, and Gregorio de la Cruz was the obvious person.

He had ended his call now, and was once again looking at her with those fiercely penetrating black eyes.

Lia's heart skipped a beat. Several beats. The blood rushed hotly through her veins as she saw something stirring in the cold depths of those dark orbs. Gregorio continued to stare at her. Something that looked like a flickering flame was growing stronger, hotter by the second, and was sucking all the air from the room as well as Lia's lungs.

She swallowed. Her heartbeat was now sounding very loud to her ears. So loud that surely Gregorio could hear it too? Lord, she hoped not! This man had kissed her once, and although Lia had slapped his face for it she had never forgotten it.

'I'm really not hungry.' She stood up to place the empty wine glass on the breakfast bar. Only to falter slightly as she realised how close to Gregorio she was now standing.

'I doubt you have felt hungry for some time now,' he acknowledged softly. 'That does not mean your body does not need sustenance.'

Why did that sound so…so *intimate*—as if Gregorio wasn't talking about food at all?

Maybe because he wasn't?

Lia recognised the flame in his eyes for exactly what it was now. Desire. Hot, burning desire. *For her.* A desire he had demonstrated four months ago and which he obviously still felt.

She took a step back—only to have Gregorio take that same step forward, maintaining their close proximity.

She moistened her lips with the tip of her tongue. 'I think you should go now.'

'No.' He was standing so close his breath was a light caress across the soft tendrils of hair at her temples.

'You can't just say no.'

'Oh, but I can. I *have*,' he added with satisfaction.

Lia blinked up at him, her heart thumping wildly now, her palms feeling damp. 'This is insane.' *She* was insane. Because a part of her—certain parts of her—was responding to the flickering flames in those coal-black eyes.

Her skin felt incredibly sensitised. Her nipples were tingling and between her thighs she was becoming slick with arousal.

'Is it?' Gregorio raised a hand and tucked a loose curl behind her ear before running his fingertips lightly down the heat of her cheek.

'Yes...' she breathed, even as she felt herself drawn to leaning into that caress.

Her father's death and David's defection meant it had been a long time since anyone had touched her, held her, apart from Cathy's brief reassuring hugs. Lia's body cried out for another kind of physical connection.

From Gregorio de la Cruz?

This man was a corporate shark who felt no compunction in gobbling up smaller fish. He was also a man who had a different woman on his arm in every news photograph Lia had ever seen of him. He bought and sold women—usually tall and leggy blonde women, who looked good on his arm and no doubt filled his bed at night—as easily as he bought and sold companies.

Lia wasn't tall, leggy or blonde.

Nor was she for sale.

She stepped back abruptly—only to give a shiver as she immediately felt the loss of the heat of Gregorio's body.

'I'm going to my bedroom to dress. I advise that you be gone by the time I come back.'

His sculpted lips curved into a smile. 'I make it a rule always to listen to advice, but I rarely choose to take it.'

Her chin rose challengingly. 'Is that because you're always right?'

His smile widened, revealing even white teeth. 'I have a feeling that however I answer that question you will choose to twist it to suit your own purposes.'

He was right, of course.

As always?

'Or should I say to suit the opinion you have formed of me without actually knowing me,' he added harshly.

Lia eyed him impatiently. 'I know enough to know I don't want you here.'

'And yet undoubtedly here I am,' he challenged.

'That's because you... Because I... You know what? Get the hell out of my apartment!' Her earlier agitation had returned, deeper than ever. 'Whatever sick game you're playing, I want no part of it.'

He sobered. 'I do not play games, Lia, sick or otherwise.'

'That's odd, because I'm pretty sure you're playing one now.'

Gregorio drew in a deep and controlling breath. Lia made no effort to hide her distrust and dislike of him. And right now her body couldn't hide her physical reaction to him.

Her breasts had plumped, her nipples hard as they pressed against the covering towel, and Gregorio's nostrils flared as they were assailed with the scent of her sweetly perfumed arousal.

Lia might distrust him, might think she had every reason to dislike him, but the response of her body told him she also desired him as much as he desired her.

He could wait to satisfy that desire. If he had to. And for the moment it seemed he must.

'I agree—you should go and put some clothes on.' He nodded abruptly. His self-control was legendary, but even *he* had his breaking point. And Lia, wearing only a towel to cover her nakedness, was it.

'Thanks so much, but I really don't need your permission to do anything!'

A nerve pulsed in his tightly clenched jaw. 'Dinner will be here shortly.'

'I've already told you I don't want any.'

Gregorio's eyes narrowed. 'Did your father have a line over which it was not safe to cross?'

'Oh, yes,' she recalled, with a wistful curve of her lips.

'And I am sure you knew to the nth degree how close to that line you might venture?'

'Yes…' She eyed him warily now.

'I have now reached my own line,' Gregorio informed her calmly.

'Is that supposed to scare me?'

Her bravado was admirable. Unfortunately it was nullified by the rapidly beating pulse visible in her throat: Lia was well aware of exactly how close she was to crossing over his line. And to paying the consequences for that trespass.

Gregorio's mouth thinned. 'You are—' He broke off as the doorbell rang. 'That will be Silvio, delivering our dinner.'

Her eyes widened. 'Wow, you must be a regular customer for the restaurant to have delivered so quickly.'

Their dinner had been prepared at and delivered by the staff at Mancini's, one of the most exclusive and prestigious restaurants in London. If Lia thought they were going to dine on pizza or Chinese food she was mistaken.

'Go and dress,' he instructed harshly. 'Unless you wish Silvio to see you wearing only a towel.'

Lia had a feeling the thought of that bothered Gregorio more than it bothered her. She was half inclined to remain exactly as she was—if only so that she could annoy Gregorio even more than he already was.

The fact that she knew she would feel more comfortable fully clothed was the deciding factor in her turning on her heel and walking down the hallway to her bedroom. But she was aware of Gregorio's devouring black gaze following her every step of the way.

Once in her bedroom, Lia slumped back against the closed door and drew in several deep breaths. Exactly what was going on here? Because something most certainly was.

Gregorio had not only kept the promise he'd made two months ago, that the two of them would talk again, but now that he was here in her apartment he was making no secret of the fact he still desired her.

Her body's traitorous response to him was harder for Lia to accept, let alone make sense of.

He was *Gregorio de la Cruz*, for goodness' sake. The man who'd had a hand in driving her father to his death.

When did I stop holding him completely responsible?

She hadn't. Had she…? No, of course she hadn't.

Gregorio was hard, ruthless, and scary as hell. He was also at least ten years older than she was, with the added experience that came with those extra years.

Dear God, she must be more desperate for human

warmth than she'd realised if she'd been physically aroused by a man she should *hate*!

'Good?'

Lia's only response was a throaty 'mmm' as she dipped another piece of asparagus into melted butter before eating it with obvious enjoyment.

Gregorio had removed his suit jacket and tie, and rolled up the sleeves of his shirt to just beneath his elbows by the time Lia had returned fully dressed from her bedroom. Her hair was loose about her shoulders, in the style he preferred—but if Lia had known that he was sure she would have scraped it back into a severe bun! She was wearing tight black jeans with a deep grey sweater that perfectly matched the colour of her eyes.

He had placed their food in the oven to keep warm, cleared the breakfast bar, found cutlery and laid two places so they were ready to eat as soon as Lia returned.

After stating that she wasn't hungry she had devoured succulent prawns and avocado with obvious relish, and steak, asparagus and dauphinoise potatoes were now being enjoyed with the same enthusiasm. The fact that she had drunk two glasses of the red wine Gregorio had ordered to be delivered with the meal—he'd had the foresight not to order one of the vintages from the de la Cruz vineyard—would seem to indicate she approved of that too.

Gregorio had found the food to be as delicious as always, but most of his enjoyment had come from watching Lia as she placed the food delicately in her mouth before eating with relish.

More colour returned to her cheeks the more she ate, and there was now a sparkle to her eyes. Evidence that she really had been starving herself the past two months? Not deliberately, but because food had simply become unimportant to her with her life in such turmoil.

Gregorio intended to ensure that didn't happen again.

Lia was enjoying the food so much, and Gregorio seemed to be enjoying watching *her*, that there had been very little conversation between the two of them as they ate together.

Which was perhaps as well. Lia felt the need to argue with this man every time they engaged in conversation.

She finally placed her knife and fork down on her empty plate. 'I'd forgotten how much I enjoyed the food at Mancini's.'

Past tense, Gregorio recognised with a tightening of his mouth. Because Lia's world had been turned upside down and she could no longer afford to eat in such exclusive restaurants.

Which was his cue to resume their conversation about her father's death. A subject guaranteed to bring back the contention between the two of them, but also one that stood between them as an invisible barrier.

Gregorio would accept no barriers between himself and Lia—invisible or otherwise. He intended knowing everything there was to know about this woman. Inside as well as out. Intimately. And he intended her to know him in the same way.

'That was delicious. Thank you,' she added awkwardly. 'But it's been a long day, and now I think what I really need is to get some sleep.'

She did look tired, Gregorio acknowledged. Well-fed, but tired. And what did a delay of one more day or so matter when he had already waited this long for her?

He glanced at the disorder about them. 'Would you

like me to come back tomorrow and help you with the rest of your unpacking?'

'Why are you being so nice to me?' Lia frowned her puzzlement, more confused than ever now that she had satisfied a need for food she hadn't realised was there until she'd begun eating.

Her stomach and her appetite had perked up at the very first taste of the food from Mancini's—a restaurant she had enjoyed going to several times in the past, alone and with David or her father.

'You are a person it is easy to be nice to,' Gregorio dismissed with a shrug of his broad shoulders.

Shoulders that looked even wider and more muscular now that he was no longer wearing his jacket. In fact the whole casual thing he had going on—losing the jacket, taking off his tie, unfastening the top button of his shirt and rolling back the sleeves—had succeeded in making him more approachable and even more lethally attractive.

Which was perhaps his intention?

Lull the poor befuddled woman into a state of uncertainty and then pounce?

Cathy was never going to believe her when the two of them spoke on the phone tomorrow as they usually did, and Lia told her friend about Gregorio's visit and the fact the two of them had eaten dinner together.

Lia wasn't sure she believed it herself.

It was becoming more and more difficult to continue thinking of this man as the monster who had helped to destroy her father when he was being nothing but attentive and kind to her. No matter how rude she was, he continued to treat her with respect and kindness.

It's just his way of worming his way into my good graces before he goes for what he really wants!

Which Lia had now realised appeared to be *her*.

He was obviously a man who enjoyed a challenge if he thought he was going to win *that* battle.

'No, I'll be fine, thanks.' She stood up as indication that he should leave.

A hint he ignored as he remained seated at the breakfast bar. 'We have not eaten dessert yet.'

'Take it with you,' she dismissed. 'I couldn't eat another thing.'

'I could not deprive you of Mancini's celebrated chocolate cake.'

Lia gave a soft gasp. 'He really sent you some of his famous chocolate cake?' The dessert was Mancini's secret recipe, and it had always been Lia's choice when she had dined at the restaurant. It was rich and decadent, and the taste of the cake was orgasmic.

'He sent *us* some of his chocolate cake,' Gregorio corrected.

'He didn't know I would be dining with you.'

'Oh, but he did. I spoke to Mancini personally and requested he send all your favourite foods.'

She widened her eyes. 'You *told* him we were having dinner together?'

Gregorio studied her from beneath hooded lids. 'Is there a problem with that?'

'Not for me, no.'

'Or for me.'

He certainly didn't *look* concerned at having announced to a third party that he was having dinner with the daughter of Jacob Fairbanks. Considering the speed with which some of her so-called friends and her fiancé had disappeared in a cloud of smoke, she found Gregorio's behaviour odd to say the least.

'You're a very strange man,' she said slowly.

'In a bad way or a good way?' he prompted as he stood up.

'I haven't decided yet.'

The grin he gave softened the harshness of his features. 'When you do, let me know, hmm?'

'You're different than I imagined.'

'In what way?'

'That night at the restaurant when you—when you kissed me, I thought you were just another arrogant jerk who doesn't like to hear the word no.'

'One out of the two, certainly,' he mused.

Lia didn't need him to tell her it was the word no he didn't like to hear. There was no doubting he was arrogant too, but there was something else. Something she couldn't quite equate with the ruthless bastard she'd labelled him. Perhaps it was the fact that, whatever his reasons, he was actually attempting to take care of her.

'You said you weren't always rich?'

'No.' He settled more comfortably on the bar stool. 'When I graduated from university with a business degree and returned to Spain it was to find that my father had allowed the family vineyard to decline. Several years of bad harvest...diseased vines.' He shrugged. 'There were still my two brothers to go to university. I put my own life on hold and set about ensuring that happened.'

'By founding the de la Cruz business empire?'

'Yes.'

'And is your life still on hold?'

He looked at her admiringly. 'Obviously not.'

Lia gave a shake of her head. 'I don't think it would be a good idea for the two of us to meet again.'

He looked displeased. 'Why not?'

Lia avoided meeting his gaze. 'Besides the obvious, I don't belong in that world any more.'

'The obvious...?'

'I hold you partly responsible for my father's death.' There—she'd stated it clearly, so there could be no lingering doubts as to her reason for staying away from this man.

Was she protesting too much?

Because of her earlier reaction to him?

Maybe. But that didn't change the fact that she really didn't want to see or be alone with Gregorio again. He...unsettled her. Disturbed her. In a deep and visceral way Lia could never remember being aware of with any other man. Including the man she had once been engaged to and had intended to marry.

'I am sorry you feel that way,' he answered evenly. 'And you can belong in whatever world you choose to be in,' he announced arrogantly.

'You really can't be that naïve! My father is dead. My engagement is over. Most of my friends have deserted me. I've lost my home. My father's business is under investigation. None of the charities I worked for want the name Fairbanks associated with them. I now live in this tiny apartment, and I start a new job on Monday.'

'None of those things changes who *you* are fundamentally.'

'I no longer *know* who I am!' If there had been enough room to pace then Lia would have done so, as she was suddenly filled with restless energy. 'I try to tell myself none of those other things matter. That this is my life now...'

'But...?'

'But I'm mainly lying to myself.' She inwardly cursed herself as her voice broke emotionally. Gregorio was the last man she wanted to reveal any weakness to. 'And you're lying to *yourself* if you think that being nice to me, buying me dinner, will ever make me forget your part in what happened,' she added accusingly.

'No barrier is insurmountable if the two people involved do not wish it to be there.'

'But I *do* wish it to be there.'

'Are you sure about that?'

When had Gregorio moved to stand so close to her? She felt overwhelmed by both his size and the force of his personality—a lethal combination that caused her heart to start pounding loudly again.

'You have to go,' she told him.

'Do I?'

'Yes!'

Despite the food she'd eaten, Lia had no reserves of energy left to resist the pull of those dark and compelling eyes. No defences to fight the lure of that hard and muscular body. Even the reminder that he was Gregorio de la Cruz wasn't working. She was caught like a deer in the headlights of a car as his head slowly began to lower towards hers.

Gregorio was going to kiss her...

No matter how exhausted and defenceless Lia felt, she couldn't allow that to happen.

'No!' She raised enough energy to put a restraining hand against his chest, and that brief contact was enough to make her aware of the tensed heat of Gregorio's body and the rapid beat of his heart. 'You really do have to leave. *Please*.'

His lips remained only centimetres away from her own, his breath a warm caress against her cheek.

His nostrils flared as he breathed long and deeply before slowly straightening and then finally stepping away. 'Because you asked so nicely...'

Lia gave a choked laugh, able to breathe again now that he was no longer standing quite so close to her. 'As opposed to threatening to call the police and having them kick you out?'

'Exactly.' He rolled down the sleeves of his shirt and fastened them before shrugging back into his jacket. 'Think of me tomorrow when you eat all that chocolate cake,' he added huskily, and then the door closed softly behind him as he let himself out of the apartment.

Lia breathed easily at last once he had gone. What the hell had happened just now? She had almost let Gregorio kiss her, for goodness' sake. She—

Lia froze as she saw the business card sitting on top of the breakfast bar.

The same business card she had refused to take from him earlier, with his personal mobile number embossed on it in gold.

CHAPTER THREE

'Good morning, Lia.'

Lia felt all the colour drain from her cheeks as she stared up at the man standing on the other side of the reception desk at the London Exemplar Hotel.

She had always thought that a person feeling the colour leeching from their face was a ridiculous concept: people couldn't actually *feel* the colour leaving their cheeks.

Except Lia just had. In fact the blood seemed to have drained from her head completely, settling somewhere in the region of her toes and leaving her feeling slightly light-headed as she continued to gape across the reception desk at Gregorio de la Cruz.

He tilted his head, a mocking smile playing about those sculpted lips as he saw her reaction to his being here. 'I did warn you that in future you should anticipate seeing me where and when you least expected to do so.'

Yes, he had—but it hadn't occurred to Lia that Gregorio might turn up at her new place of employment.

Deliberately so?

Or was it purely coincidence that Gregorio had come to the Exemplar Hotel on the morning she began working there?

Lia very much doubted that. With a man as powerful and well-connected as Gregorio there was no such thing as *coincidence*.

Which meant he had known she would be here. How he knew was probably by the same means he had acquired the address of her new apartment.

She narrowed her eyes. 'Are you having me followed, Mr de la Cruz?'

'Followed? No,' he dismissed. 'Am I ensuring your safety? Yes,' he admitted without apology.

Lia's brows rose. 'Why on earth does my safety need ensuring?'

'You are now alone in the world.'

'We both know why *that* is!'

'Lia—'

'Is there a problem here—? Mr de la Cruz!' Michael, the hotel manager, quickly hid his surprise as he greeted the other man warmly.

'Good morning, Michael,' Gregorio returned smoothly as the two men shook hands. 'And, no, there is no problem. I just came down to say hello to Miss... Faulkner,' he finished, with a knowing glance at the badge Lia had pinned on the left lapel of her jacket.

It was a surname Gregorio knew didn't belong to her.

And he also apparently knew the manager of this hotel by his first name'

An uneasy feeling began to churn in Lia's stomach, growing stronger by the second and making her feel slightly nauseous.

There was no such thing as coincidence where Gregorio de la Cruz was concerned.

Which meant he had known exactly where she would be starting her new job this morning.

He really was having her followed—might he even have had some influence in her attaining this job too?

For what reason?

The churning in Lia's stomach became a full-blown tsunami as she searched for the reason Gregorio was doing these things.

That guilty conscience she had accused him of having?

No, he had denied feeling any guilt in regard to her father's death.

The only other reason Lia could think of was to make her feel beholden to him. Not just beholden but trapped, when she badly needed to keep this job in order to pay her rent and bills as well as to buy food.

Trapped enough to give him what he wanted?

Namely herself.

'Of course.' Michael accepted Gregorio's explanation. 'If you would care to take your lunchbreak early, Lia, I'm sure we can accommodate—'

'*No!* No,' she repeated in a calmer voice as she realised how rude her previous vehemence must have sounded. 'I'm sure a busy man like Mr de la Cruz has somewhere else he needs to be right now.' Her eyes glittered in challenge.

Whatever was going on here, and whether or not Gregorio had had a hand in her acquiring this job, she did not want her co-workers seeing her on the receiving end of deferential treatment from the manager on her very first morning. There were already several curious glances being sent their way—goodness only knew what conclusions the people she had only just started working with were drawing about this conversation alone!

'Thank you for the offer, Michael.' Gregorio answered the other man smoothly. 'But, as Lia says, I have another appointment in a few minutes.'

'Oh. Okay. Fine.' The other man looked slightly flustered. 'I'll leave the two of you to talk, then.' He hurried off in the direction of his office behind the reception area.

'I do not like your hair pulled back in that style.'

Lia raised an irritated gaze. 'I really don't give a—'

'Language, Lia,' Gregorio drawled.

'Down?' she repeated abruptly. 'You told Michael you had come *down* to say hello to me…' she said as Gregorio raised a questioning brow.

'I occupy the whole of the penthouse floor of the hotel,' he admitted without apology.

Lia's heart sank down to wallow in all the blood that had already drained and congealed in her feet. 'Is it possible that you own the Exemplar Hotel?'

'It *is* part of the De la Cruz Hotel Group, yes.' He gave a smile of satisfaction.

Trapped!

Lia had absolutely no doubt now that for reasons of his own Gregorio was involved up to his arrogant neck in her being given this receptionist job.

Gregorio's satisfaction faded, his eyes narrowing as he recognised the flush gathering in Lia's cheeks for exactly what it was. Anger. White-hot burning fury.

'Do not do anything you will regret,' he warned softly as she stood up.

'The only thing I regret is actually thinking you were being nice to me on Saturday.' She bent to retrieve her bag from under the desk, her eyes glittering accusingly as she glared across at him. 'I'm going to take that early lunchbreak, after all. Perhaps you would like to clear *that* with your buddy Michael?'

'He is not—'

'Stay away from me, Gregorio!' she hissed, leaning across the desk so that only he could hear. 'Find some other mouse to ensnare in your trap, but leave *me* alone!'

Her cheeks were ablaze with colour as she marched the length of the reception desk, appearing on the other side of it before striding the length of the hotel lobby and out through the front door.

Gregorio very much doubted it was the right time to tell Lia that the staff of the Exemplar Hotel were not allowed to use the front entrance.

Well, that hadn't gone as well as he might have hoped.

Hope.

That seemed to be all he had where Lia Fairbanks was concerned, when she continued to resist and deny him at every turn.

Maybe ensuring she was employed at one of the de la Cruz hotels hadn't been his best idea, but at the time, knowing of her lack of funds and the problems she was having finding suitable employment, it had seemed the right thing to do. Besides which, he knew Lia could do the job standing on her head.

She was warm, gracious, well-spoken, beautiful... And, having been her father's long-time hostess and companion, she knew exactly what was required of a receptionist in a prestigious hotel.

He should have waited until a more suitable time, of course, to inform her that he owned the hotel where she now worked. But, having spent a frustrating day yesterday, wondering what Lia was doing and who she was with, and knowing she was downstairs working in the lobby of the hotel, Gregorio hadn't been able to resist coming down at least to look her again.

Once he had seen her—as cool, calm and collected as he had known she would be—he hadn't been able to stop himself from actually speaking to her.

Considering Lia's fury when she left, he wasn't sure she would be coming back.

'So, how was your first morning at work?' Cathy prompted excitedly the moment she sat down at the table where the two women had arranged to meet for lunch. 'Met any gorgeous unmarried billionaires yet?' she teased as she made herself more comfortable by shrugging off her jacket.

Oh, yes, Lia *had* met an unmarried billionaire. But Gregorio de la Cruz's looks were compelling rather than pretty-boy gorgeous.

But he was a manipulator. He was having her followed. He had arranged for her to be employed at his hotel. He had literally taken away all her options. Until he owned her body and soul.

Body and soul?

Lia would be lying to herself if she didn't acknowledge her physical reaction to Gregorio. She only had to glance at him to be totally aware of him. Only had to look into those dark and compelling eyes to feel her body heating from the inside out.

Much as she might wish it wasn't true, she was physically attracted to Gregorio de la Cruz.

'Never mind,' Cathy sympathised, obviously misunderstanding the reason for Lia's silence. 'It was only your first morning, after all.'

For some reason, when the two women had spoken on the phone yesterday Lia hadn't told Cathy about Gregorio's visit to her apartment the evening before. Usually she told Cathy everything—had done since the two of them were at school together—but when it came to the subject of Gregorio, Lia didn't know quite what to say.

Maybe because yesterday she had still been a little uncertain in her conjecture as to the reason for Gregorio's visit the evening before—had still been wondering if perhaps she wasn't imagining things...desires... that simply hadn't been there.

On Saturday he had said he wanted to talk to her— which he hadn't. He had told her he would feed her dinner—which he had. And he had almost kissed her. He *would* have kissed her if Lia had allowed it.

His appearance at the hotel this morning—*the hotel he owned*—left her in no doubt that for reasons of his own Gregorio was weaving a spider's web about her. One made out of expensive dinners and the job she desperately needed, but still a spider's web.

Was he only doing these things because he *wanted* her?

Because he knew he couldn't have her any other way?

Lia found it hard to believe it was because Gregorio desired her. She had been complimented on the way she looked since men had first begun to take notice of her in her mid-teens. But she didn't fool herself into believing Gregorio was so bedazzled by her he would go to any lengths to have her. He only had to snap his fingers to have any woman he wanted, when he wanted her, so why bother even trying with a woman he knew had every reason to continue resisting him?

Maybe, despite his denials, he *did* feel some guilt in regard to her father's death?

'You okay, Lia?'

'Fine.' She determinedly shook herself out of her mood of despondency as she picked up the menu. 'Let's order, shall we?'

Until she knew what Gregorio was up to she had no intention of telling Cathy she had even seen him again, let alone that he was now pursuing her.

Relentlessly.

'Can I offer you a lift home?'

'No, thank you.'

Lia didn't need to look at the driver of the dark sports car driving slowly beside the pavement she was walking along to know it was Gregorio. Illegally kerb-crawling, of course—but then he seemed to be as cavalier towards the law as he was to everything else.

'You would prefer to take public transport rather than be driven home in the comfort of my car?'

'I would prefer to crawl home on my hands and knees than accept a lift from *you*!'

'You are being childish.'

'I am being the independent woman I now am—despite your efforts to make me otherwise!' Lia's hands clenched as she turned to glare through the open passenger window at Gregorio.

She had half expected to see him at the hotel again when she'd returned from lunch, and had breathed a sigh of relief when the afternoon had passed by without any more unwelcome interruptions from him.

She should have known he wouldn't give up that easily.

The car came to a stop and she stepped forward to bend down and talk to him directly through the open window. 'I realise you're a man accustomed to taking what he wants, and to hell with anyone else's feelings, but let me assure you I can't be bought or seduced into your bed with a few expensive dinners and a job— What are you doing?' she gasped as Gregorio turned off the car's engine before opening his door and climbing out of the low-slung vehicle.

His expression was dark and thunderous as he strode round the back of the car towards her. Lia instinctively took a step back.

He was dressed less formally than Lia had ever seen him before, in a black polo shirt open at the throat and worn beneath a soft black leather jacket, with jeans resting low down on his hips. The former emphasised the broadness of his shoulders and toned chest and abs, and the latter added to that rugged attraction. Gregorio looked breathtaking in a formal suit, but in casual clothes he was even more dark and dangerous.

Gregorio took a tight grasp of her arm as he opened the passenger door of the car. 'Get in,' he bit out between gritted teeth.

'I—'

'Get in the damned car, Lia, before I pick you up and put you there.' His voice was low and controlled. As if he might start shouting if he allowed himself to speak any louder.

It made Lia even more reluctant to put herself in the vulnerable position of being alone in his car with him. At least out here in the street she had somewhere to run.

She raised her chin challengingly. 'I believe you are stepping way over *my* line now.' She reminded him of their conversation on Saturday.

Those black eyes glittered dangerously. 'You just made an outrageous accusation. One I do not intend to dignify with an answer when we are standing out here in the street, where anyone might overhear our conversation.'

Her cheeks warmed. 'You made the purpose of your interest in me obvious on Saturday evening. Or am I wrong in thinking you want me in your bed?'

A nerve pulsed in his clenched jaw. 'No, you are not wrong.'

She nodded. 'Which is why, after discovering you're now my employer, I have come to the conclusion I have.'

Gregorio never lost control. *Never.* He considered it a weakness to do so. And weakness could be exploited... manipulated.

Nevertheless, he knew he was seriously in danger of losing control at this moment. No one had ever accused him of the things Lia just had. No one would ever *dare*. No matter what she believed, he had no reason to manipulate her into an intimate relationship with him.

Not when he knew she felt the same desire for him that he felt for her...

Even if it *was* a desire she obviously didn't want to feel.

Gregorio's only motive in protecting and helping her was the fact that she no longer had anyone else in her life who would do so. The wealth she had grown up with and no doubt taken for granted was no longer there as a buffer either.

So, yes, Gregorio might have put in a word with Michael Harrington regarding employing Lia at the hotel, but his only reason for doing so had been an effort to give her back some of what she had lost.

For Lia to have reached the conclusion she had, that he was blackmailing her into a relationship with him as a result of his actions, was unacceptable. An insult of a kind Gregorio had never faced before.

The nerve in his jaw throbbed. 'We are having dinner together.'

'Did you not hear what I just said?'

'Of course I heard you,' Gregorio snapped. 'How could I do otherwise? But, as *I* said, I will not answer any of your accusations on a public street.'

His bodyguards had parked their SUV behind his sports car and the two men were now standing on the pavement a short distance away, watchful and alert to any and all danger.

'I have no intention of being alone with you. Anywhere,' Lia added with finality.

Gregorio stilled to regard her through narrowed lids. That last remark had been made so vehemently...

Lia's eyes were glittering brightly, her cheeks flushed and her lips full and pink. The evening was warm, and she had removed the jacket of her business suit as soon as she'd left the hotel. The cream blouse beneath was so sheer Gregorio could see the outline of her light-coloured bra. Her breasts were quickly rising and falling as she breathed deeply, the plumpness of her engorged nipples showed as a darker pink through the lace of her bra.

Gregorio slowly moved his gaze back up to her face. 'You want me too,' he stated.

'That's a lie!' Lia recoiled as if Gregorio had struck

her, pulling her arm from his grasp as she did so. 'How could I possibly want you?' Her breathing became even more erratic. 'When you're the callous man who helped hound my father to his death?'

Lia heard herself say the words, saw Gregorio's reaction to them—his expression hardened and his eyes were once again those fathomless black pits—and all the time knew Gregorio was right. That she'd spoken so vehemently because she *did* want him. And she shouldn't. For all the reasons she had just stated.

Except her traitorous body was refusing to listen to her. Her breasts felt fuller and more sensitive and she felt the ache of arousal between her thighs.

'You are lying to yourself, Lia,' Gregorio dismissed scornfully. 'We both know that.'

'Your arrogance is only exceeded by your conceit!'

He gave a hard smile. 'When you are ready to hear the truth about your father I suggest you give me a call. Until then...' He turned to nod at the two bodyguards, indicating his intention of leaving.

'The truth about my father?' This time Lia was the one to place a restraining hand on Gregorio's arm, able to feel his tension through the soft material of his jacket. 'What are you talking about?'

He looked at her between narrowed lids. 'As I said, call me when you are ready to listen.'

'And my job...?'

He drew himself up to his full height, a couple of inches over six feet. 'Your continued employment is not conditional upon you agreeing to see me or listen to me. Or anything else.' His mouth was a thin line.

Lia's hand slowly dropped back to her side. 'I don't understand you...'

'Perhaps that is because—as you admitted the other evening—having now spoken with me, you find I do not fit with the preconceived prejudice you felt towards me?' he taunted.

There was some truth in that. No, there was a *lot* of truth in that, Lia conceded heavily. Gregorio was arrogant, and used to having—taking—whatever he wanted. But equally there had been no doubting his anger when Lia had made her accusations about his manipulating and trying to force her into a relationship with him.

He had also been considerate and unthreatening at her apartment on Saturday evening. If he really was as ruthless as Lia had thought him to be, then surely he would have forced the issue of wanting her then? He wouldn't have taken no for an answer when there had been a convenient bedroom just down the hallway.

After all, *she* might not have been aware of it at the time, but Gregorio had already known he held all the power.

And now he had implied that he knew something about her father that she didn't.

Lia gave a slight nod as she came to a decision. 'I'll have dinner with you in exchange for you telling me what it is you think you know about my father that I don't.'

She held her breath as she waited for Gregorio's response.

CHAPTER FOUR

'I THOUGHT WE would be having dinner in a restaurant.' Lia looked dazedly around the interior of the luxurious de la Cruz jet she and Gregorio were now seated on, being flown off to goodness knew where after boarding the jet at a private airfield fifteen minutes ago. 'I don't have my passport with me.'

'We are not going to land anywhere,' Gregorio assured her. 'And we do not need to go to a restaurant when I have persuaded Mancini to join us on board for the evening.'

If Lia had needed any convincing that Gregorio was super-rich—up there in the stratosphere wealthy—then the private jet and exclusive services of the chef were proof enough.

Except she hadn't needed any further proof of this man's wealth and power.

'We're just going to fly around while we eat our meal?'

'Why not?' He shrugged. 'It ensures our privacy.'

Privacy was the last thing Lia wanted with this particular man. A man she knew was starting to get to her, in spite of herself.

Gregorio knew the information he had about Lia's

father was her only reason for allowing him to take her to dinner. Unfortunately his self-control was currently balanced on a very fine edge where Lia was concerned.

She hurled her insults at him as barbs meant to wound. They had succeeded in doing that, but her open defiance of him had also deepened the desire Gregorio felt to make love with her. To be consumed by the fire that burned between them whenever they were alone together. He wanted to strip every item of clothing from her body and gorge himself on her succulent flesh before burning in those flames.

'*Now* will you tell me what you think you know about my father that I don't?'

His gaze became guarded. 'Our agreement was that we would have dinner first.'

She gave a frustrated sigh. 'In that case we might as well eat.'

'So gracious,' Gregorio drawled as he stood up to remove his jacket.

A delicate blush coloured her cheeks. 'Why don't you just open and pour the wine?' she instructed him abruptly.

'Do you like to take charge in bed too?'

'Gregorio!' She gasped.

He raised speculative brows as he opened the white wine cooling in the galley, revealing none of the pleasure he felt at hearing her use his given name for the first time. 'I wasn't complaining. I merely wish to be pre-warned if that is the case.'

She looked more flustered than ever. 'I didn't accept your invitation—I'm only here because you promised to give me information about my father,' she reminded him flatly.

'All the while knowing how much I want you.'

'I was only— I didn't— Why do you always have to turn everything back to—?'

'My wanting you?' Gregorio finished softly. 'Perhaps because possessing you has obsessed my mind for some time now.'

She snorted. 'I find that very hard to believe!'

He poured the wine into two glasses before pushing one towards her, an indication that she should drink some of it. 'That I want you? Or that I have thought of you constantly since I first saw you?'

'I was engaged to another man!'

Gregorio gave a brief glance at her bare left hand. 'An engagement is not a marriage.'

'Obviously not,' she acknowledged heavily. 'But I find it difficult to believe you felt an instant attraction to a woman you had only just met.'

'Possibly because you prefer to continue believing me a man capable of *hounding* people to their deaths.'

She winced at this reminder of her earlier accusations. 'Talking of *possessing* someone—me—isn't exactly normal behaviour,' she defended.

'You would prefer that I flatter and seduce you with words before I attempt to make love to you?'

'That's the way it's usually done, yes.'

He gave a dismissive shake of his head. 'I have no time for such games.'

'And, personally, I would prefer it if you never referred to the subject again.'

'Then you are lying to yourself.'

'You—'

'Would you like me to show you how much you are lying?'

'No!' Lia could see the raw passion burning in his dark gaze.

He drew in a deep breath as he continued to study her for several long seconds. 'Drink some of your wine,' he finally encouraged huskily.

'And you call *me* bossy!' She eyed him impatiently.

He studied her over the rim of his glass as he took a sip of what proved to be a very good glass of white wine. He waited until Mancini had served their first course before speaking again. 'You believe me to be a male chauvinist?'

She grimaced. 'Maybe it's just a cultural difference?'

'You do not believe that any more than I do,' he observed dryly. 'And you should have met my father—compared to him I am a fully enlightened man who believes in equal opportunity for all three sexes.'

'He's...no longer with you?'

'Neither of my parents is still alive.' Gregorio inwardly berated himself for unthinkingly introducing the painful subject of the death of a parent. 'My father believed it was my mother's role to be a wife to him and to bring up their three sons.'

'And you don't?'

Lia took her glass of wine. Their conversation was far too personal for her liking. Combining that with how casually dressed Gregorio was this evening, this situation—the private jet, the personal chef—was all too disturbing for her peace of mind.

'My mother ensured my two brothers and I have a more modern attitude.' Gregorio shrugged. 'For instance, she insisted all of us learn how to cook.'

'How did your father react to that?'

'As a man who had never had to learn how to so

much as boil an egg, he was horrified,' Gregorio recalled with one of those smiles that changed his face from austerely attractive to devastatingly handsome. 'My mother loved my father enough to allow him to believe he was the patriarch of the family, when in actual fact she was the one who decided what, when, where and how.'

'She sounds amazing.'

Gregorio heard the wistful note in her voice—a reminder that Lia had grown up without a mother. It seemed as if every subject they touched upon had the potential to blow up in his face.

'She was,' he dismissed briskly.

'But you've never married?'

'There has been no time for a woman in my life.'

'That isn't what the newspapers say!'

'I was referring to a woman I might wish to marry.'

'Rather than go to bed with?'

His jaw tightened. 'Yes.'

'What happened to the woman you were having dinner with that night at the restaurant?'

'*Happened* to her...?'

Lia nodded. 'She looked nice.'

Gregorio's company had been in negotiations to buy Fairbanks Industries for some weeks before he had recognised Jacob Fairbanks in the restaurant that evening. Both of them had been dining with other people. David Richardson was known to him as Fairbanks's lawyer. But he'd never before met the woman seated between the two men.

She had been exquisite.

Gregorio had seen his dining companion seated before immediately going over to Fairbanks's table to seek an introduction to the beautiful redhead. Amelia Fairbanks—Jacob's daughter. And the lawyer was her fiancé.

When Amelia had stood up to go to the powder room half an hour later, Gregorio hadn't been able to resist following her. Or kissing her. Only to receive an angry slap to his cheek as soon as the kiss had ended.

The evening hadn't gone at all as Gregorio had originally intended it should. Not only had he mainly ignored his dining companion for the rest of the evening, in favour of staring at Amelia Fairbanks, but he had also put the other woman in a taxi as soon as they'd left the restaurant, rather than accepting her invitation to go back to her apartment for the night.

He straightened. 'I never saw her again after that evening.' Nor had he dated any other women in the past few months.

'Why not?'

He gave her a pointed glance. 'Because I saw you that night and I wanted you.'

Lia turned away from the intensity of that dark gaze. 'I can't imagine you allowing anyone—least of all me—to disrupt a single part of your life.'

'Can't you?'

She was so aware of everything about this man she was finding it hard to maintain the distance necessary if she was going to continue resisting him. Even more so after those revelations about his parents and his childhood. She didn't *want* to know things about Gregorio's life, to think of him as having been a child with loving parents and two younger brothers he had no doubt argued and fought with but would likely defend to the death if one of them was in danger. Knowing those things made him more a flesh-and-blood man and less the ruthless monster, Gregorio de la Cruz. Which had no doubt been his intention all along.

She must never forget who or what he was. Nor that he had revealed himself as someone who was not averse to using manipulation and machination to get what he wanted. And there could be no doubt now that he wanted *her*.

She glared at him. 'I'm not interested.'

'No?'

'No,' she snapped, seeing his knowing expression. But she knew he was right; she could never remember being this aware of a man before. Ever.

She had known David for over a year before he'd asked her out and she'd accepted. They had dated for another year before he proposed and she had accepted. They had been engaged for just over a month before David had invited her back to spend the night at his apartment, and again she had accepted.

Up until the night David had ended their engagement he had been every inch the gentleman throughout the whole of their courtship.

Gregorio wasn't a gentlemen, and nor did he ever *ask* for anything he wanted. He just assumed it was his right and took it.

But wasn't it better that way?

To be simply swept off one's feet and not have to think about whether or not it was sensible, or consider the possible repercussions—?

No, of course it wasn't! Now that Lia was completely on her own it was even more important for her to be on her guard. Most especially so with Gregorio de la Cruz.

* * *

'You cheated,' Lia complained two hours later as she let the two of them into her apartment.

'I merely suggested we bring dessert back here.' Gregorio followed her inside.

'And so delayed answering my questions for even longer. Well, don't make yourself too comfortable,' she warned as Gregorio sat down at the breakfast bar. 'Because you aren't staying.'

'You *are* bossy in bed,' he said knowingly.

'You'll never know,' she assured him tersely.

Gregorio made no reply. Why bother contradicting her when it would only lead to another disagreement? When he was fully aware that Lia, in spite of herself, wanted him as much as he wanted her.

Besides, he could afford to concede a single battle when he had no intention of losing the war.

'Do you *want* any dessert?'

'I couldn't eat another thing after that delicious meal.'

'That's what I thought.' She put the dessert in the fridge before straightening. 'I've had dinner with you, fulfilled my part of the agreement, now it's time for you to start talking.'

She leaned back against one of the kitchen cupboards, arms crossed defensively in front of her chest.

'Of course.'

Gregorio stood up in what was now a very tidy apartment. All the boxes had been emptied and removed, the furniture was neatly arranged, and several photographs of Lia and her father had been placed in prominent places.

'I liked your father very much—but obviously you

choose not to believe that,' he said impatiently, acknowledging her sceptical snort.

'I have no reason to believe anything you say.'

'And *I* have no reason to lie to you.' He scowled. 'Lia, De la Cruz Industries did *not* withdraw from the negotiations to purchase your father's company.'

'Of course you did—'

'No,' he stated evenly. 'Your father was the one who withdrew from our offer.'

'That's ridiculous.' Lia pushed away from the kitchen unit, her movements restless as she walked into the larger area of the sitting room. 'Why on earth would he do that when he was on the verge of bankruptcy and so badly needed to sell Fairbanks Industries?'

'In light of the current FSA investigation into the company, I think we may assume it was because he had discovered some…discrepancy.'

'What sort of discrepancy?'

'I believe several million pounds were transferred from the company accounts to offshore bank accounts.'

'You *believe* or you *know*?'

'I know,' he confirmed quietly.

'My father did *not* steal from his own company, if that's what you're implying!' Her hands were clenched at her sides.

'Of course not.'

'Then who did?'

Gregorio shrugged his shoulders. 'Only a limited number of people had the means, and access to the bank accounts affected.'

She frowned as she thought over what Gregorio had told her.

He'd said her father had withdrawn from the negotiations to sell Fairbanks Industries. That he had done so because he had discovered someone had been stealing from his company.

But who?

As Gregorio had said, only a few people had access to the company bank accounts.

Her father, obviously.

And Lia, as a precaution—in case anything should ever happen to him and she needed access, he'd explained. How ironic that was, in the circumstances.

The two vice presidents of the company...

The accounts department only had limited access—not enough to be able to transfer funds from company accounts to another one.

There was no one else except—

Lia gave Gregorio a startled glance. 'Do you happen to know who he suspected?'

'I think you have already guessed the answer to that question.'

There was only one answer, if she eliminated everyone else. But it simply wasn't an answer Lia could give any credence to.

David had not only been her father's lawyer but her fiancé when the embezzlement had supposedly taken place. Besides which, his family was incredibly wealthy. There was no incentive for David to steal money from her father's company.

Lord knew she had no reason to think kindly of David, after he had let her down so badly, but she simply couldn't believe the man she had intended to marry was capable of the things Gregorio had just revealed to her.

CHAPTER FIVE

'You're wrong.' She gave a firm shake of her head.

Gregorio had watched the play of emotions on Lia's face. Puzzlement. Dawning realisation. Shock. Doubt. Followed seconds later by this outright denial.

'Are you saying that because you *know* I'm wrong or because you hope that I am…?'

She looked at him blankly for several seconds. 'I'll admit David ultimately proved not to be the man I thought he was when I agreed to marry him, but he isn't the thief you're implying he is either.'

'Again, I ask—is that because you know for certain I'm wrong or because you don't want to believe I'm right?'

She straightened her shoulders defensively. 'David comes from a wealthy family. He's a partner in one of the most prestigious law firms in London. His father *owns* that law firm, for goodness' sake.'

'And you consider that proof of his innocence?'

'Well. No. Of course it isn't proof.' She shot Gregorio an impatient glance. 'But there is absolutely no reason why he would have stolen from my father.' Her chin rose in stubborn denial. 'David is a wealthy man in his own right.'

'My sources tell me that Richardson has a serious gambling habit.'

'Then *your sources* are wrong.' She gave a disgusted shake of her head. 'I went out with David for a year, was engaged to him for three months. David doesn't gamble.'

'I'm afraid he does. Excessively so. I am reliably informed that he lost over sixty thousand pounds in one casino alone last month.'

She gave a pained frown. 'But I never saw... There was never any hint... Can I really have been so wrong about him?'

Gregorio had known this was going to be a difficult conversation, and that was the reason he had delayed having it for as long as he could. He had known Lia would have a problem believing her ex-fiancé was guilty of theft on a grand scale, despite the other man having deserted her when she'd needed him. It was for this reason that Gregorio had been skirting around the edges of the subject for the past three days. He had known that once his suspicion was out in the open he would have no way of retracting it. That Lia would hate him all the more because of it.

Gregorio had no doubt the FSA would eventually find the missing funds, and the offshore bank account, but that would be the end of their investigation. They would have absolutely no jurisdiction in another country.

Gregorio wasn't hampered by such legalities. His own security people were even now following the money trail to the offshore bank account in the name of Madras Enterprises. He had no doubt they would eventually unravel the maze surrounding this mysterious company, and when they did Gregorio was sure they would be able to identify the owner of that company as being David Richardson.

If Richardson *was* involved, then he had probably considered it prudent to distance himself from the Fairbanks family after Jacob's death—starting with breaking his engagement to Lia. There was also the fact Lia was no longer wealthy, and Richardson was going to need a *very* wealthy wife with his obsessive gambling habit to satisfy.

'If— Whoever is responsible... My father *died* because of the strain he was put under!' Tears glistened in her eyes.

Gregorio's mouth thinned. 'I will get to the bottom of who is responsible, Lia, this I promise you,' he assured her grimly. 'And when I do they will be made to pay for what they did.'

'It won't bring my father back.'

'No.' What else could he say to a statement like that?

She dropped down into one of the armchairs. 'Then it really doesn't matter who's to blame, does it?'

She leaned her head back, closed her eyes.

It mattered to Gregorio. If David Richardson was responsible for the embezzlement then he couldn't be allowed to get away with what he'd done to the Fairbanks family. Nor could he be left in a position of power where he could do the same thing to other clients who put their trust him as their lawyer.

'Did you tell me these things so that I won't hate you any more?'

Gregorio's eyes narrowed as he looked across to see Lia now watching him guardedly. He could read nothing from her expression.

'I told you so that you would know the truth,' he said cautiously.

'But also so that I don't hate you any more?'

'Is this a trick question?' He eyed her warily. 'Do I damn myself whichever way I answer it?'

'Probably.' She gave a humourless smile as she stood. 'I think you should leave now. My head is buzzing with all that you've just told me, and I need to get my things ready for work in the morning.'

His gaze became searching. 'Are you going to be okay?'

'Yes.'

Lia wished she felt as positive as she sounded. The things Gregorio had told her tonight were disturbing, to say the least. She still didn't believe David was involved, but if her father really *had* discovered that someone was embezzling funds from Fairbanks Industries, and had withdrawn from the de la Cruz offer because of it, then she very much doubted that both men could be wrong in their suspicions.

She had only just started to put her life back together, and now she felt exposed and vulnerable again.

Moving in to her apartment and starting a new job had been positive things. A fresh start. Moving forward after weeks of feeling as if she were stuck in a quagmire of emotions with no way out.

Gregorio had given her a lot of information to think about tonight. Information about David that, if true, meant he was responsible to driving her father to his death. It also seriously brought into question the reason he had pursued her and asked her to marry him.

And her own ability to know if a person was trustworthy or not.

She had trusted David, and even if it turned out that he was innocent of Gregorio's accusations, David had still let her down by leaving her to deal with her father's death alone.

She had distrusted Gregorio the first time she met him, and yet he had done nothing but try to help her. Albeit for reasons of his own, he had apparently been protecting her this whole time—had been instrumental, she was sure, in helping her to acquire her job. By doing that he had given her back some of the pride and confidence in herself she had lost.

Was it possible that the good guy was really the bad guy and the bad guy was really the good guy?

Lia was giving herself a headache, trying to make sense of it.

'I'll walk you to the door,' she offered distractedly.

Gregorio knew he had no choice but to accept that it was time for him to leave and he slowly followed Lia down the hallway to the apartment door.

Lia had a lot of new information to think about. But he didn't doubt for a moment that David Richardson was involved in this up to his pretty-boy handsome neck.

'Thank you.'

Gregorio blinked as he focused on Lia standing hesitantly beside the still closed door to her apartment. 'Sorry?'

She lifted her chin. 'I appreciate it must have been difficult for you to tell me those things.'

Gregorio drew in a slow and steadying breath, aware that Lia was placing a tentative trust in him.

'That doesn't mean I forgive you.' Her eyes narrowed. 'Only that for the moment I'm cautiously giving you the benefit of the doubt.'

He couldn't help but smile at her begrudging trust. 'I can live with that.'

'And call off whoever you have following me,' she added with a frown. 'It makes me uncomfortable to think of someone watching my every move.'

Gregorio would rather Lia felt a little discomfort than any harm came to her. If Richardson thought for one moment she knew of his duplicity there was no knowing what he would do. For the moment the other man felt secure, with his funds in an offshore company, but if Richardson ever began to doubt that security that might quickly change.

'Gregorio?'

He grimaced. 'Your father would have wanted someone to take care of you.'

She raised auburn brows. 'I doubt he ever imagined it would be you.'

'No,' he conceded wryly. 'Am I allowed a goodnight kiss?'

Lia burst out laughing. Which was pretty incredible after the conversation she'd just had with this man. But she couldn't help her response. It was so ludicrous for a man like Gregorio to *ask* if he could do something he had decided he wanted to do.

'When did you last ask a lady's permission to kiss her?'

'Never,' he acknowledged dryly.

She continued to chuckle. 'That's honest, anyway.'

'Your answer…?'

Despite the lightness of Gregorio's tone, Lia could sense his inner tension. It was there in his expression, in the stiff set of his shoulders and the hands clenched at his sides.

Long and elegant hands she had found herself studying as they ate dinner together. Everything about Gregorio was elegant and controlled. The way he moved. The way he ate. The way he talked. All calmly and elegantly done, and all firmly under his control.

A part of Lia wanted to shake that control—if only for a few minutes.

Besides, it was very narrow in this hallway, and made even more so by Gregorio's physically overwhelming presence. She could feel the heat of his body so close to her own, and breathe in that seductive aftershave...

'Yes.' She looked directly into his fathomless black eyes.

His brows rose. 'Yes?'

Lia felt a smile parting her lips. It felt good to smile again. In a genuine show of happiness rather than the polite curving of her lips she had been showing everyone for months now. Besides, she had just succeeded in surprising the hell out of Gregorio.

'Yes,' she repeated, more firmly.

She didn't need the warmth of another human being tonight, she *wanted* it—and not just anyone's warmth either. Gregorio's. She very badly wanted to know how it felt to be held and kissed by Gregorio de la Cruz.

Gregorio hesitated no longer and moved in closer to Lia, his hands moving up to cup her cheeks as he lifted her face, his gaze holding hers as he slowly lowered and tilted his head to claim her lips with his own.

Soft lips parted slightly beneath his as he continued to kiss her. Tasting. Sipping. Lia's hands moved up to grasp hold of his wrists and she moved up on tiptoe to increase the pressure of her lips against his.

Gregorio felt as if he had been in a constant state of

arousal for days…weeks—which he had—and now he was actually kissing Lia again he never wanted to stop.

His arms moved about her waist and he pulled her body in tight against the hardness of his as he deepened the kiss. His tongue swept lightly across and then between her lips to enter the welcoming heat beyond.

It felt as if he was *inside* Lia as she sucked his tongue in deeper still, her cheeks hollowing around his invading tongue in a parody of how it would feel to have him thrusting between her thighs. Hot and wet, and oh-so-good.

Gregorio gave a groan and began to stroke his tongue in and out of her mouth, his arousal throbbing hot and heavy in response as he placed his hands on Lia's bottom and pulled her body in even tighter against his own.

Lia gave a low moan, her breathing ragged as she felt the length of Gregorio's arousal pressing against the softness of her abdomen. Heat built between her thighs in response. Her nipples felt hard as unripe berries, and achingly sensitive against the restricting lace of her bra.

She pressed in closer still as she released Gregorio's wrists to slide her hands up his chest, until her fingers became entangled in the dark and silky hair at his nape. She couldn't seem to get close enough—she wanted more, *ached* for so much more.

Gregorio broke the kiss to trail his lips hotly down the arched column of her throat. 'Can I stay?' he asked throatily. 'Please, Lia, let me—'

'Yes.'

She didn't even allow him to finish. She didn't want to talk—she wanted…*wanted*…him. She wanted Gregorio, and the mindless pleasure she already knew they would have together.

David had been her only lover to date, and Lia had always assumed that her lack of orgasm was a fault on her part, not his. Had thought that they needed time to adjust and become accustomed to each other in that way. That pleasure would come with the physical familiarity of being married to each other.

But just a few minutes of being in Gregorio's arms, of having his lips and hands on her, and Lia felt as if she was about to spontaneously combust. As if something inside her was about to burst free, taking her to a place she had never been before.

'I said yes.' She frowned as Gregorio continued to look at her searchingly.

'Are you going to hate me again in the morning?'

'I might hate you again later on tonight, but right now *hate* is the last thing I'm feeling. Can we not dissect this, Gregorio?' She frowned as those black eyes continued to question her. 'Conversation is very overrated, you know.'

His tension broke as he smiled. 'You *are* going to be bossy in bed,' he decided with satisfaction.

'I'm going to be bossy *out* of bed if we don't go to my bedroom very soon!'

Gregorio chuckled softly as he placed his hands beneath her bottom and lifted her up off the floor. 'Wrap your legs around my waist,' he encouraged.

'Now who's being bossy…?'

Lia trailed off, her breathing becoming erratic as Gregorio turned to walk down the hallway towards her bedroom.

'Oh, God…'

Her arms clung tightly about his neck and she buried her face against his throat as each step he took ground her body sensually against his, sending wave after wave of pleasure coursing through her body.

'That is so... Gregorio!'

She gasped as the tension between her thighs intensified before suddenly being released, engulfing her in heat and an overwhelming pleasure that caused the whole of her body to tremble and shake as she rode out that release to its last shuddering throb.

So *that* was what the ultimate in physical pleasure felt like!

That connection men and women throughout the ages had killed for.

Lia now understood every one of those emotions.

Her orgasm had been a pleasure such as she had never dreamed of. Pure ecstasy. It had connected her to Gregorio in a way she had never experienced before with anyone else.

There was none of the awkwardness or embarrassment she had always felt with David as Gregorio carried her across her darkened bedroom and lay her down on the bed before lying on his side next to her.

'Are you okay?' He lifted a hand to caress the hair back from her temple.

'Better than okay.' She nodded, still trying to catch her breath.

'Light on or off?' he queried softly.

'On,' Lia decided, and she turned to switch on the lamp on her bedside table.

She moved up onto her knees, wanting to see all of Gregorio as she slowly undressed him. That hard and muscled chest. The taut abdomen. The long length of his arousal. Those long and muscular legs.

She already knew he was going to look like a mythological god. All golden flesh and hard muscles.

'Arms up,' she instructed as she lifted and then removed his T-shirt completely, revealing his chest covered in a light dusting of dark hair, his nipples like bronzed pennies. She touched them lightly, glancing up at him as she heard his sharp intake of breath and felt his nipples pebble against her fingertips. 'You like that?'

'Yes.'

Gregorio had no idea what Lia's sexual experience had been before tonight, and he didn't want to know either. Here and now, the two of them together, it was so highly charged, so intensely pleasurable, that everything and every other woman he had ever known before Lia faded into insignificance. Forgotten. All he could see and feel was narrowed down to this woman. To seeing and feeling only Lia.

Her orgasm a few minutes ago had come as a complete surprise to him. He had barely touched her before she'd found her release.

He could only hope that quicksilver response was uniquely for him.

He sucked in a breath as Lia scraped her nails lightly over the hardness of his nipples, a slight smile curving her lips as she watched and obviously enjoyed seeing his response to her touch.

She could pleasure and torment him for hours if it meant he could see that smile on her lips while she did it.

Her eyes glowed dark grey, her cheeks were flushed, and her lips were curved into that seductive smile, slightly swollen from their earlier kisses.

'Dios!' Gregorio's back arched off the bed as Lia's

tongue rasped moistly across one sensitised nipple, his fingers becoming entangled in the auburn hair draped across his chest as her lips completely engulfed his nipple with the heat of her mouth and she suckled deeply.

Gregorio was used to being the lover, the aggressor, and while women always responded with kisses and caresses he had never had one take charge of him in quite this way before. It felt strange, and yet somehow liberating at the same time—a measure of the trust that was slowly building between the two of them. Fragile as yet, but growing stronger the more time they spent together.

The things Lia was doing to him with her mouth and tongue made Gregorio's body throb and ache.

Lia lifted her head to smile at him, her eyes sultry as her hands moved down to unfasten the top button of his jeans, quickly followed by the other three. Gregorio sighed his relief as his desire was no longer constricted by material, only to suck his breath in again as Lia's hand caressed the length of him outlined against his black boxers.

'I want to feel your lips and your hands on my bared flesh,' he encouraged huskily. 'Please…' He lifted himself up and pushed his jeans and boxers down to his thighs.

Lia's breath caught in her throat as her gaze feasted on his fully naked body. She moistened her lips with the tip of her tongue.

'You're— *No…!*' she cried as the ringing of the doorbell sounded, shrill and intrusive. 'God, no…' she groaned as she buried her face against Gregorio's chest.

'Ignore it—' A second loud ring, longer this time, cut across Gregorio's protest.

'It's probably one of the neighbours, come to say hello to the new tenant.' She sighed as she sat up.

'That has never been my experience.' He frowned.

'That's probably because you live in a hotel. I have to answer that,' Lia snapped with impatience as the bell rang for a third time. Whoever was on the other side of that door was *not* going to receive a warm welcome from her—that was for certain. 'Stay exactly where and how you are,' she instructed Gregorio as she got up from the bed.

'*Sí, señorita.*' Dark eyes glittered with humour.

Lia cast one last, longing look at the lean and muscular length of Gregorio's body before turning to hurry from the bedroom, straightening her clothes as she went.

The doorbell rang for a fourth time just as she wrenched the door open.

'Oh, thank goodness!' A relieved Cathy stood outside in the hallway, Rick at her side. 'I was *so* worried about you.' She gave Lia a hug.

'I'm fine,' Lia assured her, her mind racing as she wondered what she was going to do about Cathy and Rick standing on her doorstep when Gregorio was half naked in her bedroom.

No immediate answer came to mind.

'You seemed so down at lunch,' Cathy said. 'I was worried about you, and Rick and I just had to come over and see if you were okay.'

'I'm really fine,' Lia repeated distractedly, her mind racing as she tried to find a solution to this dilemma.

There was no way she could get out of inviting Cathy and Rick inside her apartment. Not when they were giving up their evening to visit her. But, conversely, she couldn't expect Gregorio to spend all evening hiding out in her bedroom.

As if that was really an option! Gregorio went where he wanted and did what he wanted. It went without saying that hiding in a woman's bedroom would *not* be what he wanted.

'You look a little flushed.' Cathy looked at her in concern. 'Maybe you have the start of a cold?'

'Er… Cat…' Rick said hesitantly beside her.

'Or maybe it's the flu?' His wife continued to fuss. 'There's a lot of it about at the moment, and—'

'Cat!'

'What is it, Rick?' Cathy turned to her husband impatiently.

Lia winced as Rick ignored his wife and continued to look past Lia into the hallway beyond. She knew without looking that Gregorio had left her bedroom, after all, and was now standing behind her.

She just hoped he had put his clothes back on first!

CHAPTER SIX

'Perhaps I should introduce myself?'

A fully dressed Gregorio—thank goodness—looked at Lia as the four of them stood awkwardly in the sitting room of her apartment. Lia really hadn't had any choice but to invite the other couple inside.

'Fine.' It was the only word she'd seemed able to say since she had opened her apartment door and found Cathy and Rick standing outside in the hallway.

'Oh, I know *exactly* who you are, Mr de la Cruz,' Cathy assured him with a sideways glance at Lia. 'We're Cathy and Rick Morton. Friends of Lia's.'

Lia winced as she sensed Cathy's censorious gaze on her after that last announcement. It was questioning why, when they were such close friends, Lia hadn't confided in Cathy regarding her friendship with Gregorio. She was going to have some serious explaining to do once Gregorio had left. Whenever that was going to be. Because of the four of them he seemed to be the most relaxed and the least intimidated by this situation. He also showed no inclination to leave.

Lia felt bad for not telling Cathy about Gregorio's previous visit, or that she was working for him. At the time she had thought it was the right thing to do—that she would be avoiding Gregorio as much as possible in future, so telling Cathy about him was a waste of time. Look how well *that* had turned out!

But at least he had all his clothes back on and had tidied himself before he'd come out of her bedroom. Although the slightly creased T-shirt and tousled dark hair indicated that hadn't been the case minutes ago.

Lia knew Cathy was going to want to kill her once the two of them could speak privately.

'I remember seeing you with Lia at the funeral,' he answered Cathy as the three of them shook hands. 'And, please, you must both call me Gregorio.'

The pleasantries over, an awkward silence once again fell over the room.

'Wine.' Lia had finally found another word to say. 'Let's all have a glass of wine. I have red or white. Which would you prefer? The white is dry, the red fruity.'

Now she'd regained her voice Lia didn't seem able to stop babbling, but at the same time her gaze couldn't quite meet Cathy's or Rick's, and she was avoiding Gregorio's completely.

She felt so stupid. Like a child who had been caught out not being honest. Not that Cathy or Rick were in the least judgemental—it was Lia who felt as if she had somehow disappointed them.

'You sit and chat with your friends and I'll pour the wine.' Gregorio spoke dryly, obviously knowing the topic of their conversation would be him.

'I'll help you.' Rick hurriedly followed the other man into the kitchen area.

'Cathy—'

'He seems to know his way around your kitchen,'

Cathy observed softly as the two women sat down, Her brows rose as she watched Gregorio remove a bottle of red wine from the rack before taking glasses from the cupboard above.

Lia tried again. 'Cathy—'

'I have to say he's an improvement on the last guy,' her friend murmured appreciatively.

Lia's eyes widened. It was the last thing she had expected the other woman to say. 'You didn't like David?'

'He was your choice, so of course I liked him.' Her friend shrugged. 'Except I didn't, if you know what I mean.'

No, Lia *didn't* know what she meant. She had always thought Cathy and Rick *liked* David: the four of them had often gone out to dinner together, and they had always seemed to get on.

'He could be rather condescending,' Cathy added with a grimace.

Thinking back to those evenings, she realised David *had* talked down to Cathy and Rick. As if they weren't quite of his social standing. Which was ridiculous. Cathy's father was a politician, currently in government, and Rick's family owned and ran a huge farm in Worcestershire. Rick himself was senior manager at a software firm here in London.

It made her wonder what else she hadn't noticed about David during the months they had dated and been engaged. Whether Gregorio's suspicions about him were well-founded. David had certainly proved himself to be a less than supportive fiancé after her father's death.

Unlike Gregorio…

She might not particularly *like* the idea of Gregorio having his security men keeping an eye on her, but there was also a certain...reassurance—a warmth in knowing that someone cared enough about her to do that.

Lia chewed on her bottom lip. 'About Gregorio—'

'Don't worry about it, sweetie.' Cathy smiled as she leaned forward to give Lia's arm a reassuring squeeze. 'It's a surprise, but not an unpleasant one. The man is *gorgeous*, isn't he?' She lowered her voice even more.

Lia glanced across to where Gregorio and Rick were chatting together like old friends—as it turned out, as she listened briefly to their conversation, they were two men who both liked football but supported opposing teams. Gregorio was laughing at something Rick had said, his dark eyes warm with humour, a relaxed expression lightening his austere features.

'Yes, he is,' Lia acknowledged softly.

'He doesn't seem at all cold and remote this evening,' Cathy added approvingly.

Gregorio had been anything *but* cold and remote in her bedroom a few minutes ago. Burning hot and very close better described the two of them together. Just thinking about all Gregorio's naked and responsive flesh was enough to cause Lia's cheeks to warm in a blush.

Cathy gave her a knowing grin. 'Do you want us to leave as soon as we've drunk our wine?'

'*No!* I mean... No,' she repeated softly as the two men turned curiously at her vehemence. 'I think I may need saving from myself,' she told Cathy with a groan. 'I don't know what I was even thinking. He's just so—'

'Overwhelming and sexy as hell?' her friend supplied lightly.

Lia's gaze could no longer meet Cathy's. 'Yes.'

'Here we go,' Rick announced in an over-hearty

voice as he handed Cathy a glass of red wine. No doubt as a warning to the two women that they were no longer alone.

'Lia.'

She glanced up at Gregorio as he stood beside her chair, holding out a glass a red wine for her to take. The humour gleaming in those dark eyes told her he had overheard Cathy's last comment—and Lia's response to it.

She turned her gaze away, her hand shaking slightly as she took the wine glass from him.

'So, what do the two of you have planned for the rest of the evening?' Rick prompted politely—and immediately had to thump Cathy on the back as she began to choke on a mouthful of wine. 'What did I say?' Rick looked bewildered by his wife's reaction.

'Never mind, love,' Cathy answered once she'd caught her breath. 'Let's just drink our wine and pick up a Chinese takeaway on the way home.'

'Lia and I have already eaten, but we could always order in food for you to eat here?' Gregorio suggested lightly. 'Alternatively, we could all go out for a drink together somewhere the two of you could have some food?'

Lia slowly turned her head to look at him. Who *was* this man and what had he done with the cold and arrogant Gregorio de la Cruz? Because *this* man certainly wasn't the ruthless businessman who swallowed up companies with the voracity of a shark. Or the playboy billionaire she'd read about in the newspapers who had a different blonde on his arm every week.

'Okay, this is getting a little weird now.'

Lia stood up decisively. She might have been in

shock since Cathy and Rick had arrived, but she was recovering fast. And the four of them spending the rest of the evening together wasn't going to happen.

'Cathy and Rick are far too polite to say so, but they don't want to spend the evening with the two of us—'

'Hey, don't put words in my mouth,' Cathy protested.

'Because they are both totally freaked out right now,' Lia continued determinedly. '*I'm* freaked out right now, so I know they have to be too.' She frowned at Gregorio. 'The two of us aren't a couple and we aren't going out for the evening with anyone—least of all my two best friends. What happened earlier…' She gave Cathy and Rick a self-conscious glance. 'Shouldn't have happened.'

'I believe *you* are the one embarrassing your friends.' Now Gregorio looked every inch the coldly arrogant man Lia had met at her father's funeral: his eyes were narrowed and no longer warm, but hard as the onyx they resembled, and his sculptured lips were thin and unsmiling.

'Not at all.' Cathy stood up. 'It's time the two of us were going anyway. Rick?' she prompted sharply as her husband made no move to get up out of his chair.

'What? Oh. Yes. Sorry.' He rose abruptly to his feet, then seemed to realise he still had a glass in his hand and looked around for somewhere to put it.

'Here.' Cathy took the glass and placed it on the coffee table next to her own. 'I'll call you in the morning, okay?' She gave Lia a hug. 'Nice to meet you, Gregorio.' She nodded. 'Say goodnight, Rick,' she instructed dryly. Her husband still looked slightly dazed by the speed of their departure.

'Goodnight, Rick,' he repeated as he was pulled down the hallway by his wife.

The apartment door closed quietly behind them seconds later.

Leaving an awkward silence.

A very cold and very uncomfortable silence that caused Lia to give a shiver as the chill seemed to seep into her bones.

'Your rudeness was completely uncalled for,' Gregorio snapped finally.

'No.' Lia's chin rose as she faced him. 'No, it really wasn't. I don't know what happened between the two of us earlier, but it isn't going to happen again. I won't *let* it happen again,' she added firmly. She was totally unsettled by their earlier passion. 'And we certainly aren't ever going out for the evening with any of my friends, as if the two of us are together.'

Gregorio was having to exert great willpower so as not to lose his temper. He made a point of never losing his temper—no matter what the provocation. But he had not encountered anyone as stubborn as Lia before.

He had been disappointed when he'd realised Lia's visitors had to be Cathy and Rick Morton, the couple he had seen her with at her father's graveside two months ago. He knew, from the daily security reports he received, that Lia had lived with the other couple before moving into her apartment at the weekend.

Rather than remaining in Lia's bedroom like a dirty little secret she was keeping hidden away, Gregorio had decided to dress and join them.

He had no experience of being in the company of a woman's friends or family, but he had thought he was doing quite well. Being charming to Cathy. Talking football with her husband. Pouring them all wine. It had seemed perfectly logical to him, as the other couple were obviously close to Lia, to suggest they all spend the rest of the evening together.

Lia's vehemently negative response to that suggestion had been immediate. And, to his surprise, her words had hurt.

He was close to his two brothers. Well…as close as he could be when he was based in London, Sebastien was in New York, and Alejandro was taking care of the estate and vineyards in Spain. He also had a large extended family, of which *he* was the recognised patriarch.

He had sex with the women who flitted in and out of his life, but he did *not* become involved with their family or their friends. He rarely even *met* any of their friends, let alone their family. He had been willing to make an exception with Lia, and he'd received a verbal and public slap in the face for his trouble.

He would not make the same mistake again.

'What happened earlier is that you used me for sex,' he bit out coldly, his accent more clipped in his anger. 'No doubt any man would have sufficed. I am pleased I was able to give you *one* orgasm, at least, before we were interrupted.'

The colour had drained from her cheeks. 'You *bastard*!'

Gregorio shrugged his shoulders. 'You were the one at such pains to explain exactly what we have between us, I am merely agreeing with you. When you feel in the need for sex again perhaps you should give me a call? If I have the time I— No, I do not *think* so.' Gregorio grasped hold of Lia's wrist as her hand arced up towards his cheek. He used that grip to pull her up close against him. 'I warned you the last time you did that I would not allow you to do it again without retaliating.'

Her top lip turned back in a sneer. 'I should have known you were the type of man who would hit a woman!'

Gregorio's jaw tightened. 'Any man who strikes a woman, for whatever reason, no longer has the right to call himself a man. My retribution will be of quite a different kind, I assure you.'

Lia swallowed. Gregorio's threat was all the more disturbing because he'd delivered it in such a calm and conversational tone. As if they were discussing the weather rather than his retribution.

'Let go of me,' she said evenly.

He quirked one dark brow. 'Are you going to slap me again?'

'No.' That impulse had passed. Besides, she had never felt tempted to hit anyone before Gregorio.

'Pity.' He bared his teeth in a humourless smile as he released her wrist and stepped back. 'I believe I would have enjoyed punishing you. Perhaps I still will…' he mused.

Lia breathed shallowly. 'Punishing me?'

Black eyes glittered through narrowed lids. 'You are not someone who likes to feel out of control, are you?'

That sounded more like a statement than a question, and Lia treated it as such. 'Neither are you,' she defended.

'I do not remember objecting when you made love to me earlier.'

The warmth in her cheeks deepened as she recalled her aggression. And her pleasure…

Which was another reason she wasn't going to allow

herself to be alone with Gregorio again. He affected her, drove her wild with passion in a way no other man ever had. Including the man she had intended to marry.

She and David had spent the night together regularly after their engagement. Nights she had enjoyed even as she had known there had to be *more*. Although she had enjoyed David's lovemaking she had never reached the pinnacle of physical pleasure when they were together.

A few minutes of just being kissed by and kissing Gregorio and she'd had her first orgasm. He hadn't even touched her. The stimulation had come from those kisses alone.

Just being with him physically excited her.

As much as it disturbed her.

Because she wasn't sure she even *liked* Gregorio.

Lia moistened her lips with the tip of her tongue. 'I really think you should leave now.'

Gregorio had given her far too much to think about. Not just what had happened between the two of them, but the truth about David's involvement in the demise of her father's company.

Because, no matter how confused she was about her feelings for Gregorio, she knew he wasn't a liar. In fact, he was the opposite: Gregorio tended to be brutally honest.

Lia knew she had to see and talk to David again. To find out for herself if what Gregorio had said about him having a gambling habit was true, at least. To try and get David to tell her the part he had played—or not played—in the downfall of Fairbanks Industries.

CHAPTER SEVEN

'This isn't part of my job description.'

Gregorio quirked one dark eyebrow as he looked at Lia, standing in the doorway to the office in his penthouse suite. 'My PA has called in sick this morning. I'm not sure it's altogether wise for you to refuse to assist your employer on only your second day of employment.'

Lia wasn't sure it was either. But neither did she think it was coincidence that Gregorio had requested *she* be the one to assist him. Although he certainly *looked* businesslike, in one of those perfectly tailored suits—dark grey today—with a pale grey shirt and striped blue tie.

After a very disturbed night's sleep Lia had tried to put yesterday evening from her mind and treat today as a new start. It had proved not altogether possible when—as promised—Cathy had telephoned her first thing this morning, wanting to know all the juicy details of Lia's relationship with Gregorio.

Lia had told her friend what she felt comfortable with Cathy knowing. Mainly that she really had no idea what last night had been about. Only that she wasn't going to allow Gregorio that close to her again.

After making another phone call Lia had forced herself to shower and dress before coming in to work today. Knowing that Gregorio might appear at any moment and shake what little self-confidence she had managed to dredge up and wrap around herself like a protective cloak.

Having Michael Harrington send her up to the penthouse floor to assist Mr de la Cruz within minutes of her arrival at the Exemplar Hotel had succeeded in tearing a great hole in that protective cloak!

'Is this what you meant when you spoke about punishing me?'

Gregorio narrowed his eyes as he sat back in his chair to look across the width of his desk at Lia. She was once again wearing a black business suit and a cream blouse—the uniform of all the hotel receptionists—and her hair was swept up in that confining style he didn't like. Mainly because it hid all the gold and cinnamon highlights amongst the red. Her face was slightly pale, but there was a defiant glitter in those dark grey eyes.

'You consider assisting your employer to be a punishment?' he challenged.

'That would depend on what he wants my assistance with.'

'The history and accounts of some of the companies I am interested in buying.'

Her eyes widened. 'And why would you think I have any knowledge on either of those subjects?'

Gregorio gave a confident smile. 'Because your father told me you very often assisted him when he worked at home in the evenings.'

Her hand reached out blindly to allow her fingers

to grasp hold of the doorframe for support. 'My father told you...?'

'Jacob and I met several times.' He nodded. 'Once we had finished our business discussions you invariably came into the conversation.' He stood up to move around to the front of his desk. 'He was very proud of you.'

Lia could find no answer to that statement. Instead she blinked back the tears stinging her eyes and prompted briskly, 'Just tell me what I can do to help you.'

Gregorio had to bite back his immediate response. Which was, *you can get down on your knees and relieve me of the throbbing ache of arousal that kept me awake all night.* He was pretty sure that wasn't the sort of help Lia was offering.

He had been coldly angry when he'd left Lia's apartment the evening before. Something that seemed to have become a common occurrence around Lia. A couple of glasses of brandy had eased some of that anger, but nothing had succeeded in taking away the sexual tension that had kept his body hard and throbbing for release.

Not even a freezing cold shower.

The moment he thought of Lia again—and that was becoming an occupational hazard too—his desire sprang back to life as if it had never gone away.

Receiving a phone call earlier this morning from Tim, his PA, explaining that he was sick with the flu, had seemed to set the tone for today too.

Until Gregorio had realised exactly *which* member of the hotel staff he could ask to assist him in Tim's place...

Was it a punishment for Lia for the fact that he couldn't seem to stop wanting her?

Maybe. Whatever his motive, Gregorio already knew that the next few hours were going to be as painful for him as they would for Lia. If for different reasons.

He had been aware of Lia's perfume the moment she entered the penthouse: that light floral scent with an underlying note of womanly musk. And he couldn't stop his gaze from returning again and again to the swell of her breasts, visible where the top two buttons of her blouse had been left unfastened.

They had been interrupted yesterday evening before he'd had a chance to remove any of Lia's clothing. He had not been allowed to see those breasts bared. His jaw clenched and his teeth ached with how much he wanted to remove her blouse and bra before gorging himself on her naked breasts. Starting with her plump and soon-to-be-aroused nipples…

'The files are on Tim's desk,' he said stiffly instead.

If he had set out to punish Lia, as she'd suggested, then during the course of the morning, working so closely with her, Gregorio knew that his intention had come back to bite him on the butt. Or on another part of his anatomy that was even more sensitive.

Despite the fact that she was sitting across the room from him, at Tim's desk, her perfume continued to fill the air and invade his senses. And Gregorio was aware of every move she made—especially when she stretched her back and arched her neck to ease the tension of sitting at a desk for several hours.

Physical awareness danced along his skin every time she spoke to him, even on such a mundane subject as company accounts.

Flu or not, Tim had better be back tomorrow, or he could start looking for another job!

'I'm scheduled to have an early lunch today.'

'What?' Gregorio scowled across the room at her.

'Michael has given me an early lunch today,' Lia repeated as she glanced at her wristwatch. 'I'm meeting someone just after twelve.'

'Who?' The demand was out before Gregorio's brain had connected with his mouth. 'We still have work to do,' he added with a scowl.

'I'm entitled to a lunchbreak,' she reasoned. 'I'll make sure I finish here when I get back.' She stood up to push her chair neatly beneath the desktop, making no attempt to answer his query as to who she was meeting for lunch.

Gregorio scowled his frustration. He wanted to tell Lia that she couldn't go. That it was more important that they finish this work and he would order lunch for them both to be brought up by room service.

Most of all I want to know who she's having lunch with!

'Say hello to Cathy for me,' he tested lightly.

Lia's smile was enigmatic. 'I'm not meeting Cathy for lunch, but I'll be sure to pass your message along the next time I speak to her.'

Gregorio stood, feeling too restless to remain seated at his desk. 'Are you going anywhere nice?'

She shrugged. 'Just a little Italian bistro quite close to here.'

Gregorio thought he knew the place she meant. It was tucked away in a side street a couple of blocks from here, and run by a middle-aged Italian couple. The food was both good and inexpensive. Something Lia no doubt now took into consideration with her changed circumstances.

'I could order some chocolate cake from Mancini's to be delivered here,' he tempted.

Her smile was rueful as she shook her head. 'I'm happy with the selection of cheesecakes at the bistro.'

Gregorio's eyes narrowed. 'Do you go there often?'

'I used to in the past, yes,' she answered cautiously.

'With David Richardson?' The offices of Richardson, Richardson and Pope weren't too far from here, so it seemed logical to assume that Lia might have met her fiancé for lunch at the bistro for the sake of convenience.

Lia frowned. 'You may be my employer, but I don't believe that where I have lunch and who with, in my own time, is any of your business.'

Of course it wasn't. And Gregorio was well aware that his questions were intrusive. It wouldn't even have occurred to him to ask another employee about their lunch plans. Tim had worked for him for two years now, and the two men worked well together, but he had zero interest in Tim's private life.

But Lia wasn't only his employee.

She was also the woman Gregorio wanted, and he wanted her more the more time he spent in her company.

Which meant it was time—*past* time—to call one of the women he'd occasionally had lunch with in the past. An afternoon in bed with another woman would certainly ease his physical frustration.

Having made that decision, Gregorio found himself still in his office fifteen minutes later, waiting for the call from one of his security team to tell him exactly who Lia was meeting for lunch.

* * *

Lia hadn't known how she would feel when she saw David again—the first time they had met since the evening he'd broken their engagement. David had been in Scotland—conveniently?—when she'd buried her father, and his own father had represented Richardson, Richardson and Pope. It had been an awkward situation for both of them, and they hadn't spoken apart from Alec Richardson's murmured condolences as he moved along with the procession of other people offering their sympathies for her loss.

Her first thought, when David entered the bistro where they had agreed to meet for lunch, was that he looked different from how she remembered him.

Or maybe she was just looking at him from another perspective? Through lenses that were less rose-coloured? After all, she had once thought herself in love with this man.

What a difference three months could make. What a difference *one evening* had made: David had shattered every one of her illusions about him when he'd walked out of her life and left her to the mercy of the media wolves.

He was still male-model-handsome. His hair was the colour of ripened corn, his eyes as blue as the sky on a summer's day. His body looked lithe and fit in his tailored dark suit, and he wore a blue shirt that was perfectly matched in colour for his eyes, and a meticulously knotted navy blue tie.

Yes, on the surface David still gave the appearance of being a confidently handsome lawyer. But Lia was able to look past that veneer today. To see the lines of dissipation beside his eyes and mouth. The slight laxness to the skin about his jaw. To note that his strides through the bistro seemed less purposeful and more full of nervous energy.

Was that an indication that David was far from comfortable with this meeting that Lia had requested when she'd rung him earlier that morning?

It was a meeting he had tried to avoid, and only acquiesced to once Lia had explained that she had found some papers amongst her father's things she thought David might be interested in seeing. It wasn't true, of course, but the fact that he had changed his mind about the meeting based on that comment had filled Lia with misgivings. Perhaps the things Gregorio had told her about David were the truth, after all.

David was a thief and a liar...

'You're looking well,' David commented, but he made no move to touch her or to kiss her in greeting before sliding into the seat opposite hers in this relatively private booth at the back of the bistro.

Lia didn't return the compliment. Mainly because it wasn't true. 'I'm very well, thank you,' she answered with cool formality.

He waited until they had placed their drinks order with the waitress and she had left them menus before asking, 'Are you still living with the Mortons?'

'I have an apartment of my own in town now. And a job,' Lia added.

'One that pays actual wages or another job at one of your do-good charities?'

Cathy was right, Lia realised. David *did* condescend. He was doing it right now.

Her fingers itched to wipe the mocking smile off his lips.

When had she developed these violent tendencies?

She had never struck anyone in her life until she'd lashed out at Gregorio in that restaurant. Now she wanted nothing more than to slap David too.

Was it because she knew, deep down, that Cathy's comments about him had been correct? That Gregorio's suspicions about David's involvement in her father's downfall might also prove to be correct…?

'I'm a hotel receptionist.'

The words instantly made her think of the morning she had just spent, working in Gregorio's penthouse suite.

The suite was furnished differently from the others Lia had been shown around on her first morning—it was part of her job as a receptionist to know exactly what each of the rooms had to offer people wanting to stay at the hotel. And the office was definitely personal to Gregorio, indicating that he really did live there all the time.

It made a certain sense. Gregorio had all the conveniences of the hotel—like room and laundry service, restaurants, a spa, et cetera—and none of the inconvenience that came along with owning his own house or apartment.

Even if it *had* seemed a little strange to know that his bedroom was just down the hallway from where the two of them were working…

'How the mighty have fallen,' David sneered.

The gloves really *had* come off today, hadn't they?

It made Lia feel slightly foolish for not having seen David's true nature before now. No doubt he had hidden the worst parts of himself from her while they were dating and then engaged, but even so Lia had always believed herself a good judge of character. Obviously she had been wrong.

Had she been wrong about Gregorio being the bad guy?

She'd already acknowledged that might be the case.

Now she was convinced of it.

Quite what she was going to do about it, she had no idea. Gregorio was…overwhelming. Forceful. And he made no secret of his desire for her.

At least he *hadn't*…

But the way they had parted last night, and the stiltedness between them this morning, seemed to indicate he might have put that feeling behind him and moved on.

Could she blame him?

He had been very polite and friendly with Cathy and Rick last night—*she* was the one who had been rude and dismissive towards *him*. In front of the other couple. No wonder Gregorio had been so angry.

She owed him an apology, Lia realised.

'Lia…?'

She narrowed her gaze on the man sitting opposite her. 'Did you ever love me or were you just using me from the start?'

David looked taken aback by her direct attack. 'The niceties are over, I take it?'

'Very much so.' She nodded abruptly. 'So answer the question. Were you using me, and my father's name and wealth, right from the start of our relationship?'

His scowled. 'I only agreed to meet with you today because you said you had some papers you needed to discuss with me.' His eyes narrowed. 'There *are* no papers, are there?'

'No.'

'Damn it.' He swore softly under his breath. 'I have no intention of hashing over ancient history—'

'It's only been a few months, David,' she snorted. 'I would hardly call that ancient *anything*!'

Their conversation stopped briefly while the waitress put their drinks down on the table. Lia shook her head when the young girl asked if they were ready to eat yet. Lia very much doubted they would get as far as eating anything. Just the thought of food made her feel nauseous.

David leaned forward across the table once the two of them were alone again. 'I don't appreciate being spoken to by you in this insulting manner.'

Her eyes narrowed. 'And *I* don't *appreciate* learning that I was going to marry a dissolute gambler!'

David reared back, a look of total shock on his face. 'I have no idea what you're talking about.'

But he did, Lia realised. The truth was there in his guarded expression and in the way his face had paled.

'Let's not play any more games, David,' she scorned. 'Your parents can't possibly know about your gambling, or they would have done something to help you.'

She had always liked the couple she had believed would one day be her in-laws, and knew that Daphne and Alec Richardson would be devastated to learn the truth about their only child.

'Are you threatening me?'

Lia felt a shiver down the length of her spine at the underlying malice in David's tone. It reminded her of something her father had once told her: a cornered animal almost always attacked. The look of rage on David's face said he was getting ready to do just that.

'Not at all,' she assured him smoothly. 'I was merely thinking how disappointed they would be if they knew the sort of man you really are.'

'Stay away from my parents!' David grated.

'I intend to. Oh, I almost forgot.' Lia turned to search through her handbag. 'You might want to give this to the next unsuspecting idiot.' She placed a ring box down on the table in front of him. The engagement ring inside had belonged to his grandmother. 'Or perhaps you could just sell it to pay off more of your gambling debts? But then, you don't need to, do you?' she continued in a hard voice. 'Not when you have the money you stole from my father's company stashed away in an offshore account.'

'You don't... I didn't... You can't possibly know...' David's face was now an ashen grey rather than just white.

'I *do* know. And, yes, you *did* do exactly what I've just accused you of doing. I don't have all the proof as yet, but I will. Believe me, I *will*,' she assured him vehemently.

She would never wish to harm Daphne and Alec deliberately by revealing the truth about their son, but neither could she allow David to get away with having destroyed her father.

'I don't think so,' David sneered as he recovered quickly. 'You're no longer the privileged daughter of the wealthy and powerful Jacob Fairbanks. Now you're just Lia Fairbanks, who has to work for a living. You have all the power and influence of a toothless dog.'

'You—'

'Sorry I'm a little late, Lia.'

Lia had recognised Gregorio's voice the instant he spoke, but that didn't stop her from staring at him as he slid into the seat beside her. Or drawing in a shocked breath as he kissed her lightly on the lips before turning his narrowed gaze on the man seated on the opposite side of the table.

'Richardson.' He nodded tersely.

If Lia was surprised at Gregorio's being there then David had obviously gone into complete shock. So much so he couldn't even answer the other man.

Gregorio turned to Lia, one dark brow raised in innocent query. 'Have you said something to upset your ex-fiancé? What's this?' He picked up the dark blue velvet ring box and flicked the lid open to reveal the two-carat solitaire diamond ring David had given her on their engagement. 'No wonder you gave it back—it isn't right for you at all.' Gregorio snapped the lid closed and put the box back where he had found it. 'I much prefer the natural yellow diamond ring *I* have picked for you.'

The ring Gregorio had picked for *her*?

A natural *yellow* diamond?

Lia had only read about natural yellow diamonds, and seen photographs of them. They were so unique, so rare, that most reputable jewellers claimed they never expected to see one in their lifetime, let alone have the privilege of selling one.

Gregorio reached over and linked his fingers with those of her left hand before lifting it up and kissing her ring finger. 'It's going to look perfect on you.'

'What...? I... You... Are the two of you...?' David at least made an attempt at speech, even if not very successfully.

Talking was still beyond Lia. It was surprise enough that Gregorio had come to the bistro at all, but that he should now be giving David the impression that the two of them were… That they were…

'Yes, we are,' Gregorio stated challengingly. 'Have the two of you ordered yet?' he continued, as if he *hadn't* just rendered the two people seated at the table with him dumb. 'I worked up quite an appetite this morning.'

The look he gave Lia could only be called intimate. Except…

When Lia looked into his eyes she could see the dangerous glitter so at odds with his pleasant tone and demeanour. Gregorio was angry. Coldly, furiously angry.

With her? Because she had met up with David?

Lia was pretty sure that was the reason.

Earlier she had refused to tell Gregorio who she was meeting for lunch, but she'd never had any intention of keeping the identity of that person a secret: how could she when she knew one of Gregorio's men would have followed her when she'd left the hotel earlier? Lia had known that the other man would report back to Gregorio as to *who* she was meeting. She just hadn't expected it to be so soon—or that, knowing she was meeting David, Gregorio would decide to join them.

Or that he would intentionally give David the impression that the two of them were *together*.

What on earth was all that about?

Did Gregorio think David would physically hurt her?

Why else would he have assigned one of his own bodyguards to protect me?

Before today Lia would have dismissed the idea of David ever hurting her as ridiculous. But the dangerous glitter in his eyes a few minutes ago, when he had taken her comment about his parents as a threat, said she would have been wrong.

David was more than capable of hurting her.

And Gregorio was obviously taking no chances.

His protectiveness really was quite... Well, not sweet, because Gregorio was the least *sweet* man Lia knew. But his concern for her definitely gave her a warm and fuzzy feeling inside.

'No, we haven't ordered yet.' She gave him a warm smile. 'I'm not sure David is staying.'

Her ex-fiancé was still staring at Gregorio, and at their linked hands, as if he had seen a ghost. Or his own demise? David must surely realise that with Gregorio beside her—literally—she wasn't the defenceless little nobody he had implied she was earlier.

He gave himself a visible shake before answering her. 'You're right. I have to get back to the office.' He slid to the end of the bench seat.

'Don't forget to take this with you.' Gregorio picked up the ring box, but retained his hold on it as David would have taken it from him. 'Stay away from Lia in future, Richardson.' Gregorio spoke softly, but he was no less threatening because of it. 'If I see you near her again I might not be quite so understanding.'

David's face flushed with annoyance. '*She* was the one who asked for this meeting.'

'Lia always tries to see the good in everyone.' Gregorio nodded. '*I* don't suffer with the same affliction.'

The other man's chin rose defensively at the challenge in Gregorio's tone. 'You don't frighten me.'

'I have no intention of frightening you,' Gregorio said pleasantly as he finally released the ring box. 'But *they* can—and will if I think it necessary.' He gave a nod in the direction of the two men standing outside the restaurant.

Lia had to choke back a laugh as she saw the look of horror on David's face as he looked at the two burly bodyguards. One of them had obviously accompanied her, and Gregorio had brought the second man with him. Both men were at least five inches over six feet in height, with shoulders that looked to be almost as broad.

David didn't say another word, pushing the ring box into his jacket pocket as he turned on his heel and strode out of the bistro. Lia saw him give the two bodyguards a wary glance before he hurried off in the direction of his office building.

Leaving a tense silence behind him.

Lia shot Gregorio a nervous glance from beneath her lashes. She could feel his tension, and see it in the stiff set of his shoulders. His eyes were narrowed, his lips thinned.

She breathed in deeply before speaking. 'I thought—'

'You didn't *think* at all,' Gregorio rasped. 'If you had then you would have known not to arrange to see or speak to Richardson alone.'

'I—'

'You will *not* defy me in this way again, Lia,' he bit out evenly. 'Do you understand me?'

'But—' She broke off as the unfortunate waitress chose that moment to come back and take their order.

'We are not staying,' Gregorio informed her abruptly as he took out his wallet to remove some money, handing it to the waitress as he slid out of the booth and pulled Lia with him.

'Where are we going?' She just had time to grab

her shoulder bag as he marched them both towards the exit.

'Somewhere we can talk privately,' came the grimly determined reply.

Lia didn't like the sound of that.

At all.

CHAPTER EIGHT

'Will you just ease up—before I either fall over or you pull my arm out of its socket?' Lia complained as Gregorio continued his march down the street, his fingers firmly around the top of her arm as he pulled her along beside him. Everyone instinctively stepped out of his way, and consequently hers too. They obviously knew from looking at Gregorio's face not to get in his way.

His expression was... Dark and dangerous. That was the only way Lia could think of to describe it. Thunderous brows were lowered over even darker and stormier eyes, his jaw was tight, lips still thinned, his jaw clenched. His whole body language said, *Get out of my way or risk being trampled underfoot.*

An impression no doubt added to by the two men who were six and half feet of pure muscle following just a couple of steps behind them.

'Gregorio—'

'It would be better if you did not speak to me right now,' he bit out, without so much as glancing at her.

'But—'

'*Dios*, do you *ever* do as you are told?' He maintained his hold on her arm as he turned to face her, his eyes glittering darkly as he glowered at her from his superior height. 'Do you have *any* idea what you risked by meeting Richardson alone?'

She did now. 'I wasn't exactly *alone* when one of your men follows me everywhere I go. Besides, David would never—' She broke off with a wince, knowing that the David she had met today was not the man who had wooed and won her. Today he had been that cornered animal. Feral. Likely to strike out and maim or kill without warning.

Gregorio eyed her scornfully. 'Do not try to convince me of something you no longer believe yourself!'

Her cheeks warmed. 'That isn't true—'

'Do you still have feelings for him? Is that it?' Gregorio snapped disgustedly. 'You want to believe he is not involved because you are still in love with him?'

'No!'

Gregorio couldn't miss the vehemence in her denial. 'Then why meet with him at all? Why would you even *do* something like that when I have told you of my suspicions regarding him?'

'Because I needed to know—to see for myself—whether or not David is capable of doing what you suspect he has!' She glared at him.

'And?'

She gave a shiver. 'He's more than capable. In fact I was about to excuse myself from having lunch with him when you arrived and started acting like a caveman.'

Given the circumstances, Gregorio considered his behaviour earlier to have been quite circumspect. What he had really wanted to do was rip David Richardson's head from his shoulders for daring to so much as breathe the same air as Lia.

If Lia thought he had behaved like a caveman when

he'd joined her and Richardson, then she should have seen him when he'd first received Silvio's phone call telling him exactly who she was meeting for lunch.

Gregorio had left the hotel immediately and walked the short distance to the bistro. Seeing Lia sitting cosily in a booth with Richardson had only made him angrier. Overhearing Richardson's scornful comments to her, mocking her social fall and her need to work for a living, had made Gregorio want to slam his fist into the other man's face.

'I consider myself to have been very restrained,' he assured her tightly.

'Is your restraint an excuse for all that nonsense about an engagement ring too?' She eyed him disgustedly.

Gregorio felt warmth staining his cheeks. 'It was my way of letting Richardson know that you aren't alone in the world, no matter what he may think to the contrary.'

'By giving him the impression that I'm now engaged to *you*?'

A nerve pulsed in his jaw. 'It worked, didn't it?'

'And what if he decides to tell someone else about our bogus engagement? Maybe the media?' Lia challenged. 'Did you even think of that?'

Of course Gregorio hadn't thought of that. His only objective had been to protect Lia.

Really?

Was he being honest with himself?

Knowing Lia was with David Richardson had filled him with a blinding rage. Seeing her in the company of the other man, her hair a loose tumble about her shoulders in the way that he liked it, had sent every thought from his head except getting rid of Richardson.

And one word.

Mine.

Lia *was* his—whether she knew it yet or not.

Perhaps it was time that she did.

'Gregorio!' Lia squeaked in protest when he didn't answer her but instead resumed pulling her along the street beside him, his face set in grim lines.

Lia wasn't sure she altogether trusted that expression. And she felt even less reassured when they entered the hotel through the underground car park, where one of the lifts for the penthouse floor was situated. Gregorio scanned his key card to open the doors and pressed the button for the penthouse floor once they were both inside.

Lia could only assume the two bodyguards would either remain downstairs or come up later. Because Gregorio obviously wasn't willing to let them travel in the same lift as them.

Lia could feel the heat and tension radiating from Gregorio now they were together in this small confined space. He didn't so much as look at her—because he was so disgusted with her?—but his harsh expression said he was every inch the arrogant and ruthless Gregorio de la Cruz at this moment.

She ran the tip of her tongue over the dryness of her lips before speaking. 'I believe I owe you an apology for the way I behaved and spoke to you yesterday evening—'

Her words were cut off abruptly as Gregorio pressed her back against one of the mirrored walls, grasping both her wrists in one of his hands before lifting her hands above her head and holding them there as he fiercely claimed her lips with his own.

The length of his body was pressed intimately against Lia's, allowing her to feel how aroused he was. And she was aware of the response of her own body.

She kissed him back with all the pent-up emotions from last night and from this morning, parting her lips to allow Gregorio's tongue to claim the heat of her mouth. Possessively. The victor with his captive. Exactly like that conquistador Lia had once likened him to.

She loved it.

Was she *falling in love* with Gregorio?

It was far too soon for her to know that for sure. Besides, right here and right now she just wanted to kiss and devour him in the same way he was claiming her. To lose herself in the desire that was never far away when the two of them were together.

She pressed even closer against him as she returned heated kiss for heated kiss. Neither of them was even aware of it when the lift doors opened and then closed again—until the lift started to go back down again.

'*Dios mio!*' Gregorio reluctantly dragged his mouth from Lia's, his forehead resting on hers as he kept her pressed up against the wall. 'You are driving me so crazy we risk being stuck in this lift for the rest of the day.'

Lia laughed softly under her breath. 'I'd much rather we spent our time in a bed!'

Gregorio drew his breath in sharply. 'Me too.'

She smiled teasingly. 'That's it? Just "me too"?'

He grimaced. 'As you said, conversation seems to be our downfall. I do not want to ruin the moment as I obviously did yesterday evening.'

She sobered. 'That was completely my fault. I felt defensive after Cathy and Rick arrived. But I should never have talked to you in that way.' She moistened lips slightly swollen from the force of their kisses. 'You drive me crazy too, Gregorio.'

'I—'

Gregorio turned away as the lift reached the ground floor and the doors opened automatically to reveal a surprised Silvio and Raphael, waiting outside.

Gregorio made no move to separate himself from Lia. 'Could you inform Mr Harrington that Miss Fairbanks will be spending the rest of the day with me in my suite?' he told them, before once again pressing the button for the penthouse floor.

Lia giggled, and buried her face against Gregorio's chest as the lift doors closed and they began their second ascent in as many minutes.

Gregorio had never heard Lia giggle before. It was pleasant. Warming.

An indication that she was happy?

Dios, he hoped so. Because there was no way he was going to be able to let her walk away from him again today.

Lia's confidence faltered slightly as they stepped out of the lift into Gregorio's suite. He was ten years older, and so much more experienced than she was. He'd had dozens of lovers, whereas she'd only had one—and not a very satisfactory one at that.

She had believed sexual compatibility to be of minor importance when she'd been with David. They'd loved each other, mixed in the same social circles, and their families had approved of the match. Her lack of sexual pleasure with David hadn't seemed that important.

What an idiot I was.

A stupid, naïve idiot who, after reaching a climax in

Gregorio's arms while still fully clothed, couldn't wait to experience that sexual release again.

David had always ensured he took his own pleasure, but what if she couldn't satisfy Gregorio? What if—?

'You think too much.' Gregorio reached up and smoothed the frown from her brow. 'First we will take a shower together.'

He clasped her hand in his as they walked down the hallway.

Was Gregorio expecting her to take all her clothes off and get in the shower with him?

Lia had a sick feeling in the pit of her stomach. She had seen photographs of the women Gregorio usually went to bed with, and although she took care of her body she knew she didn't match up to those model-thin, toned-bodied blondes. Despite her weight loss, her breasts were firm and up-tilting, but a little too big for the slenderness of her waist. Her hips were too curvy—

'You are still thinking too much,' Gregorio murmured indulgently, turning to face her as the two of them stood in the middle of the terracotta-tiled bathroom. 'You are very beautiful, Lia.'

He gently claimed her lips with his. Sipping. Tasting. *Claiming*.

Lia was so lost in her rising desire she wasn't even aware of Gregorio removing her jacket, and then unfastening her blouse before dropping it to the floor with her jacket. Or of his unfastening of the zip of her skirt before that too slid down to join her jacket and blouse.

Heat blazed in her cheeks as Gregorio ended their kiss, stepping back, making her painfully aware that she was now wearing only a cream bra and matching panties, along with suspenders and stockings. And for some inexplicable reason she was still wearing her high-heeled shoes!

Lia wondered what Gregorio saw as his hands tightened about hers. His eyes were dark as he looked his fill of her from the top of her head to her ridiculous high-heeled shoes.

'You are every one of my fantasies come to life,' he approved darkly.

Lia somehow doubted that. 'Aren't you a bit overdressed for taking a shower?' she said lightly, changing the subject.

He released her hands and stepped back and out of his shoes before stretching his arms out at his sides. 'Undress me. No—keep your shoes on,' he added gruffly as she would have stepped out of them.

'Now who's bossy?' she teased.

'Those high heels are *very* sexy.'

The burning in her cheeks seemed to have become a permanent fixture as Lia slipped the jacket from Gregorio's shoulders and down his arms before placing it neatly on the vanity: the suit had probably cost more than Lia was going to earn in a month.

His eyes glittered down at her as she stepped forward to unfasten and remove his tie before undoing the buttons on his shirt.

Lia's breath caught in her throat as she bared his chest, her fingers caressing lightly over that olive-toned flesh as she took off his shirt. His body really was beautiful—as perfect as any sculpture of a Greek god and yet, unlike a statue, warm and firm to the touch.

Her fingers were slightly clumsy as she unfastened the button of his trousers and tugged the zip down. The material slid down his hips and thighs before he stepped out of the trousers altogether, revealing that he wore a pair of black boxers beneath, the bulge of his arousal once again visible against the fitted material.

Forget all the gods: Gregorio was pure perfection.

Wide shoulders, toned pecs and abs, long muscular legs...

Just looking at him made Lia's heart beat faster and louder.

'Take them off.'

Lia's breathing became ragged as she raised her hands to the waistband of Gregorio's boxers, hooking a finger at each hip before slowly pulling the material downwards. Which, considering Gregorio's large and obvious erection, wasn't as easy as it sounded.

She had to ease and stretch the material over that pulsing flesh, before falling down on her knees in front of him as she slowly moved the material downwards and then off completely, along with his socks.

Her gaze returned hungrily to Gregorio's fully engorged and fiercely jutting arousal.

'Lia...!'

She knew what Gregorio wanted, what his husky voice was begging for. Not demanding. *Begging*.

Had Lia fallen to her knees deliberately? For just this purpose?

Absolutely.

She wanted to hear Gregorio's groans of pleasure as she took him into her mouth. To taste and lick him. To suck him.

Just thinking of that, and of how the two of them must look right now—Gregorio completely naked and fully aroused, her wearing only bra, panties and stockings—caused her own level of desire to increase achingly.

Gregorio drew his breath in sharply, his knees almost buckling as he watched Lia's fingers encircle him. She slowly licked her parted lips before bending forward to take him into the heat of her mouth.

His hands moved, his fingers grasping her bared shoulders as her other hand cupped him beneath his arousal. At the same time she took him deeper into the heat of her mouth. She pulled back again—slowly, firmly—her tongue a hot rasp over the sensitive tip, her cheeks hollowed as she sucked.

Gregorio thought the top of his head was going to explode as Lia set a tortuous rhythm. Taking all of him, deeply. Followed by the slow and tormenting drag of withdrawal. The continuous hot stroke of her tongue on his sensitised flesh. The rhythmic squeeze of her hands.

And all the while she looked so damned sexy in her bra, panties and stockings, her hair a wild tumble of auburn, gold and cinnamon about her shoulders, Gregorio couldn't take his eyes off her.

He could feel the heat of his release building, every muscle in his body straining as he fought for control of that release. The pleasure was too much…too much—

'No…!' He pushed her away from him, fingers digging into the soft flesh of her shoulders when she looked up at him with sensual dark eyes. 'Lia…' He pulled her up to her feet, his arms going about her waist as he drew her in tightly against him. 'That was incredible.'

Oral sex had been a definite no-no with David, so this was the first time Lia had ever…

Having no interest in exploring the boundaries of their sexual relationship was surely another sign that David had just been using her.

What an idiot she had been!

'I liked it too,' Lia acknowledged huskily.

'I do not want it to be over too soon.'

Gregorio gave one of those sensual smiles that transformed his face from austere to breathtaking.

'My turn,' he murmured with satisfaction, and he reached behind her and unfastened her bra before removing it completely. *'Dios!'* He spoke almost reverently as his gaze feasted on her pertly bared breasts. 'I love these...' His hands cupped beneath her breasts as he lowered his head to suckle each engorged nipple in turn.

Lia groaned, clinging to Gregorio's shoulders as she was engulfed in pleasure, heat instantly spreading to her core.

'I want to taste you...'

Gregorio straightened before lifting her up in his arms and carrying her out of the bathroom and down the hallway to his bedroom. He lay her down carefully on the bed, kneeling beside her to hook his thumbs in her panties, pulling them slowly down over her hips and thighs and then off completely, leaving Lia dressed only in the suspenders and stockings.

His eyes darkened as he looked at her. 'You are the sexiest woman—'

'You've seen today?' she teased, sure that Gregorio had been with women a lot sexier than her.

He tilted his head as he studied her. 'Why do you do that? Is it your way of pushing me away?'

She gave a splutter of laughter at the ridiculousness of that statement when they were both naked. 'Do I *look* as if I'm pushing you away?'

Gregorio didn't return her smile. 'We both have

pasts, Lia. I can no more take mine away than you can. But there is just the two of us here. Now. Together.' He lay down on the bed beside her, his hand cupping her cheek as he turned her face towards him. 'Beauty is in the eye of the beholder, Lia, and you are the most beautiful woman it has been my privilege to make love to.'

Her cheeks heated, although at the same time she still felt sceptical. 'I think we're both agreed that it's best if we don't talk.'

'Because you do not believe me?'

'Gregorio—'

'It is okay.' His thumb caressed her full bottom lip. 'I have every intention of showing you how beautiful you are to me.'

And if that was Gregorio's intention then that was exactly what he did as he made love to her tenderly, appreciatively, *savagely*. Squeezing and caressing her breasts as he drove her wild with his lips and tongue, driving Lia over the edge of release time and time again. Until she was so sensitised that his lightest touch inflamed her senses and she crashed into another orgasm.

And still she hungered for more. More of Gregorio's lovemaking. More of *him*.

'I need to be inside you *now*,' he finally rasped, his hair tousled from where Lia had grabbed hold of its darkness at the height of her pleasure.

'Please…' She arched up, needing to be filled, needing to have Gregorio inside her as much as he wanted to be there.

Lia's unease returned during the time it took him to open the foil packet he had taken from the bedside drawer and roll the condom on with an expertise that indicated he had done it many times before.

Gregorio frowned slightly, obviously seeing the uncertainty flickering across Lia's face. 'I realise this is not in the least romantic, but it is my responsibility to protect you.'

There was no arguing with that comment. None that made any sense in the circumstances, anyway.

And Lia totally forgot about that moment of unease as Gregorio knelt between her thighs and slowly, erotically, eased himself into her. Stretching her, filling her, as if they were two parts of a whole, finally joined together.

'That feels so good,' Gregorio groaned as he lay down on top of her, taking his weight on his elbows and claiming her mouth with his as he slowly began to thrust inside her. '*You* feel so good, Lia.'

Lia groaned as Gregorio's movement sent off tiny explosions inside her, wrapping her legs about his waist and pulling him in deeper still. Their breathing became loud and ragged and those thrusts became less co-ordinated as the pleasure built, higher and higher.

Gregorio broke the kiss to groan, his body tense. 'Come with me, *bella*. Now!' he rasped, and he began to pulse inside her, taking Lia with him in an orgasm so strong and intense she screamed out her pleasure.

CHAPTER NINE

'Lunch has arrived.'

Lunch? A glance at her wristwatch told her it was almost five o'clock in the afternoon, and Lia didn't want to move out of the warm comfort of the bed where she and Gregorio had spent the whole afternoon making love. They had left the bed only once, to take the shower they had forgone earlier. Gregorio had made love to her again against the shower wall once they had soaped, washed and caressed each other all over. The third time had been just a few minutes ago.

Every part of Lia ached, but it was a pleasurable ache. An ache that came from knowing Gregorio's possession so intimately, so many times in such a short time.

Which was surprising, because Lia hadn't thought a man could recover sexually so quickly. David certainly hadn't...

'Whatever you are thinking about has put a frown on your brow,' Gregorio reproved as he crossed the room to stand beside the bed, wearing a towel knotted loosely around his hips.

Probably so that he could open the door when Room Service delivered their late lunch, Lia realised.

'It was nothing of any importance.' And it wasn't. None of it. David. Their less than satisfying relationship. Their broken engagement. *My lucky escape*—that seemed more appropriate. 'I'm too comfortable to get out of bed.' She gave Gregorio a satiated smile.

His smile was indulgent. 'Would you like me to bring the food to you in here?'

'That sounds like an excellent idea.' Lia tucked the sheet about her breasts as she sat up against the pillows.

Gregorio sat on the bed beside her. 'You are very beautiful to me, Lia.' His fingertips ran lightly down one of her flushed cheeks.

Lia believed him this time. How could she not after the exquisite way Gregorio had made love to her for hours? After he had *shown her* time and time again how *beautiful she was to him*.

So why was he now the one frowning?

'I want you to promise me you will not see Richardson alone again.'

Ah.

Gregorio's eyes narrowed. 'Why are you looking at me like that?'

'Probably because I'm wondering if this is the reason you've made love to me all afternoon.' She eyed him suspiciously. 'To distract me, and also so I'd be more amenable to whatever you ask of me.'

He stood up abruptly. 'You have never for a single moment been *amenable*, Lia,' he bit out impatiently. *'Dios mio.'* He ran a hand through his already tousled dark hair. 'Is that what you think of me?' He glared down at her. 'That I would use sex to manipulate you?'

Exactly. *Sex*.

She had been making love...*falling in love*...while

Gregorio had been *having sex*. Very good sex, but nonetheless it was just sex.

Lia wondered why some women—herself included, apparently—had to pretty it up by calling it 'making love'. Maybe because that was exactly what it did—it prettied up what was basically a primal sexual urge. There was a much more crude word Lia could have used to describe it, but she was too much of a lady to use it.

Gregorio scowled his impatience at Lia's lack of a reply. 'I do not remember having to force you into doing anything this afternoon.'

On the contrary, after her initial shyness Lia had proved to be a very adventurous lover. Satisfyingly so.

So why were the two of them arguing again?

Because their conversations *always*—usually sooner rather than later—became an argument. One of them would take umbrage at something the other had said, and a disagreement would ensue.

'I think I should leave.' Lia avoided his gaze, keeping the sheet wrapped about her breasts as she moved to swing her legs out onto the carpeted floor on the other side of the bed.

'Is this how you usually behave?' Gregorio snapped in frustration. 'You run away whenever you are confronted with a situation you cannot control?'

Her eyes flashed as she turned to glare at him. 'I don't have control over a single part of my life right now. Including this part, it seems,' she added vehemently, standing up and taking the sheet with her. 'I no longer *think* I should leave—I *am* leaving.'

She kept the sheet wrapped around her as she marched over to the door.

'Lia!'

She turned in the doorway. 'Let me go, Gregorio.' Tears glistened in her eyes.

Gregorio's shoulders dropped in defeat. He knew he had no desire to force Lia into doing anything. 'As long as you agree not to see Richardson again on your own. My investigation into his lifestyle, and the money missing from your father's company, is still ongoing.'

And Lia's interference would not only put that investigation in jeopardy but also Lia herself.

'You really believe he did it?'

'I do, yes.'

'And that caused my father's heart attack?'

'Yes.'

'Very well.' She nodded. 'But you'll keep me informed?'

'I will,' he conceded tautly. 'Now I insist you allow Silvio to accompany you home and remain outside your apartment building.' After what she had revealed during her conversation with Richardson earlier today, he believed it was now even more necessary that Lia be protected.

She breathed deeply as she obviously fought a battle within herself. 'Do you really think David would hurt me?'

Gregorio's mouth tightened. 'I believe that today you challenged and cornered a man who does not like to be thwarted in any way. By meeting him, saying the things you did, you have now made Richardson aware of some of your suspicions regarding him—if not all of them. It is never a good idea to allow the enemy to know what you are thinking or feeling.'

Lia eyed him quizzically. 'Is that how you've become so successful? By treating everyone else as the enemy?'

He breathed in deeply. 'You are angry with me and deliberately twisting my words.'

Lia was angry with herself—not Gregorio. After all that had happened these past few months she had still allowed herself to be a naïve romantic where Gregorio was concerned. She was twenty-five years old, and had already been used and manipulated by one man for his own selfish purposes. It was time she stopped romanticising and accepted that she and Gregorio had simply spent a pleasurable afternoon in bed together.

And now the afternoon was over.

She forced the tension from her shoulders and half smiled. 'Let's not part as bad friends, hmm, Gregorio?'

Gregorio's eyes narrowed. Friends? Lia believed the two of them to be merely *friends*? After the afternoon they had just spent together?

'Will we be friends with benefits?' he mocked harshly.

'No.' She kept her gaze downcast. 'What happened this afternoon will not happen again.'

'You truly believe that?' he scorned. The sexual tension between them crackled and burned even now. When they were arguing or when they weren't.

She raised her chin as she looked at him, her gaze clear and unwavering. 'It's time I took charge of my own life, Gregorio,' she stated flatly. 'And that includes who I go to bed with.'

'And it will not be me?'

'No.'

Gregorio nodded abruptly. 'Silvio will be waiting downstairs to accompany you when you are ready to leave.'

'Thank you.' Lia disappeared into the hallway, and

there followed the sound of the bathroom door closing seconds later.

Gregorio made his call to Silvio and then turned to stare out of the window at the London skyline, his reflection showing him his expression was grim. This afternoon with Lia had been a revelation. She was correct in her belief that in the past twenty years he had bedded many woman. So many he had forgotten some of their names.

He would never forget Lia's name.

Would never forget Lia.

She was unforgettable.

Not because she was the most beautiful woman he had ever seen. Which she was.

Nor because she was the best lover. Which she was.

No, he would never forget her because she was Lia.

Fiery of temperament. Passionate of nature.

Lia.

'What happened to you yesterday—? Careful,' Cathy warned as Lia's hand jerked so suddenly she almost tipped her glass of water all over the table. The two women had met up at the gym after work, and were now enjoying a relaxing cold drink together in the bar there. 'I expected you to telephone last night, but now I really want to know what happened yesterday.'

The other woman eyed Lia knowingly.

'Which part?' Lia couldn't quite meet her friend's gaze.

She had gone to bed early last night—had pulled the covers over her head and slept for almost twelve hours. Today she was back working behind the reception desk at the Exemplar Hotel, so obviously Gregorio's PA had recovered enough to come in today. Or maybe not? Maybe Gregorio was doing the same as Lia? Trying to ignore her existence as she was trying to ignore his. She certainly hadn't seen anything of him in the hotel today.

'The part that's making you blush,' Cathy said with relish.

Lia winced. 'I'd rather not.'

'At least tell me if it involves Gregorio de la Cruz?'

She sighed. 'It does.'

'Wow!' Cathy had a dreamy expression on her face. 'I love Rick to bits, but being married doesn't make me blind and Gregorio is something else.'

Yes, he was. But quite what that something else was Lia had no idea.

She knew she hadn't been able to stop thinking about him since she'd left his apartment late yesterday afternoon. Since she had made... Well, it hadn't quite been the walk of shame, because it hadn't mattered that the clothes she was wearing were the same ones she had worn to work that morning. But it had certainly been an embarrassing exit from the hotel after Lia had collected her coat from the staffroom. Made more so by the fact that the other receptionists had cheerfully wished her goodnight before she left—just as if it had been a normal working day at the Exemplar Hotel.

There had been nothing *normal* about yesterday as far as Lia was concerned.

The pleasurable aches and pains in her body when she'd woken up that morning had seemed to agree with that sentiment. Which was why she had suggested meeting up with Cathy at the gym after work. The two women had been using different apparatus since they'd arrived, so sitting in the adjoining bar, sipping iced water, was the first opportunity they had found actually to chat.

'I can see by the smile on your face that he's every bit as satisfying as I thought he might be.'

'Cathy!' Lia's cheeks were ablaze with revealing colour.

'Lia!' she came back teasingly. 'You never had that cat-that-got-the-cream expression on your face after spending the night with David.'

Lia sobered at the mention of her ex-fiancé. 'I saw David yesterday too.'

'What?' Cathy sat forward. 'When? Why?'

She sighed heavily. 'Gregorio told me some things about him and I wanted to know if they were true.'

'And were they?'

'Yes.' Lia had no doubt now that Gregorio's suspicions about David would prove to be correct. Or that he was right to be cautious about to what David might do once Gregorio had evidence against him.

'More secrets?' Cathy eyed her sympathetically.

Lia blinked back the tears that never seemed to be far away nowadays. 'Gregorio thinks David is responsible for my father's financial problems and subsequent heart attack. I'm inclined to agree with him.'

'Oh, Lia.' Cathy placed her hand over Lia's and gave it a squeeze. 'I'm so sorry.'

'But not surprised?' Lia quirked a rueful brow.

'Not really, no,' her friend acknowledged with a pained wince.

Lia laughed softly. 'You really will have to be more honest with me in future regarding the men I date!'

'Gregorio has my full approval,' Cathy supplied instantly.

He had Lia's full approval too. But that didn't change the fact that she was just another sexual conquest to him. Unfortunately she had to accept that her emotions didn't function in the same compartmentalised way as his. She already cared more for Gregorio than she should, and she didn't need to have her heart broken for a second time in a matter of months.

Had David's desertion broken her heart?

If Lia was honest, the answer was no. It had hurt that he had ended their engagement so abruptly after her father's death, but she hadn't been heartbroken in the way she would be if she allowed her emotions to become fully engaged where Gregorio was concerned.

If they weren't already...

'I was wondering when you were going to arrive home.'

Lia stiffened as she stepped out of the lift and saw David standing in the hallway, directly outside her apartment. 'How did you get in here?'

There was no reception at this small apartment complex, but it did have a key-coded panel outside the front door, and a security number that had to be logged in before the door could be opened.

She had also left Raphael, her protector for the day, sitting outside in his SUV on the other side of that locked door.

David gave an unconcerned shrug. 'I told one of the other tenants I was a new neighbour and I'd forgotten the door code. She was only too happy to let me inside.'

Lia was pretty sure there had been a lot of David's false charm involved in that conversation. Although she really would have to introduce herself properly to the other tenants, so that they knew exactly who their new neighbour was in future. They also needed to be more cautious about letting unknown people into the building.

In the meantime, she had to deal with David's unwanted presence. 'How did you find out where I'm living now?' she demanded as she walked down the hallway.

He shrugged. 'It wasn't that difficult. A friend of a friend who works for the telephone company.'

Lia eyed him warily. 'Why are you here?' He was dressed casually, in an open-necked pale blue polo shirt and designer label jeans, so he had obviously been home and changed after work before coming here.

He gave her one of his most charming smiles. 'I felt we parted badly yesterday, and I wanted to put things right between us.'

'Really?' She quirked a sceptical brow.

'Yes, really.'

The smile stayed firmly in place, but Lia knew David well enough to realise it hadn't reached his eyes.

'You said some unsettling things to me yesterday, and I wanted to set the record straight.'

Lia thought saying *really* again might be a little too much. 'That's no longer necessary,' she said.

He tensed. 'Oh?'

'I think we both know the truth, David. Which means we have nothing more to say to each other.'

'You aren't being very friendly.'

She snorted. 'Do I have reason to be?'

'We were engaged...'

'*Were engaged* being the appropriate phrase.'

'Look, I know I let you down when you needed me to be strong for you. I made a mistake, okay?' His smile became ingratiating. 'I obviously don't handle sudden death well—'

'I will *not* discuss my father with you,' Lia snapped. *'Ever,'* she added vehemently. 'Now, I would like you to leave.'

'I just want to talk to you, Lia,' he cajoled. 'I've missed you.'

'Oh, please!' She glared her disgust. 'I realise now how completely naïve I was until a few months ago. Maybe I was just too busy being "the privileged daughter of the wealthy and powerful Jacob Fairbanks",' she said, repeating his insult of yesterday. 'If I hadn't been then perhaps I would have seen through you much sooner.'

'This isn't like you, Lia…'

David had returned to the condescending voice that was really starting to grate on Lia.

'You don't talk like this. I can only conclude that it's the influence of de la Cruz.' He gave a shake of his head. 'What on earth are you doing with a man like that anyway? He's a womaniser—and a corporate shark of the worst kind.'

'He's a more honourable man than you'll *ever* be!'

Lia knew that was the truth. In all his dealings with her Gregorio had been nothing but honest. Even when the two of them had spent the afternoon in bed together Gregorio hadn't made any false declarations or promises—before or after.

'Now, I really want you to leave, David.' She searched agitatedly through her shoulder bag for her door key.

'What if I don't want to?'

Lia looked up sharply, butterflies fluttering in her stomach as she realised that David had moved and was now standing much too close to her in the hallway. Uncomfortably so. There was no charm nor an ingratiating smile on his face now.

'One of Gregorio's men is sitting in his car outside this building,' she challenged tensely.

David raised is brows. 'He has men watching you?'

'Protecting me, yes.'

'Protecting you from whom? *Me?*' David questioned when Lia gave him a pointed glance. 'You never used to be paranoid, Lia,' he scorned.

'I never *used to be* a lot of things that I am now.'

'So I've noticed. And not all of those changes are for the better,' David assured her. 'But de la Cruz and his men aren't here. There's just the two of us.'

Lia was aware of that. Very much so. And she didn't like it one little bit. Didn't trust or like *David* one little bit.

'I said I want you to leave,' she repeated through gritted teeth.

'Wouldn't you like to know what *really* happened the night your father died?'

'What?' Lia gasped as she stared at him with wide eyes.

David returned her gaze challengingly. 'I said—'

'I heard you,' she dismissed agitatedly. 'What I want is an explanation of what you meant.'

He shrugged. 'I was with your father when he died.'

'I… But… There was never any mention…' She gave a shake of her head. 'I was the one to find him—slumped over his desk in the morning.'

'Our meeting was lawyer/client confidential.' David shrugged. 'When he suddenly collapsed… Well, as I said, I don't handle sudden death well.'

'He had a heart attack in front of you and you just left him there to die?' Lia reached out to place her palm on the wall for support as she felt herself sway.

'He died almost instantly.' David's mouth was tight. 'There was nothing anyone could have done.'

'You don't know that!' Lia stared at him incredulously. 'You all but *killed* him!'

'Your father died of a heart attack,' he maintained evenly.

'But heart attacks are usually brought on by stress or shock. Did you do or say something to cause his heart attack?' Lia was having difficulty keeping down the waves of nausea churning in her stomach.

'Invite me in and I'll tell you exactly what happened.'

Lia didn't like the smug expression on David's face. Smugness caused by the fact that he knew she would want to know exactly what had happened the night her father died. That she *needed* to know.

But to do that David had said she must invite him in to her apartment.

Did she dare to be alone with him in there?

CHAPTER TEN

GREGORIO TRULY BELIEVED what he had told Lia: a man could no longer call himself a man if he ever raised his hand in anger to a woman. But right now he was very angry. With a red-hot, blinding anger.

Which meant he would have to punch a wall or something to alleviate his tension before seeing Lia. Or he could just punch David Richardson in his too-handsome face and kill two birds with one stone—or one punch.

But for now Gregorio had to concentrate on driving to Lia's apartment so that he arrived in one piece.

He had deliberately avoided the reception area of the hotel today. Had avoided Lia. She had made it clear yesterday that she didn't want to continue seeing him.

That was about to change—whether Lia liked it or not.

Raphael had telephoned him just fifteen minutes ago to report that as a routine precaution he had checked all the numberplates and owners of the cars parked in the street where Lia's apartment was located. He had found Richardson's sports car parked at the other end of the street, neatly—deliberately?—hidden between two SUVs.

Gregorio had left his hotel suite in such a hurry he

had still been talking to Raphael on his cell phone when he'd stepped into the lift and impatiently punched the button for the basement car park.

If Lia had invited Richardson to her apartment, against all Gregorio's advice for her to stay away from the man...

The thought had Gregorio pressing his foot down hard on the accelerator, his expression grim.

'I'm still waiting,' Lia challenged as David stood unmoving and silent in the sitting room of her apartment.

A mocking smile tilted his lips. 'This place is a bit of a come-down for you, isn't it?'

Her gaze remained fixed on him. 'I like it.'

And she did. The apartment was compact and easy to keep clean. It was also her first very own space. She had enjoyed living with her father, but there had been a formality to it, with meals served at set times and an army of staff to cook for them and clean the house. And consequently very little privacy. Here she could do exactly as she pleased, when she pleased—including eating what and when she wanted. In the nude if she so chose.

'If you say so,' David derided sceptically.

'Well?' Lia's impatience deepened.

'Aren't you going to offer me a coffee or something?' He made himself comfortable on the sofa.

'No.'

He chuckled. 'I think I like this new, outspoken Lia after all. *Very* sexy.' His gaze ran slowly over her, from her head to her toes and back again.

Her hands clenched at her sides. 'Will you just tell me what happened the night my father died?'

David's expression became guarded. 'He invited me over. We talked. He had a heart attack. I left.'

Anger welled up, strong and unstoppable. 'You already told me that much in the hallway.'

Had her father *known* David was responsible for the missing money? Had he confronted the other man and then David had simply let her father die when he collapsed?

Why hadn't her father confided in *her*?

The answer came to Lia so suddenly and with such force she almost bent over from the pain.

David had been her fiancé. The man her father had believed she loved and intended to marry. At the time she had believed that too. She had no doubt her father had loved her enough to want to protect her from knowing the truth about her future husband.

'My father confronted you about the embezzlement of Fairbanks Industries funds.' It wasn't a question but a statement.

David's mouth twisted derisively. 'He said that if I returned the money then no one else needed to know what I'd done.'

'But you no longer have the money, do you?'

'Not all of it, no.'

'Because you're addicted to gambling.' Lia looked at him with disgust.

'I'm not addicted!' There was an ugly expression on David's face. 'I just enjoy the thrill…the excitement.'

Addiction.

'Can't you see how it's ruining your life?' Lia frowned. 'How it's turned you into a man who steals from his clients to feed his addiction?'

'You sound just like your father,' David scorned.

'He said if I returned the money no one else need ever know about it and the two of us could live happily ever after. He withdrew from the de la Cruz negotiations to give me time to make the adjustments.'

Which proved Gregorio had been telling the truth when he'd told Lia her father had been the one to withdraw from the negotiations with De la Cruz Industries, even though the sale of the company would have saved her father and the people who worked for him.

Because he had hoped to resolve the situation of David's embezzlement from the company without anyone being any the wiser. Certainly without Lia knowing what David had done.

My father confronted David alone that evening for the same reason—because he wanted to avoid hurting me.

And David—thief, liar and manipulator that he undoubtedly was—had no doubt used her in the same way to try and blackmail her father into silence. The strain had finally proved too much for her father and he'd had a heart attack.

Lia hadn't been in her father's study that evening, nor had she heard any of the conversation between the two men, but she knew with certainty that that was exactly what had happened.

'Get out,' she told David coldly.

His brows rose. 'We haven't finished talking yet.'

'Oh, we've finished,' Lia assured him evenly. 'We're *way* beyond finished,' she added vehemently. 'My father acted the way he did out of love for me, and now I'm going to do exactly the same out of my love for him. I am going to ruin you, David, as you ruined and eventually killed my father. I'll expose you for the cheat and a liar you really are— Take your hand off me!' she protested as David stood and moved across the room so quickly she was unable to avoid his painful grasp about her wrist.

Instead of releasing her David twisted her arm and held it at a painful level against her back, stepping behind her and bringing himself nauseatingly close to her.

'I don't think so,' he murmured viciously as he bent his head close to her ear. 'Why don't you just agree to be a good girl, hmm? Otherwise...'

'Otherwise?' she echoed sharply.

He shrugged. 'Well, you're grieving for your father... Not adapting well to your change of circumstances. People would understand if you were to take a bottle of pills and just fall asleep...'

'You're insane!' Lia truly believed it at that moment: no man in his right mind would threaten to kill her so cold-bloodedly.

'Desperate,' David corrected grimly. 'And you should know better than to threaten a desperate man, Lia.'

Gregorio had tried to warn her. *Had* warned her. Lia just hadn't listened.

Gregorio...

'You would never get away with killing me,' she warned him as she struggled and failed to release herself from David's painful grip. 'Gregorio would know I hadn't killed myself, and he would hound you until he caught you.'

'Wouldn't change the fact you were dead,' David reasoned.

There was no arguing with that logic.

Lia let out a scream as David suddenly twisted her

arm so viciously she thought she was going to pass out from the pain.

'Stop fighting me and I'll stop hurting you,' he ground out harshly.

Lia ceased her struggles. She slumped weakly forward the moment David reduced that painful pressure.

Gregorio tensed in the hallway when he heard Lia scream inside the apartment, not hesitating for so much as a second before he raised his booted foot and kicked the apartment door open.

He stepped through the flying wood splinters from where the lock had been detached from the doorframe and carried on down the hallway, his eyes narrowing as he took in the scene in front of him.

David Richardson stood behind Lia, one of his arms about her waist as he held her against him, his face buried in her hair, his lips against her throat.

Had Gregorio imagined that scream?

Or perhaps the reason for it…?

He knew from personal experience that Lia was a passionate lover. She was also a noisy one. She had screamed several times when they were in bed together yesterday afternoon. Usually when she had an orgasm…

Richardson and Lia were both still fully dressed. But, again, that was no guarantee that Lia's scream hadn't been a pleasurable one: she'd still been wearing all her clothes the first time she'd had an orgasm in his arms. Had he interrupted Richardson while he was pleasuring Lia?

Gregorio returned his narrowed gaze to Lia's face. The wide and startled eyes. The pale cheeks. The trembling lips.

The pale cheeks...

Lia's face was always flushed with pleasure when she orgasmed with him. Her eyes would glow. Her lips would be a deep rose colour.

He took in her body language, noting her tension and the fact that one of her arms was behind her back. Held there by Richardson.

Gregorio's jaw tensed. 'Let her go, Richardson.'

The other man's gaze was insolent as he looked at Gregorio over Lia's shoulder. 'She likes it here. Don't you?' he prompted Lia confidently as his arm tightened about her waist.

'I—' Lia broke off with an indrawn hiss as David gave her arm another painful twist.

She had been completely shocked when the door to her apartment had been kicked or shouldered open—so savagely the lock had come out of the doorframe, wood splintering everywhere, the door itself crashing into the wall behind.

And she had never been more pleased to see Gregorio as he stepped through that ruined doorway, looking for all the world like a dark avenging angel in a black T-shirt, black jeans and heavy black boots, the darkness of hair tousled into disarray.

She had no idea what he was doing here after the way they had parted yesterday—she was just grateful that he *was* there.

At least she would be if David hadn't given her arm that warning and very painful twist.

It was a threat that he intended to hurt her more than he already was if she attempted to alert Gregorio to the fact she was being held against her will.

To hell with that!

'He has my arm twisted behind my back—'

Lia broke off with an agonised yelp of pain as David jerked her arm up even further, the movement accompanied by a snapping sound.

Pain such as Lia had never known before radiated from her arm to the rest of her body. Black spots danced on the edge of her vision as she was thrust forward towards Gregorio, and then the blackness became all-consuming...

'Gently,' Gregorio warned softly as Raphael lifted a still unconscious Lia into his waiting arms where he sat in the back of the SUV.

The other man closed the door and got in behind the wheel to drive them to the hospital.

It was probably as well Lia was still unconscious, because Gregorio had no doubt that her arm was broken. He had heard the distinctive sound of bone cracking as Richardson had pushed her towards him.

Gregorio's arms had moved up and caught her instinctively. All of his attention had been centred on Lia as she'd fainted in his arms—probably from the added pain he had caused by catching her as she fell.

By the time Gregorio had lifted and cradled Lia carefully in his arms, and then looked around, Richardson had gone.

Gregorio had wasted precious more seconds placing Lia gently down on the sofa, before taking out his cell phone and calling down to Raphael. The bodyguard had reported that Richardson had left the building and already driven away. Not Raphael's fault: he couldn't possibly have known that Richardson was fleeing the building rather than just leaving because Gregorio had arrived.

It didn't matter. Gregorio would find Richardson—wherever he ran to. There wasn't a place on this earth where the other man would be safe from Gregorio's wrath for his having dared to physically harm Lia.

In the meantime they had to get Lia to hospital as quickly as possible. Her broken arm needed to be reset and immobilised.

And Gregorio knew her well enough to know she was going to be one seriously angry Lia when she regained consciousness.

The voices were fading in and out of Lia's consciousness, and the pain in her arm was making it impossible for her to make any sense of what was being said.

But she did recognise the three voices speaking. Cathy. Rick. And Gregorio.

Memory came rushing back to her.

David waiting for her outside her apartment... His threats...

Gregorio's unexpected and physically violent arrival...

The snapping sound in her arm as David had pushed her away from him.

The pain.

Blackness.

And then the pain again, when she'd woken up in what she presumed was the A&E department at the local hospital, having her arm X-rayed. Despite the painkillers she had been given, she had passed out again when they'd reset the broken bone.

And throughout all that Gregorio had been at her

side. Not speaking. Just *there*. His face had been set in grimly austere lines. The only words he'd spoken had been to the doctor as the other man had reset her arm. Before she'd blacked out again.

She had no idea when Cathy and Rick had arrived, but she realised Gregorio must have called them. There was no other way they could have known she was at the hospital.

Talking of which…

She opened her eyes to look at the three people sitting beside the gurney she was lying on, obviously all waiting for her to wake up. She seemed to be in some sort of curtained-off area—probably still in A&E. The cast felt like a heavy weight on her left arm.

'At last the lady awakens.' Cathy beamed her pleasure.

'Thank goodness.' Rick heaved a sigh of relief. 'You had us worried for a while there, Lia.'

Only Gregorio remained silent, and a quick glance in his direction showed her that his expression was as grim as it had been earlier, his eyes a glittering black.

Lia turned away to moisten her lips before speaking. 'Can I go home now?'

'Of course.'

'Yes.'

'No!'

She winced as all three of them answered her at once. 'Conflicting answers there, guys.'

'You *can* go home…' Cathy shot Gregorio a puzzled glance—his had been the negative answer.

'But you aren't going to.' He spoke up firmly. 'Not to your own apartment, anyway.' He stood up restlessly and began to pace the confined area behind the curtains.

'I have arranged for the lock to be repaired, but Richardson is still out there somewhere,' he added grimly.

A nerve pulsed in Lia cheek before she spoke quietly. 'He was threatening to kill me and make it look like suicide before you arrived,' she told Gregorio.

'God, no...' Cathy gasped.

'Bastard!' Rick muttered furiously.

Lia moistened the dryness of her lips. 'I don't think he would have done it— Okay, maybe he would,' she conceded heavily when Cathy gave a sceptical snort.

The murderous rage Gregorio had been holding in check for the past two hours threatened to overflow like molten lava from the top of a volcano.

If he could have got hold of Richardson during the past two hours...!

He had debated long and hard as to whether or not to call the police immediately in regard to Richardson's attack on Lia. He had finally decided not to do so—not this evening, at least. He would call the police once he had Lia safe. They would add assault to the rest of the charges he was going to ask the police to bring against David Richardson once they caught him.

Raphael and Silvio were out looking for the other man now, but they had already reported back that Richardson wasn't at his apartment or his parents' house. Considering the amount of money the other man had embezzled from Fairbanks Industries, there was every possibility he had decided to leave the country. Richardson had to know that, having hurt Lia in front of Gregorio, he would now be being hunted.

Gregorio had no intention of stopping that search until he had found the other man and eliminated any further danger to Lia.

'You will stay at the hotel with me,' he stated. He couldn't concentrate his attention on the search for Richardson without knowing that Lia was completely safe.

'Oh, I'm sure there's no need—'

'We'd be more than happy—'

'There will be no discussion on the subject. Lia is coming back to the hotel with me.' Gregorio spoke over the protests of both Lia and Cathy. 'She will be safer there,' he said more gently to Cathy.

Lia inwardly questioned whether she *would* be safer at the hotel.

With Gregorio.

Alone with him day and night in that sumptuous hotel suite.

Not that she was in any condition for a seduction, and nor had Gregorio shown any signs of wanting to seduce her, but even so...

She wasn't comfortable with the idea of staying with him.

'You and Rick both have jobs to go to.' Gregorio continued to talk to Cathy in that soothing tone. 'I can work from my hotel suite, and very often do. Lia will not be left alone at any time until Richardson has been apprehended.'

Oh, great—now she was going to have a babysitter— no doubt Silvio or Raphael—whenever Gregorio had to go out.

'I'd really rather not—'

'The matter is settled,' Gregorio rasped, and those glittering black eyes were challenging as he looked at her.

When Gregorio announced that a matter was settled

it was well and truly settled, Lia acknowledged a few minutes later as she sat beside him in the back of the SUV while Silvio drove them back to the hotel.

She couldn't deny there was a certain logic to her staying with Gregorio. David was obviously more dangerous than she had realised, and she didn't doubt his threat to kill her had been very real. The penthouse floor of the Exemplar Hotel was completely private to Gregorio, and he already had his own security team in place.

Besides, she accepted that going back to her apartment was a bad idea. Even though Gregorio had already had the lock and the door repaired, she didn't trust David any more.

She certainly didn't want to put Cathy and Rick in any danger by accepting their offer to stay with them.

Lia had never thought she would say it—even think it—but Gregorio's hotel suite *was* the safest place for her to stay right now.

CHAPTER ELEVEN

'You are going to need help undressing, and I will put something waterproof over the cast on your arm before you have a shower,' Gregorio informed her evenly as he unpacked the bag of Lia's clothes and toiletries that Cathy and Rick had just collected and brought over from Lia's apartment.

Lia gave a grimace as she sat on the side of the bed in what had turned out to be one of six spare bedrooms in Gregorio's suite. Not that she had expected to be invited to share Gregorio's bedroom, but this impersonal guest room told her exactly the place she occupied in his life.

She really hadn't thought things through enough when she had accepted that Gregorio's suite was the safest and best place for her to be right now. She hadn't thought about where she would actually sleep. Nor taken into account the mechanics of not being able to move her right arm properly, or the fact that she was going to be encumbered with a heavy plaster cast for the next six weeks, and a sling for two of them.

Which meant she couldn't undress herself without assistance, and showering was going to be a big problem. She would probably need to have her food cut up into tiny pieces too, so she could eat with one hand.

But right now her thoughts sounded like those of a whiny, ungrateful brat. 'I'll take a bath instead of a shower,' she announced brightly. 'And I'm sure I'll be able to take my own clothes off.'

She knew the strong painkillers she had been given at the hospital were preventing her from feeling the worst of the pain. Luckily she had been prescribed a whole plastic container full of them!

Gregorio arched a dark brow. 'I have already seen you naked, Lia…'

She shot him an irritated scowl. 'Not under these circumstances, you haven't!' She sighed as she realised she sounded ungrateful. 'I'm sorry, Gregorio. I haven't even thanked you yet for coming to my rescue earlier.'

'Luckily Raphael recognised Richardson's car and called me immediately.' Gregorio leaned back against the tall chest of drawers he had placed her clothes in, arms folded across his chest, his expression unreadable. 'What exactly did Richardson threaten to do to you?'

Lia wasn't fooled for a moment by his relaxed posture, or the mildness of his tone. 'I'm sure he wouldn't really have— No, I'm not.' She admitted with a grimace. 'He was… I had no idea he could be like that. I owe you an apology, Gregorio. Another one. Everything you said about David is true.'

'He is responsible for embezzling the money from your father's company?'

'Oh, yes.'

'He admitted this to you?'

'Amongst other things.'

She related everything David had said to her earlier that evening.

'He was *with* your father the night he died...?' Gregorio frowned.

Lia closed her eyes briefly before opening them again. 'He said there was nothing to be done. That my father died almost instantly. But—' She broke off, unable to say anything more on the subject without breaking down.

'But,' Gregorio acknowledged harshly, 'you think he is responsible for killing your father?'

'Only indirectly—in as much as he caused my father so much distress it brought on the heart attack.'

His mouth thinned. 'I will find him, Lia. No matter what rock Richardson hides under, I *will* find him.'

'I know you will.' She nodded. 'Would you mind very much if I don't take a bath or a shower tonight? I'm tired and aching and I just want to go to sleep.'

'Of course. Whatever you are comfortable with,' Gregorio reassured her as he straightened away from the chest of drawers and crossed the bedroom to her side. 'But I *am* going to help you undress.'

Lia knew that tone only too well: it was one that told her Gregorio wasn't going to be talked out of doing exactly what he said he would. And there was no arguing with the fact that he *had* already seen her naked.

'Did Cathy pack something for me to sleep in?' She stood up—only to have Gregorio reach out and grasp her uninjured arm to steady her as she tilted to one side. It was ridiculous how a little thing like a plaster cast and a sling could affect her balance.

'Something that looks like an oversized T-shirt...?'

'That's it, yes.'

Lia almost laughed at the look of disgust on Gregorio's face. No doubt he was used to the women in his life wearing silk and satin to bed—if they bothered to wear anything at all. Even when she'd been able to afford those things Lia had always preferred practicality and warmth in bed over appearing sexy.

'Thank you for calling Cathy and Rick for me earlier. I— They're the closest thing to family I have.'

'I am aware of that.' Gregorio spoke softly. 'And I have already left instructions that they are to be admitted at any time.'

'Thank you.'

He gave a rueful smile. 'You are very polite this evening.'

'About time, hmm?'

Gregorio shrugged. 'You felt you had good reason to be...less than polite to me before.'

'And I was wrong.' She sighed. 'About everything.'

'Do not upset yourself. You know the truth now, and that is the important thing.'

It was. And yet...

She didn't like it that Gregorio was treating her with the polite distance of a concerned acquaintance, rather than a lover. Not that she didn't fully deserve it, but Lia missed the intensity of passion radiating from him. That had never been far from the surface when the two of them had been together in the past.

She drew in a shaky breath. 'Let's get this over with, shall we?'

'Of course.'

Gregorio forced himself to remain detached and impersonal as he aided Lia in removing her clothes. He had never acted as nursemaid to anyone before—let alone a woman he had been in bed with all yesterday afternoon. But how difficult could it be?

More difficult that he had imagined once he had removed Lia's jacket, blouse and bra. Which had proved easy enough once he had removed the sling.

The physical removing of Lia's clothes wasn't the problem. It was being this close to her when she was completely naked from the waist up, the fullness of her nipples just a tempting breath away. That was enough to tax the restraint of any man—least of all one who had already enjoyed having those succulent nipples in his mouth.

Gregorio attempted to remove temptation by taking the long red T-shirt from the chest of drawers and quickly putting it on Lia before refastening the sling. The nightshirt covered her to mid-thigh.

He drew in a deep, controlling breath as he unzipped and removed her skirt, but his resolve to remain detached was shaken again as he looked at her wearing sexy panties, suspenders and stockings.

He could *do* this, damn it. He wasn't an animal or a callow youth. He was a man of sophistication and experience. He shouldn't be aroused just by looking at an injured woman dressed in an unbecoming red nightshirt—even if she *was* also wearing sexy suspenders.

Except he was.

Thank goodness the restrictive material of his jeans prevented that arousal from being too obvious.

'Gregorio…?'

His distraction obviously wasn't quite so easy to hide!

He dealt with the rest of Lia's clothing with the minimum of contact with the heat of her silky skin, breathing a sigh of relief once he had her safely tucked beneath the bedcovers and could straighten and move away from the bed.

Lia looked...fragile. Her hair was a silky auburn cloud on the white pillow behind her, and her face was almost as pale. The outline of her body was slender beneath the duvet.

But it wasn't just a physical fragility. Lia's eyes were a smoky and unfocused grey, with dark shadows beneath them. No doubt some of that had been caused by the agony of having her arm broken, along with the medication she had been given to relieve the pain. But Gregorio had a feeling it was also an outward show of the turmoil of emotions she had to be feeling inside.

It must have been a shock when Richardson had attacked and threatened her in that way: the animal had broken her arm, damn it. She had intended marrying Richardson once—would no doubt have done so if her father hadn't died and Richardson hadn't revealed his true colours by breaking their engagement.

As far as Gregorio was concerned Lia had escaped being married to a man who one day would have become an abusive husband.

Lia, on the other hand, must feel not only foolish for ever having been taken in by Richardson, but also disillusioned with the whole concept of falling in love.

'Try to get some sleep.' Gregorio's voice sounded harsher than he'd intended, and he made a concerted effort to control his anger. It was Richardson he was angry with, not Lia. 'I will leave the door open, and I'll be in my office or my bedroom if you need anything.'

'Thank you.' The heaviness of her lids was already making them close.

Gregorio hesitated at the door. 'Would you like the light left on or turned off?'

'On!' She half sat up again in the bed. 'Off.' She

grimaced as she sank back against the pillows. 'I don't know...' She groaned.

'We will compromise.' He nodded. 'I'll leave the door open and the light on in the hallway, okay?'

'Okay...' She sighed wearily.

Gregorio adjusted the lighting before quietly leaving the bedroom. As promised, he left the door open.

Only once he had reached the sanctuary of his office did he release the anger that had been building and building inside him by slamming his fist against the door. It hurt him more than it hurt the wooden door, but he needed the release, the physical pain, after remaining calm for Lia's sake for so long.

He wanted to hurt someone. And that someone was David Richardson. Because Lia was suffering the emotional and physical repercussions of the other man's abuse.

He had known she was suffering physically, but her emotional trauma had shown itself in her immediate reaction to the thought of being left alone in the darkness of the bedroom. Lia was frightened, but too determined to appear strong to want Gregorio to see that fear. He had seen it anyway.

His expression was grim as he flexed his bruised knuckles before pouring himself a glass of brandy, carrying the glass across the room to sit in the chair behind his desk.

He swung his booted feet up to rest on the edge of the desk and turned his head to stare out of the window at the night-time skyline. Was Richardson still out there in the city somewhere, hiding? Or had he already left the country? Not that it mattered, because Gregorio wouldn't give up the search—no matter how far Richardson had run.

Gregorio had no idea how long he sat there, sipping brandy and staring sightlessly out of the window, totally aware of Lia just feet away, almost naked in bed. He felt a certain relief when his cell phone vibrated in his jeans pocket and interrupted his reverie. His thoughts had been going round and round in ever decreasing circles, none of them pleasant.

He took out his cell phone and checked the caller ID before taking the call. 'Sebastien,' he greeted his brother tersely.

'Who's annoyed you *now*?' Sebastien didn't waste any time on pleasantries.

'It is too long and too complicated a story to tell.'

'Try...' his brother drawled.

Gregorio gave him a condensed—and censored—version of the events of the past week.

The three brothers had always been close, having shared a common enemy: their father's sometimes overbearing machismo. As adults the siblings had also become friends, and Sebastien was the closest thing Gregorio had to a confidant.

'So Jacob Fairbanks's daughter—Lia—is there with you now, in your hotel suite?' Sebastien prompted speculatively.

'She is asleep in one of the guest rooms, yes,' Gregorio stated. 'She has a cast on her broken arm and no particular liking for *me*,' he added firmly. 'Sebastien...?' he prompted at his brother's continued silence.

'Just give me a second while I choose my words carefully, Rio...' Sebastien spoke slowly. 'Our proposed deal with Jacob Fairbanks was called off months ago, and you told me she slapped you on the face at his funeral—so what is Lia Fairbanks doing in your life *now*?'

Trust Sebastien to go straight to the heart of the matter.

The heart...?

Gregorio had physically wanted Lia from the moment he saw her in that restaurant four months ago. This past week he had come to know the Lia behind that physical beauty. To like her. For her strength. Her principles. Her loyalty—even if it occasionally proved to be misplaced!—and her love for her father and her friends. Her work ethic was also exemplary: Michael Harrington had already told Gregorio he believed Lia would become one of their most competent receptionists.

Had Gregorio come to *like* her or to *love* her?

Until this mess was sorted out and Lia was safe he had no intention of delving too deeply into what his feelings for her might be.

'Taking a long time to answer, there, Rio,' Sebastien mocked.

'You are my brother—not my conscience!'

Sebastien chuckled. 'And...?'

'I feel a sense of obligation to ensure Lia's safety,' Gregorio answered him carefully.

'Why?'

'Because she is— Sebastien, her father—the only parent she had—is dead. David Richardson, her ex-fiancé, deserted her when she most needed him. He has now admitted to embezzling from her father's company, and that is the reason Jacob called off his deal with us. Richardson left Lia alone until he knew the two of us were...acquainted...' He substituted the word he had intended using. One afternoon in bed together did not make him and Lia lovers, and she had made it clear she didn't intend to repeat the experience. 'And then he attacked her, threatened her. He broke her *arm*, dammit!'

'And you feel responsible for her?'

'Yes, I feel responsible for her,' he repeated evenly.

Lia, standing outside in the hallway, overhearing Gregorio's side of the conversation with his brother, hadn't realised how much hearing those words spoken out loud would hurt until Gregorio said them. It was one thing to *think* that was what had motivated Gregorio's continued interest in her—another entirely to hear him state as much to his brother.

She had slept for a couple of hours, only to wake up suddenly, totally disorientated until she remembered where she was and why. Once awake she had realised how thirsty she was, and had got out of bed, quietly leaving the bedroom so as not to disturb Gregorio on her way to the kitchen for a glass of water.

She hadn't meant to eavesdrop on his telephone conversation with his brother, but once she'd heard her name mentioned she hadn't been able to walk away either.

Gregorio had saved her again this evening. He was always saving her from one disaster or another.

Because he feels responsible for me.

Well, that had to change. Maybe not right now, because it was far too late for her even to think of moving out of the hotel and finding somewhere else to stay tonight, and she was determined not to involve Cathy and Rick in any further acts of violence from David. But tomorrow, when she was feeling stronger and able to make other arrangements, she was going to stop being a burden on Gregorio and take control of her own life—as she had said she was going to.

Tomorrow.

'Wake up, Lia! It is not real, *bella*, only a nightmare. *Lia?*' Gregorio prompted more firmly as she continued to scream, the tears streaming from her closed eyes and down her cheeks as she fought off his attempts to take her in his arms.

Gregorio had drunk several more glasses of brandy before going to bed, knowing he was going to need the relaxant if he stood any chance of sleeping at all.

It had taken some time, but he had finally dozed off into a fitful slumber. Only to be woken—minutes… hours later?—by the sound of Lia screaming.

At first he had thought someone—Richardson—had managed to get past his security and Lia was being attacked. It was only once he had entered her bedroom and found her there alone, screaming as she tossed from side to side in the bed, that he realised she was obviously in the middle of some horrendous nightmare.

His efforts to calm her had so far been unsuccessful.

'Lia!' He was careful not to knock the cast on her arm as he grasped her shoulders. 'Open your eyes and look at me, Lia,' he instructed firmly.

She'd stopped screaming, at least, and her eyes were open, but her body was still being racked by intense sobs.

'It was just a nightmare…it isn't real,' he continued to soothe as he took her in his arms.

It seemed very real to Lia!

She was running, knowing that something…someone…was pursuing her. She couldn't see him when she dared to take a quick glance behind her, but she could feel him, hear him breathing—could almost *feel* that hot breath on the back of her neck. And then he was there—in front of her—not behind her at all. An indistinct dark shadow and yet she knew it was a man. Knew it was David. And he wanted to kill her.

'You are safe now, Lia.' Gregorio held her tightly. 'No one will harm you while I am here. I promise you.'

But he wouldn't always be there, would he? She was just a woman Gregorio felt a fleeting obligation to protect. Because she was alone in the world and she needed his help. He didn't *really* care about her. They'd had sex yesterday afternoon, and that was the reason he probably felt even this much obligation. Right now he was probably regretting that he had ever shown an interest in her at all. She brought too much baggage with her, and Gregorio de la Cruz wasn't interested in a woman with baggage.

'I'm okay now.' She was very aware of the fact that Gregorio wore only a pair of loose jogging trousers, and his chest was completely bare. The warm and muscular chest he was holding her against… 'I'm sorry if I disturbed you.' His half-nakedness was certainly disturbing *her*! 'I'll be fine now.'

She kept her gaze lowered as she attempted to pull away. Gregorio's arms only tightened in reaction.

'Lia, look at me.'

She didn't want to look at him. At any part of him. Bad enough that her hand that wasn't restricted by the sling was now pressed against Gregorio's chest, that his flesh was warm and sensual to the touch.

'Lia?'

She glanced up at Gregorio's face and then quickly

down again. His hair was tousled from sleep, his eyes black, and dark stubble lined his jaw. He looked incredibly sexy. And he smelt edible. A cross between the lingering aroma of that expensive cologne he wore and something else—a male musk that was uniquely Gregorio.

She felt her body's response to all that overwhelming male lushness.

Gregorio simply felt an obligation to look out for her, Lia firmly reminded herself. That was the only reason he had been around this past couple of months.

And in return she had slapped him at her father's funeral, been incredibly rude to him before asking him to leave her apartment, and then yesterday—yesterday she had told him she didn't want him. That she never wanted to go to bed with him again.

Liar, liar, pants on fire.

She could lie to Gregorio, but there was no longer any chance of lying to herself.

She was in love with Gregorio.

Not infatuated, not sexually enthralled by him—although she was that too!—but one hundred per cent in love with him.

He was everything a man should be. Honourable. Truthful. Protective of those he deemed weaker than himself. A man Lia knew instinctively her father had liked as well as respected. And the reason she knew that was because her father had recognised those traits in Gregorio.

In the same way her father had known that David was none of those things. If he had lived, would her father have told her the truth about David? Or would he have continued to lie and cover up for the younger man because he wouldn't have wanted to hurt Lia by exposing the true nature of the man she loved?

Lia hoped it would have been the former, and that her father would have realised she was strong enough to accept the truth.

None of which changed the fact that she had now fallen deeply in love with a man who was never going to want her as more than a friend with benefits.

'I'll be fine now,' Lia assured Gregorio lightly as she pulled out of his arms. 'Please go back to bed. *Please.*'

'Sure?' He studied her closely.

'Sure.' She nodded, keeping that bright look on her face until Gregorio had left the bedroom.

Which was when Lia closed her eyes and allowed hot tears to fall down her cheeks.

CHAPTER TWELVE

'Might I ask what you are doing here, Sebastien?'

Gregorio's brother had arrived at the hotel just minutes ago. Considering it was only eight o'clock in the morning, Sebastien had to have flown here in the second company jet overnight from New York. Almost immediately after the two men had concluded their telephone conversation the night before, in fact.

His brother stepped back from their brotherly hug. 'You didn't sound at all yourself when we spoke on the phone last night, Rio.'

He arched dark and sceptical brows. 'And that was reason enough for you to immediately fly to London?'

Sebastien gave him a boyish grin. 'That, and I wanted to see Lia Fairbanks for myself.'

Gregorio tensed. 'Why?'

Sebastien's grin grew even wider. 'I wanted to meet the woman who has my big brother so tied up in knots.'

'Stop talking nonsense,' Gregorio snapped. 'No doubt you would like a cup of coffee?'

He turned away to pour some of the strong brew he always made to accompany his breakfast. He had already drunk two full cups this morning, having been unable to fall asleep again after Lia's nightmare. He had wanted to stay alert in case Lia needed him again.

'No changing the subject, Rio.' Sebastien made himself comfortable at one of the high stools at the breakfast bar as he accepted the mug of coffee. 'What's so special about Lia Fairbanks?' He kept his eyes on Gregorio as he took a swallow.

Everything.

The thought had leapt unbidden into Gregorio's head, and once there he couldn't seem to dislodge it.

Lia was special. *Very* special. A woman who remained strong through adversity. Most women would have been hysterical after Richardson's attack last night, but Lia had remained calm. And this was after she had lost her father only two and a half months ago and her engagement had ended—although after the events of yesterday she was probably relieved that it had.

As for the way the two of them were in bed together...

Lia was like none of the women Gregorio had known in the past. She gave not only with her body but with all that she was. Gregorio had never known a lover like her before.

Would he ever know another lover like her again?

'Perhaps I'll know the answer to that once I've met her?' Sebastien was still eyeing him speculatively.

Gregorio felt an unaccustomed surge of possessiveness at the thought of Lia meeting Sebastien. Would she find Sebastien attractive, as so many other women did? The two brothers were very alike in looks, with their dark hair and dark eyes, and a similar build and height.

Would Lia find his brother easier to get along with than Gregorio?

That was a given. Gregorio was well aware that he lacked the charm and ease of manner Sebastien could so easily adopt if the need arose. And meeting a beautiful woman was definitely one of those occasions.

The thought of Lia gravitating towards Sebastien was enough to cause Gregorio's hand to clench at his side and his fingers to tighten about his coffee mug until the knuckles turned white.

'I'm guessing you don't like that idea.' Sebastien grinned.

Gregorio gave his brother an irritated glance. 'Do not see emotions where they do not exist.'

Sebastien openly chuckled now. 'If you don't stop gripping the handle of that mug so tightly you're going to snap it right off.'

He relaxed that grip. 'You would be better spending your time thinking of ways to help me locate David Richardson than commenting on things you know nothing about.'

'I know nothing about Richardson, either.'

Gregorio's lids narrowed on his brother. 'This situation needs to be resolved, Sebastien. Quickly.'

'But then Miss Fairbanks would move back to her own apartment.'

'Exactly.'

'Rio—'

'Why are you *really* here, Sebastien?' Gregorio looked at his brother searchingly, noting the lines beside his brother's mouth and eyes that didn't gel with his light-hearted banter. 'What's wrong?'

Sebastien sighed heavily. 'Nothing a hot and meaningless fling wouldn't cure.'

Gregorio winced. 'Do you have someone specific in mind?'

His brother grimaced. 'Maybe.'

Definitely, in Gregorio's opinion. 'Who is she?'

'Could we just concentrate on *your* problems rather than my own?' Sebastien prompted impatiently.

'This woman is a *problem*, then?'

'Monumentally so,' his brother conceded. 'But don't worry. I'll handle it when I get back to New York.'

'Handle it or handle her?'

Sebastien gave a hard grin. 'Both.'

'I hope I'm not interrupting?'

Gregorio turned sharply at the sound of Lia's voice, a scowl darkening his brow as he saw she was only dressed in that over-large thigh-length red T-shirt, with her arm in its sling over the top of it and her hair dishevelled from sleep.

'I'm Sebastien de la Cruz.' His brother stood politely. 'I hope we didn't wake you?'

'Lia Fairbanks,' she returned stiltedly. 'And, no, you didn't wake me. I just woke up and felt in need of coffee.'

'My big brother is in charge of the coffee pot. Rio…?' he prompted as Gregorio made no move to pour a third cup.

It was the first time Lia had heard anyone address him by the affectionate diminutive; it made him seem less the powerful and arrogant Gregorio de la Cruz and more the older brother. The casual navy blue polo shirt and faded jeans he wore added to that illusion.

She hadn't been able to help overhearing at least part of Gregorio's conversation with Sebastien—again. The little she had heard made it clear Gregorio wanted her out of his hotel suite as soon as possible.

Not that it came as a surprise. She already knew Gregorio had only insisted she come here at all because of that sense of responsibility he felt towards her. Nevertheless, hearing him reiterate those feelings to his brother made it all too real.

'You are not dressed appropriately to receive visitors,' Gregorio bit out tautly. 'I suggest you return to your bedroom and put on a robe, at least.'

Lia frowned at the censure she could hear in his tone. And at the continued lack of coffee. 'I can't manage on my own.' She gave a pointed glance at the sling immobilising her arm.

'Then I will come and assist you.' Gregorio straightened. 'If you will excuse us, Sebastien?'

'Don't bother on my account.' Sebastien resumed his seat on the bar stool. 'I think you look charming just as you are. Rio has explained that your arm is broken,' he said sympathetically.

Lia was sure, from the conversation she had overheard, that Sebastien de la Cruz was well aware of exactly how she had broken her arm. Or rather, how it had been broken for her.

Now that she was no longer in excruciating pain, and the effects of the painkillers had worn off a little, she was aware of the shock of exactly what David had done to her. Of what else he had threatened to do to her if she didn't back off.

She really hadn't known the true David at all until last night.

She gave a grimace in answer to Sebastien's comment. 'It could have been worse.'

'So I understand.' He nodded. 'I'm sorry you've had to go through this.'

'The princess had to be woken by the frog some time. It's what my father called me,' she explained emotionally as both men looked at her. 'His princess.'

A princess he had protected from seeing or hearing any of the harsh realities of life. Until he'd died from the strain of trying to protect her from the harshest reality. Well, Lia was well and truly awake to all those realities now—she had the plaster cast on her broken arm to prove it.

'I will accompany you to your bedroom and help you into your robe,' Gregorio announced into the silence.

Lia turned her frowning attention on him. 'I haven't had any coffee yet.'

'Because I have not poured you any. Nor will I do so until you are wearing your robe.'

'I'm perfectly decent as I am.' The nightshirt covered her from her neck to a couple of inches above her knees.

'I will be the judge of that.' His mouth was thin, his dark eyes glittering.

Lia gave a squeak of protest as Gregorio grasped her shoulders and turned her in the direction of the hallway and her bedroom, walking her forward in front of him. 'I can walk unassisted!'

'Then do so.' He released her, but his presence behind her continued her impetus out of the kitchen.

'What is *wrong* with you?' Lia demanded impatiently once they were outside in the hallway.

His eyes narrowed. 'You are virtually naked in front of a complete stranger.'

'He's your *brother*, for goodness' sake.'

'And you met him for the first time five minutes ago—which makes him a stranger to you.'

'"Virtually naked" would be wearing only my underwear,' Lia defended. 'And I don't remember you complaining the last time I was in your suite dressed like that,' she challenged.

Gregorio could feel that nerve pulsing in his cheek again—a common occurrence, it seemed, when he was with this stubbornly determined woman. 'And I would not complain if you were to be dressed like that again—as long as the two of us were alone together when you were.'

'Sebastien didn't seem to mind the way I'm dressed,' she taunted.

His lids narrowed to slits. 'If you are trying to annoy me you are succeeding!'

Lia snorted. 'I obviously don't have to try very hard.'

Gregorio frowned. 'What do you mean?'

'Never mind.' She shook her head before turning to continue walking down the hallway.

Gregorio caught up with her as she reached her bedroom. 'What did you mean by that remark?' he repeated as he followed her inside.

She turned to face him. 'I'm obviously nothing more than a nuisance to you. Even more so now that your brother has arrived.'

Lia was *so* much more to Gregorio than a nuisance. More than he was prepared to admit. Even to himself.

'Well?'

He scowled his irritation. 'Do not take that aggressive tone with me!'

'Or what?'

'What is wrong with you this morning?' he snapped.

'You've refused to give me my first cup of coffee of the day.'

Gregorio drew in a deep breath in order to hold on to his temper. 'Only until after you have put your robe on.'

'And I'm still waiting for the assistance you so gallantly offered.'

Gregorio ignored her sarcasm as he helped her to put her robe on. Lia was obviously spoiling for a fight this morning, and he wasn't about to give her one.

'Did you know that your accent gets stronger when you're angry?'

He finished tying the robe of the belt about her waist before stepping back. 'Then I must presume it is always stronger when I am with you.'

Lia arched a mocking auburn brow. 'Did you just make a joke?'

'Doubtful,' he drawled dryly.

'Irony *is* joking.'

'Then I must make jokes all the time.'

'When you're with me.' She nodded.

'When I am with anyone.'

Lia eyed him quizzically. 'You and your brother aren't much alike, are you?'

He tensed. 'In looks—'

'Oh, I wasn't talking about the way you look—that's a given,' she dismissed without further explanation. 'What is your youngest brother like?'

'Alejandro is…complicated,' he replied cautiously.

Alejandro's problems were not discussed outside the family.

'Like you, then.' Lia nodded. 'He was married, wasn't he?'

That was part of Alejandro's problem. And what did Lia mean by saying that *he* was complicated?

His life was an open book. He was a successful businessman. Wealthy. Single. He had a healthy sexual appetite, as the newspapers were so fond of reporting, and he didn't hide the fact that he had zero patience with incompetence or triviality. Or that he was bored very easily.

Something he had certainly never been when he was with Lia…

'You're taking too long to answer, which probably means you aren't going to.' Lia sighed. 'Can we go back to the kitchen now? The coffee is calling to me.'

Gregorio gave an exasperated laugh as he followed her out of the bedroom. 'You are obsessed with your morning coffee!'

'He left with a scowl on his face and returns smiling,' Sebastien observed mockingly as Lia and Gregorio entered the kitchen together. 'You're a miracle-worker, Lia.'

She grimaced. 'I think you'll find Gregorio was laughing *at* me rather than with me.'

Sebastien shrugged. 'A smile is still a smile, for whatever reason.'

'Is that such a rare occurrence?' Lia seemed to recall that Gregorio had laughed quite often when the two of them were together. When they weren't arguing or making love…

'I would say unique rather than—'

'When the two of you have quite finished discussing me as if I am not here…' Gregorio raised pointed brows as he handed Lia the mug of coffee he had just poured for her.

Oh, Lia was only too aware that Gregorio was there. As she'd said, Sebastien was as dark and handsome as his brother. But he possessed an easy charm that was lacking in Gregorio—although, on closer inspection, the sharp intelligence in Sebastien's eyes gave the impression that that might be a veneer over a deeper, darker nature. But it was Gregorio she was constantly aware of. Every minute. Every second.

Lia chose to concentrate on drinking her coffee rather than make any reply to Gregorio's comment. Until the silence in the kitchen became uncomfortable. 'What were the two of you discussing when I came in?' Apart from the fact that Gregorio couldn't wait to move her out of his hotel suite.

'Your ex-fiancé.' Sebastien was the one to answer her.

She winced. 'I would rather not be reminded of that fact.'

'As would we all,' Gregorio put in harshly.

Lia gave him a sharp glance, knowing she deserved the admonition in his tone. Thank goodness she was no longer that naïve nincompoop who had fallen for David's charm. 'Any news on his whereabouts?'

'None,' Gregorio answered grimly. 'Lia, the police will be coming here to interview you in just under an hour—'

'The police?' she echoed sharply.

He nodded. 'We can and will find Richardson, Lia, but it's better if the police bring him to justice for the things he has done. As such, I telephoned the police and reported his attack on you last night first thing this morning. The story will be backed up by the broken door and the hospital report on your broken arm.'

She carefully placed her empty coffee mug down on the breakfast bar. 'You should have consulted me before doing that.'

'Why?'

'Why?'

'Uh-oh—I think I'll go and take a shower and grab a couple of hours' sleep, if no one minds.' Sebastien glanced between the two of them. Lia was glaring at Gregorio and he looked genuinely perplexed by her anger. 'Obviously no one is even going to notice I've gone!'

Lia waited only as long as it took for Sebastien to leave the room before answering Gregorio. 'You had no right to contact the police without talking to me first.'

'I had *every* right.' A nerve pulsed in his tightly clenched jaw. 'I should have called them last night, once we reached the hospital, but I decided to wait until today—'

'It wasn't your decision to make—'

'God knows what would have happened to you last night if I hadn't kicked open the door to your apartment!'

She was well aware of how much she owed Gregorio. 'But the *police*, Gregorio...' She groaned as she sank down onto one of the bar stools.

Gregorio frowned as he saw how pale her cheeks had become. 'Do you not see that this is the best way to put Richardson in the spotlight of the authorities? The police will want to know the motivation for his attack on you, and I will hand over to the police all the information I have gathered so far in regard to Richardson's illegal dealings with your father.'

Lia saw *Gregorio's* motivation. It had been very cleverly done.

He had taken care of two problems at the same time. He would pass on the information he had concerning Fairbanks Industries to the police and at the same time ensure that this situation ended as quickly as possible. The two of them would then be able to get on with their own respective lives.

Which was what she wanted too.

Wasn't it?

CHAPTER THIRTEEN

LIA LAY HER head back against the sofa in exhaustion after the police had asked all their questions and finally left the hotel. But she wasn't too tired to remember that she was supposed to be working today. 'I need to contact Mike Harrington to tell him I won't be in today.'

Gregorio's brow rose at hearing Lia call the hotel manager *Mike* Harrington; he had only ever known the other man by the more formal Michael. 'I have already spoken to him.'

'Why am I not surprised?' Lia muttered.

'At the time I was unsure of what time you were going to wake this morning,' he defended.

'Fair enough.' She sighed. 'I'm just wondering whose life you ran before taking over mine?'

'Lia—'

'It's okay.' She held up a defeated hand. 'I understand.'

'Understand what, exactly?'

'That the quicker this is resolved the sooner I'll be out of this suite and your life.' She stood. 'I think I'll take some more painkillers and then follow Sebastien's example of taking a nap for a couple of hours.'

She left the sitting room.

Gregorio was so stunned by her first comment that he was barely aware of the second one.

Lia believed he wanted to hasten her departure—not just from this suite but from his life. What had he ever said or done to make her think that?

His only motivation in ending this situation with Richardson was to ensure that nothing like last night ever happened again. He also wanted to clear her father's name. Again for Lia's sake, more than anyone else's.

Lia had been very defensive this morning. Spoiling for a fight. Earlier Gregorio had put it down to late reaction to the shock of Richardson's attack last night. But what if it was for another reason entirely? Her barbs and sarcasm had been directed solely at him, Gregorio now realised. Much to Gregorio's annoyance she had joked with Sebastien a couple of times this morning. Usually at Gregorio's expense. And she had been calm and polite when she answered the questions put to her by the police.

He didn't understand why. What had he and Sebastien been discussing shortly before Lia joined them in the kitchen earlier?

Damn it!

Sebastien had been teasing Gregorio about his responses to Lia, and he had reacted defensively to that teasing. Had denied that Lia had any importance in his life amongst other things. One of those things being stating his need to resolve the situation quickly and to agree that it was so that Lia could move back to her apartment.

He hadn't meant that the way it had sounded—had only been fending off Sebastien's too-personal comments.

Perhaps he shouldn't have said it? Especially in a place where there had been a chance that Lia might overhear the comment.

Damn, damn, *damn* it.

Lia's first thought on waking up was that there was something heavy lying across her. Then she realised it had to be the unwieldy plaster cast she had on her arm.

Except… This weight felt lower down than the plaster cast. Warmer too. More flexible.

She carefully lifted the duvet so she could see what it was.

An arm.

A bare and muscular *male* arm, lightly dusted with dark hair.

An arm she easily recognised as belonging to Gregorio.

Gregorio is in bed with me!

Lia was sure he hadn't been there when she'd fallen asleep earlier, almost the instant her head had touched the pillow. She had been exhausted from talking with the police for over an hour, and then the painkillers had finally kicked in.

Gregorio must have come to her bedroom and got into the bed with her some time after that.

A part of her knew she should be annoyed, at the very least, at his having taken advantage of her sleeping. Another part of her just wanted to curl up in his arms and go back to sleep.

She also couldn't help wondering if the rest of him was as naked as his arm…

She took care not to wake Gregorio as she scooted backwards until her bottom came into contact with his groin. She was more than a little disappointed to feel the brush of denim against her skin where her nightshirt had rucked up as she'd moved about in her sleep.

'If you move back a little further you will discover that I am fully aroused.'

Lia instantly tensed at the unexpectedness of discovering that Gregorio was awake. Was it because she had woken him? Or had he already been awake when she'd been fidgeting about trying to discover what was curved about her waist? And in her careful—and obvious—efforts to discover if Gregorio was naked…?

She moistened her lips before speaking. 'What are you doing in here?'

'Until a few minutes ago I was sleeping.'

'I meant—'

'I know what you meant, Lia.' Gregorio moved up to roll her gently onto her back so that he could look at her, careful not to jar her arm. Her face had more colour than earlier, thank goodness. Her eyes no longer had that haunted look, either. 'I wanted to be here when you woke up.'

'Why?'

'Two reasons.'

'Which are?'

'Silvio contacted me shortly after you had gone to sleep. He and Raphael discovered Richardson was booked on a flight to Dubai.'

Her eyes widened. 'He was fleeing the country?'

'I believe in the beginning, with your father dead, he thought he could weather the storm and his life here in England would go on as before, with no one any the wiser as to what he had done. But—'

'But yesterday I alerted him to the fact that wasn't

going to happen.' She winced. 'I'm *so* sorry, Gregorio. I just wanted him to know I wasn't as stupid as he thought I was, but all I did was give him the opportunity to leave England as soon as possible.'

'Do not feel bad about that. Richardson's response to your warning was damning in the extreme. Besides,' he added with satisfaction, 'he is now in police custody, after an anonymous phone call informing them he was booked onto the Dubai flight.'

She gave a shudder. 'He's a lawyer, Gregorio—do you think the charges against him will stick or will he manage to wriggle out of them?'

'His attack on you will certainly stick. The FSA will also be very interested in Richardson's behaviour. Especially as I have now given them all the information I have so far on his having embezzled money from Fairbanks Industries. It may take some time but, yes, I believe eventually Richardson will be made to answer for all his crimes.'

Lia gave a shaky sigh. 'I can't believe it's over.'

'In *time* it will be,' Gregorio cautioned again.

Lia had no doubt that with the powerful Gregorio de la Cruz's involvement that time would come sooner rather than later, and that David would one day end up in jail—as he fully deserved to.

'You said there was a second reason you wanted to be here when I woke up?' she reminded him softly.

Gregorio felt the frown lift from his brow. 'I believe you are suffering under a misapprehension in regard to something you overheard me say earlier.'

Lia's tension was immediate in the wariness of her expression. 'Oh…?'

He nodded. 'I am not…comfortable with emotions.'

She smiled ruefully. 'I noticed.'

'Let me finish, Lia,' he reproved gently. 'Sebastien was being his usual irritating younger brother self this morning.'

'Obviously I can't speak from personal experience, but I believe that's part of a sibling's job description.'

'Perhaps,' Gregorio allowed dryly. 'Sebastien seems to think it is, at least.' He sobered. 'What I said to him, about resolving the situation with Richardson so that you could return to your apartment, was not meant as literally as I believe you have taken it.'

She frowned her puzzlement. 'I don't understand…'

'Nor did I until I tried to find a reason why you were being so dismissive of me,' he admitted. 'Lia, *you* were the one who brought an end to our…relationship.'

'Our going to bed together, you mean? Well… Yes.' Her gaze didn't quite meet his. 'It was clouding the issue. Obviously, having known and liked my father, you feel some sort of responsibility towards me. But I assure you—'

'I feel *concern* for you, not responsibility.'

'Oh.'

He nodded. 'I realise some of my actions and comments may have come across that way to you, but I assure you that *responsibility* is the last thing I feel when I look at you or touch you.'

'Oh.'

'Now you are worrying me,' he drawled. 'The Lia Fairbanks I know always has plenty to say on any subject,' he explained as she frowned. 'Lia, has it occurred to you that I could just as easily mistake *your* responses to *me* as gratitude?'

Her eyes widened. 'You think I went to bed with you out of *gratitude*?'

He smiled slightly. 'What I think is that we should start being honest with each other, so that in future we avoid these misunderstandings.'

The only words Lia heard were *in future*. That implied the two of them were going to *have* a future. Maybe not as anything more than friends, but even friendship was better than *responsibility* or *gratitude*.

'I'm waiting for you to start being honest,' she prompted after several long seconds of silence.

Gregorio chuckled at her guardedness. 'I have been honest with you from the beginning. I told you when we met again last week that I'd wanted you from the first night I saw you in Mancini's with your father and Richardson.'

'And now you've had me.'

'Yes.'

'I… This is in the spirit of honesty, you understand?'

'I understand.'

'Well. I… You're only the second man I've… Well, that I've…'

His brows rose. 'I am only your second lover?'

'Yes.' Lia breathed a sigh of relief that she didn't actually have to say the words. 'And in comparison the first one was awful,' she said with feeling. 'Not that I'm comparing you to David in any way,' she added quickly. 'I just want you to know that our lovemaking was spectacular. Wonderful. Special.'

'In the spirit of honesty?'

She frowned up at him. 'Are you mocking me?'

'Not at all.' Gregorio chuckled. 'In the spirit of the same honesty, can I say that our lovemaking was—

Lia…?' He prompted against the fingertips she had placed over his lips.

'I really don't want to hear how I measured up to the legion of women you've had in your bed.' She grimaced.

'I seem to recall that a Roman legion comprised about five thousand soldiers, and while I *have* been sexually active for some years, I very much doubt the total of my bed partners comes anywhere near that number.'

'You *are* mocking me!'

'Only a little,' Gregorio acknowledged huskily. 'And only because I am honoured to have been your second lover—especially as the first was such a failure.' His voice lowered. 'What I would *really* like above all things is to be your last lover too.'

'Sorry?' Lia's mouth had gone dry. Did Gregorio mean…? Was he asking…?

No, of course he wasn't. Gregorio didn't *do* for ever. She must have misunderstood him.

'Lia…' His hands moved up to cradle each side of her face as he looked down at her intently. 'Beautiful Lia. Our lovemaking was spectacular to me too. Wonderful. Most of all, special.'

'It was?' Lia wasn't sure she was still breathing. She couldn't possibly be awake.

'It was,' Gregorio confirmed gently. 'I wanted you from the moment I saw you, but in just a few days I have also fallen in love with you.'

Her eyes widened. 'You *love* me?'

'So very much.' Gregorio had only realised how much earlier, when he had contemplated the huge gap Lia would leave not only in his hotel suite but in his life, his heart, when the time came for her to leave and return to her own apartment.

Lia swallowed. 'Really?'

'Really,' he confirmed. 'Perhaps I always did. I have never believed in love at first sight, but...' He leant over to pull open a drawer in the bedside cabinet and remove something from inside. 'This is the handkerchief I used to wipe the blood from my cheek the day you slapped my face at the funeral.'

'You keep it in your bedside drawer?'

'Silvio gave it to me that day.' He smiled ruefully. 'I placed it in this drawer when I returned home, and it has been here beside me every night since.' He dropped the handkerchief back in the drawer. 'I couldn't bear to part with it.'

'You *love* me?'

'I do.' He nodded. 'More than life itself. Rather than wanting you to leave, as you believe, if I could I would keep you here with me for ever. But all of this is too soon for you.' He sighed. 'You lost your father such a short time ago. Your engagement ended badly. You need time to heal. To make a life for yourself. To prove to yourself that you *can* make a life for yourself.'

'You can understand that?'

His smile became warmer. 'You would not be the Lia I love if you did not feel that way.'

She looked up at him searchingly, noting the love and pride shining in his eyes as he steadily returned her gaze, leaving himself and his emotions wide open for her to see.

'Gregorio.' She reached up and touched his cheek. 'I've fallen in love with you, too.' She spoke clearly, firmly, wanting there to be no more misunderstandings between them. 'I love you,' she said. 'So very much.'

Gregorio felt as if someone had punched him in the

chest, stealing all the breath from his lungs and rendering him incapable of speech. Lia *loved* him?

'How can you possibly...?' He was finally able to force words past his shock. 'You cannot possibly... You believed... You accused me of...'

'Yes. Yes. Yes. And yes,' Lia acknowledged emotionally. 'I did, and I believed all of those things. And *still* I fell in love with you. Because you're none of those things, Gregorio. You're honourable. Truthful. Protective. You have been nothing but kind to me even in the face of my less than gracious behaviour towards you. How could I *not* fall in love with you?'

'Dios mio...' Gregorio continued speaking in Spanish as he buried his face against her throat.

'I have no idea what you're saying, but I don't care because I'm sure it's something beautiful.' Lia laughed happily, her arm about his shoulders as she clung to him.

He lifted his head, his mouth now only inches away from Lia's. 'I said you are beautiful. My heart. My world.'

'I love you, Gregorio. I love you so very much.'

She lifted her head and claimed his lips with her own.

'I said you would be bossy in bed,' Gregorio murmured indulgently a long time later, when the two of them were lying naked in bed together, Gregorio on his back, Lia nestled against his side with her head on his shoulder.

Their lovemaking had necessarily been gentle, because of the cast on Lia's arm, but no less beautiful because of it. Perhaps more so, because they had taken the time to explore and appreciate every inch of each other. Not just in passion and pleasure, but in love.

'Lia, when this is over there is a question I wish to ask you.'

Lia felt as if her heart had leapt into her throat. 'Why can't you ask me now?'

'For all the reasons I stated earlier.' He sighed. 'I want you to be sure—*very* sure—when you give me your answer.'

She frowned. 'And what happens in the meantime? Between us, I mean? Do we go our separate ways and meet up again in three months' time, say, to see if we both still feel the same way?'

'No!' Gregorio's arms tightened about her possessively. 'Absolutely not. We will see each other every day. And we will share the same bed every night,' he stated firmly.

Lia could barely hold back her smile of happiness.

Gregorio loved her. She loved him.

And whether Gregorio ever asked her that question or not was unimportant, because she had absolutely no doubt they would be spending the rest of their lives together.

EPILOGUE

Three months later

'YOU LOOK BEAUTIFUL,' Cathy said emotionally as she adjusted Lia's veil outside the church in her role as matron of honour.

Today was the happiest day of Lia's life. The day she and Gregorio were to be married.

She glanced down at the engagement ring she had transferred to her right hand for the duration of the ceremony. A solitaire yellow diamond, as Gregorio had said it would be. To Lia it was a symbol of their love and happiness together, and a promise for their future.

'Do stop fidgeting, Rick,' Cathy teased her husband as he stood beside Lia, ready to escort her inside the church and give her into Gregorio's safekeeping for the rest of their lives together. 'You look gorgeous,' she reassured him with a light kiss to his lips.

Lia found it hard to believe that this was happening. Six months ago she had thought her world was coming to an end—now she knew it was just beginning.

This was the first day of the rest of her life with Gregorio, as his wife.

'Ready?' Cathy prompted brightly.

'Oh, yes,' Lia confirmed without hesitation.

The last three months had been a rollercoaster of emotions. Gregorio's telling her he loved her. David's arrest and charges of embezzlement and fraud having been added to the charge of grievous bodily harm for his attack on Lia. Her days being occupied with making a success of her job at the Exemplar Hotel—which she had. And all her nights being spent in Gregorio's arms.

Throughout it all Gregorio had been the constant. Always there. And always, *always* assuring her of his deep love for her.

Today was their wedding day. A day when they would reaffirm their love for each other before family and friends.

She placed her hand on Rick's forearm before stepping forward, which was the signal for the two ushers to open the church doors and for 'The Wedding March' to be played.

And there, waiting for her at the altar, stood Gregorio, love and pride shining unreservedly in his eyes as he looked at her.

An unshakable love Lia knew she would return for the rest of her life.

* * * * *

COMING SOON!

We really hope you enjoyed reading this book. If you're looking for more romance be sure to head to the shops when new books are available on

Thursday 21st May

To see which titles are coming soon, please visit
millsandboon.co.uk/nextmonth

MILLS & BOON

TWO BRAND NEW BOOKS FROM
Love Always

Be prepared to be swept away to incredible worldwide destinations along with our strong, relatable heroines and intensely desirable heroes.

OUT NOW

Four Love Always stories published every month, find them all at:

millsandboon.co.uk

FOUR BRAND NEW BOOKS FROM
MILLS & BOON MODERN

Indulge in desire, drama, and breathtaking romance – where passion knows no bounds!

OUT NOW

Eight Modern stories published every month, find them all at:

millsandboon.co.uk

LET'S TALK
Romance

For exclusive extracts, competitions and special offers, find us online:

- **f** MillsandBoon
- **X** @MillsandBoon
- **◉** @MillsandBoonUK
- **♪** @MillsandBoonUK

Get in touch on 01413 063 232

For all the latest titles coming soon, visit
millsandboon.co.uk/nextmonth